Baking with a Rockstar

Baking with a Rockstar

A BROOKSVILLE NOVEL

JASMIN MILLER

Baking With A Rockstar

Copyright © 2018 by Jasmin Miller

Published: Jasmin Miller 2018
jasminmillerbooks@gmail.com
www.jasminmiller.com
Editing: Jenn Wood, All About The Edits
Proofreading: Judy Zweifel, www.judysproofreading.com

To my husband,
my very own rockstar.

CHAPTER ONE

THE SOFT GLOW OF THE MORNING SUNLIGHT AND A fresh breeze stream through the open window into the kitchen. The canyon stretches out beyond the backyard, accentuating a sky splattered with beautiful hues of pink, orange, and blue. I turn away from the window and walk over to the big island in the middle of the room, grabbing the radio remote on the way.

Even though I enjoy the soft and comforting humming of the oven in the background, I prefer having some music on too. Almost everything is better with music, especially baking. Since there's a nice pile of dough waiting for me, I wash my hands thoroughly then dig into the soft mass, my whole body instantly relaxing at the sensation.

"Charlie, it smells amazing in here. What are you making?" Hannah startles me as she walks into the kitchen, stopping to casually lean against the refrigerator. Her gray hair is piled loosely on top of her head, making her look younger than she actually is. But since she was my grandmother's best friend, I know exactly how old she is—not that she acts like she's in her seventies. If there's one woman who portrays the saying of "You're only as old as you feel," it would be her.

"You're as stealthy as a cat." I shake my head and laugh, my hands automatically going to my now racing heart. Removing them from my shirt a moment later, I feel the material lift and immediately know I've made a mess. One look at my chest, and it's confirmed—several pieces of dough stick to the faces of my favorite *Supernatural* actors. I let my head fall in shame dramatically, not the slightest bit surprised about it.

I should have known better. Sorry, guys. Poor Dean and Sam.

"Sorry, honey, I didn't mean to sneak up on you. I always forget how easily you scare." She walks over and looks at the array of ingredients in front of me, especially the big jar in the middle with the hazelnut chocolate spread. "It's that kind of day, huh?"

We've only lived together for a few weeks, but she already knows me well enough to understand I crave specific kinds of food when I'm in need of some emotional comfort.

"I didn't get a lot of sleep last night, and the little I got was mediocre at best. So, I thought I could use a little pick-me-up this morning and decided to make some Nutella puffs." I smile at the silliness of it all. "You know how much I love that stuff. There's already some cream cheese Danish bread in the oven. I know you have a weakness for that too."

Hannah chuckles, the laugh lines around her eyes dancing with the movement. "You know I do. I hope you'll save some of both for me for later."

"Of course." After grabbing a rolling pin to roll out the

dough, I look back up at her. "Where are you off to this early anyway? I was hoping you could sample the new cupcakes I want to make later."

Grinning at me, she grabs a banana from the large fruit bowl on the counter. "No worries, I wouldn't leave you alone with that task. The ladies from the quilt club talked me into joining them for their Sunday morning hike, but I won't be gone for long. Just a quick round around the lake."

"Oh, that sounds like fun."

She shrugs her shoulders. "I'm not sure I'd call it fun, but with all of the sampling you've put me through over the last few weeks, I have to up my workout routine if I want to continue to fit into my clothes." She winks at me, and I give her a big smile.

This woman has been my lifesaver, and I'm not sure what I'd do without her. I know for a fact I wouldn't be standing in this kitchen right now, more content than I've been in a long time, if it wasn't for her. Right when I hit rock bottom in my life, she swooped in and not only did she talk me into moving across the country on a whim—from New York to California —but she also provided a roof over our heads.

She took me and my little baby in like family, no questions asked. There will never be enough words to show her how grateful I am for all of the help and support she's given us. Life certainly wouldn't be the same without this guardian angel.

When I focus back on her face, I catch her staring at me.

"Stop thinking about it. You know I can tell." Her hands are on her hips, her lips pinched together in a tight line.

A quiet snort escapes my mouth, and I hold up my hands in surrender. "I know, I know. I just can't help it sometimes.

But I'm trying not to fall into that trap if I can help it, I promise."

We share a knowing look, one we've shared many times over the last few weeks. This wasn't the first time my mind slipped into the past—voluntarily or not—but we both know it won't be the last time either. Thoughts from the past have a weird way of sneaking up on you at any time. Sometimes it's a fleeting thought that's gone before you can grasp it, but other times, it's so overwhelming, you feel like it's going to suffocate you.

Beep. The baby monitor sitting on the far side of the kitchen bar sends a warning tone, letting me know it lost its signal.

"I didn't think I'd ever live in a house big enough for this thing to lose the connection." Sighing, I quickly wash my hands to check the monitor.

By the time I push the button to turn on the screen, the signal is already back on. Weird technology.

"Is she all right?" Hannah's voice is laced with a hint of concern as she tries to peek over my shoulder.

"Yep, still sound asleep." The screen is bright, showing the crib with my little baby girl, Mirabelle, in it. Seeing her lying on her belly with her butt high up in the air makes me smile—sometimes it still feels weird that she's become my everything so quickly. There's no denying we had a rocky start, one I wouldn't wish on anyone, but we pulled through and came out stronger on the other side.

My thoughts wander to last year, when my ex-fiancé, Sebastian, left me—left *us*—at the worst moment of my life. Just the thought of it makes my insides churn.

Sometimes I wonder what would've happened if he

hadn't left me with a newborn, but in hindsight, I'm glad. Without a doubt, he was a complete asshole for doing it the way he did, but we're better off without him. It took me a while to realize that, but once I did, life got a little easier. Thankfully, Mirabelle has been a great baby from the beginning, almost like she wanted to help me through that rough patch in our lives.

A hand on my arm snaps me out of my thoughts, and my eyes focus back on Hannah.

"You okay there?" Her eyebrows draw together as she looks me over.

I nod quickly and return my focus to the dough in front of me so she can't study my face any further. There's no need to indulge my brain in that part of my past any longer than I already have.

Hannah drops her hand from my arm and walks over to the fridge. "Do you want me to bring any of the girls back with me after our hike? You know how much they love you and your baking."

Just thinking about those women makes me chuckle. "Not today, but thanks. I just want to make a small batch for us later today. But if we deem them good enough, I can make a big batch next week at the bakery and we can invite them over then."

Even though my bakery won't be open for a while, I use every chance I can to bake big batches in my beautiful massive industrial ovens.

"Sounds perfect. I can't wait." She grabs her water bottle from the fridge, waving at me as she leaves. "Now, enjoy the little break, and I'll see you later."

"Have fun, and say hi to the rest of your squad for me." I

smirk at the term like I always do, but it's just perfect. The six seniors who make up the quilt club are worse than a group of teenagers sometimes. It definitely never gets boring when they're around.

For the next few minutes, I'm completely focused on my baking. It's something that centers me, no matter what mood I'm in. Once I'm happy with the dough, I cut it into equal pieces. The brown hazelnut spread is next, and I smear it on generously with a knife, because there's no such thing as too much Nutella.

After folding each piece to form an open tube, I place them neatly next to each other on a baking sheet. Since the oven is still occupied, I put the baking sheet on the counter and move on to the next bowl of ingredients that's already waiting for me. I love days like today, where I can just bake one thing after the other. It calms me down while also allowing me to think clearly about what the week ahead will bring.

Since I've decided not to rush things with the bakery, I still have a few months until I'm going to open it here in this small California town. Not only is there a lot of preparation that needs to be done, but I've quickly figured out that trying to raise an infant at the same time isn't the easiest thing—even with all the help I've been getting.

The song on the radio ends, and the host interrupts my thoughts. "Sources claim that our very own Brooksville citizen, rockstar Hudson Mitchell, was spotted at the airport this early morning. If it's true, and he's really back in town, please be kind, folks. Remember he's one of us."

"Rockstar?" I snort to myself. "I've been here for several weeks now, and no one has mentioned anything about a rockstar living here—not that I've been out much. And here I thought we could have a quiet life in this place. Thank goodness Monica didn't move with us, she'd be all over this." My best friend is the worst celebrity gossip, even though she knows to keep it to the bare minimum with me.

I shake my head, as I realize I'm talking to myself, a habit I don't think I'll ever stop—something Sebastian wasn't very fond of.

Stop it! No thinking about him, he's not worth the time.

The oven timer beeps, successfully distracting me from my thoughts. I take out the baking sheet with the Danish bread, and after carefully placing it on the stove, I put the next sheet in. The sweet smell of baked goods drifts into my nose, and I let out a loud sigh just as my stomach lets out a growl. I put my hand on my belly absentmindedly, immediately noticing Hannah might have been right about us having to up our workout routine.

Focusing back on my work, I lose myself in the bread dough once more. Swaying gently to the music coming from the radio, I startle when the front door shuts with a loud *bang*.

"Weird." I stop, my hands still deep in the soft dough, and listen. "Maybe Hannah forgot something."

"Gosh, what smells so good in here? I would've come back earlier if I'd known this was waiting for me." The voice —male, and *definitely* not Hannah—gets louder with every spoken word, indicating the person is coming closer to the kitchen. A man is coming closer to *me*. A stranger.

I'm frozen in my spot—certain I look like a deer caught in the headlights—and I'm afraid my heart will burst out of my chest in a second if it keeps beating this wildly.

Who on earth could that possibly be?

Hannah and I have been living here for the past few days while her kitchen gets renovated. All she's ever said was that it belongs to a family member who doesn't use it right now. She didn't mention anyone else would be here with us.

"Seriously, so good. I'm starving."

Before I can even think about running or hiding, the person walks around the corner and into the kitchen.

The man's wearing a pair of black basketball shorts and nothing else—I repeat, nothing else.

What on earth?

To complement the set of wide-open eyes that are practically jumping out of my sockets, my mouth hangs slightly open now too. Perfect.

The smart and rational side of my brain seems to be on a break because all I'm capable of doing is raking my eyes over Mr. Basketball Shorts. He's tall with broad shoulders and the most pronounced abs I've ever seen up close. The baseball cap on his head is turned backward, and he's currently wiping his face off with what I assume to be his shirt. That is the only reason he hasn't seen me yet, and why I haven't seen his face yet either. But I'm going out on a limb here and say it's probably as gorgeous as the rest of him.

My eyes drift back to his magnificent chest, following the beads of sweat that are slowly running down his torso to the V-shaped lower abs until they disappear into the pair of shorts that sits low on his hips.

Sudden heat shoots through my body, making my cheeks tingle from the force of it. My brain uses that moment of distraction to finally kick back in again, reminding me of the situation at hand.

A total stranger is standing in my kitchen.

Half-naked.

And we're all alone in this house.

He could be *anyone.*

"Aaaaahhh!" The strangled cry rips out of my throat, startling not just me but my drool-worthy intruder too.

He removes the shirt from his face in one swift motion, his brown eyes immediately finding mine—not that it's a hard thing to do after the war cry I just let loose.

The noise of blood rushing through the veins in my ears is loud and distracting, and my body seems to have a mind of its own, doing things I'm not even realizing until—

Smack.

I look down at my now empty hands in utter shock before slowly looking back up to take in the crime scene I just created.

The big ball of dough I just threw—without any conscious thought of it—landed square in his face.

Oops.

CHAPTER TWO

*T*HUD.

The ball of dough hits the floor with a soft *plop*, leaving a surprised-looking man standing in front of me. At least, I think he's surprised since he still hasn't said another word. He's just staring at me with his eyes wide and his mouth slightly agape. Since the dough was still wet enough when I threw it, little pieces are now stuck to almost every inch of his face.

"Oh my gosh." My hands fly up to slap over my mouth while I try really hard to keep a straight face. I still have no clue who this guy is, but man, I can't remember the last time I've seen something this funny, and I practically have first row seats. My attempt at keeping my feelings about this situation to myself remains unsuccessful when I burst into a bout of laughter—fully complemented by the occasional snort.

This might quite possibly be the worst first impression I've ever made on a human being. Maybe I should be worried about that fact, but I just can't bring myself to care. It's been a very long time since I've laughed like this, and it almost feels cathartic.

The guy clears his throat, touching his face with a shake of his head. "Well, I'm glad you're enjoying yourself, at least."

At first, I'm not sure how to take his comment—and for a moment, I'm afraid he's mad—but then I see the corners of his mouth lift into a smirk. All I can do is stare at him, my eyes blinking rapidly, basking in the fact that I'm pretty sure he has dimples.

Freaking dimples. They will be the end of me.

I guessed he'd be good-looking, but this man goes above and beyond that level, making him easily the most handsome man I've ever seen—even with dough plastered all over his face. Before that thought can spin into something bigger, I stop myself. Taking a deep breath, I tell my hormones to stay far away, not that I can blame them for wanting to come out to play.

"I'm so sorry." The mortification is slowly starting to sink in, and I'm ready to hide somewhere to escape this embarrassing situation.

He arches an eyebrow, and a piece of dough that was stuck to it falls to the floor. "Huh. Are you sure? You could have fooled me when you were doubled over with laughter just a moment ago."

Heat immediately shoots into my cheeks in response, and a huge grin spreads across his face. I momentarily forget how to breathe because it's that blinding. I clearly haven't been out in a while, especially not around ridiculously handsome men like him. Now that I think about it, it's actually been years since I felt attracted to someone this quickly, not that it's ever been this strong before. My grandma always used to say there are two kinds of attraction. One is the instant one, that usually happens before you even know the person, and the other is the kind that grows with your feelings as you get to know a person better.

I'm pretty sure we have an instant winner, since I can't seem to think straight and words just start pouring out of my mouth. "Who are you anyway?"

There are a lot of ways he could have reacted to that question. What I don't expect is for him to start laughing so loudly I'm sure they can hear him a few houses down—and the properties in this neighborhood are pretty big. He clutches his stomach as he continues to shake with laughter, and naturally, I can't help myself and track his every movement with my eyes. And for the love of...there are those perfect abs again, practically begging me to devour them with my gaze—at the very least.

"Could you, uh, could you maybe cover yourself up a little bit more? It's a bit inappropriate, if you ask me. Don't you feel uncomfortable like this in front of a stranger?" More random—and albeit pretty inane—words come out of my mouth. I barely refrain from slapping myself on the forehead, trying to pretend like I'm actually in control of my own brain. My eyes stay trained on him, never letting him out of my sight.

This time, I can tell he's trying to keep his laughter at bay, not that I can blame him for wanting to laugh at me again. I'm obviously doing a pretty lame-ass job at this whole impression thing, and I wouldn't be too surprised if I ended up with a dough ball in my face too.

Since I'm uncomfortable with the silence right now, I'm trying to fill every second of it. "So, who are you?"

I don't always make such an idiot of myself, so I might as well know who I have to bribe to never speak a word about what happened here. I mean, this guy is nothing but a bad distraction I definitely don't need in my life, but for right now, he can at least be a distraction with a name. Once I know that, I can properly bid him farewell when he leaves—fascinating abs and all.

He studies me for a moment before crossing his muscular arms over his chest. "Well, I've been gone for a few months, but the last time I checked, this was my house. So"—he points a finger straight at me and I gulp—"the real question is, who are you?"

Crap. His house? Hannah said this house belongs to one of her grandsons. After taking another good look at him, I can actually see some family resemblance. His eyes definitely have the same mischievous glint that Hannah has so often.

"Oh." My mouth stays in a perfect O-shape for a few moments—not only because I'm perplexed but also because I'm even more embarrassed now about my previous behavior. I just "doughed" the owner. Only me. Ugh. "Hannah didn't mention anything about you coming back. She said we'd have the place to ourselves."

"That's probably because I didn't tell anyone I was coming home. It was supposed to be a surprise." His eyes roam over my face, and I briefly wonder how he sees me. What an odd thought. "But it looks like I'm the one surprised instead."

Before either one of us can say another word, a loud wail comes from the monitor, blaring through the room.

He looks around the kitchen, his eyebrows drawn tightly together. "What the hell was that?"

"That was the baby monitor. Looks like my baby is up." I'm not sure how I feel about leaving him alone right now, or turning my back to him, but I hate having Mira cry even more. Taking a big breath, I give myself a little pep talk before walking over to where he stands, trying to maneuver my way around him without actually touching him. That would be too awkward. "If you'll excuse me, please."

He finally moves a little to one side, allowing me to push past him—barely. The close vicinity allows me to not only feel his body heat but to also smell his intoxicating scent. My heart skips a few beats, and I chastise myself for reacting to him at all. I like to be in control of things, and right now, in this situation, I feel anything but—least of all, my own body.

Without looking back, I halfway sprint up the stairs to the second level, panting by the time I make it all the way up. At the end of the long hallway, I open the door to the makeshift nursery—we just added a crib to the otherwise normal guest bedroom—and turn up the dimmed light.

Mirabelle—who we call Mira pretty much ninety-nine percent of the time—is sitting up, the tears from a moment ago already replaced with a big toothy grin. "Ma-ma." She draws out the syllables, clapping her little, pudgy hands together with an enthusiasm only a ten-month-old baby can have.

"Hi, cutie pie. Look at you clapping. Good job." The compliment for her newfound skill makes her squeal, which is the cutest thing ever. Seeing the joy spread across her whole face is something that will never get old.

After a diaper change and a fresh set of clothes—thanks to Mira's uncanny ability to have managed a second poop blowout today, all before ten o'clock—we go back downstairs.

Thankfully, our visitor is nowhere to be found when we get to the kitchen. I pick up my phone to call Hannah and ask her about him, but it goes straight to voicemail. In that moment, I realize I still don't even know the guy's name.

How embarrassing.

Now that I think about it, I don't think Hannah has ever mentioned it either. She likes to talk about her family, but usually doesn't mention any names or occupations. I certainly never imagined such a fine specimen as her grandson, that's for sure.

I put my squirmy girl on the floor in her little playard, so she can play while I clean up the mess I left behind in the kitchen. After wiping random strands of hair out of my face, I throw the last bits of crumbs from the counter into the trash. Mystery man must have taken it upon himself to clean up the floor since I can't see any more dough leftovers. The front door slams loudly just as I'm starting to prepare Mirabelle's late breakfast.

"Charlie?" Hannah's voice carries through the house, and I let out a loud breath of relief.

Finally, I'm about to get some answers. Hopefully.

"In the kitchen." I watch Mirabelle crawling over to the side of the playard that's closest to the entrance of the kitchen. Just hearing Hannah's voice has put the biggest smile on her face, making me chuckle.

Watching children get all excited about something has become one of my favorite things. There really isn't anything quite like it. The pure and raw joy they feel is reflected so clearly on their faces. It's both a miracle and a sad truth at the same time—a miracle that we're born with such an easy instinct to be happy about the simplest things, but also sad that we seem to lose the ability to hold onto that little piece of magic when we have to face the world we live in.

Hannah walks into the kitchen, her face sun-kissed, her eyes immediately lighting up at the sight of the wiggling child on the floor that's trying very hard to get her attention—doing a little bouncing dance and squealing as loud as she can.

"Where's my favorite little girl?" Hannah clasps her hands together before opening her arms wide as she walks toward the playard, egging Mira on even more. Mira's little booty is bumping up and down so quickly, it looks like she might prepare for take-off in a minute.

In less than thirty seconds, they're reunited when Hannah picks her up. After snuggling for a while, Mira babbles like she's filling in her replacement grandmother on everything she's missed since they saw each other last—which was only a few hours ago, early this morning. I could watch them do this all day long, because it never ceases to melt my heart. Underneath the surface, it hurts a little bit sometimes, knowing my own grandmother—the woman who basically raised me—will never have those moments with her great-granddaughter.

For some reason, that thought brings me back to our shirtless intruder, and I'm trying to think of the right words to ask Hannah about him. "So, Hannah, uh…"

Well, this is going well so far. She stares at me as I try to figure out how to ask her about her grandson without sounding stupid. At least, I really hope he was telling the truth about that. The alternative wouldn't be very good.

But before I can get out another word, we all turn toward the sound coming from the hallway, where someone is clearly walking down the stairs.

Hannah's eyes go wide and she shrieks. Mira joins her without a second thought, and I giggle at her excitement, even though she has no clue what all the commotion is about. "Hudson! Oh my goodness, I can't believe it. What are you doing here?"

Hudson? Mmmm. I like it.

Now, why am I thinking about liking his name?

"Hi, Grandma. Surprise?" His voice goes up a little at the end, making it more of a question than a statement. Hudson —it's good to finally know his real name—walks up to her, giving her as good of a side hug as he can manage with the baby occupying the other side of his grandmother. Of course, Mira is clapping and squealing, almost falling out of Hannah's arms from all the excitement.

What a traitor.

After a moment, Hudson lets go of Hannah but stays close, peeking around his grandma to smile at Mira. "And who do we have here?"

I'm still behind the kitchen island, completely engrossed in their exchange.

Hudson looks freshly showered, a few droplets of water still shimmering in his hair—brown, just like his eyes. The black jeans and white T-shirt combo don't do much to hide his incredible physique, and I have to remind myself to keep my eyes above the shoulders. Or maybe I shouldn't look at all, but the jury is still out on that. Either way, there is no need to stand here and ogle his incredible upper body.

Cut it out, ovaries.

Hannah looks at me as if for confirmation, and I give her a smile in response. I love that about her. She wants to protect Mira just as much as I do, which is the only reason I trust her so much with her. Turning back to her grandson, Hannah points at my baby girl, who's still happily sitting on one of her hips.

"This is Mirabelle, but we call her Mira." She tickles her little belly, making her giggle with delight.

They both stare at Mira in fascination, and I completely understand why. This little girl seems to wrap everyone around her little finger in five seconds flat. I have yet to meet someone who's immune to her charms.

Hudson takes Mirabelle's little hand in his and shakes it gently. She takes that as an invitation, of course, and halfway leaps into his arms. They gaze adoringly at each other before Mira nestles into his neck.

I can't believe it.

Hannah suddenly points at me, clearing her throat as she looks in my direction. "And this over here is Charlie Peterson. Well, it's Charlotte, but she goes by Charlie."

"Charlie?" There's undisguised curiosity in his voice as he tilts his head a little to the side and looks at me.

"Yes." I nod, and for some inexplicable reason, I'm trying to sound as indifferent as possible. Someone like him must be used to women throwing themselves at him, left and right, and I don't like to be a part of that fan club.

Not in this house. Well, unless you count a baby and a grandma—it seems like they've already signed up for the club.

"Charlie is opening her bakery here in a couple months. It's right on Main Street, and it's going to be beautiful. They've been living with me since they moved here from New York a few weeks ago. And since my kitchen is being renovated at the moment, I just moved them in here with me. I told you about my kitchen renovation and my visitors when we last spoke on the phone, didn't I?" Hannah taps her chin with her finger as she looks up at the ceiling for a moment.

Hudson shrugs his shoulders. "Not that I remember."

My stomach plummets at his words because the last thing I want to be is a burden.

"Oops. Sometimes I don't remember who I tell what anymore. Sorry about that." Hannah puts one of her hands on his arm. "It's not a problem though, is it?" Her eyebrows are drawn together as she looks up at her grandson.

Now, I definitely feel like I need to chime in. After all, I'm the intruding non-family member he didn't even know about. "Hudson, we'll move out and find another place to stay, no problem at all. I wouldn't have agreed to stay here had I known you were coming back."

Hudson throws his head back and laughs so much he has to wipe the corners of his eyes.

What on earth was so funny about what I said?

His whole body is shaking, and the sound of his laughter shoots little bouts of excitement through me. It's one of those laughs that makes you want to join in, even if you don't find it funny or don't know what it's about.

It's beautiful and infectious. Just like this man.

Oh goodie.

Hannah chuckles now too, jabbing her grandson in the ribs with her elbow. "I bet that's a first for you."

He finally calms down, but a big grin remains on his face. "It sure doesn't happen often."

Why am I starting to feel like I'm missing something big?

When Hannah looks at me, she slaps one of her hands over her mouth while her eyes go so wide, I'm afraid they might pop out of her sockets at any moment. "I can't believe it. You have no clue who he is, do you?"

Her eyes shimmer with glee, making me uneasy with that look alone. I shake my head, deciding it might be best to stay quiet. There really is no need to embarrass myself any further than I already have.

Hudson looks at her and chuckles. "Grandma, have you been keeping us your dirty little secret again?"

Hannah slaps him lightly on the arm. "Stop saying it like that. You know I don't like talking about what you do when you're not around."

They stare at each other for a moment before turning their attention back to me.

After that little exchange, I'm extra nervous.

"Charlie." Hannah stands up straight and clears her throat almost dramatically. Here we go. "This is my grandson, Hudson Mitchell, the famous rockstar you like to listen to on the radio."

Well, butter my butt and call me a biscuit.

CHAPTER THREE

Hannah's smile falters, a big frown settling on her face instead. "Charlie, are you okay?"

My first thought is no. I mean, I've never been one to fangirl much, but it still takes me a moment to swallow past the big lump in my throat.

Hudson is a freaking *rockstar*—and not just any rockstar either, but one of the most famous ones out there. And if I remember correctly from one of Monica's celebrity rants, the ones I usually tune out, he's only twenty-five.

If I don't pay attention, that little fact can give me a complex. Even though I'm only twenty-three and about to open my own business, it's nothing compared to Hudson.

Okay, deep breath. None of this is a biggie, right?

Oh, who am I kidding? Of course, it's a big deal—though, if I'm honest, my issue is more with his good looks than anything else. I have a feeling that if I don't pay attention, Hudson can be a distraction for me—even if I just stare at him all day long. Which definitely wouldn't be a hardship. I'm already getting distracted just thinking about him.

Giving myself a mental shake, I snap out of this moment, realizing I've been staring at the two of them like a total moron.

"Uh...what?"

Two big thumbs up for me. Surely, no one knows how to make a first impression like I do. Between the flying dough and the rest of my behavior, he probably thinks I'm a total nutcase.

I close my eyes for a moment and take a deep breath, begging for my brain to please let us get through this day without any further embarrassments.

"You look a little pale there." Hannah lets go of Hudson and walks over to me. I try to put on a small smile, but I'm not sure I succeed. "I'm sorry. I didn't mean to throw you under the bus like that. I just have this weird rule that I don't tell anyone what my family does for a living until they meet them."

She looks sincere, yet at the same time, I spot a hint of a mischievous glint in her eyes. At this point, I can only hope she isn't up to something.

Shaking my head at her, I feel a little guilty for worrying her. Because let's face it: her family, her rules. "No, no, you're fine. I was just surprised, that's all."

Both Hannah and Hudson wear identical frowns. It doesn't seem like I've convinced either one of them. Even Mira—who's been oddly quiet in Hudson's arms—looks at me like she can see straight through my lie.

I let out a little sigh, rearranging things on the counter so my hands have something to do. "Well, under those circumstances, we should definitely move out. I'm sure the last thing you need right now is two extra guests in the house, especially when they're strangers and one of them is a loud baby." I glance at Hudson, only to look away again quickly.

Taking advantage of other people bugs me, even if they only mean well. I think I declined Hannah's offer to temporarily live with her for a little while about fifty times before she finally wore me down. I don't want to be in anyone's debt—or way—unless I absolutely have to.

Hudson is still frowning when I peek up at him through my lashes. There's no denying the irresistible vibe that surrounds him, and I'm sure there aren't a lot of people who refuse him anything—probably more so the opposite. Usually, I don't have any issues telling people no, but for some reason, I already feel like Hudson will test me more than anyone else has ever done before.

What if I can't handle it?

The last year has been an absolute nightmare, and I'm so glad I've finally started to slowly get back on my feet. The last thing I need is some sort of scandal involving this super popular rockstar, especially when he taunts me in his workout gear like this morning. I'm not a robot. I'm sure even I can't resist that forever.

"No, Charlie, please don't." The way he says my name, gentle yet with a certain resolve, makes me lift up my head to look at him. His voice is melodic and very alluring, and I wonder if it's a natural quality or one he's acquired over the years.

But I'm totally getting ahead of myself here.

When he takes a few steps toward me, I realize, much to my horror, why Mirabelle has been so quiet. That little bugger is happily sucking on Hudson's T-shirt, and I'm not sure if he hasn't noticed it yet or if he just doesn't care.

Just when I decide to mention something about little Miss Slobber-mouth, Hudson beats me to it. "This issue is completely my fault, and I take the blame. I should've called to announce my plans, at least to Grandma, so she knew I was going to come back. You're a guest, and I don't want to make you uncomfortable. I'll just grab a few things and move into a hotel. It's no problem at all."

This time I gape at him, baffled. Absolutely floored. I cannot believe what he just offered. I shake both my head and my finger in front of me for emphasis. "Don't be ridiculous, Hudson. You're not going anywhere. This is your house, and you don't have to tell anyone you're coming home. And just for the record, you're not making me uncomfortable at all."

Gosh, I'm such a liar. From the way the corners of his mouth twitch, he might already know that too.

Fantastic. I've always sucked at hiding my emotions.

Hannah looks back and forth between Hudson and me, quietly chuckling to herself. "Stop that nonsense, you two. You're both staying here. This house is big enough for all of us. Charlie, you can look for a place once the bakery is open. The last thing you need right now is even more stress. I want to have you close, so I can help you with Mira as much as I can."

She's got a point. There's no way I can get the bakery opened in just a few months without her help.

I sigh in defeat. "I know, you're right. At least let me pay rent or something. I definitely can't stay here for free."

"I like her, Grandma." Hudson chuckles, looking adoringly at Hannah. "You always know the best people." His dimples pop again, and I'm biting the inside of my cheek before I do anything stupid like...sigh—or worse, ask to be the new leader of his fan club.

I'm afraid either would be rather telling.

Hannah gives me a big smile that I return easily. "Charlie is one of the very best."

My heart swells from her statement, but that's only short-lived when I realize both of their gazes are on me, openly studying me. Since I've never been a big fan of being scrutinized by others, I quickly grow uncomfortable, relieved when they finally snap out of it.

I decide to push the rent topic again at a later time. Right now, other matters are more urgent—such as Mirabelle's sucking noises that become louder by the second. I flinch a little when I look at the big, wet stain on Hudson's T-shirt she's been working on this whole time. His gaze follows mine, and I'm mortified. "I'm so sorry about that. I should've warned you that she puts everything in her mouth right now, especially when she's hungry. Let me feed her quick, and then I can wash your shirt."

Hudson doesn't say anything, and I turn to Hannah. "And then I'll start those cupcakes I promised you." Maybe focusing on baking will help me feel more like myself again.

She grins at me. "Sounds perfect. Let me take a quick shower, and then I can help you."

I silently watch her leave the kitchen, trying to swallow away the nerves that bubbled up the second I realized she's going to leave me alone with Hudson—Mira doesn't really count yet.

Despite the fact that I'm not into the whole celebrity world at all, even I've heard of Hudson Mitchell and know he's a big deal.

There's no reason to be nervous. I mean, Mira has been sucking on his T-shirt, for goodness' sake. If that isn't the ultimate test of a prissy person, I don't know what is. Let's just pretend he's a normal guy—albeit a very attractive one.

Most importantly, he's *not* Sebastian. That unwelcome thought brings me back to reality faster than anything else ever could. Rationally, I know not all guys are bad, I just need to remind myself of that. Plus, he's Hannah's grandson, so he at least deserves the benefit of the doubt right now.

After taking a moment for another silent pep talk, I close the distance between me and my newly acquired—and very temporary—celebrity roommate, so I can take Mirabelle from him.

When I start to hold out my arms for her, Hudson shakes his head. "I can feed her if you want."

"Really?" This man keeps catching me off guard. Surprised by his offer, my arms are still halfway up in the air. "You don't have to do that."

"I know. But I really don't mind, I promise." He shrugs before turning to look at Mira, who's so delighted by all the attention that she starts hitting her little fist on his chest. "I mean, look at her. I might even be willing to change a diaper for this cutie. It's okay though, if you don't want me to, I get it. No hard feelings."

Oh dang, this beautiful man. His words and actions hit me right in the rib cage.

There really aren't a lot of things that are more heart-melting—and also incredibly sexy—than a man and a baby. Match made in heaven right there. And who am I to deny the handsome rockstar what he wants—at least with this simple request of feeding Mira.

Willing to give him a chance, I nod. "All right. If you really don't mind. But don't complain about your shirt later on."

"My shirt?" His eyebrows draw together.

Looking at his confused expression, I can't hold back a quiet chuckle. "Maybe you'll be fine. We'll see. On the other hand, Mira has already done a job of getting you messy anyway."

He only shrugs. "It's just a shirt."

Interesting. "Do you want me to put her in the highchair?"

"No, I've got it." He looks over to the big dining room table where Mira's chair is pushed against the wall. "Or maybe you can do it quickly?"

The pleading look on his face is adorable, and I can't help but smile. "Of course."

I take Mira from his arms, cuddling her to my chest, since it's one of my favorite things to do. She faintly smells of Hudson even after such a short time, and I'd be a liar if I said I didn't just take a deep whiff. No one should smell this good —woodsy with a hint of fruit. It's a very masculine and rather memorable scent I'm sure I'll start to recognize from now on.

"Sweetie pie, your new friend Hudson is gonna feed you some yummy food now, okay? Be good for him, will ya?" I buckle Mira into her chair while she keeps patting my cheeks with her little hands. After giving her a quick kiss and a toy to keep her occupied for another moment, I turn around to walk back to the kitchen to get her food. I stop short when Hudson stands only a few feet away, watching me intently with those chocolate-colored eyes of his. "Thanks again for helping."

"Don't mention it. I like kids, so I really don't mind." He

smiles at me, one dimple popping out—almost daring me to look away. I briefly wonder if he has issues being under a microscope too, but then I remember he's probably used to people staring at him all day long.

I finally snap out of my daze when he walks around me to pull a chair out from the table, so he can sit in front of Mirabelle.

Almost on autopilot, I go back into the kitchen and start whipping up Mira's meal—a small portion of oatmeal mixed with some mashed banana, and a few little pieces of soft pear for those little fingers to pick up.

The two of them are playing with some blocks when I walk over, but the second Mira sees me, the toys are forgotten and her focus is completely on me—more importantly—her food. She wiggles her arms and legs as much as the highchair allows. There's no doubt this girl likes to eat. She's squealing, already trying to reach the bowl and plate that I put on the wooden dining table next to Hudson.

"What is that?" He wrinkles his nose and points at the bowl.

His obvious distaste makes me laugh. "It's just oatmeal and banana."

He keeps eyeing the mixture suspiciously. "Huh. It doesn't look like someone should be eating it."

I had the exact same thought at first. "Well, that's most baby food for you. But you'll see, she absolutely loves it. It's actually not half bad," I reassure him and head back to get started on those cupcakes. I hope the coconut cupcakes with frosted coconut frosting will taste half as good as they sound, because *yummy*.

"Very yummy indeed." The quiet murmur comes from

across the room, and when I look up, Hudson's eyes are on me.

Did I just say that out loud? What is it with me today? My gaze is still locked with Hudson's, and there's something in his look I can't quite decipher. Before I can try to figure it out, though, my attention briefly flicks over to Mirabelle. The alarm bells go off in my head, my eyes going wide as I gasp.

"Watch out." I try to warn Hudson, but it's already too late.

For the second time in the past few hours, I break out into laughter so high it almost harmonizes with Mirabelle's little giggles. I might even sound like a dying hyena, but I honestly couldn't care less at this point. "You might not believe me right now, but I really am sorry." I clutch my stomach and try to get a few more words out, gasping like I just ran a marathon. "I should've given you better instructions when I set her loose on you."

After another round of laughter, I finally get a grip on myself. Wiping the corners of my eyes, I carefully open them to take in the crime scene in front of me. My restraint is tested the second I lay eyes on him again, but by some miracle, I manage to stifle my laughter this time.

Most of it, at least.

Hudson is covered in oatmeal. The brown goop is dripping off his hair and face, all the way down onto his shirt and pants. There isn't a lot of visible space left that's unharmed and free of the sticky goo.

He looks back and forth between Mira and me and shakes his head slowly. "You girls should come with a warning."

"I'm so sorry. I forgot to tell you that she can get quite

impatient if you don't shove food into her mouth fast enough." I feel more than just a little bad about everything that's happened to him today—and it isn't even noon yet.

We might have to move to a hotel, after all. I'm sure not everyone wants to share a house with a messy pair like Mira and me. I sigh and step closer, so I can start cleaning up the mess.

"Please don't get mad at Mira, though. She's just a little baby." Bile rises in my throat when I remember the way Sebastian blamed this precious little baby for everything that went wrong. I swore to myself I'd do whatever it took to shelter Mira from anything similar happening again.

Getting protective in this moment might seem a bit odd, but I've seen people get worked up over way less than some spilled oatmeal.

A lot of people have a sad tendency to blame others for just about anything that goes wrong.

"Hey." Hudson touches my arm for a second to get my attention, and the unexpected contact startles me. "Of course it's not her fault, please relax. Don't worry about it, okay? It's all good." His tone is soothing and his touch gentle.

My chest deflates as I exhale loudly, and his eyes are still on me when I look up. They are such a beautiful mixture of dark honey and chocolate tones, blending together perfectly. Dark, long eyelashes surround them, and I can't help but marvel at them for a moment.

Once I snap out of my trance, I'm relieved to see he seems genuine. If I'm honest, I don't think I *really* expected him to react badly. My reaction was more of an automated reply, like I want to make sure people know what's acceptable and what isn't *before* anything happens. Hudson's presence has been nothing but relaxing from the first moment—just like it was with Hannah.

I still feel Hudson's eyes on me, but I choose to ignore him. Instead, I make quick work of cleaning up the mess, or at least as fast as I can since cleaning up oatmeal is a total pain in the butt. Hudson wordlessly takes the extra paper towels I hand him, just as Hannah comes back downstairs.

She stops abruptly when she walks into the kitchen. "What's going on?" When she sees us in all of our messy glory, she immediately doubles over in laughter. Pointing at me, she's still trying to get her laughter under control. "You didn't tell him about our little Miss Impatience, did you?"

I shake my head in chagrin, feeling heat seeping into my cheeks.

"Oops." Hannah shrugs her shoulders and we all laugh, even Hudson.

After a quick face wash in the kitchen sink—and despite his current state of messiness—Hudson keeps feeding Mirabelle the rest of the food she didn't manage to splatter all over him. I'm more than just a little surprised and keep shooting glances in their direction because not everyone would be in such good spirits after the morning he's had.

No, no, no. Don't do it.

My brain is alerting me, knowing full well that if I don't watch out, I'll be having hearts in my eyes before I know it. That's the last thing I need right now. But since I'll probably see a lot of him over the next few weeks, I might as well enjoy the scenery, right? Nothing wrong with that—not at all.

As long as it's just looking.

Hannah sits down on the other side of the table, opposite Hudson. "How long are you planning on staying home this time?" She taps her fingernails on the table and doesn't look at her grandson, making it pretty obvious she's trying to act nonchalantly.

I'm sure if she can't fool me, she can't fool her own family either.

Hudson's quiet for a moment and looks down at the table. When he lifts his head again, the expression on his face has changed. Gone is the carefree, happy guy I just met. In its place is someone more closed-off, with eyebrows drawn together so tightly, I'm afraid it might leave a permanent crease on his face.

The corners of his mouth lift in a weak smile. The curiosity burns inside me, wondering what's going on with him. After the way Hannah just acted, she seems to know something is up too, or at least suspects it.

His shoulders lift once before he focuses back on putting more pear pieces on Mira's tray. "Not sure yet. Probably a few weeks, maybe a few months."

"I see." Hannah rubs her fingertips together, studying him openly. She's not trying to hide her scrutiny, and I'm actually a little surprised she doesn't ask him straight out what's going on. Instead, she gives him a wide smile. "Actually, I'm glad you'll be here for a while. It's been too long since you stayed with us for more than just a few days. It's perfect."

Wait, what? That definitely wasn't the reaction I expected.

His eyes narrow. "Why?" The suspicion in his voice is so evident I have to suppress the urge to chime in and ask her the same question while also high-fiving Hudson.

The wariness in my chest only grows when Hannah

looks like the cat that ate the canary. "Well, I just thought you could help Charlie with the bakery." The words come out of her mouth faster than usual, but her tone stays casual like she's talking about the weather.

I'm in the middle of cracking eggs into my mixing bowl when I hear her drop that bomb, and manage to accidentally let some eggshells fall into the flour.

Crap. Crap. Double crap.

What the heck is she doing?

Waving my hands in front of me, I brush my hair out of my face with the back of my hand. "Oh no, Hannah. That's not necessary. We're already enough of an inconvenience living here, I don't want to impose on Hudson any more than we already are. I'm sure he didn't come back to slave away in my bakery anyway. Plus, we're not in a time crunch either. I planned it out far enough in advance, so there wouldn't be any issues." I try to sound confident and convincing, but I'm not sure that's enough for Hannah.

This woman seems to be on a mission.

My worries are confirmed when she shakes her head before I even finish my last sentence. "Nonsense. It wouldn't hurt to be done earlier than you had planned, would it? That way, you can relax some more before the chaos starts. And I'm sure Hudson can make time for it, right?" She gives him a pointed look before getting out of her chair. "I just realized I forgot my phone in my room. You two discuss this, I'll be right back."

I'm pretty sure I saw her grin right before she left the room and disappeared down the hallway.

My chin drops as I stare after her. "Unbelievable." I shouldn't be surprised because in the time I've known her,

I've learned one thing about this woman—she loves to meddle, absolutely *loves* it.

I try to focus on getting the cracked eggshells out of my mix, hoping maybe Hudson and I can both just ignore the whole topic.

"Grandma is right, I really don't mind helping."

Well, so much for that.

Hudson walks over to me with a neutral expression on his face. After putting Mira's empty plate and bowl in the sink, one side of his mouth lifts up and the traitorous dimple pops out. "But I have one condition."

CHAPTER FOUR

ONE CONDITION.

Hudson's words crawl over my skin in an uneasy way, making the hair on the back of my neck stand up as a shiver rushes through me involuntarily.

Of course there has to be a condition. There always has to be something. Why can't people do things just because they want to help, not because they want something in return? Sebastian was a master at this game, positively making me distrustful toward anyone asking for a favor, or offering help.

"Just spit it out, Hudson." The words fly out of my mouth a bit harsher than I intended, and I grind my teeth in an effort to calm down.

I know he doesn't deserve my anger. He hasn't done anything mean or malicious—yet. The look on his face confirms I might have taken it a bit too far, or at the very least, confused him. He can't possibly know why his words trigger such an abrupt change in my behavior. Instead of reciprocating my frustration, or going beyond that and slipping into anger, the look in his eyes softens. One corner of his mouth lifts up the tiniest bit as he takes a step back, holding up both of his hands as if to placate me.

Crap.

This is not how I've wanted to start things with him. He's probably a second away from declaring me crazy and kicking us out of the house after all.

I let out a big breath and stumble back onto a kitchen bar stool. "I'm sorry."

I know he isn't like Sebastian, not even in the slightest. But sometimes it doesn't matter when our brain and body react to triggers from the past, which actually makes it pretty unfair for others in our lives.

The subconscious can be a bitch, there's no doubt about that.

Hudson's expression turns somber, and I have no clue what he's thinking. But the way he studies me makes me wonder if he can read my feelings to a T.

Shaking his head, he rakes one of his hands through his hair. "No! I'm the one who should apologize. I didn't mean to make you uncomfortable."

"I know." We're staring at each other, and I realize I'm already trying to figure this guy out, not sure how to feel about him. So far, he doesn't seem like a jerk. And to be honest, I would expect a lot of people of his status to be—even though they shouldn't be—but there are bratty people everywhere.

My gut seems to think he's a nice guy though, so I'll just go with that for now. It's a sobering thought since I haven't exactly been thinking about guys in any capacity in almost a year. My brain cells return from whatever planet they disappeared to, and I'm glad I can stop staring at him like an idiot now. "You didn't deserve that. It just hit a nerve, I guess."

His eyebrows draw together so much they almost touch, and I hate knowing I'm the reason for that frown. I usually consider myself a pretty friendly and easygoing person, contrary to how I just acted in front of this famous stranger. Embarrassment at this whole situation rushes through me, and I avert my gaze.

The sudden wail coming from Mira makes me feel crappy for a whole other reason. During this short exchange with Hudson, I forgot everything around me. I just met this man, and he's already invading my senses. We both look over as Mira complains about her bottle that fell off the highchair.

Hudson holds up his right hand. "I'll get it."

"Thank you."

I watch him as he picks it up from the big mat we put underneath the highchair and hands it back to Mira. She looks at him for a moment before going back to happily drinking her water while also using the spout as a teething toy. Apparently, watching Hudson and me while also playing with her bottle is entertaining enough for her right now.

Hudson stays close to her this time, probably in case she needs help again, but turns in my direction. "I was going to say I probably could have worded it better—actually, there's no probably about that. What I should've said is I could use your help for something too. But only if you're up for it."

Without a doubt, this sounds miles better. It doesn't make my body jump straight into panic mode, and makes me feel more like an equal, maybe even a friend instead of a subordinate. Since I promised myself to never feel like that again, it's indispensable.

When I respond this time, I manage to keep my tone light and friendly. "Well, it depends on what it is." The corners of my mouth lift into a small smile before I realize it, and I'm surprised at how I'm once more back to feeling at ease with him.

Maybe it's not such a big surprise, after all though, considering I felt the same way with Hannah too. It may very well be a family trait.

"Let's hear it." My curiosity has taken over, and I'm blatantly staring at him now, the mix in front of me completely forgotten.

He doesn't say anything for a moment, almost as if he wants to give me a chance to openly study him first. His features are all dark—from the dark hair on top of his head that's pushed back carelessly after his shower, to his brown eyes that feel like they can burn a hole in my body with a look alone—or at the very least, set me on fire—down to the chiseled jaw that's all sharp angles and covered in a light dusting of dark hair. He looks like the epitome of rugged and manly, making me groan inwardly.

Of course, after swearing off men until Mira is at least a teenager, I end up with one of the sexiest *roommates* alive.

Heck, he probably *was* voted "Sexiest Man Alive" at some point.

Without a doubt, women around the world—and probably plenty of men too—have been drooling all over him during the lifetime of his career.

I snort at the thought, pretty sure Monica, who's obsessed

with all things celebrities, would jump on the next airplane to California if she knew what was going on here.

"What are you thinking about?" With a hint of a smile, Hudson's smooth voice interrupts my thoughts about my best friend, making me aware I'm still staring at him.

Great. I've officially moved into awkward territory, and he probably thinks I'm going to turn out to be just another groupie.

"Nothing really." Clearing my throat, I tell my mind and body to stop ogling him. It seems like I've lost control over both the second this man walked into the house. It's not like I haven't seen a gorgeous man before.

And let's face it. At the end of the day, they all poop, right? Yes. *Yes!* There you go. He poops like everyone else, problem solved.

Hudson smirks, like he knows exactly what's going on behind my probably flour-coated forehead. "Well, I was hoping you'd agree to spending some time with me." He leans casually against the table, folding his arms across his chest.

Losing my inner battle, my eyes flicker momentarily to his bulging biceps before I tear my gaze back to his face. If I didn't know better, I'd think he's doing this on purpose to taunt me.

Actually, I *don't* know better. *Mmm.*

His words finally register, and I stare at him in disbelief. "What?" Before I know what I'm doing, I shake my head, almost violently. "Sorry, Hudson, but I don't date. Don't worry though, it's no big deal. I can get the bakery ready by myself, like I've been planning on anyway. That's why I gave myself several months to get it ready for the grand opening, so I wouldn't run into any problems."

Just thinking about going on a date with this man sends my body into a frenzy, and I'm sure the slight panic is visible on my face.

Mira chooses that moment to fling her water bottle to the floor again, and I'm pretty sure she's done this time. After washing my hands in the sink, I get a washcloth ready to wipe her off.

Hudson clears his throat and presses his lips together. "As much as I wouldn't mind going on a date with you, that's not exactly what I meant."

Oh my goodness.

Mortification rushes through me, and I bow my head as the familiar heat rushes into my cheeks. Please, oh please, please, *please*, where is that hole in the ground to help you escape when you really need it?

Embarrassment about my wrong assumption battles with the slight annoyance of wondering if he did this on purpose, or if he just naturally likes to talk in riddles.

"Well, could you please tell me *what* exactly you meant then?" My voice squeaks a little at the end, and I hate to admit he's already getting to me. I've known him for less than a day, and he's already gotten a rise out of me—not to mention the drooling I've already done over him too.

But that's beside the point, because I'll continue to pretend that never happened.

"I want you to spend a little bit of time with me every day —if possible, just the two of us." There's no trace of a smile on his face. Nothing that would hint at him joking or making fun of me.

I'm all but ready to huff and puff. "Let me get this straight. You want to hang out with me as your condition, but you don't want to date. What exactly would we be doing then? And does it really have to be every day?"

Either something I just said was unintentionally funny or my facial expressions must be amusing enough to make him burst into laughter.

After a few moments, he takes a deep breath and closes his eyes briefly to stop his outburst. "Oh, Charlie, you're really something. I know what I'm about to say might sound a little strange, but let's just say that I think you're my muse."

"Your what? Muse?" My eyebrows shoot up, and I'm not sure I heard him correctly. I'm more than a little confused though because all my brain can come up with are artists' muses, the naked ones we've all heard about before.

I'm *definitely* not going to do that.

Nope. No. No way, Jose.

"Yes. Apparently, my brain finds you very...uh...stimulating." He says the last word casually, like it doesn't hold a highly suggestive double meaning that my brain catches right away. "Coming back to the whole dating thing, though. I'd love to take you out sometime. Are you sure I can't convince you?"

His grin is so beautiful with a hint of a mischievous glint that I can almost hear my heart go *pitter-patter*.

Without a doubt, I'm one hundred percent sure this man is trouble.

So. Much. Trouble.

I ignore him for a moment while finally taking care of Mirabelle, who's been getting more impatient by the second.

After cleaning her up, as well as the mess she made with Hudson, I pick her up under her pudgy little arms. She gives me the biggest smile and presses her face into mine. "Hi, sweetie. Do you want to play a little?"

Her answer is a loud, excited squeal followed by a round of clapping, making both Hudson and me laugh. I walk over to the playard with her. When I'm about to put her down, she suddenly tries to reach behind me. I turn around to see what she wants and almost bump into Hudson. I didn't hear him walk over to us, but now I'm pretty sure I know exactly what —or rather, *who*—Mirabelle is trying to reach.

This little stinker is already smitten with the rockstar.

"Mira, should we go play with your toys?" Hudson's voice has turned soft and soothing as the two of them stare at each other. I haven't dated since Mira was born and Sebastian and I split up, so I've never been confronted with the sheer power of an attractive man combined with a baby.

Somebody, please have mercy, because I'm not sure my ovaries can take this any longer.

"Of course, only if it's okay with your mommy." His brown eyes bore into mine, and I'm uncertain I can form a cohesive sentence right now.

Luckily Mirabelle wants his attention again, and he breaks our eye contact. Taking a deep breath, I try to find my dignity and look for some self-control along the way too. It seems like I lost both the second Mr. Abs-and-Dimples popped into the kitchen this morning.

Brain to body, no more googly eyes for the rockstar.

"So, what do you say, Charlie?" It doesn't escape my notice that Hudson keeps pushing the matter, and somehow, I have no doubt he usually gets what he wants.

"Yes." My voice is shaky, and I can't positively say I know what I just agreed to.

"Yes?" He turns my answer into a question, and I'm stunned that he seems surprised. Maybe I'm not that easy after all.

After clearing my throat, I try again. "Yes to playing with Mira, and yes to the muse meetings." My voice is firm this time, and I feel a little proud of myself for sounding confident and strong instead of weak and insecure.

Look at that, Mr. Rockstar. No starstruck fan here.

I decide then and there this will be my new mantra. I have a feeling I'm going to repeat it a lot over the next few weeks, but he's just a normal guy after all—a normal guy who poops.

The corners of his mouth lift into a triumphant smile. "Really? Okay then. Great."

Pop. And there are the dimples.

Dang it.

New rule: no more looking at Hudson's cheeks. These dimples are hazardous for my sanity.

"Great. I'm glad we got that settled." I'm not really glad, and I think he knows that.

My stomach is filled with nerves, but I just couldn't handle his extreme gaze anymore.

Let's face it, listening to him talk to Mira in that gentle way might have turned me into putty a little bit too. Ironically, she looks just as happy as Hudson, giving me a huge grin, which I automatically return. There's no way I cannot smile back at this girl.

"Beautiful momma you got there." Hudson leans closer to us, so he can stage whisper to Mira. "Maybe you can help me convince her to go on a date with me sometime. What do you think, cutie pie, are you in?" He winks, and naturally, Mirabelle giggles happily in response.

Even though I shake my head, I'm unable to keep the smile off my face.

Hudson holds out his hands to Mirabelle and she moves over to him easily. Our arms and hands touch in the process, making my skin tingle everywhere. I hurry to get away from all this walking temptation and back into the kitchen, happy to be back in what I consider my safe place. At least the cupcakes won't test my willpower like a certain rockstar already does, even though I have no one to blame but myself.

What on earth did I just agree to?

CHAPTER FIVE

DAYDREAMING ABOUT MY BAKERY HAS BEEN ONE OF MY favorite pastimes ever since I was a young teenager. It also helped me through the sometimes grueling study sessions and exams involved with my business degree over the years, the degree I knew would be the most useful, albeit the most boring one. There is no doubt it's saved me, though, especially during this last year.

Being able to stand in my very own bakery now—even if it's still mostly naked and dirty—I can clearly imagine how it will look once it's done, and it's one of the best feelings. Just the thought of the glass cases filled with delicious-smelling pastries and cakes, and the front area buzzing with people eating my food, is so overwhelming sometimes I'm ready to explode from excitement.

"Charlie, where do you want me next?" Hudson's voice sounds from behind me, making me jump.

The hairs on the back of my neck rise at the sound of his rich voice—the deep timbre almost echoing across the room—

as I spin around to face him. "Gosh, Hudson, can you please stop sneaking up on me like that?"

I slap his shoulder lightly, leaving a nice flour mark on his black T-shirt.

Good. Serves him right.

Today is our second day together at "work," and I still have to get used to him being around. Thankfully, I barely saw him yesterday, since he was helping one of the contractors fix a few things outside the building while I hid in my office, hunched over a pile of papers to make sure everything's going according to plan. I wonder if Hudson stayed away from me on purpose, giving me some time to get used to him. I'm almost certain he knows how easily some people get overwhelmed by his presence.

He grimaces, but the mischief is clearly displayed in the way his eyes sparkle. "Sorry, I didn't mean to, but you were so absorbed in your work. There could be a meteor coming your way, and you wouldn't know it until it hit you."

Well, he's got me there. When I focus on something, it's easy for me to zone out. "Very funny."

I glare at him playfully and study him for a moment, taking him in, from his black T-shirt all the way to his dark gray jeans that are paired with black boots. His whole outfit is covered in dust, dirt, and a few specks of paint. He looks every bit the busy worker bee he's been, and since I'm not blind—and my hormones practically demand it—I have to admit, he couldn't look sexier.

Somehow, I have a feeling this man could be covered in mud and still wreak havoc with women's baby-making machines. "You don't have to do anything else today.

Seriously. You've already done so much these last couple days, I feel bad enough as it is."

Shaking his head with what looks like determination, he brushes his hands off on his thighs. "Don't even mention it, it's nothing. And just between the two of us, it actually feels good to be active and helpful like this. Don't get me wrong, I love my music stuff, but it's different. This is a nice change for me, and it feels good to put my hands to use."

He looks genuine, and I'm surprised by his statement. He raises one eyebrow and tries to peek around me at the counter. "What are you still up to? Maybe I can help *you* with something?"

"All that's left is making some croissants for tomorrow and decorating a set of cupcakes once they're cooled. Easy peasy. I'll just see you back home later."

He's staring at me, shoulders pulled back and jaw set, not saying anything for a moment.

I'm not always the best at reading people, but Hudson seems to be an extra hard case for me. Is he waiting for something? One thing I do know is that holding eye contact with him for long periods of time feels weird. Normally, I wouldn't think of myself as socially awkward—not more than average, at least—but I'm afraid I might start stress-sweating soon under his intense gaze.

I clear my throat, hoping to get rid of this awkwardness between us. "Unless you...you know—"

Before I can continue, he interrupts me, taking a small step toward me. Seems like he doesn't take the term "personal space" too seriously.

"Unless I what, Charlie?" He says my name in a way that

makes my whole body shiver, and I'm almost positive he did that on purpose.

I wave my hand around nonchalantly. "Oh, you know, cash in your muse payment for the day."

Hudson throws his head back and laughs loudly. "You sound so happy about our arrangement."

"It's not that. But you've helped me for two days already without getting anything in return. That wasn't part of the deal, and I'm starting to feel guilty about it. I don't want to be in your debt." I swallow repeatedly, always feeling uneasy with any form of confrontation.

His laugh vanishes as quickly as it appeared, now firmly replaced by a big frown. "You know, if it really makes you so uncomfortable, you don't have to do it. I'm not going to force you to spend time with me if you don't want to. Just say the words. I wasn't thinking things through the other day, and maybe I shouldn't have suggested it. Or pushed it, for that matter." His shoulders slump a little before he breaks eye contact.

"No! It's really not a problem." Now it's my turn to frown. "I'm just a bit nervous I guess, because I still have no idea what to expect from these sessions. I don't do well with the unknown. I like to know what to expect, so tell me, and I'll feel better about it. Do you need us to sit down, or is it enough if we're just in the same room? I'm not sure what the exact rules are—not that I know what you need me for anyway."

"No rules, Charlie." He stares at me with an expression I can't decipher, almost like his words are supposed to have a deeper meaning. I'm not sure if they do, but my insides definitely feel like they got the memo, turning all soft and squishy.

"Well, okay then. If you just want to hang out, you can sit down on the stool over here while I finish up?" The words rush out of my mouth in rapid-fire, making me sound as nervous as I feel. To make it worse, I pat the silver metal stool next to me, like he isn't capable of figuring out which one I'm talking about—especially since there's a total of, well, one stool in the room.

Just shoot me now.

He sits down at the edge of it, his long legs outstretched in front of him with his feet crossed at the ankles. Relaxed, carefree. It might seem odd, but I don't remember the last time I've had someone this laid-back in my life. The confidence mixed with a slight level of cockiness makes for an interesting combination that might just be the tiniest bit intriguing to me. Throw in the smell of his delicious cologne, that practically surrounds me like a little cloud, and my hormones are ready to party.

Not even half a minute later, he starts squirming around. "Are you *sure* there isn't anything I can do? I'd love to help."

Since we're pretty much at eye level right now, I only have to turn my head to the side to look him straight in the eye. Like I knew it would, his gaze catches mine immediately, holding it prisoner for a long moment before I give in and nod. "All right. Go wash your hands. I'll show you what to do."

Let's bake with the rockstar. No biggie at all.

Yeah, right.

Not only does he wash his hands, but he also grabs a black apron from the hook behind the door. He looks

49

adorable in his little get-up when he stands beside me again, an eager expression on his face.

"I'll show you how to make the croissants, okay?" Since the dough needs to rest for several hours beforehand, I prepared it this morning. All that's left to do is the easy part of the process. His eyes are focused on my hands as I explain how to roll out the dough and cut it with a dough cutter.

"Why are we doing rectangle shapes? I thought croissants are triangles." He looks genuinely confused when I look up at him.

No one's ever asked me that before, and I can't hold back the big grin. "Well, there's a really easy explanation for that. The rectangle ones hold more chocolate than the triangles."

Hudson stares at me like I just told him the secret of life before he starts laughing. "Oh, Charlie, I like the way you're thinking. More chocolate. Gotcha. Rectangles, it is."

With matching grins on our faces, I show him how to slice the baking chocolate before placing it on the dough and rolling it all up. "There, a little sleeping bag for the chocolate." When I look up at him, Hudson blinks at me, his head tilted to the side. The intensity in his gaze makes me feel self-conscious, and I absentmindedly brush at my face. "What is it? Do I have something on my face?"

Without saying a word, Hudson's hand stretches toward my face, and my heart starts beating erratically. *He's going to touch me*, and I'm pretty sure I'm only one step away from hyperventilating. Just the thought alone sends my body into a frenzy. It's like everything's suddenly on high-alert—my skin feels hypersensitive, awaiting the unexpected touch to happen while there's a rolling feeling in my stomach. My lips are dry but I refrain from licking them when Hudson is in such close proximity.

When his fingers touch my cheek, I can't keep my eyes from fluttering closed. He lingers there for a few seconds, and I don't dare open my eyes, too afraid of what I might or might not see in his.

"There. Just a little flour." One more brush of his thumb across my cheek and jaw, and then his hand is gone.

"Oh. Yeah. Of course. Thanks." The words come out in such a mumbled mess, I'm not sure he understood me.

Thankfully, he shifts his body, focusing on the task in front of him. "Could you show me one more time?"

Without questioning it—as well as thankful for the distraction—I go through all the steps one more time. Then his hands are next to mine, mimicking my movements alongside me, innocently brushing my fingers. The room suddenly feels too hot, and my knees feel weak. The hair on my arms has risen, and I'm sure I'm not the only one who's noticed it.

Before my nerve endings go into complete overdrive—or worse, I suffer a cardiac arrest—I decide to go back to my cupcakes, a.k.a. my new safe zone. Despite having several feet between us, it doesn't feel like my body is ready to calm down yet.

I need a better distraction.

"What's the craziest thing that's ever happened at one of your concerts?" For some reason, this question has been swirling around in my head, so why not use the chance and ask?

My eyes flicker back and forth between Hudson and the

cupcakes, unable to look at him for more than half a second. At least the cupcakes are ready for me to decorate now.

Apparently, Hudson doesn't have to think long since he answers almost immediately. "Definitely one of my stage-diving experiences a few years ago. It was a hot summer day, and the crowd was crazier than usual. A woman twice my size pulled me down into the audience and put me in a chokehold before I even had a chance to stand. She said she'd only let me go if I promised to marry her. Needless to say, that was my last stage-dive."

"What?" That certainly got my attention, the disbelief of it temporarily making me forget about the moment we just shared. My hands stop in the middle of filling up the icing bag. "You're kidding."

He shakes his head and chuckles. "Nope. My band members thought it was hilarious, and the press had a field day with it too. Sadly, that means I've got plenty of proof."

"Wow." It's crazy to imagine anything like that happening. Quite impossible actually, for me.

He shrugs, his hands busy again. "It's okay. The good moments usually outweigh the bad ones."

"Did you always want to play music?"

"For as long as I remember." Hudson's staring at the wall opposite him, his eyes shimmering with an expression I haven't seen before. "Every single time I was with my grandpa, there was music—either on the radio, or he played it himself with one of his many instruments. It made him incredibly happy, and I guess it kind of became our thing."

A cloudy look crosses his face, his lips almost white from pressing them together so tightly. "When he passed away, I was only thirteen. And let's just say, I didn't take it well. The pain was almost unbearable, and music the only thing that helped. I ended up playing on a daily basis and never looked back."

"I'm so sorry, Hudson." Losing someone you love is the absolute worst.

"Thank you." He's still not looking at me, and the urge to reach out and comfort him is hard to resist. His chest heaves up and down, like he's inhaling big bouts of air, before he continues. "Anyway. Shortly after, my friends and I formed our band. We were discovered only a few years later after posting some videos online."

It's easy to tell he's trying to move on from the uncomfortable topic, and I'm trying my best to help with that. "That's cool. I bet that made things a lot easier to be discovered that way."

"It did."

I'm still mulling over all this newfound information when I feel his eyes on me.

"Since we're playing this game, can I ask you a question too?"

Dread overcomes me immediately. When someone inquires if they can ask you something, it's most likely a loaded question. My instinct wants me to say no, but that would be rather hypocritical.

"Okay." I draw out the word, not sounding sure at all. This time, I don't look away, ready to face whatever he's planning on throwing my way. Noticing the way he's biting his cheek, I'd say it's going to be something embarrassing or upsetting.

After rubbing his jaw with the back of his hand, he finally

spits it out. "Does Mira see her dad often? I haven't heard you talk about him."

Well, that conversation just went in a totally different direction rather quickly.

"Nope. It's just us." For some reason, I'm actually glad he asked me that question, happy this little bit of information is out in the open, even though it makes me uncomfortable.

This conversation is making one thing crystal clear—I'm starting to like Hudson, and I'm not sure how I feel about that yet.

Even though his curious eyes are still on me, I try to stir things away not only from myself but also into safer territory. I decide to ask the first thing that comes to mind. "What job would you be terrible at?"

Hudson doesn't react at all for a moment, making me anxious I hit another nerve with my question, but then he throws his head back and laughs.

I release a sigh, at the same time wondering what's so funny.

After calming down, he shakes his head. "I'm afraid there are a lot of things I'm bad at, but right now, I have to say I'd be the worst baker ever."

He motions toward the counter, and my eyes go wide when I see what's in front of him.

CHAPTER SIX

Laughing doesn't seem to be enough for the sight in front of me, so I snort a little too. "What on earth have you been doing over there?"

Hudson joins in, and it feels good to crack up over something, to completely let loose without a care in the world. It feels like it's been forever since I've done that.

Folding up a few pieces of chocolate-stuffed dough into rectangles was apparently more than our rockstar could handle. Instead, the croissants have no recognizable shape whatsoever. Each one is just a big blob with chocolate bits and pieces sticking out at every possible angle.

"I can't...I don't know what to say." My voice comes out in almost a shriek, and I have to look away from his baking attempt before I start crying from all the laughing.

He pokes my arm with his finger. "Hey, don't be mean. I have no problem owning my weaknesses." The corners of his eyes crinkle with laugh lines, and I like that he doesn't take himself too seriously.

That's a big plus in my book. It might even earn a gold star.

Patting his arm, I try my best to refrain from more laughter. "No worries at all. No matter what they look like, they'll still taste delicious."

He lets out a big breath. "Phew. I'm so happy to hear that. I was actually worried for a moment I ruined them."

"Nope, we're all good." I smile at him and can't keep the grin off my face for the remainder of the time we work in silence.

Once we're done with everything, I point toward the abandoned stool. "Why don't you relax now and do your...musing thing—whatever that entails. I'll just clean up quickly."

Turning around, I walk over to the big sink but not without hearing his low chuckle behind me. This man is a walking ray of sunshine, and I can't remember the last time I've smiled this much. I try to focus on the huge pile of dirty bowls and other equipment that has piled up over the past few hours rather than how his laugh reverberates through my entire body—well, at least I try to. With determination, I shove up the sleeves of my shirt and turn on the faucet.

Hudson suddenly appears next to me, nudging me aside with his hip. "I clean, you dry."

My breathing hitches and I tell myself to use caution—a huge amount of caution—after the way everything went down with Sebastian. I've had more than enough time since last year to dissect my past relationship with him, making me realize how toxic and bound to fail it was from the beginning. Being careful seems to be the last thing on my mind when it comes to Hudson though. No, that's actually not true. It's on my mind, prominently so, but shoved back into the corner and all but forgotten within the first minute of him being around me.

"Sponge?" He holds out his hand, and I silently place it in his palm, trying hard not to touch his skin in the process.

Been there, done that. With my luck, a moan might just slip out of my mouth at the contact this time, or something equally embarrassing. "You really don't have to do this. You already help me at the bakery, and let Mira and me stay at your house too. I feel like I'm taking over your whole life. I don't want to be even more of a burden."

I lower my head a little, not wanting him to see the vulnerability I'm sure is visible in my eyes. I've been trying hard to not let the past rule my present, but that's always easier said than done.

Words stay with us, no matter how hard we try to forget them.

The feeling of not being enough has lessened over time, but it's moments like these that bring it all back. Doubt is an ugly part of the brain that should stay hidden forever, but seldom does.

I look up just as he lifts one of his hands to my face before dropping it at the last moment. His gaze holds mine, determination unabashedly portrayed in his eyes. "You listen to me, Charlie. Neither of you are a burden to me. No, I didn't expect to come home to a couple of roommates, but I'm glad you're here. Very glad, actually. I know it sounds completely crazy, but these couple of days with you guys have been better and far more fun than most of my last year. So please stop apologizing and saying negative things about you or this situation. I really don't like hearing them."

I blink, disbelief rattling my very core. I swallow a few times to try and get past the lump in my throat that's suddenly keeping me from breathing properly. I'm not sure if he can see the emotions on my face, but if he does, he doesn't let it on. "Thank you, I appreciate that."

"It's nothing. Really." His hand touches my arm lightly, only for a second, but long enough to still feel his warm fingers imprinted on my skin moments later.

Sebastian's hands were usually cold.

I'm not sure where that thought just came from but I shake it off. Rather, I'm trying to think of something else to say, needing the distraction before I turn into an emotional mess from his words. "So, why don't you tell me what exactly you mean when you talk about your muse sessions? That way, we can avoid further confusion about it. The other day, it seemed like you didn't want to talk about it in front of your grandma. Is it a secret?" I lean in a little, curiosity taking over.

He doesn't laugh like I expect him to, so I watch him for a moment as he adds a few drops of soap into the water. When he finally turns my way, I'm surprised to see the serious expression on his face and a sigh escape his lips. "Actually, I'd really appreciate it if you could keep this between us. It would make my life a lot easier if no one else knew about it."

This new bit of information stuns me for a moment. "Oh okay. Sure, no problem at all."

"Thank you." He lets out another big breath, and I wonder what's up with all of this.

There's clearly more to these sessions than I thought there was. Or maybe I just don't get it because let's face it, this isn't my scene at all. I mean, I didn't even know who he was when we first met.

The comforting sound of the running water stops when Hudson turns off the faucet. With the sponge in his hand, he starts washing one of the mixing bowls I used earlier. I'm not sure what I expected, but this seems more normal than I thought it would. Somehow, I thought I'd find the picture of my rockstar roommate washing the dishes to be hilarious, and maybe even slightly odd. Instead, it feels like no big deal—just two people sharing a completely normal and mundane task.

While I'm still clueless about what's going on, I'd really like to change that if possible. "Can you at least tell me what exactly it is you're planning on doing during these sessions?"

"Sure." It seems like taking a few minutes was all he needed to get out of his funk, and he's back to smiling. In the short amount of time we've spent together, he seems like a normal guy—contrary to the moody, brooding, or just plain arrogant kind of musicians you hear a lot about in the media. "Let's just say that my creative juices haven't been flowing very well over the past few months, and I need to rectify that. Very badly and very quickly."

"Huh." And here this man surprises me again with his answer. That was definitely not at all what I thought he was gonna say. "Are you talking about writing songs?" I stop drying the bowl in my hand, tilting my head to look up at him. "Wait. You do write your own songs, right?"

Without warning, my face is suddenly covered in water drops and soap bubbles.

I blink at him for probably a solid minute while my brain is trying to catch up with what just happened. "Did you... Did you just flick water at me?" I wipe my hand over my face and look at Hudson incredulously.

"Sorry." He's laughing—big, loud belly laughs that make me want to join in too. "Strong reflexes to being insulted, I suppose, or maybe it was payback. I still owed you one for the fun welcome home with the dough."

Well, what can I say to that? He's got me there. Holding up my hands, I point my finger at him. "All right, I can't argue with that. But now we're even."

"If you say so." He keeps chuckling, and we go back to doing the dishes. After a few minutes, he's the first to break the silence, his voice filled with sadness and frustration. "To answer your question, though, yes, I do write my own music. But it seems like I've been having a bit of writer's block hit me out of the blue. It's nothing I'm proud of, and no one really knows about it either, not even my bandmates. To be honest, I'm not even sure why I'm telling you all of this right now." He shakes his head, not looking at me.

I try to keep my voice quiet and calming. I obviously don't have any experience with this sort of thing, but I can imagine what a tough and vulnerable subject this must be for him. "And you think I can help you with that?"

When he turns around to look at me this time, his gaze is soft, holding an emotion so strong, my heart skips a beat. "You already have. Just spending time with you seems to do the trick. The second I saw you, I had music and words floating through my head." He pauses for a moment, lost in thought. "I can't even tell you how incredible it feels. Nothing like this has happened in the past six months. And even before then, inspiration never seemed to hit me this hard."

Hudson swings his hands around in the air as he continues talking, his excitement almost palpable.

His words leave me speechless for a moment, and the

look on his face as he recalls the experience has me slightly entranced. There's no doubt about the level of pure joy he's been feeling about this, and it's almost infectious.

That feeling is crushed into a pile of dust though, as the realization of this whole situation hits me. Hudson needs me to save his career—or at least he thinks he does—and that knowledge settles in my stomach with a sour taste. A rush of disappointment makes its way through my body while I keep telling myself there's no reason for it.

It's great I can help him with his career, right?

I mean, what more could I want?

CHAPTER SEVEN

I can't believe it's only been twenty-four hours since Hudson dropped Mira and me off at the airport. When we got home from the bakery the other day, I got a phone call from my best friend's mom, informing me that Monica had been in an accident. After getting all the details and the hospital info from her, I immediately went online to book a flight to New York—after profusely declining any sort of private air transportation or upgrades Hudson was offering me.

Thankfully, my nerves finally settled a little after I was able to see for myself that Monica's okay—at least, as okay as anyone can be after getting hit by a car and needing immediate surgery for their broken leg, which was especially bad with Monica's career as a dancer. But my best friend seems to be the same—loud, boisterous, and slightly inappropriate at times, if the male nurse's flushed cheeks were anything to go by when we walked into Monica's room.

My phone vibrates from where I set it on the windowsill, and I snatch it up quickly to silence it. Mira fell asleep on the way to the hospital, and the last thing I want to do is wake her up. Spending half the day traveling across the country yesterday—from Los Angeles to New York—and spending the night in a hotel didn't make for the best sleep for either of us.

"What does Mr. Sexy Rockstar want now?" Monica's eyebrows are raised as she waits for my answer. Her strawberry blonde hair is piled on top of her head, her green eyes looking a little tired on her pale face.

Sitting back in the chair next to her bed, I prop up my feet on the side rail of the bed. "How do you know it's Hudson?"

She shrugs her shoulders, a smirk on her face. "Just a hunch, I guess. Am I wrong?"

I unlock the screen and shake my head. "Nope."

"I knew it." Her voice sounds triumphant, and I have to laugh at the big, goofy grin on her face.

"You're impossible." I roll my eyes at her, still smiling.

"What? Why? I mean, come on, give a girl something. I was just in an accident, and you know how much I love him and his music. And umm, you just fucking moved in with him."

That comment makes me sit up straight again. "I did not *move in* with him. You know I never would've taken Hannah up on her offer had I known it would be anyone but us in the house, let alone someone like Hudson."

She sighs and plops back against her pillow. "Gosh, do I ever. You'd probably be the last one jumping on an offer like this. I'm not sure if that makes it better or worse. Anyway, what does he want?"

I look down at my phone to read the message.

**Hudson: When are you guys coming back home? It's
so quiet here without you. To be honest, it's actually
pretty boring. Grandma threatened to take me out
with her squad later on if I don't get busy. I'm
officially scared.**

I chuckle at his text. I mean, how can I not? Monica is
surprisingly quiet, but I can almost feel the curiosity radiating
off of her. I'm also pretty sure she's trying to burn a hole in
the side of my head with her gaze.

**Charlie: We're gonna fly back the day after tomorrow.
Hudson: Is your friend gonna be okay?**

I want to call and tell him everything that happened to
Monica, but I don't think we have that kind of relationship
yet. It seems like we're on the way to becoming friends,
though, despite our "muse deal." I haven't had real friends in
many years—besides Monica, of course, but she's been busy
with her career and traveling ever since we graduated from
high school.

Despite my earlier reluctance, I have to admit I like the
idea of Hudson and me becoming friends. I love both Mira
and Hannah to the moon and back, but it feels nice to have
someone my age around to talk to.

**Charlie: Yeah, it's gonna be a while for her to get
back to normal, but she'll be okay. She's gonna
transfer to a rehabilitation facility in two days, so
that'll keep her busy for a little while.**

I'm sad to leave Monica again so soon, but I know she has to focus on getting better, and sadly, I can't help her with that. There's no point in denying I'm excited to go back to my new home, though. In just the few weeks since we moved, I've felt better and more relaxed than most of last year. It's been a real life-changer.

A change of scenery really does do wonders sometimes.

"Hello? Are you going to talk to me or what?" Monica's dramatic voice cuts into my conscience, but I ignore her for another moment while Hudson's next message comes in.

Hudson: I'm glad to hear that. You're a good friend for being there for her. Let me know which flight you're gonna be on (or when you stop being stubborn and let me get you better tickets at least), so I can pick you up from the airport, okay?

"Come on, Charlie, don't leave me hanging." Monica's voice has turned whiny.

Deciding to throw her a bone, I look up from my phone. "He wants to know when we're going to be back."

"Aww, that's so sweet. He misses you." Putting a hand over her heart, she sighs. She looks so completely smitten and happy I can almost see the hearts in her eyes. I try to keep my eyes on her face, since I want to flinch every time I see her bruised body that's covered with bandages.

"I'm sure he misses his new best friend, our little Miss Mira here." I point over to the stroller on the opposite side of the room, where Mira's snoring softly. "You should see those two together, Mo. It's quite the sight. The best way to describe it is like two old souls that have been separated for ages and are finally together again. They absolutely adore each other. It's almost like nothing else exists around them. I've never seen Mira get attached to anyone this quickly."

"Looks like someone's jealous." Monica sing-songs the words as she points at me.

"Who? *Me?*" My eyebrows pull together, and I have to laugh.

Monica chimes in, the occasional snort thrown in for good measure, and I press my index finger to my lips to remind her we have to be quiet.

She nods and puts her hands around her mouth to form her own kind of megaphone. "*You,* my friend, are jealous of the relationship between Hudson and Mira," she whisper-shouts.

"No, I'm not." Despite my request to her, my voice comes out louder than I intended, and Mira stirs in her stroller. Thankfully, she snuggles back into the other side without waking up. "It's just sweet to see them together, that's all. I told you I'm helping him with his career. You know better than anyone that I'm not looking for a relationship. I don't need a guy, even though I don't mind him being my friend."

Letting out a sigh, she shakes her head at me, all the playfulness suddenly gone from her face. "I know you don't *need* a guy. And I never said you should throw yourself at Hudson and ask him to marry you either." She puts a finger to her chin and gazes past me out the window. "Even though that would definitely be super awesome. Could you imagine the headlines? My best friend and the hot—"

"Mo!" I interrupt her before she can finish that sentence,

knowing full well I just lost her to her own little world of all things celebrity.

Rolling her eyes at me, she stretches her arms across her chest, wincing at the movement. "What I wanted to say was that I think it would be good for you to get back into the game. You don't have to commit to anything. Just go out and have some fun. It's been almost a year since Sebastian, that stupid dickhead, and I don't like that he did such a number on you. I still wish I would've kicked him in the balls when I had the chance. He deserved it, and then some."

"Okay. Calm down, tiger. This has nothing to do with my ex and everything to do with Hudson. Aren't you the one always telling me about all these famous guys changing women like their underwear? I don't think I want to be another notch on a bedpost. That's just not who I am, and you know that. Plus, let's not forget I'm not a single deal either. The last thing he needs is a woman with a baby getting attached to him." My feelings are scattered all over the place from this conversation, and I let out a big sigh.

"Hey, hey. None of that!" Monica's voice is firm. "You know how I feel about you saying stuff like that. Just because you've had bad experiences in the past doesn't mean you have to give it up altogether. You deserve someone good in your life, and you deserve to have some fun too, you both do. End of story."

"Hudson said something similar." I belatedly realize I'll probably only encourage her with this admission. "Well, not really, never mind." I make a face, hoping she'll just forget about all of this.

"Honestly, if he said something close to this, I like him even more. Not everyone is bad, but I understand it's hard for you to believe in good guys. I promise you they're out there, though. I truly believe it for you." Her smile is reassuring, and I almost want to believe her.

As usual, I ignore the fact that she only believes there's someone out there for me but not her. It's been a battle between us for ages, since she refuses to talk about her love life.

"I know you do, and I'm sure I'll find someone eventually, but I don't think that someone for me is Hudson. I mean, *look* at him. We're completely different, it could never work. Plus, I could never compete with the long list of prospects he can choose from on a daily basis either. I'm not sure I'd ever be able to handle that." I sigh again, feeling defeated and a little upset with both Monica and myself for allowing the conversation to go down this road. All week long, I've successfully avoided thinking about Hudson this way, knowing it would only frustrate me.

"It seems like *he's* interested in *you*, though." Leave it to my best friend to push my buttons even more.

I throw my hands up in the air, feeling the irritation burning under my skin. "How do you know that? I've known him for less than a week. I'd like to think we're on the way to becoming friends, but that's it. I doubt he's looking for anything more anyway. He's very focused on his songwriting, which is quite captivating to watch. A lot of the time, he just sits there, completely engrossed in his music sheets."

Monica doesn't say anything, which strikes me as weird. Instead, she's grinning from ear to ear.

"What? What did I say?" I pause, mentally going over what I just said but coming up empty. "Why do you look like the cat that ate the canary?"

"You like him." Her statement is short and simple, so unlike my best friend's usual declarations.

Something about that makes me nervous, especially since she's still grinning. "Stop smiling at me like that, it's creepy. And yes, of course, I like him. Why wouldn't I? He seems like a nice guy."

"You *really* like him."

Rolling my eyes at her—something I seem to be doing a lot in her presence today—I take in the self-satisfied smirk that's telling me exactly how happy she's with herself. "You're annoying. Now stop it." I can't help myself after all and grin at her.

"I just wasn't sure you'd ever like anyone again. I was so worried about you after Sebastian." Her voice softens, and I know exactly what she's talking about because I was worried too. I wasn't sure I could ever like another guy again either, or if I even wanted to.

Now, I'm not sure about anything—all because of Hudson.

"Mo, as much as I like him, I don't think he's the right guy for the job." Monica has been my best friend since elementary school, and we've always been honest with each other. No need to change that now. "And this is not just about me anymore either. Not only could he break my heart ten times worse than all the other guys before him combined, I also have to think about Mira. How could I ever risk her heart?"

Monica studies me for a moment before speaking. "Because love is worth it, and you both deserve a good guy in your lives." She says it like a statement, like it shouldn't be questioned, and I'm guessing in her eyes, that's the case.

I shake my head at the crazy girl I call my best friend.

"And because you have the chance to get down and dirty with Hudson freaking Mitchell, Charlie. Just do it for me, girl. You can't let a chance like this pass." She levels me with a death stare, and I burst into laughter before slamming my hands over my mouth to stay quiet.

Only Monica would do a one-eighty like this.

It's like she knew I needed her craziness because, just like that, my weird mood is gone. "Of course you'd say something like that."

"Come on, you can't blame me. I mean, have you seen his ass?" She sighs loudly, a dreamy expression on her face.

"Nope. But how about his abs?" I giggle as her gaze snaps to my face, her mouth wide open as she stares at me.

"You've seen his *abs*? You better not be toying with me right now, or I will never ever forgive you for such a lie."

Even though she's glaring at me, I can't deny I'm enjoying this just a little bit. I don't get these moments often, so I take my time to relish in this one. "Did I not tell you how we met? Oops."

"You better spill the beans, or I'll come over there, broken leg be damned."

I have no doubt in my mind she'd actually do it too, so I quickly fill her in on everything, having a hard time making it through the story without bursting out laughing at her stunned expression.

"I cannot believe you haven't told me about this before. You are the worst best friend ever." She smacks her lips a few times, shaking her head at me, like I did something far worse than not telling her how I met one of her favorite musicians. "Unbelievable."

"Sorry, Mo." I can't help myself and chuckle again, earning another death glare from her. It's not easy to surprise Monica like this, let alone make her speechless.

"Does he have a happy trail?" She wiggles her eyebrows at me, her face lighting up with excitement. And just like that, she's getting over her own shock by shocking me.

I hide my face in my hands, absolutely certain I have a healthy flush on my cheeks. "Oh my gosh. I can't believe you just asked me that." I peek at her from between my fingers, confirming she's still waiting for an answer, her big grin firmly back in place. "Yes, okay? Yes, yes, yes. He has a freaking happy trail, framed by the perfect V-cut, all of it disappearing into a probably very impressive happy place."

Monica looks at me, her eyes wide as saucers, her head cocked to the side. A second later, she laughs. "Wow. Look at you, I'm impressed. This one's really done a number on you, hasn't he?"

If I thought I was confused about Hudson before, I'm completely puzzled now. Talking to someone about him makes him even more compelling. I blink at my best friend. "I guess so."

"Well, I can't wait to meet him soon." Her smile is wide, but just when I'm about to ask her what the heck she's talking about, Mira whimpers.

"Hold that thought, we're not done here." I point at Monica before getting up to walk over to the stroller. Mira looks at me through droopy eyelids, one of her little hands rubbing her eye. Her fine, blonde hair stands up in every possible direction, a sight that still makes me smile every single day. "Hi, sweetie pie. Did Aunt Mo wake you up?"

Monica huffs behind me as I bend down to get closer to

Mira. She stretches her hands up in the air before reaching for me. I unbuckle her so I can get her out, and she immediately puts her head on my shoulder. My eyes close instinctively, cherishing these small moments with her. Rubbing her back for a moment, I walk over to sit back down in the chair. It usually takes her a few minutes to fully wake up, but then she's ready to go.

My gaze zooms back in on Monica. "What exactly did you mean when you said you can't wait to meet him soon?"

She clasps her hands together in her lap. "Well, the doctors said I'll be out for quite a while, and my dance group already knows about that. Obviously, they weren't happy about the news, but it's not like anyone can change what happened."

"I'm sorry, Mo. I know this must be hard for you." I try to keep my tone as gentle as possible.

Shrugging her shoulders, she waves me off. "It's okay. It could've been a lot worse, so I'm happy there's a possibility of recovery, at least—even though it's gonna be a pain to get there. Literally. But anyway. You know I love my parents, but my mom's already driving me crazy just visiting. There's no way I'm gonna stay at their place for longer than I have to. And since I don't have a place in the city anymore, I thought I could come see you guys for a bit. Only if that's okay with you, of course. The doctors said they'd like me to start in the rehabilitation facility here, but that I should be okay to continue my physical therapy anywhere, as long as I stick to it."

My smile is so big, I'm afraid my face will crack at any moment. "Are you serious right now?"

Monica nods, and I want to jump up and run over to her,

but refrain from doing that with Mira in my arms. Instead, I squeal a little, hoping my voice portrays all the enthusiasm I feel. "Best news ever. Of course we'd love to have you. You don't even have to ask that. I'm so excited."

"Me too. I was ready for some time off anyway, even though I wasn't planning on spending it this way. At least I'll get to be with you guys. Plus, I've heard you've got some nice eye candy in town." She sits up further in her white hospital bed, wiggling her eyebrows.

I let out a loud sigh. "You're gonna be after him, aren't you?"

"Not if you snatch him first." She winks at me and giggles. "I might still have to squeeze that fine ass, though, if I get a chance."

"Goodness. Please don't. I actually live there now and have to show my face around town."

She throws up her hands in exasperation. "Come on, you can't tell me you haven't at least thought about it. I mean, that man is pretty much perfection. Have you actually looked at him? Like, *really* looked at him?"

"Of course I have, I'm not blind. There's no denying he's freaking gorgeous. Actually, he might be the most beautiful person I've ever seen in my life. If I could get away with it, I'd just stare at him all day long. There, are you happy now?" I look out the hospital window at the sunny New York sky, suddenly feeling a little embarrassed by my admission. It's so unlike me to blurt out things like that.

"Very." Her one-word answer makes me look back at her. "Does that mean you'll go on a date with him?"

"I don't know, Mo. Maybe, possibly. He might not even

ask again." A little ache settles in my chest at the very real possibility.

Monica's studying me, silently urging me to take the chance, to venture out of my comfort zone and take a risk. "Somehow, I have a feeling he's going to ask again."

I can't even blame her for being pushy, because if the roles were reversed, I'd most likely do the same. That's what best friends are for, to sometimes help each other make uncomfortable decisions when they think it's for the best.

The realization hits me that I'm actually contemplating this crazy idea, but perhaps she's right. Maybe it *is* time for me to move on with my life, and try and get over my past in every possible way.

When I meet her gaze again, a few moments later, her eyes go wide in excitement. She starts clapping and cheering before I even get the next words out of my mouth.

"Yes, if he asks again, I will."

CHAPTER EIGHT

THE CALIFORNIA SUN IS BLINDINGLY BRIGHT WHEN I step out of the airport terminal. I push the stroller and suitcase to the side, deciding to give my eyes a moment to adjust since it's probably safer than walking straight into someone, or worse, traffic. I *still* manage to almost trip over my own two feet, as a set of strong hands grab my waist tightly from behind, saving me from eating the ground.

"Easy there." A shiver runs down my spine at the low voice whispering in my ear as he lets me go, and I immediately miss his touch.

I'm not sure my heart knows what's going on, but it seems to think we're in the middle of running a marathon.

Betrayed by my own body. That could certainly be the new theme song of my life, at least whenever a certain rockstar is around.

"Hi, Hudson. Thanks for catching me." My voice sounds hoarse and my cheeks heat up. From the sound of his chuckle, he's still right behind me, and I'm not sure I'm capable of facing him this close without going into cardiac arrest.

"No problem, happy to help."

While I'm still debating if I should turn around or not, he takes the decision out of my hand by walking around me. When he's standing in front of me, I'm confused by the serious expression on his face, instead of the friendly and welcoming one I expected. His baseball cap sits low on his forehead, and dark sunglasses hide his eyes. I'm not sure that's actually providing him with any sort of anonymity, but it seems to be better than nothing.

His chin lifts a couple inches, nodding toward the crowd of people walking in front of the terminal. "Who was that?"

"Who?" His question takes me by surprise, as I'm still busy re-memorizing his face, like I could've forgotten it in the short time we were gone. It's still nice to stare at, though.

His eyebrows are knitted together tightly, and I'm not sure if he's looking at me or something over my shoulder since I can't see his eyes. "The guy who waved at you when you left the building."

Oh, that guy. I already forgot all about him. "That was Martin. We met him on the flight. Thankfully. He helped us with our luggage and the stroller. You wouldn't believe how hard it can be to navigate a stroller while dealing with all the luggage too." I blow a strand of hair out of my face, slowly starting to get a little hot.

"Well, that was *nice* of him." His lips press into a thin line before he shifts his focus to the stroller. The canopy is pulled down as far as it goes, covering most of Mira's body. "Is she sleeping?" He peeks through the clear cutout in the top before turning back to me.

Nodding, I let out a big breath. "Yes, finally. She fought it the whole flight, started crying when we started our descent, and then finally passed out ten seconds before we landed. She has the worst timing, but it's all over now." I grab the water bottle from the stroller and take a big gulp.

"Poor thing, she must be exhausted." He looks at Mira one more time before holding out his hand to me.

I stare at it for a moment, my breath catching in my throat. He can't possibly—

"Let me carry your suitcase."

The sound that comes out of my mouth is a mix of nervous laughter and a cough. Heat spreads up my throat and onto my cheeks, and I can only hope the combination of the bright sun blasting down on us and Hudson's dark sunglasses make it impossible for him to notice my embarrassment. "Of course. Thank you."

He nods and leads us through the airport labyrinth to the correct parking lot. His huge, dark SUV stands out like a sore thumb, but I appreciate the spacious inside once we've got everything stowed away. By some miracle, Mira didn't wake up and is safely seated in her car seat in the back. I hope she stays asleep on the hour-long drive back home.

We hit the freeway a few minutes later, and Hudson glances at me for a moment before turning on the cruise control. "So, how's your friend doing? Did the transfer to the rehab facility this morning go well?"

"Uh-huh. From what she's texted me, she's already made her nurse blush a few times, and her physical therapist is a charmer, so it sounds like she's doing great."

Hudson chuckles, one of his hands lightly tapping on his knee. "She sounds like fun."

"She's the best. She actually said she's going to come out to visit us in a few weeks when she gets the okay to travel. Her fracture was a bit more complex, so it'll take a while to heal."

"That must be hard for her. I can't imagine if something similar would happen to my voice. It's a scary thought." He's quiet for a moment, probably lost in thought. "I'm glad she seems to be in good spirits, though, that counts for half of it. And I'm sure it'll be great for you guys to spend some time together."

"Yes! Everyone in Brooksville has been so welcoming to me, but nothing replaces a best friend. I'm used to not seeing her a lot, but I still miss her. Monica's been so busy touring the world for the last few years, she usually only makes it home every few months, for two or three days. Thank goodness for social media and video chats." I turn to him. "But you know, more than anyone, what that's like."

He nods, adjusting his sunglasses. "It's the most incredible experience to see so many beautiful places and to meet so many wonderful people from around the world. Yet, at the same time, it gets tiring after a while to be cramped up in a bus, or to live in one generic hotel suite after the other. Your values, and what's important in life, changes a lot over time."

"How has it changed your life?" I study him, unable to hold back the question, even though I feel like I might be invading his privacy. On the other side, I know he wouldn't answer my question if he didn't want to. Hudson doesn't seem like a pushover.

"I think what changed the most was the urge for adventure. In the beginning, the excitement to get out into the world and see every last bit of it was exhilarating. Add the people you meet along the way to the mix, and it makes it almost addicting. As cliché as it sounds, you're young, wild, and free."

He stops talking, and I wonder if he's contemplating how much he should share with me. We've definitely gotten to know each other better this last week, but when it comes down to it, we're still strangers for the most part—even though it doesn't feel that way. I also wonder if he was talking about women when he mentioned the people he met along the way. I mean, that's what the whole rockstar title comes with, right? Lots and lots of women.

Changing lanes smoothly, he clears his throat. "Once some sort of routine settles in, life and priorities shift around. Playing your music in front of a crowd is still the best thing ever, but suddenly, you crave waking up at home in your own bed every day, maybe even with the same person next to you. Variety all of a sudden doesn't sound as much fun anymore, but uniformity does." His voice is barely a whisper when he finishes the sentence, and a hint of melancholy lingers in the air.

Just like that, the atmosphere has changed. If the constant glances Hudson keeps sending my way are any indication, he feels it too. I'm not sure if he regrets sharing all of that with me, so I try to think of a way to steer the conversation back to neutral territory.

Giving him a small smile, I focus on the part of the conversation that seems the safest and least sad. "Are you trying to tell me that the famous Hudson Mitchell is trying to settle down?"

Apparently, that was the wrong thing to say after all,

because his expression turns even more somber. "Is that so hard to imagine?"

Way to go, Charlie.

"What? No. No! That's not at all what I meant. I'm sorry. I guess I thought you meant it as a joke."

The car fills with silence again, but this time, it's a rather uncomfortable one. My nerves kick in, and I start to throw out the first question that comes to mind. "So, why isn't there a Mrs. Mitchell? I'm sure you aren't lacking prospects."

Seriously, Charlie? Seems like the filter between your brain and mouth is malfunctioning once again.

He turns on the blinker and takes the next exit off the freeway, stopping at a traffic light at the bottom of the ramp. His gaze is on me, but I avoid it, being a total chicken. I can't blame him if he's getting annoyed with me either, because even I'm shocked I've been asking him all these personal questions. Monica wouldn't hesitate for a second to dive into his life like she's known him forever, but I, on the other hand, don't normally act this way.

Until now, I guess.

"I apologize. Again. It's really none of my business, so just forget I asked." I can't stop the all-telling flush from creeping up my neck, and I'm grateful Hudson's paying attention to the road and not me.

"No, it's okay." Hudson clears his throat, and after a quick glance, I'm glad to see he doesn't look mad. "I know this will sound awkward, but if I'm honest, I've actually wondered the same." He shrugs, like he didn't just make a statement that tugged at my heartstrings.

"You have? Really?" My voice sounds squeaky, not hiding the disbelief and shock.

"Most people think it's easy to meet someone special when you're in my position, like you just snap your fingers. From my experience, it's actually the opposite."

I'd be lying if I said I wasn't especially curious now. I'm leaning toward him in my seat, just enough to put my elbow on the armrest between us, propping my chin up on my hand. "How so?"

Gripping the steering wheel with both hands, Hudson's knuckles are almost white from the pressure he puts on them, the muscles in his forearms rigid and strung tight. "Quite frankly, it's hard to tell who's interested in me as a person, or just the famous rockstar. Some people just want to be seen with me, have their picture taken, or maybe even snag a gig somewhere in the entertainment industry. There are a lot of leeches out there, I had to learn that the hard way."

I'm stunned for a moment. "That doesn't sound like fun. How old were you when you started your career?"

"I had just turned eighteen, and was only out of high school for a few months when I went on my first tour." A frown is deeply etched into his forehead, his lips pressed together in a tight line.

The sudden urge to make him feel better stuns me for a moment. I want to reach out to reassure him, to make him feel better, but I'm not sure he wants that sort of comfort, or if it's even my place to give it to him.

"I was such a kid, young and impressionable, believing everything people told me. I've definitely learned my lesson since then." He grits his teeth, and I'm torn between wanting to go back in time to take my question back and wanting to find out more about what happened to him.

He lets out a big breath. "Sorry. Let's talk about something else, okay?"

I feel like someone just dangled a treat in front of my nose, only to snatch it away the last second. I want to ask a million more questions, but instead, I do the right thing and nod. "Of course."

"Thank you." He opens and closes his hands a few times, clearly trying to shake off his frustration. "So, Grandma told me you're going to make the birthday cake and some other delicious treats for my mom's birthday next week?"

The birthday party for Hannah's daughter. Hudson's mom. I feel like a total idiot, but I didn't even think about the connection between them. Actually, I haven't even thought about the party and the birthday cake since Hannah asked me a couple weeks ago. Who would've thought this turned into such a family affair?

Well, I'm definitely not going to tell him that realization just made me a nervous wreck.

I know most people would say it's just a cake, but it's more to me. I try to get every cake perfect for the individual recipient. I want it to match. I want them to think back to whatever big day they celebrated and remember how much they loved my cake. It's silly, but that's how it's always felt to me.

Since I can't exactly say this kind of stuff to Hudson—who would undoubtedly think I'm as nutty as a fruitcake—I plaster on a big smile for him. "Yeah, I'm excited. This will be the first big cake I'm making here, so it'll be perfect to test the oven in the bakery for a bigger crowd."

His eyes crinkle at the sides when he chuckles. "That makes sense. I suck at baking, as you know, so I can't even imagine creating anything that big. Mom likes to be social, so I'm sure it's gonna be a good-sized party. The more people are there, the more she can meddle too. I wouldn't be surprised if she already has a few possible prospects for me invited too."

I look at him, trying to figure out if he's serious or not. "She does that?"

He shrugs his shoulders, scratching the back of his neck. "Wouldn't be the first time. Though, that was a while ago, so maybe she's given up."

"Huh." Thoughts race through my mind at Hudson being set up with different women at the upcoming party.

Why does that thought make my stomach churn? It's not like it has anything to do with me.

The SUV slows down when Hudson turns into the driveway of his property. "Maybe you could come with me, Charlie?"

"To the party?"

He nods, his voice hopeful. "Yes. The rest of my family has been dying to meet you, and I'd love it if you were there with me."

I suddenly feel a little lightheaded because that sounds an awful lot like a date.

As if Hudson read my mind, he turns my way and pushes his sunglasses up and into his hair. His beautiful eyes focus on me, his gaze drawing me in. "It can be a date if you want it to be, or not. Your choice. You know what I want."

My mouth falls slightly open, both his admission— wanting a date with me—and the promise I made Monica to say yes if he ever asked me out again swirling around smack center in my brain. To be honest, I'm not sure I would've made this promise to Monica had I known he'd ask again so soon.

But it can just be easy and fun, right? No expectations or anything. Just two friends enjoying each other's company. No biggie at all.

I lean my head on the headrest and look at him, studying his breathtaking face. He turns his baseball cap around, which is my absolute weakness, and mimics my position.

Gosh, he's handsome.

A small smirk crosses his lips, making the dimple on his right cheek appear. "So, what do you say, roomie? Want to go on a date with me? I promise I'll make it worth your while."

I swear, this man will be the end of me. No one should be this sexy and utterly charming, not to mention adorable, all at the same time. It's like he's bulldozing every defense I've built up like it's nothing.

There really is only one right answer. "Yes."

CHAPTER NINE

THE FOLLOWING WEEK, I TURNED INTO A MASTER OF pretense—to me, the conversation with Hudson didn't happen. Of course, I know it *did* happen, but I pretended otherwise so life would be easier for me. If I'd acknowledged the fact that I actually agreed to go to his mom's birthday party *as his date*, I might have ruined the cake purely out of nerves. Hudson was a lifesaver by not mentioning it either. I'm sure my anxiety was easy to spot, even from miles away, most likely waving around a big, fat "Caution" sign.

One thing that definitely changed is the tension between us, which isn't a surprise considering we work side by side at the bakery and live in the same house. Everything has become more intense. The accidental touches of two people still getting to know each other, the intentional touches of friends who have learned so much about each other. The secret glances, the obvious glimpses.

I've also learned a lot about his habits and routines, which makes living together a lot easier. Much to my ovaries' delight, one of my favorite routines of his is the shirtless run he goes on every morning, right before he has his muse session with me. Since he said he doesn't mind when Mira is around, the three of us have come to start our mornings together most days.

The day of the party has arrived, though, and my nerves are back in full swing, ready to kick me in the butt.

"Ugh." The groan echoes in my closet, not making me feel any better. My body is strung so tight with jitters, I feel like I might unexpectedly pass out or puke at any moment.

A knock on the door makes me jump.

"Charlie?" Hannah's muffled voice comes through the thick wood, and I call for her to come in.

When she enters, I look her up and down and whistle. She's wearing a floral-patterned maxi dress with a cream-colored cardigan on top. "Look at you. You look amazing. We're gonna have to beat the guys off of you with a stick tonight."

She chuckles, shaking her head. "Stop it, you're making me blush."

"Good. You deserve it." Giving her a big smile, I feel a great sense of gratitude wash over me for having her in my life.

"I just wanted to see if you're all set before I leave. Hudson is already over at his mom's to help, and I'm headed there now too. Are you sure you don't want me to wait for you?"

"No, I'm all good, thank you. I'll just meet you there in a little after Mira wakes up."

"Sounds good." She looks past me, probably inspecting the mess I made when I threw about every piece of clothing I own all over my room. I mean, what do you wear to the party of your client—who also happens to be the mother of your roommate slash date for today, *and* a major rockstar—to make a good impression?

She points her finger toward the bed. "Wear the navy blue dress, it looks stunning on you." With a huge grin on her face, she waves goodbye before she turns around to walk away, then stops once more and looks over her shoulder. "Also, stop worrying so much, everyone's going to love you."

I'm equally nervous and relieved when I finally make it to the Mitchell House an hour later—nervous to meet Hudson's family and relieved I made it with the cake still intact. Maybe it would've been smarter to have someone help me, after all, but it's too late for that now. Last night, I had nightmares about the cake getting smashed, making the worst possible impression on the Mitchells. Hudson's family. My date's family.

Yikes.

I'm still not sure if I've lost my marbles to agree to this, since my brain's still entirely undecided.

"Charlie." Hudson's loud voice pulls me out of my thoughts. He's jogging down the driveway toward the curb where I parked. He's wearing dark jeans, dark boots, and a plain white T-shirt. I've come to think of this as his signature rockstar look. It definitely suits him.

Who am I kidding? It's hot as hell, melting my insides pretty much every time I see him.

Without a doubt, he looks good enough to eat, and I'm pretty sure he knows it too.

Stepping out of my car, I smooth out my blue dress. Of course, I ended up picking the one Hannah told me to.

"Hey, Huds—" His big arms come around me so tightly and unexpectedly, that the air whooshes out of my lungs. A tingling sensation spreads through my entire being while Hudson's body heat seeps through both of our clothes, making my own temperature rise in response. And it might be weak on my part, but I shamelessly lean into his touch, realizing how much I've wanted this. Needed even. Not just a hug from a super hot guy—the one I also happen to like a bunch—but a hug from a friend.

After giving me one more squeeze, Hudson pulls back just enough to give my cheek a tender kiss. He lingers there for a moment, and I'm starting to feel a little dizzy from breathing in his delicious aftershave.

"I can't tell you how glad I am you're finally here. Everyone's going nuts."

My body is going completely crazy at this contact—the most we've had so far—not sure if it should be shocked or ecstatic. He stays close to me, remaining in my personal bubble, which is totally fine with me right now. I actually welcome it. I'm sure I'm smiling like a lunatic, and my inner voice is yelling at me to pull him closer again. Even though it's only been a few weeks since we've met, it feels like we've spent as much time together as other couples do in the first several months.

Not that we're a couple, of course.

This time, he takes several steps back, his eyes raking up and down my body. "Did you know blue is my favorite color? You look beautiful in it. Absolutely breathtaking."

"Thank you." I can neither help the blush spread on my

cheeks nor the fast pounding of my heart. This man gets under my skin like no one else, and it's a sheer miracle I haven't jumped him yet.

No, we're not going to make out on the front lawn of his mother's house.

A loud noise from behind me makes me chuckle. "I guess Mira's awake. She had a bad night and passed out again on the way over here, even after taking a nap at home already. Teething is evil, I'm telling you. *Evil.*"

"Poor baby and poor mama. Let me help you." He steps around me to the back door of my silver car. "Is it okay if I get her out?"

I nod. "Of course."

"Perfect. I've been wanting to get my hands on that little cutie pie anyway. My mom's been dying to finally meet both of you too. Grandma has been telling her nonstop about you guys. If my parents hadn't gone on their extended cruise, I'm sure Grandma would've dragged you over here already. I'm actually surprised she hasn't paraded you around everywhere."

Even though I'm nervous, I'm genuinely excited to meet his parents and the rest of the family. "I can't wait to meet everyone."

As Hudson disappears halfway into the car, he leaves me to stare at his backside like a starving lunatic.

"Uh. Do you remember how to loosen the straps of the car seat?" I showed him last week how it works when we went grocery shopping together. Sometimes it feels like you need a special degree in baby devices—one's harder to figure out than the next.

"Yup. Already got it."

More staring at his butt then, I guess.

I wrack my brain for a distraction before I say something embarrassing, and remember what he said when we arrived. "What happened, by the way? You seemed a little frantic when we got here."

He emerges from the car with Mira in his arms, and I'm sure not a lot of women would remain calm at this sight. Super hot rockstar plus cute baby make a killer combination. All that's missing is a little adorable puppy.

"Nothing major, just my mom going a little nuts."

I try to ignore my hormones and focus on Mira. "Hi, sweetie pie. Do you feel a little better?"

Giving me a tired smile, she extends her arms toward me. I grab her, holding her close to me. When I look back at Hudson, there's something in his gaze I don't think I've seen before. "Sorry, what were you gonna say about your mom?"

He shakes his head and slips his hands into the front pockets of his jeans, leaning back against my car. "This is her fiftieth birthday, so I think the whole age thing is getting to her. She keeps talking about wrinkles, gray hair, and grandbabies. I think she's having a little meltdown and is driving everyone crazy."

I put my hand on his forearm and squeeze gently, wanting to reassure him and let him know I'm here for him. "Oh. Your poor mom. I bet she's just a little overwhelmed. Some women don't take changes like that very well, but I'm sure she's gonna be all right. Let's get everything inside, and we'll see how we can help her, okay?"

"Really?" He tilts his head to the side, a habit I've seen him do several times before.

"Of course. I mean, why not? Isn't that what friends do?

Help each other?" I'm not sure why I say the whole "friends" thing, or why the word feels a little sour in my stomach when it leaves my mouth. Something about it doesn't feel right, and if his flinch is anything to go by, he feels the same.

He continues to study me, not breaking eye contact as he takes a small step closer. "Is that what we are? Friends?"

I inhale loudly when he lifts his right hand to touch my cheek, gently tracing my jaw with his fingers. The sparks from earlier come back tenfold, making me squirm from the close proximity of his body.

He smirks at me, knowing full well what he's doing. "Does this feel like friends to you? Because it doesn't to me."

Smack.

Mira's little hand rests on his cheek where she just slapped him. A second later, it's on the move again, grabbing his nose. She's clearly enjoying herself, if her little giggle is anything to go by.

I can't hold back my chuckle and wink at him. "Sorry. You know better by now. Anything within reach is fair play."

"What's so funny?" Hannah steps out of the house and walks down the driveway. "Hudson, help Charlie get the cake inside before your mother has an anxiety attack. She's finally calmed down, so let's try and keep it that way. And find your siblings, I think they're hiding."

"We're not done here." Hudson's voice is low enough that Hannah can't hear him. This time, he's the one winking at me before he gives me the big smile I've dubbed his panty-melting smile.

Somehow, all of this feels like foreign territory. The nerves, the butterflies, the endless blushing and talking nonsense.

Despite the fact I've been in relationships before—one even almost landed me at the altar—nothing has ever felt this way.

This feels normal and natural, even though it apparently comes with feeling like a teenager again at times.

If it wasn't for Hannah only a few feet away, I might just throw all caution to the wind and jump him like one of his groupies, everything around us forgotten.

"Let's get this party started, folks." Hannah reaches us and claps her hands together, Mira copying her right away. "Want me to take her so you can grab the cake?"

"That would be perfect, thank you." I hand over Mirabelle, not that she needs an invitation for that.

Waving Hudson around to the trunk, I hand him a few pastry boxes while I take the biggest of the cake boxes, not wanting to take them all at once. The last thing I need right now is to ruin the cake.

Hannah leads the way, and I follow her into the beautiful, white country-style house. We walk briskly through a sitting room and into the kitchen. I don't have enough time to take in everything around me as I try and keep up with her. This woman sure is speedy for her age. I'm relieved to find the large room empty, not particularly ready to face a lot of people yet.

Hannah points to a big, empty spot in the far corner of the dark granite kitchen counter. "Just put the boxes over there. I'll help you set up everything in a minute."

"Thank you! I'm just gonna go back to the car to get the other ones. I'll be right back." After declining both Hudson's and Hannah's help multiple times, I practically run out of the house.

When I come back into the kitchen, I'm greeted with a scene so sweet it makes my heart swell to endless boundaries.

Hudson has Mirabelle in his arms, going back and forth between blowing raspberries on her belly and blowing the hair out of her face. Mirabelle is giggling, squealing, and clapping her hands in pure happiness. My steps falter, and I swallow the big sigh that wants to escape my throat. Hurrying up, I put the remaining cake boxes next to the other ones before something really bad happens, like me dropping them.

Hannah has set out big serving platters for me. I walk over to the sink to wash my hands when she walks up next to me. "They need me out back for a minute. Do you want me to take Mira with me? Hudson can help you with things in here."

"Whatever works for you. It shouldn't take us long, so I can come and find you when I'm done."

"Sounds perfect. See you in a minute then." She claps her hands a few times again to get Mira's attention, who's happy to switch arms again. "Hudson, be a dear and help Charlie, please. I'll be on damage control duty out back."

"Don't worry about us, Grandma. I've got Charlie covered."

"I'm sure you do." Hannah laughs at him before leaving with Mira in her arms.

Hudson and I work silently side by side for a few moments. While he puts the pastries and cupcakes on platters, I get the different pieces of cake out of the box, making sure it really survived the drive without any damages before putting the tiers back together.

After disposing of the empty boxes, I turn around to find Hudson right in front of me.

He scratches the back of his neck before looking me straight in the eyes. "I wanted to apologize if I came on too strong outside. But I haven't been able to get you out of my head, especially since you agreed to be my date for today. All I've been able to think about is how badly I want to kiss you."

I laugh nervously, not sure where to look. "Well, no one can say you aren't direct."

Shrugging his shoulder, he leans in another inch. "I know what I want, and I'm tired of pretending this insane chemistry between us doesn't exist."

He's definitely right about that. I've tried so hard to ignore any kind of attraction I might feel for him, but I think I've gotten to the point when even I have to admit defeat.

Closer than ever before, I feel Hudson's warm breath on my face, reminding me of chocolate and mint.

"Hudson, where are you?" A female voice comes from the back of the house, loud, followed by fast footsteps approaching.

He groans and his head drops, hanging low between us. "Soon, Charlie." Displeasure is written all over his handsome face as he steps away from me with the promise hanging quietly between us. "I'm in the kitchen, Mom."

CHAPTER TEN

BEFORE I CAN EVEN BEGIN TO MISS HUDSON'S CLOSENESS or think about what almost happened between us, a woman enters the kitchen through the white French doors. She's wearing a flowery summer dress with a jean jacket over it. Her blonde hair is cut in a long bob, swinging with every step she takes.

"Oh, thank goodness I found you. I've been looking for you everywhere. Could you come outside and help your brother with some last-minute tent changes, please?" Her eyes swing from Hudson to me, as if she didn't see me before. "I'm so sorry, how incredibly rude of me."

Her hand goes up to her chest as she walks over to us. The corners of her mouth lift into a big smile, the same beautiful smile Hudson has.

"Mom, this is—"

"Charlie." She finishes Hudson's sentence, and before I can say a word, she pulls me in for a hug. "I'm so happy to finally meet you. I've heard so many great things about you."

After a moment, she steps back, holding me out in front

of her at arm's length. Her gaze sweeps over me from head to toe, and I almost expect her to twirl me around. Instead, she pulls me in for another hug. This time, she holds me tighter, her mouth close to my ear. "I hope I'm not overstepping any boundaries, but I wanted you to know I'm incredibly sorry for your loss. I've heard so many wonderful stories about your family over the years. I'm thrilled my mom talked you into moving to Brooksville. We all love having you here."

The whispered words pierce right into my heart, and I have to swallow hard to keep the tears at bay. I didn't even think about the fact that Hannah might have told her about my family, even though it makes sense. My grandmother and Hannah were best friends for a very long time, so it's not surprising she knows about my grandma and sister.

"Thank you, Mrs. Mitchell." I feel Hudson's eyes on me, so I keep my voice low. I don't think he knows anything about my family, and I'd rather keep it that way—for now, at least. I need more time before I feel ready to share that part of my life with him.

She squeezes my shoulders one more time before letting go. "Please, call me Rebecca. And you really are just as beautiful as my mom told me. You're her favorite person to talk about at the moment, besides your little cutie pie, of course—who I still have to meet too." She gives me another big smile, probably trying to lighten the mood, and I'm grateful for it.

I feel my cheeks heat up, and if Hudson's chuckle is anything to go by, my blush is pretty apparent. "You're very kind, thank you."

"It's just the truth, dear. I'm very happy you're here. Also, thanks so much for making all the treats, and the cake. Everything looks perfect."

I shake my head, trying to deal with all the compliments this woman is throwing my way, and also remembering the reason for today's party. "It's nothing at all. And happy birthday."

"Thank you."

Hudson steps forward and winks at me. "Just wait until you try it, Mom. Once you've had it, you can't ever get enough of it. You just want more and more and more. It's an insatiable hunger she instills." Even though he's speaking to his mom, his gaze is locked with mine.

Somehow, I can't shake the feeling he's not just talking about my baking skills here, and the thought alone makes me squirm.

What has gotten into this guy all of a sudden?

I feel like the rules have changed, but I didn't get the memo.

Before I can try to dissect his behavior, Hannah comes back in with Mirabelle. "Sorry to interrupt, guys, but I'm afraid they need you out there again, Rebecca. Hudson, you should probably go help too."

She sighs, promising we'll talk more later before leaving with Hudson in tow—but not before gushing over Mira for a moment. When Hudson and Mira giggle over something, I'm almost certain I heard her sniffle a little. I'm glad she's just as awesome as the rest of the family. Somehow, it feels like a huge weight has been lifted off my shoulders.

"Are you all done over here?" Hannah peeks over the kitchen bar after the other two finally leave, looking happy when she sees the cake, and all the platters filled with various treats. "You've done a great job. Everything looks fantastic, and I'm sure you'll make a lot of future customers today."

"I hope everyone will like it." I feel a little nervous about so many people judging what I made, but I better get used to it—fast.

"They'll love it. Let's go outside, and you can meet the rest of the family—at least the ones that are already here."

Letting out a big breath, I rub my hands on my thighs. "All right. I'm as ready as I'll ever be, so let's do this."

When we stand right in front of the French doors, I catch my first glimpse of the backyard and gasp. I've never seen anything this beautiful before—it looks straight out of one of those garden magazines my grandma used to have.

Big mature trees frame the huge, green lawn, and there are flowers surrounding it everywhere. The strong scent drifts into my nose immediately, making me sigh in a mixture of pure bliss and happiness. Tents are set up about halfway down the yard, but I'm sure whatever lies beyond is just as beautiful as the rest.

"Grandma would've loved it here." The words come out of my mouth without me thinking about it.

Hannah nods in agreement beside me. "I agree. I always think of her when I'm out here. I wish she could've seen it."

"Me too...I miss her."

She squeezes my arm for a moment before setting her hand back on Mira, who is suddenly getting all squirmy. "I'm sure you do, honey. Just remember, they're always in your heart. My favorite spot is all the way in the back, where the gazebo is. There's a little pond, and it's the most peaceful place. I like to sit there and think of your grandma and all the shenanigans we got into over the years. She truly was the best."

Nodding at her, I try to see where she's pointing.

"It's hard to see from here with all the party tents in the way. I can show it to you, if you'd like."

"Show her what, Grandma?" Hudson is suddenly right in front of us, startling me yet again.

I'm seriously starting to wonder if he's had some sort of ninja training, with all the appearing out of thin air acts he keeps doing.

Hannah shifts Mirabelle around in her arms. "I was just telling Charlie about the pond."

"Ah. Let's go see it, shall we?" He looks from me to Mirabelle. "Wanna come with us and look at the fishies, Mira?"

With little to no hesitation, she leaps into his outstretched arms, and I'm quietly wondering how I feel about that fact. They both beam at me, making me smile in return. Without a warning, Hudson takes my hand, pulling me after them. The skin contact has sparks shooting through my whole body.

We walk down a little stone path on one side of the yard. It leads us past the party chaos—that we thankfully ignore—all the way down to the little pond. A few sea roses float on top while some fish swim around, poking out their little heads here and there. It's beautiful, just like Hannah said.

"Look, Mira, there are the fishies." Hudson points toward the water, and we know the exact moment she sees them too. Her eyes go wide, and a huge grin spreads across her face. She starts babbling in excitement, and it's the most adorable thing.

A sense of overwhelming emotions for this little human

overcomes me, and I softly brush my hand over her hair and cheek. "Gosh, you're so cute."

"Truest thing I've heard all day." The male voice comes from behind me. "Who's this lovely young lady, Hudson?"

Hudson looks over my shoulder and turns around to face whoever is approaching. "This is Mira."

The man has come up beside me, and I try to peek over as unsuspiciously as possible. Even though I can only stare for a moment, I notice right away his profile looks strangely familiar.

"Hi, Mira, it's a pleasure to meet you." He holds out his hand and after staring at it for a while, Mira puts her own little one in his, as if she knows exactly what she's doing.

Then his attention shifts to me. "And who do we have here?"

He turns to face me, and my mouth drops open when I get a good look at him. I'm so shocked that I'm not even embarrassed about the gasp that comes out of my mouth.

Hudson clears his throat, apparently realizing he has to do the introduction for me. "This is Charlie. Charlie, this is Gabe—"

"Shut up. Shut up. Shut up." I momentarily space out, not even feeling bad for interrupting him. My brain feels like total mush, and I don't think I can control whatever is coming out of my mouth, even if I wanted to. I point a finger at the man standing in front of me, restraining myself from poking him in the chest. "*You* are Gabe Mitchell. You're freaking Gabe Mitchell. I can't believe it. You're, like, my favorite author in the whole world. You have no idea how much your books have helped me get through this last year. Wow."

The man in front of me chuckles, and I'm immediately mesmerized by the sound of it. Reluctantly, I pull my gaze away to look at Hudson. "This is *Gabe Mitchell*. What the heck, Hudson? Why didn't you tell me you know him?" Realization finally hits me, and I slap both of my hands over my mouth. "Wait a second. Oh, no freaking way, this is your *brother*?" I'm not sure what's possessing me, but I punch Hudson lightly on the arm.

In response, his eyebrows draw together tightly while his mouth sets in a grim, straight line. "Last time I checked, he was, but that might change soon. How in the world can you know who he is when you had no idea who I was?"

Gabe holds up his hands in a time-out position. "Wait a second. Please tell me you aren't kidding right now. She really didn't know who you were when you met?" Gabe doesn't need to wait for an answer from Hudson because the sour expression on his face says it all. Gabe throws his head back and laughs loudly. He claps his thighs a few times too, probably making a few heads in the backyard turn our way. "This is the absolute best thing ever. Was poor Hudson baby not recognized?" Gabe uses a baby voice for the last part, making me and Mira giggle while Hudson frowns even harder.

"What's going on over here?"

"We could hear you laughing all the way at the house."

I turn toward the female voices, stunned by the sight in front of me.

Hudson grumbles behind me. "Great, just what I needed."

"You won't believe what I just found out." Gabe points toward me. "My lovely new best friend here recognized *me* right away but didn't know who Hudson was when she first met him."

The two women burst into laughter, their high-pitched tones almost harmonizing. I take a closer look at them, blinking as I take them in.

First of all, they are both quite tall—definitely taller than my five foot, seven inches, from the looks of it—and they must be twins. While one has blonde hair piled up high on top of her head, the other one has long dark brown hair with a rainbow assortment of colors mixed into it. Other than that, they both have the same beautiful face, their features identical mirror images of each other.

"Charlie, these are my sisters, Dahlia and Rose." Hudson is standing beside me now, groaning like it actually pains him to make this introduction.

"*This* is Charlie?" Rose—the one with the colorful hair—shares a look with her sister, both of their eyes going wide.

Not sure how to take their little exchange, I nod and shake hands with both of them. "It's nice to meet you." Since my hand is shaking, I put it behind my back the second I can. These Mitchell siblings all seem bigger than life, and I'm not sure how to deal with that at the moment.

The twins grab each other's arms before Rose turns back to me. "Oh no, trust me, the pleasure is *all* ours." She leans over to her sister without taking her eyes off me. "Grandma is right, she really is perfect."

Well, if my nerves weren't shot before, they definitely are now.

If there's one thing I've learned about this family, it's that frankness is a Mitchell trait.

Dahlia takes a step toward Hudson. "So, this must be

little Mira then. Gosh, Rose, look at her. She's absolutely beautiful." Dahlia plays with Mira's fingers while Mira soaks up the attention, and after looking at me for reassurance, she climbs into Dahlia's arms.

Apparently, I'm not the only one who's enthralled by this family.

I watch Gabe and the twins gush over Mirabelle while Hudson silently stares at me.

When I finally acknowledge his burning gaze, I can see a whole lot of determination in his eyes—I'm just not sure for what. "Hudson, what—"

Before I can say anything else, he grabs my hand. "Can we talk for a moment?"

CHAPTER ELEVEN

Hudson pulls me toward the little gazebo that's only a few feet away. He walks so fast down the narrow path that I have a hard time staying on my two feet—cobblestones and heels definitely don't mix well.

"Slow down, Hudson. What's gotten into you? You're acting like someone's after us." After I say the words, I turn around quickly to make sure there actually isn't anyone behind us.

Not a good idea.

I should've known better than to move that much when I already have such a hard time walking straight. That little movement starts a domino effect, and everything goes down the drain within a few seconds. Not only do I lose my balance —big-time—but I also fall sideways. Hudson, the helpful guy he is, tries to catch me before I go down. Sadly, even he can't save me this time.

Instead, I take *him* down with me.

That would be embarrassing enough by itself, but of course, luck doesn't seem to be on my side lately. Rather than landing on the hard ground, we fall into the pond with a big splash, a loud shriek coming from my lungs as I hit the water. Hudson follows close behind, landing halfway on top of me. Thankfully, he quickly rolls off before crushing me, and is now quietly sitting a few feet away in the shallow water.

"Oh my gosh." Crossing my arms over my chest, I try to rub away the goose bumps that have already formed everywhere. Despite the warm spring temperatures, the water is surprisingly cold. I shudder and close my eyes for a moment when I feel slimy algae all around me. Because that's not enough, I also have hard, pointy rocks poking into my butt, and I'm pretty sure some fish just swam by my feet.

No doubt, this is one of those moments where it would be incredibly helpful if the ground would open up and swallow me. I'd really appreciate that. So so very much.

Hudson is still as a statue and just stares at me with wide eyes before he shakes his head and chuckles. "Things are definitely never boring when you're around, Charlie."

Despite my cold body, my cheeks flush at his statement. I'm relieved when rushed footsteps come our way, but it all fades into the background when Hudson stands up to carefully walk over to me. Even though we're both completely soaked, I have a feeling I look more like a wet dog whereas Hudson looks like he's ready for a sexy wet T-shirt photo shoot.

His white T-shirt clings to his upper body like a second skin, reminding me of his perfect body I've seen on an almost daily basis for the last few weeks. My cheeks heat up even more, but this time not from embarrassment.

He sinks halfway back into the water, kneeling down in

front of me. "Are you okay? You didn't get hurt, did you? I should've checked first."

I shake my head and let out a big breath. "No, I'm good. I wouldn't mind vanishing into thin air, though—just in case you know that trick. Being the big party laughingstock wasn't on my list for today."

He pretends to think for a moment. "Sorry to disappoint, but I don't have that one in my repertoire."

"Mmm, of course not. Figures."

His eyes move over my body, stopping at my arms crossed tightly over my chest. "You're shivering. Let's get you out of here and warmed up. I'll run back to the house to get us some towels."

Gabe clears his throat, standing at the edge of the pond with a smirk on his face. "Rose already went to get some. She should be back any moment. You guys okay?"

I sigh loudly. "Besides my pride, everything's just peachy."

All three of us start to chuckle—being clumsy definitely does make for good entertainment sometimes. Dahlia joins the party, quietly laughing too while Mira is completely oblivious to the whole situation, happily occupied with the drawstrings of Dahlia's top.

"I'm back." Rose comes running toward us, a big pile of towels in her arms. "I hope I didn't miss anything funny." She winks at me, trying to catch her breath.

Hudson holds out his hands to me, standing up again to his full height. "Come on, let's go inside and get cleaned up." My hand is securely wrapped in his as he pulls me up and we trot over to the edge of the water. When we get there, he lets go and walks around to stand behind me. "I'll lift you up, so you can get out first. Okay?"

"Sure, thanks."

In my haste to get out of this wet situation before anyone else can see me, I don't think twice about how exactly Hudson's planning on helping me. Before I know it, his hands grip my waist tightly, the contact sending my whole body into shock. I don't have the chance to react though when Gabe grabs my wrists and starts pulling me up. I'm halfway in the air when I slip through his hands, immediately afraid to either land in the cold water again or on Hudson's face—not sure which one would be worse.

Without warning, Hudson's hands are on my butt, pushing me up enough for Gabe to pull me all the way out. I thank Gabe and spin around to gasp at Hudson, who, of course, has the nerves to shrug and laugh. In one swift move, he hoists himself up on one of the surrounding rocks and stands behind me two seconds later.

Show-off.

He leans closer, putting his mouth right next to my ear. His hot breath is fanning my neck, and this time, I shudder for a completely different reason. "At least now I can say I got you all wet."

I snort and shake my head before I look at him over my shoulder. "Probably more so the other way around."

"Well, you won't hear me complain about that—either way works for me." His dimples are on full display, turning this into a completely unfair playing field.

I turn around and slap his bicep lightly, the muscle immediately responding and flexing under my touch.

Reluctantly, I take my fingers off him after a few seconds. "Goodness, stop it."

Someone coughs behind us, and I'm reminded of where we are. I step away from Hudson. I clearly can't think straight when he's around.

Rose hands me a towel, and after thanking her, I cling to it like it's a security blanket. She smirks at me, but thankfully stays quiet. I'm not sure how many more comments I can take from this family right now before my head explodes from total embarrassment.

She throws the other towel in Hudson's direction and gives my shoulder a squeeze. "Come on, I'll show you around inside. I'm sure we can find something dry for you to wear somewhere."

"Thanks, Rose. I really appreciate it."

"No problem at all. It's the least I can do, he's *my* idiot brother, after all." We both snicker at that comment.

She starts walking, but I look around for Mira first.

"Go ahead, Charlie. I've got her." Hannah must have joined our little impromptu party without me noticing, but I'm beyond grateful she did. "She's chewing on her hand. Is it time for her to eat?"

I pull the towel closer around me, trying to shield myself as much as possible from the wind. "She wasn't very hungry when we left, so probably. Would you mind feeding her? The diaper bag is in the kitchen."

Hannah nods and waves me off. "Of course, don't worry. You take care of yourself, the munchkin and I are gonna have a great time, as always." She takes Mirabelle from Dahlia, snuggling her tightly.

Somehow, I have a feeling she's going to be the most spoiled baby—at least when it comes to the Mitchell family.

"Thank you." I share a look with her and smile.

"Don't even mention it. Now go before you turn blue." She shoos me away, making me laugh. I do as she asks because I really do want to get out of these clothes as soon as possible.

Hudson is still behind me, but he's been uncharacteristically quiet during this whole exchange. Maybe it's better this way. With every interaction we have, my resistance crumbles away some more, and I still can't decide what to make of it. I haven't come across a guy that's intrigued me in the slightest since Sebastian ended things last year.

This whole time, I thought the reason was because I'm better off without a guy, that it's not worth risking my heart as well as Mira's. But ever since Hudson walked into our lives—his half-naked state not helping in the least—my resolve has been tested to the extreme. Even though his looks definitely don't hurt, there is so much about him that draws me in.

We make it back to the house, where Rose swiftly guides me through the kitchen and up the grand staircase. The long hallway stretches ahead of us, and she opens the first door on the left. The bedroom she reveals is decorated in a nautical theme, white and navy blue everywhere.

"Wow, it's beautiful." I walk in and look around. Big ocean canvases line the wall above the dark wood bed that is almost overflowing with white and blue striped pillows. There are small decorations scattered around the room, some made out of rope, and even a stunning shadow box filled with sand and seashells. "I love this."

"Isn't it awesome? It's my favorite bedroom here. Mom loves to decorate, and Dahlia and I help her sometimes. We had the best time with this house when Hudson bought it for our parents."

My mouth drops open, apparently ready to catch some flies. "He bought this house for them?" It's not that the thought of Hudson buying his parents a house seems farfetched, more so the opposite. From everything I've learned about him so far, this seems exactly like the thing he'd do.

So sweet.

"Yup. First thing he bought after he got his initial record deal. He wanted to make sure everyone else was taken care of before he bought stuff for himself." She gives me a proud smile.

It's the first time I realize she doesn't have the same smile as Hudson and their mother, making me wonder if the twins look more like their dad, since I still haven't met him.

I'm staring at her, still a bit shell-shocked after the news that Hudson bought this house.

"Well." Rose rubs her hands together. "Let's get you taken care of. I'll be back in just a minute with some clothes. The bathroom is right over there through that door. I'm sure you wouldn't mind a hot shower. I'll just leave the clothes on the bed for you. Pick whatever you want." She gives me another smile before she heads toward the door.

"Thanks so much, Rose."

"Anytime." She looks back at me, studying me for a moment. "I like you, Charlie, I really do. Somehow, you're...different."

With that, she walks out the door, leaving me to wonder what the heck she meant by that.

After a quick shower, I'm relieved to see Rose left me a few clothes on the bed, just like she said. I pick a beautiful blue flower dress that thankfully fits—well, mostly. It's a little snug around my torso, but it'll work for the next few hours.

When I open the door, Hudson is waiting for me, casually leaning against the opposite wall.

"Hi." I take him in, all freshly showered. His hair is still damp and pushed back unruly, like he just raked his hands through it a few times—his signature look. It looks good on him—very good—and maybe it's made me wonder a time or two if this is how he looks in the morning when he wakes up.

"Hi yourself." He looks me up and down before his gaze lands back on mine. "Man, blue suits you so well. You look absolutely stunning. Remind me to thank my sister for finding this dress. It looks like it was made for you."

This time it's not just my cheeks that are hot, it's my whole body. I feel like someone just dumped me in front of a heater. "Thank you."

"Charlie?" His voice is as smooth as honey as he pushes himself off the wall, stalking toward me. The hallway is bright enough for me to see the determination in his eyes.

"Hm?" I suddenly feel a little dizzy—I think.

On second thought, has someone put a spell on me?

"Did you want me to kiss you earlier?" The directness of his question stuns me for a second, but I can't dwell on that since I'm lost in his gaze as he comes closer. His movements are painfully slow while my heart feels like it's going to gallop out of my chest at any moment.

Anticipation. Pure, unapologetic anticipation of what's to come.

I open my mouth to say something, but nothing comes out.

"Do you want me to kiss you now?" Another step closer.

My heart starts beating even faster, and I'm sure there's a group of hummingbirds in my stomach, flapping their wings wildly against my insides. It's like someone pressed my ON button because my body is coming alive *everywhere*.

Why is this starting to feel like foreplay?

My gaze darts back and forth between his eyes and his mouth. His lips look beyond inviting—all soft, pink, and full —practically begging me to do something about this tension that is starting to consume me. I try and swallow past the big lump that has formed in my throat while my eyes track him like a hawk.

"Charlie?" His voice has an edge to it I haven't heard before. It's short of a growl—impatient, and so incredibly sexy.

For a moment, I stop thinking and just feel.

Then, I wet my lips and nod. "Yes. Kiss me."

He closes the distance between us faster than I thought possible, and then his mouth is on mine. He kisses me like he's starving for me, like he needs me to breathe. His lips are soft yet demanding.

Exploring, wanting, taking.

The kiss deepens, and I'm completely lost.

"Hudson." His name leaves my lips in a soft moan.

My hands are in his hair, pulling and tugging, while he

holds my face protectively before his fingers slowly wander down my body, landing on my hips. He pulls me away from the open doorway and over to the side, pinning me against the wall with his whole body deliciously pressed into mine.

This is the kind of kiss I've heard and read about. After all these years of never experiencing one, I thought they didn't exist.

Boy, was I wrong.

This kiss is everything. It makes me feel alive in a way I've never felt before—all-consuming and powerful. It goes deeper than just a physical connection, making me drown in the overwhelming sensation of it all.

Hudson pulls away slightly, kissing my jaw all the way over to my ear. "You taste like fucking heaven."

A shudder runs through my entire body when he finds a sensitive spot, and my eyes roll back into my head. My hands have a mind of their own and grip his hair even tighter, pulling him as close to me as possible, so I can savor this feeling for as long as I can.

A voice is trying to break through my subconscious, but I'm in a bubble. The only thing I can hear is us—all the little moans and groans mixed with whimpers and harsh breaths.

He's kissing his way back to my mouth, and I welcome him like it has been years instead of mere seconds when I last kissed him.

"Uh. So sorry, guys, but, Hudson, your phone's been ringing nonstop. I think it might be important." The words finally pierce our bubble as someone walks around the corner.

Hudson's lips stop moving, and his whole body freezes while I stare straight at Gabe as he averts his eyes to the ground. I'm still so caught up in the moment, it takes me a minute to fully snap out of it.

"This better be good." Hudson's unhappy groan is loud enough to echo through the hallway as he pushes away from me to walk over to his brother.

CHAPTER TWELVE

Like Gabe suspected, the phone call was indeed important. Hudson had told me last week that he was supposed to fly out to Los Angeles for a meeting with the big bosses of his music label a few days after the party. Apparently, it was an extremely important meeting that got moved up several days without anyone telling them. Hence, his manager was losing his mind, trying to get the band flown out to L.A. that very evening. Sadly, that meant our night ended right then and there, in the hallway at Hudson's parents' house.

Even though I understood, I was also upset about it, barely able to get any sleep that night. Maybe it was a premonition of some sort.

He's been gone for two days now—one of them filled with drama coming from L.A.—and despite everything, I miss him. I've gotten so used to him being around practically twenty-four seven that the unexpected trip threw me a bit for a loop. At least it's given me the chance to focus some more on my baking, especially since that's one of the only things that helps me work through my emotional chaos anyway.

Since Monica wants to catch up with me—and probably gossip like there's no tomorrow—I took my laptop to the bakery and set it up in my kitchen, a few feet away from me and all the ingredients, safely propped up on a little crate I found.

Hannah has proven to be a lifesaver once again, taking Mirabelle out for a trip to the zoo. That way, I can focus on my baking and my best friend—who happens to think I'm trying to bake my little heart out.

Sadly, she might have a point.

Looking around the bakery, I'm not sure who's supposed to eat all the cakes, pies, and pastries I've already made and still plan on making. Since I'm an emotional eater, I know I'll make a big dent in it for sure, even if it means I'll end up with a stomach ache.

Monica's been a little ball of barely contained irritation ever since I took her call a minute ago. She skipped pleasantries all together and jumped straight into what's been on my mind the last twenty-four hours. "Mo, would you please calm down? Take a deep breath and stop cursing for a moment, so we can get through this together, okay?" I sigh, frowning at the screen in front of me. I give her another moment because I know why she's so worked up.

Hudson's ex.

The one I had no clue about, not a bleep of knowledge of who she was or what she looked like, or that she almost became Mrs. Mitchell at some point.

Now, I know all about it. Not only did Monica fill me in on everything she knows, but there's also been no escaping the social media pictures and comments that have surfaced since yesterday. The same ones I've been trying to avoid and forget as much as I can.

No one needs to see pictures of the guy you've come to like and his ex-fiancée, especially when he just left your arms hours before.

Seeing them after we had our moment—at least *I* thought we had a moment, a very hot moment—hurts more than I thought it would. It has also made me question everything between us.

The last time I saw Monica, she talked me into letting go and having some fun. But those few minutes with Hudson felt like more than just fun, and I'm not sure I'm okay with that, or ready for it yet—especially after this new development.

"All right. Give me one moment to get comfortable, and then I'm ready to talk shit about you-know-who." The screen wobbles, and I hear her moan and groan as she settles in—at least, I think that's what she's doing. She's still wearing a big frown when her face appears on the screen again. "Okay, I'm all ears now. So, you were at the birthday party, almost making out with Hudson twice. Then you got wet with him in the pond, and after getting all cleaned up, you got it on in the hallway. Is that correct?"

Monica never fails to make me laugh, even when I'm in a weird mood like right now. "I guess that about sums it up."

Getting it on in the hallway. Her words repeat in my head, and a burst of heat shoots through me as the memories of Hudson and me flood my mind. It still seems surreal, almost like a dream, like it never actually happened.

When his hands and lips were on me, it instantly wiped

away any trace or conscious thoughts of previous men. It felt like Hudson was my first touch, my first kiss, every other memory just floating away into nonexistence, not even worth comparing anything to it.

"Will you snap out of your hot thoughts? I can see you blush from over here." She taps her fingernails on the laptop, impatient as always. "Well, I'm glad you actually did follow through on your promise of going on a date and having fun. But what I don't like is everything that happened in L.A. yesterday."

And just like that, my hot thoughts are replaced with the harsh reality of what went down.

I know Monica wants to talk about it, and weirdly enough, this time, I do too. Even though I'm usually the last person to gossip, I can't help myself and dive into the topic headfirst. "I don't really know what happened, Mo. The only thing I know is that he's in L.A. until tomorrow for some important meetings, and yesterday, all these pictures of him and his ex having dinner surfaced, spreading like a wildfire even I couldn't escape."

I inhale deeply, the anger and hurt bubbling up all over again. "I mean, did you see the pictures? They looked so dang cozy. Did they look cozy to you too?" Throwing my hands up in the air, I fling little pieces of dough everywhere.

She lets out a big breath before rubbing her hand across her forehead. "Shit. They did look cozy. What a son-of-a-mothertrucker. I can't believe he gets you all hot one day, and then the next day, he's out dining with his ex-fiancée when he knows there's paparazzi everywhere. He better watch his ass when I come to Brooksville. Sexy ass or not, no one messes with my best friend. Didn't she pull a number on him when they split last year?"

I shrug my shoulders. She knows I have no idea about that kind of stuff. Torturing myself with yesterday's pictures was already more than enough for me. "No clue. That's your territory. You're the celebrity fangirl, not me." Staring at my dough, I suddenly feel a little overwhelmed with everything. "Thanks, Mo."

Her voice is soft this time. "Hey, hey. You're not crying, are you? None of that, all right? Gosh, I will most definitely kick his butt."

I can't help it and laugh. Monica has a way about her which is why we get along so well.

Letting out a long sigh, I rub the back of my hand across my forehead, careful not to smear dough all over my face. "I don't know what I was thinking, to be honest. Me and a famous rockstar? In which universe does that ever work? Maybe in fairy tales and cheesy chick flicks, but not in real life. Plus, I'm not even sure if I'd want that after the last few days. This is totally normal in his world, isn't it? All the media attention and seeing these posts about the 'dream couple reuniting' and stuff like that. So much drama. I'd have to deal with this constantly. I mean, this is his life. With this new development, there will probably soon be paparazzi everywhere, including here, hoping to catch a glimpse of the power couple. Or one of them alone, at least. I'm actually surprised they haven't been here yet."

Monica's eyebrows draw together so tightly, they almost look like one big unibrow. "Ugh, I don't know what to say. I'm sorry. Even though I'm extremely pissed about the whole spiel, I really don't think there's something going on between these two. I've learned over the years how much the media obscures reality. I wouldn't put it past that woman to meet up with him and calling all the paparazzi herself. I think her spotlight has been rather dull since she and Hudson called it quits, so I wonder about her motives in all of this."

I only shrug, not sure what to say. All I know is that I feel incredibly disappointed and just plain sad. For a very short moment, I thought that maybe, just maybe, I might have something special with him. But that feeling is long gone. "I don't think I can deal with this spotlight life."

She points her finger at me. "Remember you told me Hudson said the media usually leaves him alone when he's home? I think that's true. I barely found any pictures online about him in Brooksville. It's just too far away from the main celebrity scene for the paparazzi to care about. I mean, who wants to spend hours on the road to take a picture of him grocery shopping or something boring like that? Besides, I'm sure his family would've said something otherwise, especially Hannah. Even though I have a bone to pick with him, I don't think he'd mislead you like this."

"I have to agree with her on that." The deep voice comes from behind me, making me gasp.

Thankfully, I recognize it after the initial surprise and turn around. "Gabe! What is it with you guys always sneaking up on me? I'm starting to wonder if that's a family trait."

Gabe stands in front of me with a boyish grin on his face. He's wearing a pair of light blue ripped jeans and a dark gray T-shirt. This family definitely knows how to wear casual clothes and look like a million bucks.

I still can't get over the fact that I now know my favorite

author—personally—and that he's actually standing right here, in the middle of my bakery. He's still as good-looking as he was a few days ago—short, messy brown hair, brown eyes, and a slight stubble on his face.

Taking his hands out of his jeans pockets, he holds them up. "Sorry. I wasn't planning on being sneaky."

"Sooooo..." Monica's voice surprises me as she draws out the word. "You're the famous Gabe, huh?"

For a moment, I actually forgot about my best friend.

Oops.

Her eyes move around, and I know she's checking out Gabe. "Nice."

At this point, she's almost purring.

Oh boy. I know what that means.

She's found a new target, and I'm not sure how I feel about that. Since I can't say anything about it right now, though, I'll file it away for later. "Mo, this is Gabe. Gabe, this is my best friend, Monica."

He stares at the screen, lifting his right hand a little. I don't know him well enough yet to read him, but to me, it almost looks like he's mesmerized.

Interesting.

Monica's beaming at him. Despite not wearing any makeup, she's as stunning as always. "So, Gabe, do you also live in Brooksville, or are you just there for a visit?"

Gabe chuckles, scratching the back of his head.

I can't believe these two.

What is this? Chuckling and beaming-at-each-other central?

Sticking his hands back into his front pockets, he takes a small step closer. "Actually, I just moved back to town last year. I tried living in Los Angeles for a while but I missed my family and the tranquility of this place. There's nothing like it."

She nods as if she completely understands what he's talking about. "That makes sense. And it's perfect too, since I'll be in town sometime in the next few weeks."

"Oh really? For a visit?"

"For now, yes."

What on earth is happening? For now? What does she even mean by that? I'm so surprised by her answer, that I hold up both of my hands before either one of them can say another word. "All right, you two chatterboxes, you can talk more when she gets here." I remember something and turn back to Monica. "Before I forget it, have you checked into the hotel you told me about?"

She shakes her head. "Not yet. I'm waiting until after my doctor's appointment at the end of the week, so I know the correct dates."

At that, Gabe's head whips around, and he looks at me. "She's not staying with you guys?"

I shrug my shoulders. "Nope. Hudson said it wasn't a problem, but Mo declined."

An awful noise comes from the laptop when Mo moves hers around, and I flinch.

"Hey. Don't say it like it's a bad thing. I just don't want to be the third wheel, that's all. Nothing wrong about that."

Gabe is quiet for a few moments before he looks at my best friend. "I have a little guest house, if you're interested. I don't live far from Hudson, so it's probably more convenient than a hotel anyway. It's yours if you want it."

"Really?" Both Mo and I say at the same time, staring at Gabe.

"Really." He gives her a small smile, and I'm oddly fascinated by this whole exchange.

Sometimes in life, you realize you meet people that are different than others. There's just something about them that makes them special. By now, I think it's safe to say the Mitchell family has hit the jackpot in that area. And by some lucky star, I'm fortunate enough to be surrounded by them.

Mo has a hard time containing the excitement in her voice, and maybe there's a hint of eagerness too. "Deal."

They stare at each other silently for what feels like forever. The urge to clear my throat is so strong, tickling in the back of my throat, I make myself cough in the process. Time to wrap this up before they throw me out of my own bakery, so they can keep staring at each other.

I focus on my best friend first. "All right, we'll figure out the details when you know more. I know your therapist appointment is coming up, so I'm gonna let you go."

She picks up her phone from somewhere beside her and looks at the screen. "You're right, looks like it's time to meet the slave driver." She points a finger at me. "Don't let Hudson walk all over you when he gets back, or I'll have his balls." Her gaze shifts to Gabe, and she gives him a dazzling smile. "Sorry, I know he's your brother, but I have to watch out for my loved ones first. Thank you again for your generous offer, Gabe. I really appreciate it, and I'll see you soon. Charlie can give you my phone number, so we can arrange things for my arrival."

She blows me a kiss, and then she's gone.

At least, I *think* the kiss was for me.

I chuckle nervously. "Mo is something else. Do I need to apologize for her already?"

His shoulders shake with laughter when he turns around. "Being different is good, and I'm more than happy to help." He leans back against the work table. "The guest house will be a lot better for her than some boring hotel room."

I nod. "I agree. I didn't want her in a hotel room either, but she can be stubborn. So, thank you. That was very sweet of you to offer."

"No problem at all."

"Ready for that phone number before I forget it?"

"You bet." He gets his phone out of his back pocket and enters Monica's number as I ramble it off from memory.

Once the phone is back in his jeans, his focus shifts back to me. He studies me silently, folding his arms across his chest.

Man, those Mitchell men sure know how to work their muscles.

He switches the position of his feet. "Apropos offer. I stopped by to see how you're doing, and if I can help with anything. We all saw the media coverage, and I wanted to make sure you're all right. We're used to it by now, but you probably aren't. And trust me, no one was as shocked about seeing the pictures of Hudson and Addy as we were. Just remember to not believe everything you see. She's always been one to play the media every chance she gets, and sadly, they eat out of her hand."

Monica filled me in on every bit of gossip she knew about this woman the media seems to love so much. It left me slightly nauseated, to say the least. The person she pretends to be in the public eye, and the person she seems to be in private—according to a few sources—are apparently two different people.

Talk about being two-faced.

Gabe rubs his forehead. "That's probably not helping right now, sorry. Anyway, I just wanted to apologize and make sure you're doing okay."

"Why would you apologize?"

"He's my brother."

"That's nonsense, Gabe. None of this is even remotely your fault." Then I nod, maybe a bit over the top, but I can't seem to stop it. "But yes, sure. Everything's *just* fine."

He throws his head back and laughs. He reminds me so much of Hudson that a sharp pain shoots straight through my chest.

Dang it.

"Charlie, if there's one thing I've learned about women over the years, it's that *something* is usually wrong when they say they're fine."

Got me there, sucker.

Before I can stop myself, the truth slips out of my mouth. "Well, what do you want me to say? That I'm freaked out about everything happening right now, and beyond annoyed and hurt by your brother? I haven't heard a peep from him, except for a few messages to check in with me—like nothing has changed. And let's not even talk about those lovely images of the two of them online that I can't seem to escape for some reason." With a heaving chest, I look at Gabe in pure shock.

What the heck was that?

Spilling my guts is completely unlike me, especially to a guy like Gabe who's, in most aspects, still a stranger—even though it doesn't feel like it. My shoulders slump a little. "I'm sorry. I wasn't planning on unloading this on you. None of this concerns you. Let's just pretend I didn't say any of that stuff."

"What are you talking about? Of course it concerns me, and I'm glad you're honest with me. You're one of us now, so I want to be there for you and help however I can. We all do." He looks sincere, so extremely genuine, it makes me feel all warm and fuzzy.

Swallowing back the lump in my throat, I try very hard not to get all emotional in front of him. He might be able to tell anyway, though, because he opens his arms for me without another word.

I only hesitate for a second, before walking straight into them, immediately feeling safe and secure.

He gently puts his head on mine and gives my back a few soft pats. "Sorry, my brother is such a dimwit sometimes."

The back door of the bakery slams shut and footsteps approach.

A familiar scent hits me, and I close my eyes, knowing exactly who it is, even before his melodic voice fills the room.

"Please, Gabe. Tell me how you really feel."

CHAPTER THIRTEEN

Gabe gives my shoulders a squeeze before letting me go. He turns around to face his brother, who's not looking happy at all. "Well, well. I guess you're back, huh?"

"Looks like I interrupted something." Hudson's voice is more of a growl than anything else as he glares at his brother.

Gabe's nostrils flare the smallest bit as he stares down Hudson. "If, by interrupted, you mean me trying to see if Charlie's okay, then hell yes, you interrupted something. There's no need for you to come in here and act like the wronged party."

I'm stunned by this exchange, and all I can manage to do is look back and forth between the two brothers, not sure what's going on. Am I supposed to step between them to break up whatever this is? Hudson's acting like I did something forbidden with Gabe, which is obviously a big joke. Plus, he's the one who was schmoozing with his ex, less than twenty-four hours ago.

His face is drawn into a grimace—his lips almost white from pressing them together, eyes little slits, and his dark eyebrows are drawn together so tightly, the crease between them looks like a crater. He looks like he's ready to pounce on his brother.

They both actually appear ready to explode, their hands clenched into tense fists at their sides.

"What are you talking about? I only call it like I see it." Hudson's almost yelling at this point.

Gabe laughs once, but there's not an ounce of humor in his voice. "Obviously, I'm talking about you and Addy having a jolly old time at dinner, giving the paparazzi, and therefore the world, a wonderful show. Apparently, you don't give a crap what those pictures do to the people in your life."

"You have no idea what you're talking about, so just shut up."

Wait. Is Hudson shaking? I'm pretty sure his nostrils are flaring too. The only thing that's missing is steam coming out of his ears to complete the picture of an angry cartoon character.

Let's hope he isn't going to explode out of his skin in a second and turn into Hulk, or we're really screwed.

Taking a step closer to Gabe, I pat his arm gently. Someone has to diffuse this situation, and it looks like I'm the unlucky winner. "It's okay. I've got this."

Hudson's eyes dart to me, going wide for a moment. When he blinks a few times, I wonder if he momentarily forgot I was there. His shoulders sag, and he almost seems to visibly deflate.

Gabe turns to face me in a way that blocks Hudson from my view, almost as if he doesn't want him to see me. "Are you sure? I can kick him out if you want to, or I can stay here, if you prefer not to be alone with him right now."

Gratitude washes over me for having added another great person to my life, and I give him a small smile. "That's very sweet of you, and I can't tell you how much I appreciate your concern, but I'll be fine. Promise."

He still doesn't look convinced, but nods anyway. He turns around and points a finger at Hudson. "You better be nice to her, or you're gonna have to deal with me."

To my surprise, Hudson holds up his hands in surrender. "Fair enough."

Gabe pulls a card out of his back pocket and hands it to me, his fingers brushing mine briefly in the process. "Here's my card. My cell number is on the back. Call me, and we can talk about the guest house and whatever arrangements need to be made, okay?"

"You bet. Thanks so much again for helping out." I put his card in the front pocket of my apron.

"It's no problem at all." He bends down and gives my cheek a quick kiss without lingering. "Take care of yourself. Call me if you need anything."

When he walks over to Hudson, they silently stare at each other, before Gabe speaks up. "You're an idiot, bro."

Less than five seconds later, he's out the door, letting it shut loudly behind him. That leaves Hudson and me in an eerie silence as I try to avoid his blazing look.

Of course, he's the first to say something. "So, you're moving into my brother's guest house? You could've just said something if you didn't want to live with me anymore."

"What?" His question throws me off, and my hand shoots out to the counter to give me some extra balance.

"He just said to call him so you can talk about the guest house." His hand is up in the air in a questioning gesture.

Oh, that.

I could set the record straight—probably should, since I'm not one for playing games—but for some reason, I'm stubborn right now. First, he wines and dines his ex the day after we make out, and then he comes back to throw accusations around.

A sudden bout of irritation at his behavior overcomes me, and I bite the inside of my cheek to stay calm. "I know what he said, but I don't want to talk about it. Is there a reason you're here?"

He might as well stew a little in his attitude.

When he rubs his hands over his face, it's the first time since he walked in that I get a good look at him.

His eyes are slightly puffy, framed by dark circles, making it look like he hasn't slept in a while. Exhaling loudly through his nose, he shakes his head. "Of course, I'm sorry. This weekend wasn't fun, and it feels like I was gone for years instead of just two days. I didn't stop by to make it worse." He runs his hand through his hair. "Can we sit down and talk?"

I try as hard as I can to stay strong, but the urge to comfort him is hard to resist. I want to reach out and give him a hug, and tell him everything is going to be okay, even though I felt very different about that just a few minutes ago. Seeing him makes my resolve weak, but I fight the impulse—I have to.

"All right." I walk over to one of the small tables that line one of the walls and pull out two bar stools from underneath before dragging them back over to my workbench. I pat one of the stools while sitting down on the other. "Here, sit down."

Once we're both situated, I hand him a fork and point at

the table with the array of baked goods I managed to produce in record time today. "Might as well join me in this sugar massacre. Since you're partially at fault, you deserve the fat hips right now just as much, if not more."

The corners of his mouth twitch when he takes the fork from me. He looks at the food in front of us, his eyes wide. "You made all of this?"

"Yup. Some people take a relaxing bath or work out when they're frustrated or need to let off some steam. I bake." I shrug matter-of-factly, since it's been *my thing* ever since Grandma started teaching me how to bake when I was younger.

"I guess that makes sense." That's all he says before digging into the cherry pie, his eyes fluttering closed for a long moment. "Wow. So good."

At least I think that's what he said around the mouthful of food.

"I've missed this, Charlie."

I snort, digging into the pie myself. "What? Getting fat with me?"

A lopsided grin adorns his beautiful face. "No, silly, just enjoying your company without any added stress. Things are different with us. We can just be Hudson and Charlie, and nothing else. There's no pressure for me to be the 'famous rockstar,' or to fulfill whatever other weird box people put me in. Not once have I felt like that with you, which is why I enjoy my time with you so much. Being thrown back into the business world this weekend, after this tranquility with my family and you, has been more of a shock than I was prepared for."

"Mmm." I pause for a moment with the fork at my lips,

allowing his words to sink in. Theoretically, I completely understand what he's talking about, but I'm not sure it's a safe topic for me right now because my resolve is already weak.

Diversion it is.

I don't look at him, but push a cherry around on my plate instead. "So, how's the writing going?"

He sighs and shrugs his shoulders. "I was away from you, so I'm sure you can guess the answer to that. But I'd rather not talk about it right now."

Looks like we both have a list of taboo topics.

I can't help myself and feel a little bad that his career is suffering alongside all this chaos. "Well, what did you want to talk about?"

"I came to apologize, Charlie. I can't tell you how hard the last few days have been for me, and how incredibly sorry I am for everything that happened."

And just like that, my irritation is back in full force. "Really? *You* were having a hard time? How do you think I've been feeling? Everything's been just peachy here, right?"

Two emotional outbursts in half an hour. That's a record.

One of his hands extends my way, but he drops it last minute. "I'm sorry. First, I had to leave you out of the blue like that, and then this whole shitshow with Addy happened. I just wanted to forget about that disaster and come back home."

"Oh right, Addy, your *fiancée*." I might sound a little childish, but I don't have it in me right now to care. My hurt pride feels like I have the right to sulk.

He tilts his head to the side and frowns. "*Ex*-fiancée, Charlie, *ex*. A very, *very* important distinction."

That stops me in my tracks for a moment, my fork now

covered with some delicious cheesecake that's halfway to my mouth. A stray thought comes to mind, wondering if it might be better to stop eating now before I get sick, but I decide I'll deal with whatever later on. At least the food will distract me from the emotional turmoil that's been raging inside me for the past few days.

A sudden and unexpected urge to know everything overcomes me. Why not torture myself some more and hear all about his weekend?

"So, why exactly did you have a fancy dinner with Addy then?" Saying her name makes me want to throw up, and I try to keep it to a slight snarl when her name leaves my lips.

"I didn't. That's what I'm trying to tell you. I'm still not sure what strings she pulled, but she knew where I was and just invited herself. When I told her to leave, she said she'd make a scene, and sadly, I know she'd have totally done it. I was exhausted from my day of meetings, and the last thing I needed was one of her public outbursts. Not to mention, the field day the media would've had with that, which probably would have played right into her hands."

He takes a deep breath and puts his fork down on his plate. "So instead, I decided to listen to whatever she had to say and get the hell out of there as fast as I could. She isn't a good person to have around, and I didn't want her to cause any more drama than she already has just by being there. That woman *loves* creating chaos around her; it's one of her absolute favorite things to do."

I huff and barely refrain from rolling my eyes.

His eyes lock with mine, the look in them intense. "Somehow, she knew about you, Charlie. She knew we live together, and about Mira too. I couldn't *not* listen to her after

133

she dropped that piece of information on me. All I wanted was to figure out what she was up to. The last thing I want is her dragging you guys into some fabricated mess."

Saying I'm stunned by Hudson's explanation might be a bit understated. It's so far from all the scenarios I've been coming up with ever since I saw the first photo online that I need a minute to digest it. All the while, he looks at me with big puppy eyes, making it extremely hard not to dissolve into a puddle from that look alone.

"So, dining with her for the whole world to see was just for my sake?" The words feel wrong, and my stomach clenches with unease.

"Sadly, yes. I had to figure out what she wanted. The only way to get any info out of her is by schmoozing her. I know it doesn't sound right—and trust me, I really didn't enjoy my time with her—but things with her are never easy. The saying 'you catch more flies with honey than vinegar' was created for people like her."

"You could have explained things to me. One simple message or phone call would have been enough, Hudson. Instead, I had to watch this show happen online, like the rest of the world." My voice sounds like it's about to break, and I hate it. I don't want my emotions to get the better of me, because I don't want to come across as weak.

After things ended with Sebastian, I promised myself I'd never let anyone walk all over me ever again. I owe it not only to myself but also to Mira. My life has changed dramatically with her in it, and I have to make all my decisions depending on what's best for both of us.

He rubs a hand over his face. "I know, I should've known better. I panicked and didn't think about how it might look in the media. I just wanted to do the right thing."

"Is she gonna leave you alone now, at least? Did you figure things out with her?"

He shakes his head and actually looks defeated. "I wish I could say yes, but for some reason, I have a bad feeling about her. She wasn't happy when she left, and she isn't one to easily give up."

Swallowing hard, I put my fork down too. I doubt I could get another bite down right now anyway. My brain's a mess, going over everything I just learned, getting stuck on one thought specifically that makes the unease in my stomach multiplying. "She wouldn't come here, would she? I mean, she wouldn't do anything stupid, right?"

Sadly, there are some crazy people out there, and you can never be too careful.

"I don't think so. She's never been here, always said she wouldn't get caught in a small town so far away from the spotlight, so I doubt she'd do it now." He stops talking and stares past me into nothingness. "I still wonder how I could've been so blind about her. It's all so blatantly obvious to me now, whenever I see her. I mean, even my own family only met her once. At that point, we were already engaged, and that took weeks of persuasion on my part."

"That's sad." I actually mean it. I can't imagine being engaged to someone when I haven't met his family or vice versa. She just doesn't sound like a nice person, and Hudson still seems to have a hard time dealing with the past.

"It is, but it's my own fault. I fell for her whole charade. She's like a siren. She lures you in and sounds pretty much perfect until she strikes completely unexpectedly." Shoving his hand roughly through his hair, the frustration is written all over his face.

He closes his eyes for a moment before looking straight at me. "That's exactly how Addy is. She's a fantastic manipulator, and she has absolutely no problem using that skill to her advantage whenever she deems necessary, which is pretty much all the time. When I first saw her, she was so beautiful and funny, and I never thought she'd be capable of doing all the appalling things she did."

He's lost in his memory again, and I hate seeing him like this. No matter what happens with us now, he's still become my friend, and no one should be treated like that. I still don't know the whole story, but I trust him enough to believe what he just told me.

Hudson clears his throat, shrugging like it doesn't matter.

He can't fool me though. The ugly mark she's left is still clinging to him like a nasty rash.

"Anyway. I've learned that beauty can be very misleading, especially when it's paired with lies and pretensions." He says it so nonchalantly now, like I'm not sitting here, burning with curiosity about what exactly happened.

I'm so into the story that my mind is demanding more information. But before I actually get a chance to ask him, I suddenly have to cough really hard.

Leave it up to me to choke on my spit. Fabulous. And so classy too.

"You okay?" Hudson jumps up from his seat to pat me on the back. "One second, let me get you some water."

The contact shouldn't have sent a shockwave through my body—especially since it wasn't intimate in any way—but I can still feel the lingering warmth of his handprint on my back. A moment later, he hands me a glass of water, and I take it eagerly, still coughing between sips. I'm sure my face is beet red as I try to get my cough under control. How embarrassing.

He remains right next to me, and the urge to turn my head and look up at him is almost impossible to resist. Taking the decision out of my hands, he puts his fingers under my chin to gently turn it his way. I'm surprised when he's suddenly at eye level since I didn't expect him to bend down for me. I momentarily get lost in his brown eyes, so drawn in by the depth of emotion shimmering right beneath the surface, my resolve chipping further and further away with each additional second I spend with him.

"Charlie, I really am sorry about everything. I know I didn't handle the situation very well, and hurting you was the last thing I wanted to do. I thought I was doing the right thing, but I can easily see now that there would have been a million better ways to handle it. I underestimated the media, but I should've known better."

Even when his fingers drop back to his sides, our gazes stay locked, this connection—or whatever it is between us—buzzing around us like its own entity. "Just know I really believe that there's something special between the two of us, and I want to explore that. I *need* to explore that."

"Hudson, I—"

He holds up his hand. "Please, let me finish first."

I nod.

"I know I made a mistake, and I know I'm far from perfect. If you want confirmation on that, just ask my family. I'm sure they'd be *more* than willing to provide you with lots of stories." He chuckles once and my lips curve up a little at the corners at the thought of hearing all kinds of stories about Hudson.

Even with everything going on, this family has grown on me already, making the dark hole in my heart a little smaller.

His fingers reach out for mine, softly grazing the tips. "Even though we've only known each other for a few weeks, you've already become a very important part of my life. And I hope I didn't screw that up."

"I feel the same way." The words are out of my mouth before I can stop them.

The hope in his eyes shines brightly. "Does that mean you forgive me?"

Chewing on the inside of my lip, I feel the weight of his question trying to crush me.

What on earth am I supposed to do?

CHAPTER FOURTEEN

MY SPINNING THOUGHTS ARE ONLY INTERRUPTED BY MY pounding heart. The blood is rushing through my ears as I take a deep breath and try to focus. "I forgive you."

The words come out of my mouth easily, even though I was terrified of saying them.

"Thank you." Hudson studies me intently for a few seconds before he lets out a loud sigh. "Why do I feel like there's a 'but' coming, though?"

I give him a sad smile, still a little torn about everything. "Probably because there is. I'm sorry, but we can't be more than friends right now. After everything you just told me about Addy, I can't risk it. You said yourself that you have a bad feeling about the whole situation, and that you don't know what she's up to. I have to think about Mira too. I can't deliberately put a target on us, knowing what I now know about your ex. I hope you can understand."

He rubs both of his hands roughly over his face. "I don't like it, but I understand it. You guys mean a lot to me, and I'd never do anything to intentionally hurt either one of you."

He's quiet for a moment before he gives me a look so full of emotions, I can feel it in my own heart. "This isn't the end though, right?"

"Hudson." His name falls from my lips in a plea, because I don't know what to say. He wants to hear the same thing my heart wants too, but I can't let anything other than my brain decide in this situation. Since I can't give him a definite answer, I don't say anything. I can only hope we can get through this in one piece and come out on the other side together.

A frustrated growl rips from his throat and he gets up, the metal stool scraping against the floor as he pushes it back. "I don't even know what she wants. It's beyond frustrating to wait for the other shoe to drop. I just want her to go away already, so I can have my life back. I wish she'd never found me in L.A."

Me too, Hudson, but it's too late for that now.

I try to keep the pain and sadness over losing what we had at bay, at least until tonight. I'm sure it will all come crashing down on me later, when I'm in bed by myself. Instead, I try to focus on the one thing that allows me to channel all my anger. "So, she didn't actually tell you much when you saw her?"

"Nope. When she left, she said she'd see me soon, which is what makes me so nervous. Addy is pure evil and loves to play games with people. Thankfully, I discovered all of that before marrying her. That would've, without a doubt, been the biggest mistake of my life."

Disbelief is probably written all over my face after everything he just told me about her. "I still can't believe you actually *wanted* to marry her."

"Things were different, *she* was different. It was actually pure coincidence I didn't tie the knot with her, or I guess maybe more so, luck."

"Why? What happened?" I wonder for a moment why I asked that question. I'm undeniably curious to hear what she did, but I'm also just happy Hudson's still talking to me, so I want to keep him talking. Quite possibly I've also developed a liking for self-torture.

Hudson seems to be wondering the same. "Do you really want to know?"

I don't trust my words right now, so I nod.

"All right." He lets out a deep breath and pulls the stool back to him. "We met on the set of one of her movies about two years ago. I was going to write a song for the movie, and the director invited me to watch them film the scene he wanted the song for. He introduced me to the cast, and Addy and I seemed to click instantly. We were pretty much inseparable from the very beginning. Because of our busy schedules, we didn't see each other very often, but I was hoping that would change eventually, sometime down the road. On our first anniversary, I proposed to her, feeling like the luckiest man alive when she said yes."

Even though Hudson's looking at me, I don't think he really sees me. The pain in his eyes is raw and real, and I'm dreading to know the rest of the story.

After swallowing loudly, he tears his eyes away from mine and focuses on his hands instead. "Despite being so young, we talked a lot about our shared dream of having a big family. It was one of the first things we bonded over. A few weeks before I proposed, we decided to try and start our family. Several months later, I came back home early after a canceled meeting and heard Addy talking in the study. She was on the phone, telling the other person that she'd wrapped me around her little finger, promising me kids, even though she hated them and never wanted any. She said she'd never allow a little pest to ruin her perfect body like that."

My heart is hurting for him. I can't imagine the kind of pain and betrayal he must have felt during that time. Having the person you love do something so cruel and heartless to you must not only be hard to accept, but also incredibly hard to overcome.

Maybe that's one of the reasons we get along so well.

Maybe our pasts are why we connected so quickly.

"I guess she had some sort of medical explanation lined up for me that would explain why she couldn't get pregnant, and I'd have never been the wiser. I stood in front of the door, listening to her as she laid out her whole plan to the person on the phone, laughing the whole time. This was a side of her I'd never seen before.

"At that moment, I realized the strong possibility of not even knowing the real her. The reality of that hit me so hard, I thought someone punched me in the gut. I also must have made a noise because she suddenly looked straight up at me. The terror in her eyes was real, I know that much. She ended the call immediately and tried to apologize, giving me one lame excuse after the other, but we both knew her game was over. She moved out the next day, and I hadn't seen her since."

My head is spinning so wildly, all I'm capable of is staring at him for what feels like an eternity before I get up and give him a hug.

Because he deserves one.

I pull him close. "I don't know what to say. I'm incredibly sorry that happened to you. I still can't believe someone would actually do something like that."

He hugs me back so fiercely a little corner of my heart breaks for him. At this moment, I feel like I'm his lifeline, the pain and sorrow almost palpable between us.

We stay like this for a while, neither one of us saying a word.

When we pull apart, he looks me straight in the eye with a cautious expression. "Thank you. I... You're actually the first person I've ever told the real reason we broke up."

That immediately gets my attention and to say I'm stunned is an understatement. Did I hear that right? He's never told this to *anyone*? Not even his family? That can't be right. "No one?"

Shaking his head, he bites his lower lip. "I was hurt, and I guess also embarrassed about falling for Addy's whole spiel. I told you, my family never liked her much, and my bandmates merely endured her when she was around, so that made me the only idiot to fall for it. Man, I was so incredibly blind, I still want to kick my own ass for it. Badly. I'd only ever known her as this sweet, caring person and nothing else."

I give his arm a reassuring squeeze before sitting back down. "I totally get it. I think sometimes things like that just happen, and we're almost unable to see behind the façade." I shrug, understanding him so much better than he knows, but not wanting to go down memory lane myself. "How did she take it?"

"Not well, as you can probably imagine. The gossip magazines were running their mouths like crazy about our breakup, posting rumor after rumor. I think the worst ones were about me cheating, a pregnancy I wasn't happy about, and alcohol and drug problems. The list was endless. Of course, it was all from anonymous sources, but I think everyone who knew the real Addy knew she was behind it. That's probably why my siblings react so extreme whenever her name pops up. I quickly learned Addy doesn't shy away from dragging others through dirt, if it benefits her in any way. All that matters is her career and how she looks in the public eye."

Sometimes it's hard to wrap my head around the fact people like that actually exist. Now, everything he told me about her is starting to make a lot more sense. He really was telling the truth when he said he wanted to protect us. "I'm so sorry you had to go through all of this, especially by yourself. I wish you'd have told someone the real reason. You didn't do anything wrong."

He only shrugs, giving me a sad look. I feel like a jerk for doing this to him, to us, but I don't know how else to handle the situation.

When Hudson goes to the bathroom, he gives me a few minutes to process the new information. By the time he gets back, the puzzle pieces are slowly coming together. "Is that when you started having problems with your music?"

It's hard to explain, but it's oddly rewarding to see this vulnerable side of him since it's so different from the funny and carefree Hudson I've seen so far. Even though I'm sad he had to experience all of this, I'm glad it allows me to see him in another light.

"Not so much at first, but it pulled me down further and further with each passing month, as the media kept talking and speculating. I guess, at some point, it got to be too much and really kicked my inspiration in the ass, which made me hate Addy even more. I fell into a deep hole for a while, not knowing what to do with myself or my career. What she'd done, mixed with what I'd lost, was too much for me to handle. And to make matters worse, I couldn't even write music to deal with any of it. It was, without a doubt, one of my lowest points in life."

His gaze meets mine, his faint laugh lines framing those beautiful brown chocolate eyes as a shy smile slowly takes over his face. "Can you understand now why I was so ecstatic when I met you? It felt like I just got ten years' worth of birthday and Christmas presents combined. It was like seeing *you* unlocked that box in my brain, and you've inspired some of the best music I've written. *Ever.* To top it off, you turn out to be this amazing person with the most adorable baby girl in the world. These last few weeks have felt like a miracle to me, like I've won life's jackpot."

Well, *dang it.*

Emotions threaten to close up my throat, and I swallow several times to stop them. Memories from my own awful last year flood my mind, the thoughts of getting back up after hitting the lowest point of my life so overwhelming, I get dizzy for a moment.

Hudson steadies me, his hand firmly holding onto my elbow.

I want to tell him I feel the same, that my life has gotten so much better since I met him because it's true. But I don't want to make this any harder than it already is.

I blink at him. "Thanks for saying that. I can't tell you how much that means to me, especially after the year I've just had."

"Will you tell me about it?" His voice is quiet, but I love this newfound connection and openness between us.

Despite everything that just transpired, I have to chuckle. "I don't think I can handle any more crazy-ex stories for today. But I will another day, if you still want to know."

"I'll take anything you're willing to share. At least I won't be the only one with a crazy ex then." He winks at me, making the suppressed butterflies in my stomach stir again.

"Oh, don't you worry, I certainly got you covered."

He picks his fork back up and plays with it. "So, friends, huh?"

Nodding, I give him a small, uncertain smile.

When I look at him, it's hard to remember why I'm putting on the brakes. But all it takes is one thought about Addy and the things she might still bring upon Hudson, and therefore possibly people close to him too.

He spreads one of his hands out wide to stretch before relaxing it. "I'm not even going to pretend I'm happy about it, not after everything I just told you. But I understand it and respect your decision. Just know I'm right here, waiting for things to go back to normal. Because the second we've got this whole chaotic mess off the table, I want us to pick up right where we left off."

"Thank you, Hudson." My voice is quiet but strong. Despite this annoying situation—or maybe because of it—I'm grateful for his reaction.

His fork lands in a piece of lemon pie. "We better get going if we want to finish all of this today. Want to eat some more cake with me now?"

"I thought you'd never ask."

CHAPTER FIFTEEN

"Mira, could you *please* hold still for a moment so we can get this over with? I love you very much, sweetie pie, but sometimes you drive me crazy."

Gathering another ounce of patience, I tackle her again, trying desperately to change her diaper—which is easier said than done. Babies at this age are so active, it's ridiculous sometimes. Even being still for two seconds is too much to ask.

"Ma-ma, ma-ma." She gives me a big toothy grin when I hand her yet another toy, hoping that'll keep her occupied long enough this time.

A soft chuckle makes me lift my head, my eyes immediately trained on the open door without taking my hands off the little wiggle ball in front of me.

"So young and so much trouble already, huh?" Hudson's voice sounds raspy, like he just rolled out of bed and appeared in my doorway—which is actually a possibility. He's casually leaning against the doorframe, his arm and chest muscles on full display in a snug light gray T-shirt.

I'm so distracted by him I realize, too late, I loosened my grip on Mira enough for her to flip over. She's using this moment of freedom to her advantage, crawling off to Hudson as fast as she can—her diaper hanging awkwardly off one side of her little booty.

What can I say? That was all I managed to secure before my thoughts went on a field trip to Hudsonland—the one I tend to get lost in so often.

Chuckling at Mira, he bends down to pick her up. "Good morning, you little rascal. Are you giving Mommy a hard time?" She's so excited to see him, she keeps hitting him on his shoulder. After snatching her little hand and pretending to eat it, much to Mira's delight, his eyes lock with mine. "Want some help?"

"Gosh. Yes, please." I half-groan, earning another amused chuckle from him. The closer he gets, the more Mira squirms in his arms, probably knowing what's about to happen. At least she's happy to see Hudson, squealing louder by the second—especially when he talks.

Looks like we both have a thing for his voice.

Sitting down on the plush cream carpet next to me, he lays Mira down in front of us before picking up one of the toys from the floor. He shakes it in front of her, and she's smiling up at him with a big, goofy grin.

Completely mesmerized by him.

That's pretty much the only thing I notice since I'm attempting to win my own battle over here—trying to ignore the skin of our naked arms almost touching. On top of that, the scent of his signature aftershave infiltrates my senses, making my body almost hum in appreciation.

How can a scent do something like that?

No, Charlie, stay strong. You wanted to be friends for now, remember?

If it was just that easy.

I should have known better, should have expected this to be a lot harder than I anticipated.

I mentally shake myself out of the haze I'm in, putting in some extra effort to focus on the task at hand.

Rubbing my hands together, I peek over at Hudson. "All right, let's do this. You entertain her while I close that diaper and put on her leggings, okay? You're captivating enough, so I should get it done quickly."

He looks at me like he's trying hard not to laugh. "Am I now?"

"Are you what?"

"You said I'm captivating."

"No, I didn't." Crap. I totally did. "I mean, I said it, but I didn't mean it like that. What I wanted to say was that you'll keep her attention well enough, like a good toy."

Oh no. Abort mission, *abort mission.*

I think the close proximity of him has made my brain malfunction because *that* definitely wasn't the right thing to say either.

This time, he bursts out laughing, not that I blame him. He probably thinks I'm a little nuts this morning.

"Wow. You're really good for my ego." He turns to Mirabelle. "Did you hear that, sweetie? Your mama thinks I'm a captivating toy."

I close my eyes. How embarrassing.

Why does everything this man says sound like it's interlaced with sex?

Or maybe that's just me, faltering under this extreme tension between us.

Poking him in the arm, I can't help but laugh too. "I didn't say that, stop it." I touch one of my cheeks to find it as hot as I thought it was. "Let's just forget about it and get this done."

"Oh, trust me, I will remember this *forever*." He winks at me, and I'm powerless against the flutter in my rib cage in response to his teasing.

It's been getting harder and harder with each passing day to stay strong, and it's only been a week since we had our "friends talk." Maybe it's time to admit I'm a sucker when it comes to him. He's different than any guy I've ever met before, but I've known that for a while.

By now, it's useless to deny my weakness for anything Hudson.

I guess you could say he's my flavor.

Doing the right thing feels more like torture than anything else. Real painful torture that leaves me sleepless at night. And when I do finally fall asleep, I wake up in the middle of the night, all sweaty and tangled up in my sheets. I'm not sure that's the right solution either because there doesn't seem to be any doubt as to what my body and heart seem to want. My brain, on the other hand, is still trying to hang on to the control—even though that might not be more than a thin thread by now either.

Hudson's voice pulls me out of my thoughts. "What are you thinking about so hard?"

He's studying me intently, lifting one of his hands slowly up to my face.

"Please, don't." My voice is quiet, and I close my eyes,

knowing it would only make things worse if he touches me right now.

Pulling his hand back immediately, the corners of his mouth turn down into a sad frown. "I'm sorry. I didn't mean to make you uncomfortable."

"You didn't. You don't. But it's already hard enough without you touching me."

He nods, even though I'm not sure he understands what I'm talking about. I leave it at that, though, not seeing a point in explaining it any further, spiraling myself deeper into this misery. The fact is, nothing has changed with the whole Addy debacle, and that's what I need to focus on.

Lying down next to Mira, he stares up at me. "Let's just get your little stinker here ready, okay?"

This time I nod, happy for the diversion. All week long, we've turned into masters of distraction, pretending as best as we can that we're doing all right with this unfortunate situation. "Sounds good."

After that, we make quick work of Mira, and once she's all done, I let out a big breath. "I didn't know they would be so much work at such a young age already. That was quite a reality-shock when I figured that out."

"I can imagine, but you're doing such a great job. Mira is thrilled to have such an awesome mom—no doubt about that. She wouldn't be this beautiful little person without you as her mom."

His words hit me so deeply, I have trouble breathing for a moment. I avert my eyes away from his, because there's no way I can keep the emotions out of mine. His words mean more to me than I could ever tell him—despite the fact they're also incredibly bittersweet to hear.

"Thank you." Fanning my eyes, I try hard to laugh it off instead of crying. "I guess I'm a little emotional this morning."

Sitting up right away, he ducks his head to catch my lowered gaze. "Hey, I'm sorry. Is everything okay? Did I say something wrong?"

He doesn't know he hit a nerve, but I'm not sure he's ready for my story yet—or rather, I'm not sure if I'm ready to tell him yet. Instead of explaining anything from my past, I chicken out. "No, I'm all good. Sorry. I just haven't been sleeping well."

"Nothing you need to apologize for. Why don't you go and get ready while I stay here with Mira. Take your time and try to relax some, all right?" He grabs a few blocks and stacks them up in front of Mira.

I'm confused by his statement. "Do I need to get ready for something?"

Hudson chuckles and points to my head. "Not really. You can stay like this all day long if you want, I don't mind one bit."

My hand reaches up, immediately feeling the thick towel still wrapped around my hair. "Oh goodness, I completely forgot about that. I really think I'm losing my mind."

He shakes his head. "Don't worry about it, I've got your back. Now go, we'll be fine."

Hudson is such a natural when it comes to Mira. The two of them play together all the time, and it's actually become one of my favorite things to do—watching these two together in the living room while I bake in the kitchen. Hudson's repertoire of nursery rhymes has expanded quickly, much to

Mira's delight, and they enjoy each other's company tremendously.

"Thank you, I'll be right back." After giving Mira a quick kiss, I rush out of the room before I do something silly like bend down to kiss Hudson too. Even though he does deserve some sort of reward for all his help. Life without Hannah and him—heck, without this whole family—would not only be ridiculously lonely but also incredibly listless.

Not only does Gabe check in with me constantly, getting everything ready for Monica's impending arrival, but even Hudson's sisters have already told me they consider me a part of the family. I can't remember ever having so much love and support surrounding me, which can be quite sobering at times—yet it also endlessly warms my heart.

Just like Hudson told me, I take my time to get ready. It doesn't sound like much, but sometimes even taking five more minutes without checking on your baby every two seconds feels like a game changer.

When I get back to Mira's room, the two of them are crawling on the floor, both of them laughing. It feels like months, rather than days, since we had our friends talk, and the more time passes, the harder it seems to get for me. My strength to resist Hudson is tested on a daily basis, especially in situations like this where he's playing with my little girl like it's the best thing in the whole world.

I mean, come on, is there anything hotter than a guy being adorable with a baby?

Hudson looks up when I walk in. "Was that you taking

your time? I really meant it, you didn't have to rush. You know I don't mind playing with this little bugger here."

Mira stops mid-crawl and turns around to look at me. She's happy to see me, but at the same time, it almost looks like there's a little bit of accusation in her eyes too.

Which is nuts.

Or maybe she wanted some more alone time with the hunky rockstar.

Get in line, kiddo.

I give her a big smile that she returns before I focus back on Hudson. "I know you do and I really appreciate that. We're a bit in a hurry, though. There are some important deliveries coming in at the bakery today. The opening is only a few weeks away now, so things are starting to get a bit more chaotic."

He sits up. "Why didn't you say so? Let me grab my things, and I'll come with you."

"Thank you. Are you sure?" Taking a deep breath, I try to find the courage to say what's on my mind. "Would you mind meeting us there? I... I just don't think it's a good idea to be seen together in public right now." His face visibly falls at my confession. I feel horrible, absolutely terrible, but I needed to say it.

More and more paparazzi have come to town this week to get a look at their rockstar. I'm not worried about being seen with Hudson, per se, but I am worried about what that would mean for his ex. The last thing I need in my life is the kind of drama, or worse, she'd bring with her.

Bottom line, I'm scared out of my mind—like "wanting to pack my things and move back to New York" scared. "I'm really sorry."

He shakes his head but avoids my gaze, and I'm starting to feel a little sick. "Stop apologizing for things that aren't your fault. I really understand why you're doing this. I'm not a hundred percent sure how far she'd go either, so I'd rather be safe than sorry too."

"I wish things could be different." I'm not sure if that's the right thing to say but it *is* the truth.

He stands, bringing Mirabelle with him. "Trust me, me too." After handing me my baby, he walks over to the door. Before he leaves, he turns around, looking at me for a long moment. "I'm going to fix this, I promise. I'll see you in a little bit, okay? Bye, baby girl."

I nod at him and then he's gone. For some reason, I suddenly have a bad feeling in my stomach, really hoping he isn't up to something.

After grabbing everything we need, we head downstairs into the kitchen to eat something before heading out. I'm surprised to see Hannah sitting at the bar, sipping a cup of tea. "Oh, hey. I thought you were going out with the other ladies this morning."

"Hey, girls. I'm going to leave soon. You know how they are, always running late." She tickles Mira for a moment before I put her down in her bouncer.

I turn on the music and give her a teether from the freezer, all the while feeling Hannah's gaze on me. When her eyes meet mine, there's something in her gaze I haven't seen before. It almost feels like she can look straight into the deepest corners of my soul. She gives me a warm smile, reminding me so much of my grandmother that my heart aches a little.

Brushing a strand of hair out of my face, I suddenly feel very raw and vulnerable. "What is it? Is everything all right?"

"I'm good, if that's what you mean." She takes a deep breath and leans my way. "You know, I usually don't like to put my nose where it doesn't belong, but it seems like things have gotten a little out of control. Charlie, he might not always do the right thing, but just know his heart is in the right place." Without mentioning Hudson's name, we both know she's talking about him, so I nod. "His life is anything but easy with being in the public eye so much, but he's a genuinely good guy, one of the best I know. And you, my friend, you more than deserve a good guy."

My chest actually hurts from her words. "Hannah, I—"

She shakes her head and stands up. "No, you don't need to explain anything to me. I know you're scared after everything that happened. I get it, I *really* do. And there's a lot happening right now. All of this drama surrounding his career and private life is exactly the reason why I never tell anyone who my grandchildren are. It puts so much pressure and prejudices on them, which I don't think they deserve. But anyway, just think about it. I have to run now, or I'm going to be the one late this time and will never hear the end of it. You guys have a good day, okay? Call me if you need anything."

With that, she's out the front door, leaving me alone with my jumbled thoughts and a rockstar to meet at the bakery.

CHAPTER SIXTEEN

"CHARLIE, WHERE DO YOU WANT THESE?" GABE IS barely visible when he walks in the back door of the bakery, a stack of boxes piled up high in his arms.

I rush over, ready to help. "Just over there on the counter, please."

After putting all the boxes down, he looks at me and shakes his head. "How does she sleep in this chaos?" He points at Mirabelle who is strapped to my back in a carrier.

I chuckle and peek over my shoulder. "I have absolutely no idea. Sometimes the noise actually seems to be soothing. Go figure. Seems like it's just one of those things. Some babies sleep through everything while others wake up from the slightest noise."

"Babies are such a mystery. Good thing they're cute." He's looking at her with a smile on his face. From the looks of it, the whole Mitchell family is a little baby crazy, but I'll keep that fact to myself.

The oven beeps, and I walk over to turn it off, taking the baking sheet full of apple cinnamon muffins out to slide it onto the counter. I point my oven mitt at Gabe. "They have to be cute, or we'd all be extinct, trust me. Remember those words for whenever it's your turn."

"Yeah, thanks." He looks a little uncomfortable, and I have to chuckle. It's actually pretty adorable.

I press my lips together to keep from laughing. "Gabe, are you still in the phase where you love babies as long as you can give them back after a while?"

His cheeks turn slightly red. "I guess so."

I clearly embarrassed him and feel a little bad about it. "Nothing wrong with that. You're only a year older than Hudson, right? You still have plenty of time."

He nods. "Tell that to my mom. She loves to whine about wanting grandbabies. Thank goodness you guys are here now. Mira should quench her baby thirst, at least for a little while."

That makes me snort. "Yeah, Hudson told me about that."

Gabe looks taken aback when he studies me. "He did? Really?"

Taking the muffins out of the baking form, I put them on a cooling rack. "Yeah, a while ago. Is it bad that he mentioned it?"

"What? Oh no, I didn't mean it that way. He just has this weird thing where he usually doesn't like to talk about babies, so I guess I'm just surprised he talked about it with you."

Something inside me snaps, and I get defensive. "Maybe he has a reason for his behavior, don't you think?"

Gabe raises his eyebrows, picking up on my tone.

"You know what? You're right, maybe he really does." He

studies me for another moment before shrugging his shoulders. "Speaking of Hudson, do you know where he is?"

I sigh and shake my head, feeling like a jerk for lashing out at him. "He said he was going to meet us here, so I'm guessing he got caught up somewhere."

"Dang it, he didn't answer his phone either. I'm worried he's going to do something stupid."

Hudson acted completely normal earlier, but I can't help and feel a little nervous at Gabe's remark. Maybe I didn't imagine it then, or Gabe knows something I don't. "Why? Did he say something to you?"

Shaking his head, Gabe looks everywhere but me.

I stare at him until he finally turns around to look at me. "You're keeping something from me. What is it?"

He throws his hands up in defeat, letting out a big breath of air. Well, that didn't take long. "You're just as bad as Grandma. Can't get anything past you guys."

"Well, you obviously know something... I'm waiting." I'm barely refraining from tapping my foot in annoyance.

"Something about wanting to make things right. I'm not sure what exactly he was referring to. The phone call lasted all but a minute. I'm guessing it has something to do with Addy, not that he'd tell me if it was, since he doesn't talk about her." He shakes his head. "We still don't even know why they broke up."

I stare at him as we study each other for a moment in silence, and I'm afraid I'm gaping a little too much. Then he points a finger at me. "I can't believe it. He told you, didn't he?"

The last thing I want to do is create problems in this

family because of this whole situation. But I'm also not going to lie, so I nod.

Gabe's voice is quiet when he speaks again. "Is it as bad as we think it is?"

What on earth is the right thing to say here? It *is* pretty bad, after all. "Maybe...probably."

His face transforms in seconds, a light layer of red coloring his face. This time, it's definitely out of anger, though. He looks like he's ready to blow steam out of his ears.

"Man, I really can't stand that woman. You should've seen Hudson when she was done with him. I've never seen him like that before. *Ever.* It was like his body was just this empty shell, and we were so worried he wasn't ever going to go back to normal." His eyes flicker to Mira on my back, and I wonder how much worse his outburst would be if it wasn't for her.

Hearing about Hudson's pain from Gabe feels like a little stab right into my heart again. "I can imagine how down he was. He told me it didn't end well."

Gabe's looking at me with pleading eyes, making it rather easy to guess what he wants from me.

Pinching the bridge of my nose between my thumb and my index finger, I exhale loudly. "I can't, I'm sorry. I totally understand why you want to know, and I really think you should—all of you, actually—but it's not my place to tell."

He rakes his hands roughly through his hair, and it's hard seeing him like this. It's clear how much his brother means to him and that they all have each other's backs. Feeling helpless is probably one of the worst feelings out there, no matter what situation you're in. "No, I completely understand. I should be the one apologizing, not you. I shouldn't have put you on the spot like that."

"Hey, I'm sure it'll be all right. If not right now, hopefully soon." I squeeze his arm gently, hoping it'll reassure him, at least a little bit.

He gives me a small nod. "You're right. And I'm happy he's got you now to confide in. That's a million times better than not having anyone."

If he keeps saying things like that, I'm going to cry.

Gabe reaches out to snatch one of the muffins. Sneaky little thing. "I'm just worried about him, that's all. It's so typical of him to just dive into situations headfirst without thinking things through. I'm sure that's what got him into this mess in the first place."

"I don't know, Gabe. Maybe it was a part of the issue, but from what I know, Addy was sneaky and untruthful about everything. I feel incredibly sad for Hudson. He didn't deserve any of it."

Gabe looks down at me, and I realize what I just babbled about.

My hand darts up to cover my mouth. "Shoot, I shouldn't have said anything."

"Relax. You didn't say anything we didn't already know. Believe me, we sat down as a group several times, trying to put the puzzle pieces together. We were so desperate to help him."

They did? Wow.

I can't deny that it feels weird to know something so personal about Hudson when his own family doesn't. "You guys truly are the best family I've ever met. I really hope Hudson will tell you everything that happened one day. It sounds like it would be good for all of you to get some closure on this."

"Charlie, you are absolutely right, as usual." The sound of another voice in the room makes me widen my eyes, and Gabe and I both turn to look at Hudson.

"Is this a regular occurrence now, to eavesdrop on us?" Gabe walks over to Hudson, studying his younger brother. "Dude, you look like crap."

"Thanks, I appreciate your honesty. Speaking of, I know I should've told you guys what happened last year." He peeks around Gabe to look at me. "For some reason, it took this lovely lady over there to make me realize that."

Automatically, I hold up my hands. "I didn't do anything."

Hudson gives me a small smile, and our gazes lock for a long moment. "You've done so much more than you'll ever realize. Trust me."

Gabe clears his voice. "So, did you take care of things, like you said on the phone earlier?"

Hudson lets out a big breath, shoving his hands through his hair, so similar to what his brother just did a few minutes earlier. "Yes and no. I did take care of things, but it was too late to stop the avalanche that Addy had already set in motion. I should've gotten on her case right away last week."

"Why? What happened?" The bad feeling that's been following us all week hits my stomach with a heavy *thud*—especially after getting the confirmation he was indeed dealing with Addy when he wanted to come help me. I need to sit down.

I pull out one of the stools from under the table, but right before I lower myself, I feel Mirabelle stir on my back. A few seconds later, she starts babbling sleepily.

Hudson walks over to us. "Did I wake her up? I'm so sorry, she usually sleeps through all the chaos."

Nothing about this moment is special or significant, but it hits me like a brick wall just how well he knows Mirabelle and her habits. They've gotten so close, and for some reason, that scares me a little. I guess the only good thing is that she's still so young and wouldn't remember if Hudson suddenly wasn't in her life anymore. We've done it before and we can do it again—if we have to.

What am I saying? Would I really want that?

Taking a deep breath, I try to forget the negative thoughts that momentarily took over my mind. "She probably heard your voice and woke up. It was time though, anyway. You know how she is. If she naps too late, she's ready to party at bedtime."

He chuckles quietly. "She is quite the party animal, especially at night." We look at each other for a silent moment. "Want me to take her out?"

I nod. "Sure."

Hudson unbuckles the carrier in the back, and I take off the straps in the front before he carefully takes her out of the carrier.

Mirabelle immediately snuggles into his chest, and they both sigh. I brush her hair out of her face, smirking at the sleeping lines on her pink cheek.

Hudson gives her a small kiss on the head. "Ah, much better."

The sight of the two of them warms my heart and inexplicably also makes me want to cry like a baby.

How ironic.

In an effort to distract myself, I say the first thing that comes to mind. "So, tell us what happened."

Gabe has silently moved next to me, leaning against one of the big work tables behind us. He's watching the exchange between his brother and Mira, and I'm pretty sure he's just as curious as I am.

Hudson clears his throat. "Well, there's good news and bad news."

Gabe and I shift around nervously before looking at each other. Then, like the dorks we are, we mutter the same words. "Good news first."

Hudson doesn't seem surprised by our little twin magic. "All right then. I called Addy and confronted her about everything. She had a huge meltdown, and we ended up talking for a while. And let me tell you one thing, that woman is screwed up. Like, a lot worse than I actually thought."

Absolute silence.

Out of the corner of my eye, I see Gabe looking at me, probably just as confused as I am right now.

I cross my arms over my chest. "And how exactly is that good news?"

Hudson grimaces. "Sorry. I guess I kind of forgot about that part. So, like I said, we talked for a while and at some point, she finally understood that she needs help, like, professional help. I used some of my connections and got her checked into some rehab center, so hopefully, she can get better. And she said she'd leave me alone now."

I never asked him, and he never mentioned anything, but I'm pretty sure Addy was the one who blew up his phone all week long with messages and calls.

"If that's the good news, I'm not sure I want to hear the bad." Gabe shakes his head, and I don't blame him one bit.

Well, the self-torture part of my brain is having one hell of an active day today. "I already know I'm going to regret this, but what's the bad news?"

Hudson shifts Mirabelle around so he can hold her with one arm while grabbing something out of the back pocket of his pants.

A magazine.

"The bad news is that it was too late to prevent this from being printed."

He throws the familiar gossip magazine down on the table in front of us, the cover staring straight at us.

It shows a picture of Hudson and Addy from their dinner last week. I'm sure no one cares about the picture though, once they've read the headline.

Dream couple Addy Parker and Hudson Mitchell secretly reunited for months, now expecting their first child together.

CHAPTER SEVENTEEN

"WHAT THE F—"

I slap my hand over Gabe's mouth in speed record. "There's a baby in the room. I don't need that word to be one of her first."

He looks at me with big eyes. "Sorry. I wasn't thinking about that." He turns back to his brother. "What the freaking heck, dude? You're having a baby with that evil...witch?"

Despite the topic at hand, I have to smirk. Gabe is obviously having a hard time keeping the language baby-friendly, making this whole situation a little comedic. Not that I blame him. I'm sure all three of us want to use *all* the swear words right now.

Hudson rolls his eyes in response. "Really?"

Gabe throws his hands up, clearly frustrated. "I'm sorry, I know better. I'm obviously having a hard time dealing with this crap right now, okay?" He takes a deep breath, putting a lot of effort into calming down. My guess is he would've exploded if it wasn't for Mirabelle and me being here.

"Is she really pregnant?" It almost pains me to force the words through my clenched teeth.

Hudson nods, and I feel like I might be sick. His face has turned an ashy gray, and I can't imagine what he must be going through right now. This situation has to hit home worse for him than anything else.

"You've got to be kidding me." Gabe's voice echoes through the room, making Mirabelle snuggle deeper into Hudson's chest.

"Could you please get a grip on it, Gabe? You're starting to scare Mira." Hudson's voice is quiet but laced with a warning undertone. He turns to me. "Do you think she'll be okay to play in her playpen for a bit?"

"I think so. As long as she can see us and has her toys, she should be good for a little bit."

"Good, let's try it. I don't want her in the middle of this right now."

I blink. There he goes again, being all considerate, hammering away at the walls I've built up around my resistance and determination. "Sounds good."

After getting the playpen out of my office, I push it to the side of the room and put a few toys and her sippy cup in it. Hopefully, that will buy us at least ten minutes to talk.

Hudson's next to me, humming so quietly I can barely make out the melody. For some reason, he still seems completely collected—his behavior, at least—which baffles me more than just a little bit. I'm not sure if it's because he's still holding Mirabelle, or if this whole situation just doesn't faze him as much as it does me. I mean, who's okay with having something like that on the front page? Especially after the past they share.

Hudson sets Mirabelle into the playpen, gently brushing her hair out of her face. "There you go, baby girl. Here's some water for you and your favorite toys. We're right over there." He points toward Gabe, like Mira understands exactly what he's talking about. "Have fun."

"Such a good girl." I bend down and give her a kiss before walking back over to the two brothers.

Gabe looks like he's ready to pounce on Hudson. "Now, tell us exactly what happened, please, before I explode."

I've never seen him looking this grim and on edge before, and I'm glad I'm not on the receiving end of it.

Hudson lifts his hands up in surrender, chuckling a little. "All right, I will. Now calm down."

Calm.

He really is completely calm, and it makes me want to shake him. Is he in some sort of shock or what's going on? I'd expect him to be furious and going out of his mind over this. Having this on the cover of one of the biggest gossip magazines out there seems huge to me. I know, if the roles were reversed, I'd want to hide under a rock for a very long time, preferably with a big stash of desserts and some Nutella.

Hudson mimics Gabe's stance and crosses his arms over his chest. "I already told you I talked to Addy. At first, we mainly just fought over the whole media circus she's created, and that she has to stop harassing me constantly. Then, out of the blue, she suddenly broke down and started sobbing. I didn't think she'd ever stop. When she finally did, she started telling me all sorts of crazy stories about her childhood. It seems like her extended family took her in after her parents died, amongst lots of other things. Anyway, I don't really want to go into it, but it was pretty messed up. I'm guessing the issues from that time play a major part in everything that's been happening."

"Always a screwed-up childhood to blame." Gabe's comment is quiet when he mutters it, but loud enough for me to hear, making me freeze next to him.

Unwanted thoughts of my own childhood flood my mind. Growing up without a dad and being left with a mom who couldn't care less about her children definitely wasn't fun. As much as I hate to admit it, I guess Gabe is right. Most adult problems can be traced back to something that happened in childhood.

Hudson shoots Gabe a disapproving look before continuing. "She went on to tell me about the pregnancy." His composed face slips for a moment, but he tries hard to push through it. "Apparently, she got involved with someone on the set of her last movie. She wouldn't tell me who it was, so I'm not sure what exactly happened. She wouldn't tell me his name either. But in the end, it doesn't matter."

Gabe lets out a big puff of air, and I hope it helps to calm him down some. "Well if that's what happened, why the heck do we have such a crappy media headline about the two of you?"

Hudson sighs loudly. "She panicked about being pregnant and thought I'd happily take her back since she can now offer me everything I wanted. She thought it was all going to work out. When I turned her down in L.A., she was furious. Add a gossip reporter on speed dial, and you've got yourself a cover story like this faster than you can say Hollywood."

I gasp loudly, having a hard time wrapping my head

around Hudson's explanation. "I can't believe she did something like that. That is so low."

"Uh, guys." Gabe looks confused, his gaze going back and forth between Hudson and me. "I'm a bit lost here. What are you talking about, her giving you what you wanted?"

Hudson looks at his brother before peeking my way. His eyes glaze over with sadness once more, making me want to do a lot of bad things to his ex for causing him this much pain —the old and the new one. I'm not sure what Hudson wants or needs from me right now, but I try to give him a reassuring smile and nod.

He runs his hands through his hair once before looking back at Gabe. "I'll tell you guys the whole story together as a family, but let's just say, I wanted to have kids, and she didn't. Unfortunately, she wasn't exactly forthcoming about that piece of information."

Gabe snorts in response. "Figures. Of course she'd be a snake like that. Why am I not surprised? I knew it must have been something big like that. Who jokes around about having children? Seriously. Some people just shouldn't be allowed to have a relationship at all. It's just not fair. There are so many good people out there who deserve to be happy and who genuinely want a partner and children in their life. They should just be left alone in their search to find someone instead of being deceived and used as a pawn. It definitely sounds like Addy needs some serious help."

Hudson and I look at each other when Gabe is done with his mini-rant. We're both equally perplexed, so we burst out laughing.

"What's wrong with you guys? This is serious." I expect Gabe to stomp his foot in annoyance any second now, which

170

makes me laugh even harder. Mira pulls herself up on the side of her playpen, curious to see what all the commotion is about.

I know there isn't really anything funny about this, but it almost feels cathartic. Had someone told me just a few months ago what my new life in Brooksville would be like, I'd have laughed in their faces at how ridiculous they sounded.

Wiping away a set of stray tears, I try to calm down with a few deep breaths. "I'm sorry, but all of this just sounds like a bad soap opera—totally scripted and with lots of drama. And somehow, I'm smack in the middle of it all."

The look on Hudson's face makes me stop laughing immediately. He takes a hesitant step toward me without doing anything else. "I'm so sorry I've dragged you in all of this. That was never my intention."

"Stop blaming yourself. You didn't do anything. Yes, you made a bad choice with your partner, but that was last year. That's in the past, and we all make mistakes from time to time. I have a skeleton like that in my closet too."

Hudson's eyes go wide, mirroring my own as I realize what I just said.

This filter system between my mouth and my brain definitely needs a checkup. It has been pretty faulty lately, happily babbling while I try to play catch-up.

Gabe is staring at me too, curiosity burning brightly in his eyes.

I wave my hands in front of me as I try to distract everyone once again. "Anyway, how exactly do you guys plan to solve this crazy mess now? I mean, you do have a plan at least, right?"

Thankfully, Hudson nods. "Yes. Addy will get her PR

people to release a statement that the media claims are false. I'll ignore the paparazzi as best as I can and stay silent for now."

"Do you think that's going to work?" Gabe doesn't sound happy or convinced, and I can't really blame him. It's a lot to take in, none of it positive in any way.

Hudson's jaw is set as he stares into my eyes with a determined gaze. "I promise I'll get this back to normal somehow. If it was just about me, I'd let it blow over. But that's not the case anymore. You and Mira are a part of my life now, and I'll do whatever I can to protect you guys."

There he goes again, including Mira and me in his life choices, like we're a team—or a family.

I'm lost in his intense gaze, barely noticing when Gabe leaves my side, muttering something that sounded a lot like, "Damn straight you are."

Since this is slightly awkward, and I don't know what to say, I blurt out the first thing that comes to mind. "Are you guys hungry? I think we could all use a cupcake or two. How does that sound?"

I breathe a sigh of relief when they nod, because why shouldn't they? It's food.

Better yet, it's cupcakes, for crying out loud.

Everything's better with cupcakes.

Mira's starting to complain—still hanging on to the side of the playpen—and Hudson picks her up without a word. I watch the two for a moment before Gabe clears his throat. He has the biggest smirk on his face when I turn to him, and I want to slap the smug expression off his face.

Instead, I duck my head to avoid his knowing gaze.

While they sit down at the table, I walk over to the

counter to get one of the boxes I packed up earlier. When I open it up on the table, the sight and delicious smell in front of me make my mouth water. "Red velvet or lemon blueberry?"

Both Hudson and Gabe raise their eyebrows at my question, giving me identical expressions.

I press my lips together, silently chuckling, my shoulders shaking. "I'm guessing that means both?"

They both nod, and we all laugh. Mirabelle chimes in with her high-pitched giggle, clapping excitedly. That's the beauty about babies. They laugh when you laugh, thinking you're the funniest person around. Most of the time, at least.

As if she feels my eyes on her, she turns and stares me down. "Ma-ma." The smile she gives me is so wide my heart swells, like it does every time she says it.

Before I can react, she looks away from me and to Hudson instead. She's laughing and hitting his chest with her little fists. All of a sudden, she stills and studies his face for a moment. "Da-da."

Her little voice seems to echo through the room while I stand there, feeling like the world just stopped moving.

My heart didn't get the same memo though, since it's beating wildly in my chest.

In the meantime, my hands start shaking so badly the cupcakes fall out of them, landing on the table with a soft *thud*.

CHAPTER EIGHTEEN

AFTER GIVING BOTH MITCHELL BROTHERS NEW cupcakes, I focus on cleaning up the mess I just made. My gaze stays firmly locked on the table while my cheeks continue to burn hot. I still haven't found the courage to look up at Hudson, I just can't. Hearing Mirabelle say Da-da to him—as unintentional as it most likely was—is enough for my stomach and my heart to perform simultaneous somersaults, making me a little dizzy.

Out of the corner of my eye, I see Hudson snuggling Mira close to his chest. "Mira, you are the cutest baby I've ever seen."

Gabe, on the other hand, is awfully quiet. When I sneak a peek at him, I find him staring at me curiously. He immediately catches my gaze and gives me a warm smile. I'm not sure I want to know what he's thinking. My brain feels fuzzy, and I'm a nervous ball of energy. Usually, I'd start baking in a situation like this, to deal with my inner turmoil, but that's not going to happen this late.

"Well, guys." Gabe's chair scrapes against the floor when

he stands up too quickly, and I look back up at him in confusion. "I just remembered something, so I have to go. Hudson, I'm guessing you walked here earlier, so you can catch a ride home with Charlie, right? It's way more convenient anyway. All right. I'll see you guys later."

He barely takes a breath before snatching one more cupcake from the open box. He tickles Mirabelle's belly, winks at me, and claps Hudson on the shoulder. Then he's out the door in record time.

Talk about a speedy exit.

"Bye, Gabe." The words come out in a quiet mumble, seconds after the door closed.

After a minute of silence, I risk a glance at Hudson, but luckily, he's engrossed in playing with Mirabelle. I watch them for a moment until he looks up at me. From the look in his eyes and the smug smile on his lips, he knew I had my eyes on them all along.

Clearing my throat, I wipe my hands off on my pink apron. "Are you ready to leave? You look tired."

He chuckles in response. "You always know how to make me feel better."

"You know what I mean." I make a motion with my fingers like I'm locking my lips and throwing away the key. "I'll stop talking for now."

"Please don't stop on my account. I love listening to your babbling, it's always very entertaining. And let's not forget about it being dang cute too." He smirks before looking down at Mirabelle who's playing with his shirt, pinching it between her little fingers and letting it go before doing it all over again. "Don't you agree, sweetie? Your mama is the cutest thing ever, besides you, of course."

As usual, she gives him a big drooly smile, and they both laugh.

His words make my stomach churn restlessly, and I have to close my eyes for a moment to calm my nerves.

How am I supposed to resist this man when he says the sweetest things all the time? All the while playing with my little girl like it's his most favorite thing to do.

Dang it. That's so unfair.

Apparently, it takes this moment, and seeing these two together for what must be the millionth time, to realize something. If I really want to take our relationship to the next level, I have to tell him about my past first because he deserves to know what happened.

Otherwise, it will all feel like a big lie, and I wouldn't want him to feel trapped or deceived by me in any way. Even less after knowing about what happened with his ex.

A relationship with him and his profession would already be challenging enough, there really is no reason to make it even harder.

Brushing the hair out of my face, I promise myself to come clean soon. Otherwise, none of this will mean the same. It will lose meaning faster than I can build the memories, and neither one of us deserves that. "Just give me a minute to get our things, and we can leave, okay?"

"Sure thing." He gives me a big smile, making the butterflies in my stomach swarm around in excitement.

I busy myself for as long as I can, suddenly dreading the drive home. Being in close proximity to the man who's been occupying my thoughts more and more with every passing day, seems like the last thing I need right now.

When I can't stall any longer, Hudson holds Mirabelle out to me, confusing me.

His face turns into a grimace. "Sorry. Just in case there are still some paparazzi left outside."

Oh. I already forgot about the paparazzi again. "Stop apologizing. It's not your fault."

It seems like we keep apologizing for something that is neither one of our faults.

"Did you...did you want me to go out first and meet you around the corner?" He looks like it hurts him to say the words, and I hate seeing him this way. My heart breaks for him because no one should feel like that.

To make it worse, I just added to it too.

I don't say anything for a long moment. All I do is look at him. This man has been nothing but kind, sweet, and understanding to me. He's been a great friend from the moment we've met. He helps me at the bakery and with Mira as much as he can, and asks for virtually nothing in return—having him sit somewhere while I work is really no hardship in any way.

Yes, I was scared about his ex, but that problem is probably solved for good now, and I believe him when he says he won't let anything bad happen to us. This friendship between us obviously means a lot to him.

I think it might be time for me to show him the same courtesy in return, because he more than deserves it. "Nope, not on my account. They already know we live together anyway. Seeing us together really shouldn't be a big deal."

I shrug my shoulders, suddenly just wanting to be home. I'm slowly but surely growing more than just a little tired of the paparazzi dictating my life. Everything seems to be going well until someone brings them up. They're spreading the dreary wearies like nothing else, and I'm done with them.

Plus, we *are* friends.

"Just know I support whatever decision you make because this is completely your choice."

"Thank you. Let's go then." I know this is one of the downsides of fame, but it still doesn't change the fact that I just want to give him a big hug. Feeling the need to hide in public while wondering if your friends want to actually be seen with you just doesn't sit right with me.

"Are you sure?"

I poke him in the arm. "Yes! Now stop asking me stupid questions, or I'm gonna lock you in here and leave by myself after all."

Hudson chuckles, finally relaxing some.

Mission accomplished.

Without a warning, he closes the distance between us and wraps me in a gentle hug, Mirabelle sandwiched between us. She giggles, totally enjoying the attention.

He gives me one more squeeze before letting go. "Thanks for being you. I don't think I've ever met someone like you. So very special. Don't ever forget that."

Well, dang it. There he goes again.

I'm starting to think there's no wall high enough I could possibly build around my heart that this man couldn't demolish in record time.

A few minutes later, I plop into my driver's seat, happy there was only one stray photographer waiting for us. Even though I'm pretty sure he got a shot of my butt when I put Mirabelle into her car seat.

These are the things I live for.

We drive in silence, except for Mira's constant babbling in the back seat, but I feel Hudson's gaze on me. My nerves get the better of me, and I continuously wipe my hands on my jeans. Chances are, he's wondering if I've lost my mind or if I already regret leaving the bakery with him.

That couldn't be further from the truth.

When the silence finally starts to get to me, I decide to break it. "Do you really think the statement will help take care of the whole situation?"

Leaning his head back against the headrest, he closes his eyes. "Honestly, I have no idea. I really hope so, but I can't deny that I have my doubts. Those paparazzi and reporters are like piranhas. They try to suck as much as possible out of a story, no matter how false or damaging it might be for the involved parties. So, they might keep running it, not caring if I give a statement or not."

"That sounds awful. There's really nothing you can do?"

"Nope. Sadly, it's part of the game. I'll just lie low for a few days and hope they disappear, especially when they hear about Addy checking into the rehab center. I hope that fact, paired with the statement posted online tomorrow, will have most of them leave for good."

"I really hope so. This must be hard for you."

He shrugs his shoulders. "You get used to it, just like with everything else. The craziness of the business becomes your new normal, and you learn to live with it. Some things and some people are worth making those sacrifices for."

"Mmm." I stay quiet, focusing on the road while my thoughts are scattered all over the place. It's hard to imagine being in his shoes. I can't even wrap my head around living like that. For most of my life, I've been trying so hard to be a quiet and reserved person who can easily blend into the background. I did it for so many years, it became second nature at some point. I can't help but notice how opposite that makes us, even though I'm not that person anymore either.

Staying out of trouble and away from people that cause trouble used to be my number one priority.

Sometimes, I wonder if I even know who I am anymore after molding myself so much to become the person I thought I should be in order to be happy—anything to be the opposite of my mother.

"What are you thinking about so hard?" Hudson interrupts my thoughts, making me startle in my seat. "You always bite the inside of your cheek when you're deep in thought, it's adorable."

I chuckle under my breath, my senses on high-alert, as if I've been caught with my hand in the cookie jar. Sometimes it's eerie how well he already knows me, even though I shouldn't be surprised after spending so much time with him for weeks on end. By now, he's aware of pretty much all of my annoying, little habits, and he loves to tease me about them—often.

That realization, mixed with the thoughts of my past, makes me feel a little queasy. "It wasn't really anything important. Just something from my old life in New York."

Such a load of crap. I'm such a chicken, and I'm sure he knows that.

His elbow grazes mine for a nanosecond on the armrest. "Will you tell me about it, Charlie?"

I'm still distracted by the small shock the skin contact

elicited. I want to tell him all about my past, but I know this isn't the place nor the moment for it. "I will."

We finally reach the house, pulling up the driveway to the gorgeous two-story home.

Once the car is parked in the garage, Hudson turns my way. "Good, I can't wait. I've been dying to know more about you too."

I know, Hudson, I know.

I'm just afraid things won't be the same way anymore.

CHAPTER NINETEEN

A FEW DAYS HAVE PASSED SINCE THE INCIDENT AT THE bakery, and we haven't talked about any of it anymore. Sometimes ignorance truly is bliss, but sadly, that hasn't prevented Hudson's predictions from coming true. The media's been having an absolute field day with the chaos Addy created, so everyone's been trying to lie low. Hudson is putting on a brave face, but I know he hates it as much as everyone else does.

"Isn't your friend Monica coming soon?" My rockstar roommate looks at me from the other side of the kitchen bar. He's having his breakfast, while I work on some business stuff I've been pushing aside for way too long. Of course, he looks his usual put-together, sexy self, making it extremely hard for me to focus on anything else.

A big smile forms on my face at his question, successfully wiping away my previous thoughts. "Yes. She's going to be here as soon as the doctors clear her. She's thinking it might be next week. I can't wait." I can barely contain my excitement, wanting to jump up and down and clap my hands. I'm afraid that might be a bit too much for Hudson, especially this early, so I refrain.

Apparently, I'm not doing a very good job though, since he laughs.

The look he gives me over the rim of his coffee mug is filled with pure amusement. "I couldn't tell at all."

My gaze drops to the counter, even though there really isn't anything wrong with feeling happy about my best friend visiting. "Sorry. It's just going to be so nice to have her around. I miss her like crazy."

His voice turns gentle. "Nothing wrong with that. Having someone special in your life is always a good thing. Not everyone's that lucky."

I look up from my laptop to fully focus on him. His plate is already empty, not that I'm surprised. We quickly figured out he devours pretty much anything I bake. We also realized we're both coffee junkies, which actually comes in pretty handy. There always seems to be some brewing when we're home, or even better, we bring each other coffees from our favorite places when we're out and about.

He's pushed his plate aside and is now hunched over a bunch of papers spread out in front of him, a pencil ready in his hand.

Our muse sessions have become a normal part of our daily lives, even though we haven't stuck to any sort of schedule. Now, he just gets his music sheets and whatever else he needs when I'm around and he feels like it.

It's not like I actively have to do anything for him to be inspired.

I've asked him a few times what exactly he's doing and how these muse sessions work, but he always says he can't explain it. Melodies and lyrics just magically come to him whenever he's around me. So far, he hasn't shown me anything though, despite my never-ending curiosity.

I mean, it's only fair to know what he creates from all my musing vibes, right? Especially since he gets the most intriguing expression on his face whenever creativity has struck. I'm not even sure if he notices, but he either sticks the tip of his tongue out of the corner of his mouth or he nibbles on his bottom lip.

It's adorable, and maybe even a little hot.

Okay, it's *really* hot.

Needless to say, our sessions have become more and more distracting to me. No one in their right mind could resist looking at those impeccable, full lips, with a cupid's bow shaped so perfectly I have to resist the urge to touch it and trace it with my fingers—or better yet, my tongue—over and over.

There, I'm already getting distracted again. Shoot.

Trying to snap out of this alternate reality, I nod my chin toward Hudson's papers. "Are you ever going to actually show me what you're doing there?"

He looks at me for a long moment before smirking. "Maybe, when I think it's good enough."

I barely contain the loud sigh that wants to bubble to the surface at seeing him this carefree and happy. I'm getting to the point where I have to admit to myself just how much this man has gotten under my skin over the last few weeks.

Definitely a lot more than I'd planned.

It seems like there's nothing I can do about it either. Not that I'm sure I'd even want to.

Studying him, I try to figure out if he's serious right now

or not. "Don't be shy. Obviously, I've heard your music before. It's awesome and beautiful, and I love it. Plus, I don't think you could write a bad song, even if you wanted to."

His eyes widen and his mouth opens a little. "You think so? We've never really talked about my music before, I guess. And with you not recognizing me when we first met, I just assumed you weren't into it."

"Are you crazy?" Now *I'm* the one who looks at him in shock. Now that I think about it, I realize he's right. We haven't talked about it before. "I *love* your music. The only reason I didn't recognize you was because I'm not big into the celebrity scene. I never know who's who when I see pictures. That's Mo's specialty. And to be fair, I was a little distracted by your half-naked entrance."

Hudson's grin turns into a smug smile. It's pretty obvious he knows exactly what I'm talking about and probably how much it affects me too.

Way to go. Might as well tell him more about his abs and happy trail while you're at it.

I laugh nervously, then take a sip of my coffee. "Anyway. We were talking about Monica. My friend Mo."

I definitely deserve an award in awkward conversation skills today.

Just then, Hannah walks into the kitchen with Mirabelle in her arms, and I sigh in relief.

Hannah to the rescue.

She walks over to me, barely able to hold on to Mira, who's jumping around in her arms at the sight of us.

Holding out my hands for Mira, I give her some cuddles. "Hi, sweetie, did you have a good walk?"

Hannah chuckles. "You should have seen her at the pond when she saw the ducks. She loves them."

"She does. We have to take her there more often." I look at Mira, brushing the hair out of her face. "Did you see the duckies, sweetie? Quack, quack."

Just as expected, she laughs and wiggles around in my arms, having become slightly obsessed with animal sounds lately.

After getting a drink, Hannah sits down next to Hudson, looking at me. "Has Gabe set everything up for Monica?"

I hand Mira one of the toys from the counter, then turn to Hannah. "I think he has everything prepped. At least that's what he said the last time we talked. I offered to help him several times, but he wanted to do it by himself."

She chuckles and shakes her head. "He's always like that, don't worry. He loves to help others, but when it comes to his own stuff, he likes to do things alone and his way."

Hudson puts down his pencil and looks at me with furrowed brows. "I still don't understand why she doesn't want to stay here. Wouldn't that be so much more convenient for everyone?"

Now that Mira's around, I close my laptop, not wanting to break it. I've had to learn quickly that even though older babies are still super small, they can break just as much as a bull in a china store if given the opportunity. No need to chance that. "She knows that Mira and I have already set up camp here. She didn't want to add another person to *your* house."

Hudson opens his mouth to say something, but I hold up my finger.

Mira grabs my outstretched finger and laughs as I

continue. "Plus, Gabe offered, so it's totally out of my hands anyway."

"Yeah, I know he did."

"Something's obviously on your mind, so spit it out already."

His gaze flicks over to his grandmother. "It's nothing, really. Don't worry about it."

Hannah eyes him suspiciously too, but apparently makes the decision to let it slide when she turns back to me. "I think it's a great idea. Gabe has been alone for way too long. It'll be good for him to have a friend around. I know she won't be staying with him at the house, but at least she'll be on the same property. Monica's a lot of fun. Exactly what Gabe needs."

It's useless to say I haven't been a little worried about the arrangement, but I won't get in the middle of it. I can only hope everything will work out. "I hope so. It sounds like Mo and Gabe are very similar when it comes to doing things their own way though, so I hope they won't clash."

Hannah gives me a reassuring smile. "They're both adults, so they'll figure it out. Stop worrying about it."

I snort. "I know, I know."

Hudson clears his throat and walks over to me with his arms outstretched. "I haven't seen this cutie pie all day. Let me have her for a few minutes before I have to leave." In less than a minute, he bounces her around the kitchen, his laughter mixing with Mirabelle's giggles.

The sweet sound fills the air and makes my heart swell. Seeing them together like this has become an almost daily occurrence, making it nearly impossible to imagine a life without any of it.

But, as always, reality likes to come knocking on my door.

Hannah just told me last night that her kitchen will finally be finished in the next week. She wants to wait with her move back home until after the bakery opening, though, so she can help me with everything as much as possible.

That means I have to be realistic about finding a place to stay too. I can't just stay here and play house with Hudson since there's really no valid reason for that. Hannah said we can stay with her as long as we want, but I don't want to take advantage of her. The last thing I want to be is a burden. Mira and I lived by ourselves in New York, so there's no reason we shouldn't be able to do it here either.

"Earth to Charlie." Hannah waves her arms in front of my face. "Are you all right? You look a little pale all of a sudden."

That woman can read me like an open book sometimes—it's scary. "What? Me? Yeah, I'm all good. Just a little nervous about everything coming up, I guess." No need to divulge my worries right now.

Hannah nods, even though she doesn't look convinced. Maybe it's the fact I zoned out while staring at Hudson and Mirabelle that made her suspicious.

She grabs her purse from the bar stool next to her and swings it over her shoulder. "Well, I'm going to leave. I'm meeting up with the ladies first, and then Paul and I are headed to the movies. No need to wait up for me." She winks at me, and we both laugh.

"Sounds like fun." I might be just a little jealous of Hannah having more of a social life than I do, a very doting boyfriend included.

"Do you have anything fun going on for the rest of the day?"

I shake my head. "Nothing major. I just need to respond to a few more work emails. You need to be after people so they can get their job done on time. The bakery opening is getting closer, and there's still so much to do."

"I'm sure it'll all work out. People here always pull through things together. It's a great community."

"I've noticed. Everyone's been very helpful and accommodating, so I'm not really worried."

She tilts her head to the side and gives me a smile. "Good. Maybe try and relax some tonight. Have some good food and a glass of wine once Mira's in bed? I bought that rosé wine you like so much."

I walk over to her and give her a hug—she more than deserves one for everything she constantly does for us. "Thanks so much. You're an angel."

She pulls back after a moment of us clinging to each other, her eyes suddenly looking as misty as mine feel. She waves me away with her usual air of nonchalance, sniffling a little. "Oh please, it's nothing. Don't even mention it." Clearing her throat, she squeezes my arm lightly. "Just try and take the night off, okay? You've been working so hard, I know you must be exhausted. You deserve a little break."

Hudson walks over to us with a smile on his face, Mira chewing on something he must have given her. "Don't worry, Grandma. I'll make sure Charlie won't be working tonight."

"Well, I'm happy to hear that. Take good care of our girls. Don't let Charlie anywhere near her computer tonight." They both chuckle like they're super masterminds at work.

I can't stop the smile from appearing on my face though.

Instead, I shake my head at them. "You guys are impossible. Someone has to do the work. The bakery won't get done by itself."

"We know that, we're only teasing." Hannah looks at her watch. "Sorry, guys, but I've got to run. Have a good night."

Hudson and Mira wave at Hannah's departing figure. "You too, Grandma. Tell Paul to be good to you, or I'll have a word with him."

Hannah laughs loudly at his comment. "I will. Bye, guys."

Once the front door closes, Hudson walks over to the corner of the living room where we put part of Mirabelle's toys and sets her down on the big foam mat on the floor. The whole house is baby-proofed to the ninth, at least the areas Mirabelle spends time in.

All thanks to a certain rockstar.

Even though I told Hudson it wasn't necessary, he insisted. Apparently, he didn't want her in a "baby cage," as he calls it, all day long, so he took matters into his own hands. A few weeks ago, when we came back home from the bakery one day, the house had turned into one of the safest places for babies I've ever seen.

Mirabelle loves the newfound freedom, happily banging around with her toys when Hudson walks back over.

It's fantastic being able to still see Mira everywhere in the living room and dining area while I'm in the kitchen. I'm utterly in love with this open floor plan. It makes life so much easier.

"So, pretty mama." He plops down on one of the bar stools across from me and puts his elbows on the bar, leaning forward as much as possible. "Seems like it's you and me tonight, huh?"

Gaping at him and the way he makes such a simple remark somehow sound the tiniest bit dirty. It makes my cheeks immediately flush with heat, and I press my palms to them, feeling how hot they are.

He chuckles softly. "Don't look so surprised. You know I think you're absolutely breathtaking."

"I don't know, Hudson." I can't deny I'm flattered, but doubt and fear still creep into my system, almost on autopilot. I know his offer sounds harmless, but deep down inside, I know things will change after our time together tonight.

"I won't take no for an answer. I promised Grandma, and I believe you still owe me a story too." His tone is playful, which makes me a little anxious. I think he still assumes the story about my past won't be worse or crazier than his. Otherwise, I don't think he'd be so lighthearted about it and that scares me.

If only I knew how he'd react.

But when are things ever that easy?

He's right, though. I did promise I'd share my story with him too.

Usually, I keep my word.

"I'll order us Chinese takeout." Hudson knows that's my weakness.

"All right! You've got yourself a deal. You and me tonight."

He grins in triumph while I cross my fingers behind my back, hoping this won't end badly.

CHAPTER TWENTY

Hudson's peeking over my shoulder at the monitor in my hand, his warm breath hitting my neck. "Is she asleep?"

Closing my eyes, I take a deep breath, needing a moment to collect myself. "Yeah. She was exhausted after an extra early morning and being active all day. She passed out the second she hit the mattress."

I put the baby monitor on the patio table in front of me. Hudson thought it would be a great night for us to spend outside in the backyard, and I have to agree. One side of the patio has a canopied sitting area with comfortable sofas and chairs—there's even a little mini kitchen next to the barbecue —all of it surrounded by twinkling lights that will look lovely when it gets dark. The sun will be setting soon, which also means a drop in degrees, but Hudson has thought of that too, having turned on the heaters around us. The warmth is already seeping into my body, making me all cozy and comfortable.

It seems like Hudson thought of everything. The Chinese takeout is spread out on the table, looking like we could feed at least five families with it. The bottle of my favorite wine Hannah mentioned is right next to a bottle of water. I always like to have some water with my wine, yet *another* thing Hudson has picked up on over time. We've known each other for about a month now, but it definitely feels more like years.

Sometimes, I wonder if that's a good or a bad thing. I know it definitely scares me a bit at times. It makes me feel vulnerable to have someone in my life know me so well already, and who oftentimes seems to see straight through me —almost like he has a direct connection to my thoughts and heart.

Hudson rubs his hands together, grinning like a little school kid. "I hope you're hungry."

"Yes! Starving, actually. What did you get? It smells delicious." I'm curious and lean over the numerous bags, the exquisite aromas wafting in the air around me. My stomach lets out a big growl, and I quickly cover it with my hands.

Hudson chuckles beside me. By now, he knows I'm not like some of his previous dates—who, according to Mo, mostly looked stick-thin—because I love to eat. Not that we're having a date of course, at least not a real one. We're just having dinner together.

A date-dinner amongst friends. That's totally a thing, right? No matter how attracted you are to said friend.

He starts opening a few boxes and tips them in my direction, so I can get a good look. "I know you like to have a variety, so I wanted to cover my bases and got a bit of everything."

My throat suddenly feels dry, making it hard to swallow, and it takes a lot more effort to get my words out. "Thank you. That was very sweet of you."

The smile he gives me in response is absolutely breathtaking. It reaches his eyes, making them sparkle as the sun slowly goes down around us. I'm unable to do anything but stare at him—completely and utterly mesmerized.

I snap out of it when he holds out a fork to me. "You pick first."

After taking a quick sip of water, I clear my throat. "If you insist."

"I do." The words come out of his mouth in a sweet whisper, making my heart clench.

Gah. This man.

Those two words have always been a bittersweet reminder of my past, but for the first time, I don't feel any discomfort. I avert my eyes from his intense stare and focus on the food in front of me, piling up all of my favorites on my plate. After Hudson does the same, we eat in comfortable silence with the occasional secret glance between us. Mostly, we both appear to be in deep thought, which neither one of us seems to mind.

We make a much bigger dent in the food than I thought was possible for two people. Apparently, I wasn't the only hungry one.

Leaning back on the couch, I rub my belly with a satisfied grin on my face and my eyes close for a second, enjoying this blissful moment. "That was *so* good. Thanks again, Hudson. I'm so full, I could go to sleep right now."

He shakes his head. "No way. You owe me a bedtime story first."

There it is. I can't blame him for being after me with this. I've been dropping enough cryptic comments over the past few weeks that his curiosity must be through the roof. Not to mention he already told me his story, and I've promised him to tell him mine too.

Taking a deep breath, the doubts bounce through my mind like kangaroos on steroids. "I can't guarantee a happy ending, though."

The smile is wiped from Hudson's face, his voice filled with worry. "It's not that bad, is it?"

Shrugging my shoulders, I'm not sure what to tell him.

Yes, I think it's that bad? More than bad. The worst possible time of my entire life?

Right now, I'm hoping I can even get through the story.

Well, here goes nothing. "I don't know where to start, to be honest. There's so much to tell, and I'm not even sure you want to hear all of it because it's just so much garbage. On the other side, I don't want you to hear about it later on from someone else, or think I was lying to you, especially after you were so honest and open with me."

He takes both of my hands in his and squeezes them gently. The warm skin contact is such a weird and unexpected sensation that I gape at our intertwined hands for a moment—his so much bigger and tanner than mine. The blood buzzes through my veins at a speed that almost makes me dizzy, yet the contact still offers me some comfort too.

"Heeeey, take a deep breath. I'm here for you, and whatever it is, we'll get through it together, okay?"

"Promise?" I can't help but ask the one thing that's on my mind in a constant loop, because I really want that to happen. I want him to know the truth and to get to the other side *together*.

"Of course! Come here." He lets go of my hands, and before I can react, Hudson pulls me over to him and engulfs me in a hug. His arms circle tightly around my body without making me feel constricted. Despite my position, I let out a deep breath and relax into him.

Although my nerves and hormones are going a little crazy, feeling him so close and having his scent surround me calms me almost instantly. When he starts rubbing my back in gentle, hypnotizing circles, my breath slows down even more.

I feel like he's just become the Charlie-Whisperer. Is that a thing? It should be.

"There." More rubbing. "Much better."

My face is squished into his shoulder. "Thank you—for everything. You've been nothing but awesome." Perfect really. So incredibly good for me, and Mira too.

"Anytime. No need to thank me at all." Something touches my hair, and I stiffen.

Did he just kiss my head?

Pulling back from him slowly, I slide away from him a little. There's a momentary flicker of hurt in his eyes when I put distance between us, but I feel vulnerable right now. And under no circumstances is Hudson someone I want to have regrets with.

Not to mention I can't think clearly when I'm that close to him.

First, I need him to know about Mira's and my life before anything more happens.

He deserves to have a choice.

I swallow loudly, the lump in my throat barely moving. "Okay, let's start at the beginning then."

Leaning back in his seat, Hudson tries to get into a comfortable position, his gaze solely focused on me.

My voice is shaky, but I push the words out anyway. "I guess, like most stories, mine starts with my childhood too. My mom has always been more absent than present. Once, when I was older, she told me that both my older sister and I were accidents, that she never wanted to have children. She didn't know who fathered either one of us, which shouldn't have been a surprise since she was usually either high or drunk. That's also the reason she couldn't ever hold a job, so we lived with my grandma for as long as I can remember.

"And thank goodness for that woman. My mom went in and out of our lives like a flimsy little mouse, until I was almost ten. That's when she left for good. On my sister's eleventh birthday, she decided it was a great time to tell us that she was going to get married and leave us to travel the country with her soon-to-be husband—a guy we'd never even met. That was the last time I saw her."

Hudson hasn't so much as blinked yet, and I'm not sure if that's a good or a bad sign. I decide that continuing is the best solution.

Might as well just get it all out before I chicken out.

"We never talked much about her, and Grandma did the best she could to raise us girls on her own. Sadly, once my sister was old enough—or at least she thought she was—she started to follow in our mom's footsteps with her lifestyle. I swore then and there that I'd never be like them. I wanted to control my life, not have it control me. I never wanted my emotions to dictate my decisions and my goals in life. I wanted to have a good life and a family one day, not end up in a gutter, with alcohol poisoning or an overdose."

Telling this story to Hudson is strange. Besides talking to Monica about it, I've never seen the point of reminiscing about all the negative aspects of my past. On some weird level, I have to admit that it feels good, almost freeing.

Hudson comes a little closer, as if he can sense I might need the support. "I'm so sorry. I can't imagine how hard that must've been for you—for all of you. And I totally get the emotions thing. I've chosen to turn my emotions off a few times over the years, especially after the whole Addy thing, when it just became too much. But then I learned something very important. Without the negative, I'd also miss the positive, and wouldn't that be quite tragic."

"You're absolutely right. Mira has taught me that much already." We both have matching smiles on our faces at the mention of my baby girl.

Sadly, it also makes me think of what I have to tell Hudson next, and my smile vanishes again. Looking down at my hands in my lap, I play with the seam of my shirt. "I got into a routine that worked for me, even though my life was rather monotonous—school, studying, work, and helping my grandma—until I met Sebastian my first year of college. He was a few years older and everything I thought I needed and wanted."

I was such an idiot. "We both had similar values and goals of what we wanted out of life—his law career was the most important thing to him, but he also wanted a wife by his side and some children in the future. He was calm and level-headed, and very matter-of-fact. He also didn't drink excessively or do drugs, so he was a winner in my book. We started dating and one thing led to another. We got engaged a couple years later, and we were going to get married last summer."

Hudson inhales sharply when I glance up at him, and he

looks like he hasn't decided which emotion to express first. His eyes show a hint of anger while the softness still remains in them. Rubbing his hands over his face, he gives me a pleading look. "But you didn't get married, right?"

I shake my head. "No. I spent part of my summer in France last year, learning from some of the best pastry chefs in the world. I had been back for a few days when Sebastian canceled the wedding. It was only two weeks before we were supposed to get married."

He jerks back a few inches. "Seriously? What the hell? What kind of person does something like that? That's so messed up. What an asshole."

My heart is racing in my chest like a herd of wild horses. "Sadly enough, at that moment, I couldn't give a crap about not getting married to him anymore. What broke my whole world apart was what had happened the day before, when my life as I knew it shattered."

CHAPTER TWENTY-ONE

HUDSON'S FACE IS A DISPLAY OF CONFUSION AND ANGER, and I don't blame him one bit. I can almost see the wheels turning in his mind, coming up with all sorts of different scenarios to what I've told him.

He's probably wondering why in the world I wouldn't care about my canceled wedding.

What could possibly be worse than that?

After all, that was a big part of the bad experience he had with his crazy ex—on top of the whole faking to become pregnant, of course.

My mind is in overdrive too, trying to prepare me for what's to come. I want to back out on my word so badly, get up right now and run away from this whole conversation, because this sucks. It *never* gets easier. It feels like something is blocking my airways, making it suddenly hard to breathe.

I try to swallow but without a lot of success.

"Shh. Hey, it's okay. I'm right here." Hudson puts his arms around me, rubbing my upper arm gently, almost as if he's afraid he might break me otherwise. "Please, you don't have to tell me if you don't want to. I never would've asked had I known it's that bad for you. I can't stand to see you like this." His voice breaks at the end, and I make myself look up at him and his clouded expression.

Sniffing loudly, I force the tears away. "I have to, Hudson. It's going to break my heart all over again, and I'm afraid of your reaction, but you deserve to know. *I* need you to know."

He shakes his head. "I don't know. Are you sure? It's clearly hurting you, and I hate that."

I nod, not trusting myself to talk about how I feel right now. Instead, I return my focus to my story, all of a sudden just wanting to get it all out and over with.

"You might have guessed that Sebastian wasn't too fond of my family, especially my sister, Rachel. She was the problem child, turning out to be just as bad as my mom always was. She saw a lot of different guys, got into drugs, drank a lot, and never even tried to keep a job. I found her passed out on my grandma's doorstep more than once, and she barely ever remembered how she got there. My grandma was an angel to keep a roof over her head. I'm sure a lot of people would've kicked her out, but luckily for my sister, our grandma was different."

The thought of Grandma and her kind nature makes me smile. Thinking about her still makes me sad, but the good memories of her are so much stronger that it's gotten easier to focus on those.

"She sounds like she was an extraordinary person. I'm so sad you lost someone that special, especially after everything you had to go through already." His hand finds mine, and I hold onto it like it's my lifeline.

"She was my rock. She and Mo kept me alive all those

years when life wanted to pull me deep under. Everything that happened with my mom and my sister was very overwhelming to me. At times, it almost felt too much to deal with. If it wasn't for them, I might've given up at some point, I'm not sure." I shrug, stunned at the words that just came out of my mouth.

Before now, I don't think I realized those thoughts were there, at least not on a conscious level, and it's pulling the ground away from under my feet. But now isn't the time to digest that. "Forget I just said that. I don't...I didn't mean it the way it came out."

He's rubbing one of his eyebrows, his gaze flitting over the backyard for a moment before returning to me. "Are you sure? Sometimes we say things out loud without realizing they're true until then."

I keep nodding, not wanting to even think about that possibility.

Instead, I focus back on that horrible day in my past, the words ready to replay it all. "The day before Sebastian called things off was my final wedding dress fitting. My grandma and Rachel came with me to the bridal shop. It was a lovely day, and I could finally enjoy time with my family since Rachel had changed drastically over the previous year. She had distanced herself from her old friends and their lifestyle. She was more like the old Rachel from when we were younger, the one I had loved and missed so much. Everything was finally falling into place, and life was good."

Hudson sat as close to the edge of the couch as possible without falling off. I wonder if he'd be pacing around if it wasn't for me and my obvious nerves. "What happened then? What changed things so drastically?"

"When we were done at the bridal store, I parted ways with my grandma and Rachel and headed back home to my small apartment."

Hudson holds up a hand, his eyebrows pulled tightly together. "Wait a second. You didn't live with...with Sebastian?" He spits out the name, the dislike obvious in his voice.

"He didn't think it was appropriate until we were married."

The confusion on his face grows after that statement.

Giving our hands a quick squeeze, I remind him of the connection we still have, the one that gives me the strength to get through all of this. "I was okay with it. To be honest, I actually liked it. I stayed the occasional night at his place after he threw a dinner party or some other social gathering, but it felt good to still have my own four walls too."

He nods, but from the looks of it, he might be biting his tongue.

"Since I needed a few things, I stopped at the store on my way home. It took a little longer than I thought, and when I walked through the front door of my place, my phone kept ringing. It was the police, telling me about an accident that my family had been in."

Hudson lets his head hang low for a moment before he snaps his gaze back to mine with a distant look in his eyes. "No."

"My grandma died on impact, and Rachel was at the hospital with severe injuries. It didn't look very good for her, and they told me to get there as soon as possible." Taking a deep breath, I'm unable to look up at Hudson. I need all the strength I can muster to get through the rest of the story, my words now barely a whisper. "Mira was in the car too. By some miracle, she didn't have a scratch on her."

That last bit must have been too much for Hudson because he drops my hand and jumps up from his seat. I don't say a word and let him walk around a bit before he comes over to my side of the couch. He kneels down in front of me and takes both of my hands in his.

A single tear runs down my cheek this time. "Rachel didn't make it. I was able to see her for a minute before they took her away for surgery, but she never came back. I saw her long enough to make her a promise, though—the biggest one I've ever made in my whole life."

My hands are shaking, or maybe it's Hudson's. His eyes look glassy, and it's almost too much for me to handle at the moment.

"I promised Rachel I'd take care of her baby girl. Mira isn't my baby, Hudson, she was Rachel's. She's my niece." There. I said it. The words are out, and I feel lighter and completely heartbroken at the same time.

His eyes go as wide as I imagine they can possibly go. There are only a few people that know about this and that's for a good reason. It's a big pill to swallow, too big for some people.

Without uttering a word, he sits down next to me and pulls me onto his lap. We sit without speaking for a long time when he starts humming a melody into my ear. It's beautiful but also sad, which makes me cry even harder. I don't think I can fully grasp what this man is doing for me tonight. Letting me share my story with him while caring and offering so much support is truly a gift. Not a lot of people are willing to give something like that.

When my tears finally slow down, I pull back to look at him. I'm painfully aware I must look like a mess, but I take comfort in the fact that he's still here.

His eyes shine with so much sympathy, I have to bite the inside of my cheek to keep more tears at bay.

Our faces are only inches apart, and I wish we were in a different situation than we're currently in.

If I want to finish the story, I need to put some distance between us. Hudson lets me go reluctantly when I slide off his lap and back over to my seat.

"Sebastian was on a business trip when it all happened and didn't get back until the next day. Since I hadn't been able to reach him, all I could do was leave him a message to come and see me at my grandma's house. It was easier for me to stay at their place, with all the baby stuff already there. Despite what just happened, I also found some comfort in being there. By some miracle, Mo was in the city at that time. She cleared her schedule immediately so she could stay with me for a while to help."

I swallow. Hard. "She'd just left to get a few things from her place when Sebastian dropped by. We sat down and I explained to him what had happened. It took him all but two minutes to look at all the baby things around us before he turned back to me with what I had dubbed the ice-cold lawyer face. He told me he didn't want to deal with my problems and that the wedding was off. And then he left. He had the few things I left at his place packed up and sent to me."

A noise is coming from beside me, and I'm almost sure Hudson just growled.

I glance up to see his jaw is set in a grim line, and his

hands are balled into tight fists at his side. "That worthless piece of shit."

CHAPTER TWENTY-TWO

Since it seems like it's going to take Hudson a while to cool down after everything I just told him, I give him the time he needs. I let him roam around, his steps heavy, his fists only unclenching so he can shove them roughly through his hair, pulling on strands in between.

Losing both my sister and grandma in one day, and then having Sebastian leave me the day after in what was, without a doubt, the absolute worst moment of my life was beyond devastating. Just when I thought I'd already hit rock bottom, his betrayal had me spiraling down even further. His reaction showed his true self, unwaveringly cruel and cold-hearted, a person I didn't know existed until that very moment. He purposefully decided to be appalling, to abandon me and a little baby at a point in life where I needed his help and support more than ever before.

Hudson's calm voice startles me; it's so contrary to his still tense form. "How old was Mira when it happened?"

"She was only a few weeks old, not even a month. I'd only seen her a couple of times before that day. Mira wasn't even supposed to be born until I returned from France. But she seemed to have different plans and came early while I was still gone—even though my trip was almost over at that point. I wanted to book an earlier flight back, but my sister insisted I stay overseas and finish my course first. We skyped a few times until I flew home, so I was able to spend some time with her and Mira. You should've seen Rachel. She was already such a proud mom. It was clear as day that she loved her little baby with all of her heart."

Another rough shove through his hair. "I... I really don't know what to say. I can't put into words how sorry I am about all of this. Shit. You lost your family, especially when you'd finally just gotten closer to your sister again. Then you're left with her baby, and your scumbag of an ex-fiancé leaves you hanging like that. I hope, more than anything, that karma is going to bite his ass extra good. How cruel and heartless he must be to do something like that. To anyone, but especially to someone like you—someone wonderful, caring, and just genuinely good. Not to mention, an innocent little baby. I can only hope he and I will never cross paths, or I won't be responsible for my actions."

Jumping up, I walk over to him, putting a hand on his chest in an effort to calm him. "He's not worth it. I was angry and devastated for so long until I realized one day that it's useless. It's not worth it, and more importantly, it sadly won't change what happened either. So, I decided to stop thinking about him as much as I could, because, to be honest, I'm not even sure if he ever so much as spared me a thought after he left me at my grandma's house that awful day, so—"

Hudson is opening his mouth, probably to tell me exactly what he thinks of Sebastian's behavior, but I shake my head.

"Don't. I'm pretty sure I know what you want to say, and trust me, I've felt all of it and worse. It took me a while, but I eventually realized that I was only making myself and my life miserable. He didn't care I was unhappy and so incredibly mad at him—he didn't even know about it. The only thing it did was take away from my life and with that, from Mira's too. Mo said she wouldn't leave me alone until she thought I could handle everything, so I had to get a grip on it. As much as I didn't want her to leave, I didn't want her to throw away her career for me either."

Hudson lifts his hand and gently cradles my cheek. "You're a good friend. A very good friend." Without thinking, I lean into his touch and briefly close my eyes. We stay like this for the longest moment, and I enjoy every second of it. "And you're obviously way more mature than I'll ever be. I can't imagine I'd have calmed down after all of that. You're an extraordinary woman, an incredibly strong one."

Despite everything, his comment makes me laugh. That's actually one of the things I... what, like so much about him? "You would've eventually too. Maybe not as fast as I did, but even you would've realized how much it can change your life for the better if you did." I wink at him, enjoying this more playful moment after all the sadness.

"Ah, there's my sassy Charlie again. I've missed you." He rubs his thumb over my cheek.

Once.

Twice.

Three times before he drops his hand.

All the while, I stand as still as a statue.

My heart thumps wildly in my chest, reminding me once more of how much I like this guy.

Then it hits me.

He's still here.

Still supportive and nice to me, even after everything I just told him. A couple new tears form in my eyes while I try to smile up at him.

"Hey, none of that anymore." He wipes away the tears that have already escaped, not bothered by it in the slightest. "I don't think I can handle seeing you sad anymore."

Sniffing as quietly as possible, I chuckle. "Those are the good tears."

"Happy tears?"

I nod fervently. "I just realized you're still here after hearing my story."

He blinks. "Of course I am. Did you think I wouldn't be? Did you expect me to just get up and leave?"

Since I'm not really sure, I shrug. "Honestly, I don't know. I was just terrified of your reaction."

"Come here." He pulls me closer to him, and I easily relax into his body. "I'd never react badly to anything you told me. You're one of the strongest and bravest people I've ever met. Not everyone would've done what you did or turned their whole life upside down to make the most of it. You could've easily fallen into your mom's footsteps or taken five million other wrong steps somewhere along the line. Instead, you kicked life in the butt and made it a great one for yourself —all built on determination and hard work."

Pulling back, he stares into my eyes for a long moment, almost as if he wants to convey the meaningfulness of his words. "And you're still the best and most wonderful mom to Mira, and an incredible woman on top of it. Nothing can change those things. You hear me? *Nothing*."

His gaze is intense, completely backing up his statement. I'm drawn to him like he's got a magical spell over me. The sincerity is written all over his face, making me bite my cheek again. Even though it seems like I still have plenty more tears left, neither one of us needs any more today.

"Thank you." My voice is quiet, but I need him to know I really mean it.

When his all-consuming gaze becomes too much, I avert my eyes, suddenly having the strong urge to kiss him. I know from experience it would be incredible, but I don't think it would be a good moment after a conversation like this.

"Looks like it might be time to call it a night, huh?" Hudson brushes a strand of hair out of my face. "I'm sure you're ready for some sleep by now."

A big yawn escapes me at his words, making both of us laugh. Emotional conversations and tears always make me overly tired. "Sleep *does* sound good."

He goes to the table and starts putting empty cartons into the takeout bag. "Why don't you go inside while I clean up."

"Don't be silly, I can help you. You were already sweet enough to get everything ready."

"It was nothing."

This man makes me want to sigh constantly. "Well, then it's nothing for me to help put it all away either."

Hudson chuckles. "Is this how it's going to be? You all stubborn about this?"

Putting my hands on my hips, I smile up at him, enjoying this new, light feeling now that my past is out in the open. "Yup. No one needs to clean up after me, especially not some hot rockstar. Now stop being so charming already, and let's get this done."

The words have barely left my mouth when Hudson freezes, the air around us becoming charged with emotion. He sets down the few things he was holding and slowly comes back over to me. For some reason, he reminds me of a predator stalking its prey. His strides are precise and powerful while his eyes are solely fixated on mine.

My feet start moving on their own accord, slowly walking backwards. "What...what are you doing, Hudson?"

"Nothing. Why do you think I'm doing anything?" The smirk on his face tells otherwise, practically screams it.

Since I backed myself into a counter next to the grill, he's almost right in front of me, still not slowing down. Just when I think he's going to run into me, he stops mere inches away. His breath is warm on my face, his eyes studying me intently.

"I... I..." I can get neither a coherent thought going nor a full word out of my mouth.

He leans in, touching my forehead gently with his. "Charlie! You can't say something like that and expect me not to react. I respect the hell out of you and try to do things right by you, but I can only take so much."

Closing my eyes, I enjoy his nearness so incredibly much. "Every now and then, it's hard to bite my tongue around you. You're making my brain all mushy. Sometimes I don't even know what I'm saying, let alone what thoughts rush through my brain."

He chuckles, obviously enjoying what I said. "That's good. I like that. A lot. That means you're being honest without a barrier between us, and that's exactly how I want you to be with me."

My hands start shaking next to my thighs as he gently takes them into his. Before I can react, he raises his head and lifts both hands up to his face, placing a soft kiss on the back of each of them.

For a moment, I think my brain short-circuits as I look back and forth between his face and my now tingling hands. This man might have his flaws, just like we all do, but at this very moment, he's pretty perfect.

My mouth does its own thing again, babbling out what's on my mind. The only difference is, this time, my heart is on the same page, beating rapidly with nerves and anticipation.

"Hudson, I don't think I want to be alone tonight."

CHAPTER TWENTY-THREE

SELF-DOUBT SHOWS ITS UGLY FACE, THREATENING TO consume me when Hudson doesn't immediately reply. He's staring at me, and I'm not sure I can handle a rejection from him right now. After what feels like forever, he finally nods. His expression is soft and his gaze gentle. My guess is he knows exactly how much of a mess I am right now.

No matter the reason, relief floods through me, and I let out a big breath.

One of his hands brushes over my hair and pauses at the back of my neck before he leans in to kiss my forehead, his lips lingering on my skin for a moment. I can't deny I'm a tiny bit disappointed it's only my forehead, but I also understand it's probably not the best moment for more.

He lets go of me after squeezing one of my hands. "Let's finish this up then."

I nod. "Sounds good."

We clean up in silence, making quick work of everything while I try to keep my thoughts focused on the task in front of me instead of what I'm about to do. Even though I'm the one that made the offer, I'd normally have a major freak-out over it. Thankfully, I'm too exhausted though, and my emotions are on the down low. At least for now.

Once we're inside, I take the big notepad from one of the drawers. "I'm just going to leave a note for Hannah. I want her to know what's going on, just in case she needs anything. Is that okay with you?"

Hudson shrugs his shoulders, looking at me like I'm a difficult puzzle he's trying to solve. "Of course. It's pretty much pointless to hide anything from that woman anyway."

With a small smile on my face, I write my note. "There, all done." Ripping it off the pad, I tape it to the fridge, spinning on my heels to face Hudson.

"She'll be happy to know that everything's okay." Hudson holds out his hand to me. "She knows, doesn't she?"

"She does." I'm not sure how he's going to feel about that piece of information, but his expression doesn't change. "She flew out to New York to see us last year after everything happened. She stayed with me and Mira for a few days after Mo left to make sure we were doing all right."

"That sounds like her. Grandma is a very special person." He walks over to me and pulls me into him. "Just like you, Charlie."

Our bodies are flush together, and I lean my head on his chest. He's lazily caressing my hair and back, and I close my eyes to enjoy the moment.

This evening has broken down a barrier between us, bringing us closer together in a way that feels both natural and, if I'm honest, it also feels right. It's like we're meant to be like this, and it's been way too long since I've felt this content, if I've ever actually felt close to this good before. "I'm so happy she talked me into moving over here."

"That woman deserves a medal of some sort. I'm thrilled you guys are here, I can't even tell you how much." He holds me tightly for a moment before letting go. "Ready?"

I nod, heat shooting through my body and into my cheeks. When I told Hudson I didn't want to be alone tonight, I wasn't really thinking it through. Now, I'm not sure what to expect at all. Nerves zap through my body, suddenly making me aware of just how close we are, how close we've been all night.

Despite everything I told Hudson, he's been very attentive and kind. I'm not positive I would've been able to get through the whole story without him by my side and his constant reassurance. He deserves to know that.

"Thank you for tonight, Hudson. As you can imagine, I was more than just a little anxious to tell you everything, but you've been nothing but wonderful."

"I appreciate your trust, it means a lot. I love knowing more about you, even though I hate you had to go through so much in your life. I can't help but be incredibly happy, though, that Sebastian was such a major jerk. Because look at you. You're here now, with *me*. As far as I'm concerned, that's the most important thing."

Apparently, it takes this wonderful man to allow me to look at my past in a way I haven't been able to before. For some reason—maybe because I was so wrapped up in the negative parts of my life—I've never even thought of seeing the positive of it like that.

Without a doubt, there are a lot of good things that have come from it.

As the realization rings true, I feel the inside of my chest burning in pure glee.

"Plus"—Hudson taps my nose lightly with his finger —"now I think you're even more awesome. And let me tell you, I already thought you were pretty spectacular beforehand. Now, you're above and beyond that, in superwoman territory."

I touch my hot cheeks, feeling extremely embarrassed by all the praise. "Stop it. You're making me blush."

"Why would I do such a thing? I *love* making you blush. You look so damn cute with your flushed cheeks, not to mention, incredibly beautiful and sexy too."

"Oh gosh, enough now." I hide my face behind my hands until he peels them off slowly.

We both chuckle at my obvious discomfort. Trying to laugh it off always seems to be one of the best ways to deal with embarrassment.

The laughter quickly turns into another big yawn.

Hudson takes my hand. "Definitely time for bed. It's been a long day."

I don't complain when he pulls me through the kitchen and the entrance hall toward the staircase. When we're at the top of the stairs, I pull my hand out of his. "I'm just going to change and get my things, okay?"

He nods and winks. "You know where to find me."

A quick glance toward his bedroom door brings back the nervous flutter in my stomach, and I swallow loudly. "I do. I'll be quick."

I can feel his eyes on me all the way down the hallway until I disappear behind my bedroom door.

After a quick cleanup, I take way too long to figure out

what to wear. I finally give up, deciding to keep it simple with some pajama shorts and a tank top.

Stop overthinking it, Charlie. This is Hudson. You basically just poured your whole heart out to him, and he's still there.

If that doesn't show what a good guy he is, I don't know what does.

Making sure I have Mirabelle's baby monitor and my phone, I head to his room.

My heart beats like crazy when I stand in front of the big white double doors, and a moment of doubt creeps in.

Before I can think about backing out last minute, the door opens, revealing the subject of my nervousness.

Hudson takes a step forward and leans against the doorjamb. "I thought I heard something. You okay there?"

Blinking at him, I nod. "Yes." It comes out more like a shriek, but either he doesn't notice or he chooses to ignore it.

Pushing off the side, he takes my hand. "Good. Let's get you in bed then. You look like you're ready to pass out. I'm sure tonight was exhausting as hell."

"Maybe a little." I bite my lip as I take a step forward.

He chuckles as he pulls me inside and closes the door quietly behind us. "I wasn't sure if you prefer a specific side of the bed, so I'm leaving it up to you to pick first. I want you to feel comfortable."

I look at him in awe as he points toward the large king-size bed, as if it's the most normal thing in the world. Who would have thought this huge superstar would turn out to be this sweet, humble, and considerate person? He could have just about any woman he wants by his side, but he's here. With *me*. Letting me pick which side of *his* bed I want.

Without a doubt, this man is one of the best people I've ever met in my whole life.

Unequivocally.

Turning to him, I pull on his hand until he faces me. "Has anyone ever told you how special you are?"

The light is dimmed in the room, but I'm almost sure I can see a faint blush on his cheeks.

He coughs awkwardly, almost as if the air got stuck in his throat. "Besides my family and my fans, no one has ever said anything like that to me. At least not anyone that actually matters to me."

Who would have thought? It's mind-blowing how blind people can be—not seeing what's right in front of their eyes.

That thought makes me stop right in my tracks. Isn't that what I've been doing this whole time?

Maybe a little bit. This whole time, I've been aware of how great of a guy he is, but I guess I didn't realize just how genuinely *good* he is until tonight.

Looks like it's time to put on those big girl panties and take a chance—albeit a very slow and cautious one. Just to be on the safe side.

"Well, Hudson. You *are* very special—like extraordinarily special. You've been there for me from day one, even though you didn't know who we were or what was going on with us. You never asked questions or tried to be pushy. You gave me the time I needed to open up to you, and I can't tell you how much that means to me. It's not easy to share your own four walls with a stranger, let alone when that stranger comes with a baby in tow too. You're very different. Nothing like I thought you'd be, but in the best possible way."

"Thank you, even though I didn't really do anything." It's

easy to tell he's flustered by the way he avoids my gaze and plays with my fingertips.

It's cute. It's adorable. And it's also incredibly sexy.

My heart.

He's cute. *He's* adorable. And *he's* so incredibly sexy.

Oh, how the tables have turned. No wonder he enjoys doing this so much to me.

He clears his throat and pulls on my hand. "Now stop talking nonsense and get into bed."

Laughing in response, I notice for the first time that he changed into different clothes too—a pair of workout shorts and a plain white T-shirt. I briefly wonder if that's his usual sleep attire, or if he put on more clothes than usual for my benefit. I wouldn't put it past him wanting to make me comfortable, especially tonight of all nights.

Maybe he usually sleeps naked?

Oh, the possibilities.

That's something to figure out another time.

Maybe. Hopefully.

We stand in front of the bed, shoulder to shoulder, our hands linked between us. I nudge his shoulder with mine. "Where do you usually sleep?"

"Probably right in the middle."

"Same."

We both chuckle.

I point to one side of the bed. "I'll just take the right side then. It gives me quicker access to the door in case Mira needs me."

"Sounds good. Hop in then." But before I can even make a step, he spins me around by my shoulders, pulling me close to him. "Wait. There's one more thing."

Gazing into my eyes, he closes the distance between us, his lips meeting mine in a soft, feathery kiss. A quiet sigh escapes both of us at almost the same time, making me smile against his mouth. When he starts moving his lips gently on mine, I'm immediately lost in the sensation and feeling.

This kiss is different than our first.

It has been an emotional evening for both of us, and it shows in every single one of his movements. He's tender and sweet, yet careful while still making sure he conveys how much he enjoys doing this with me.

It's about more than just physical needs, it's about healing and making me feel wanted and needed in a way I haven't felt before—ever. This man, and everything he does, is exceptional and rare to me.

I try to soak it up as much as I can, unwilling to waste any more time with him.

Consequences be damned.

If tonight could have a theme song, it would be "Don't waste your life, you never know how long you have."

Maybe I needed to relive my past to get that reminder.

I pull back slightly, planning on telling him exactly what I want from him when he beats me to it.

He brushes his thumb across my cheek, his touch soft as a feather. "I want so much from you that it's hard to put into words, but I'm not sure you're ready to hear it yet. Tonight, I just want to hold you. No pressure. You hear me?"

Speechless.

I'm utterly speechless.

My brain seems to have stopped working, and all I manage to do is nod.

He gives me his breathtakingly beautiful smile. "Perfect."

Without another word, and after picking up my things from where we dropped them at the foot of the bed, he walks me to my side of the bed. He pulls the covers back for me and watches me slip in before going over to the other side. *His* side.

A moment later, the lights are off, and the mattress dips next to me. My heart flutters wildly in its cage like a huge charm of hummingbirds as I try to steady my breath.

"You okay over there?" I hear the smile in his voice, but if I'd have to guess, there's a slight edge of nervousness in it too.

"Uh-huh." Another squeak from me, and I'm grateful he can't see my red face.

He chuckles again, making me feel a little more at ease. "What are you waiting for then? Come over here."

We move at the same time, scooting together in less than two seconds. I'm still on my side, and just as I'm about to turn around to face him, he puts his arm around my middle and pulls me close to him. He holds me so tightly I feel his chest move against my back every time he takes a breath.

It's heavenly.

It's perfect.

It's exactly what I need.

Where my nerves were going crazy a minute ago, a new calmness has settled in—some form of rightness that makes me close my eyes in pure content, snuggling closer into the most perfect cocoon of blanket and Hudson.

I barely hear Hudson's whispered, "Good night," and a soft touch to my neck as I drift off to sleep.

CHAPTER TWENTY-FOUR

WE EASILY FALL INTO OUR NORMAL EVERYDAY RHYTHM the next day. Except this time, it's filled with little touches and lots of kisses whenever possible.

After talking about it, we've decided to keep us on the down low for now, especially when we're out and about. There's no reason to draw any unnecessary attention to us while the crazy media circus is still going on. .

We want the paparazzi gone, not more of them to come.

After a busy morning at the bakery and a quick grocery run, we're back home for an afternoon with my favorite group of crazy ladies.

Hannah comes up behind me, clasping both of my shoulders. She laughs quietly into my ear, automatically making me chuckle too. "I'm so sorry. I didn't think they'd be that bad. I'm gonna get them out of your hair now, I promise. Thanks so much for being so patient, you're an angel. At least they all had a blast baking with you. Not sure I can say the same about poor Hudson, but he was a champion too."

Blowing a strand of hair out of my face, I turn around to

look at her. "No worries at all. I had a fun day. You know I love your friends, it's always very entertaining when they're here."

"It definitely never gets boring, that's for sure." With a big smile on her face, she turns around to face the others. "Okay, girls, gather your things, we need to head out. Our reservation at the restaurant is in half an hour, and we don't want to miss it." She claps her hands. "Chop-chop."

Laughing at Hannah's authoritarian method, I watch her as she reins in her squad—her six senior friends she's in a quilt club with—all of them gathering up their purses, jackets, and miscellaneous accessories.

After I walk over to them, Hudson and I give everyone a quick hug and three kisses on the cheeks—something the women insist on, especially with Hudson. "Bye, ladies. It was so good to see you. Have a fun dinner."

They all say goodbye, some of them snatching another cupcake on the way out the door.

Once we hear the door shut, Hudson and I look at each other.

His eyes are wide as he exhales loudly, making me laugh. "I can't believe that group. How can old, little, cute women be so naughty and exhausting? I feel like I got run over by a bus."

The chuckle escapes me before I can hold it back. "I was thinking the same."

"I mean, did you see them? Edna and Shelly both squeezed my ass—several times. They're worse than some of my fans."

Pinching my lips together, I lean forward and rest my forehead on his shoulder, so he can't see my face. The quiet laughter shakes my whole body until I can't hold it in any longer. "I did see it. Your face was absolutely priceless. It was totally worth all this chaos."

His whole body goes rigid for a moment, right before his hands move to my waist and he starts tickling me. "Oh, that's how it is, yeah? You think that was funny? I'll show you funny."

"No!"

He's relentless, tickling me up and down both sides of my torso. In an effort to get away from him, I quickly move backward across half of the living room until we hit one of the couches and fall onto it. Hudson lands on me, his hands suddenly stopping at my sides as we stare into each other's eyes.

The silly atmosphere is suddenly gone, a heated tension that's sure to drive me insane in its place instead.

Unable to tell who moves first, our lips clash. Where I had more than enough air mere seconds ago, I'm missing it now as my body goes into overdrive. Hudson's lips are relentless against mine, his tongue delving into my mouth with a skill set that has me clawing at his back, ready to rip off his clothes right now if he'll let me.

His hands move under my shirt, caressing my skin in a grip so deliciously tight and possessive I'm starting to see stars behind my closed eyelids. We're both pulling at each other at this point, not able to get enough from one another. When he breaks the kiss, I finally take a much-needed breath as his mouth travels down my face and throat—determined and unapologetic in its exploration.

Without a doubt, he wants me as much as I want him, both of us more than ready to take this to the next level.

To be honest, I was ready this morning when I woke up in his bed—but the spot beside me was already empty and cold when I turned around still half-asleep. So, this morning's missed opportunity is almost literally a dream come true right now—one I wouldn't mind doing, over and over again.

Hudson's kissing his way back up to my face, all the while pulling me by the hips, so he can get us both into a more comfortable position on the couch. When he leans down, pressing part of his weight and his rock-hard body into mine, I'm almost ready to combust right then and there. I haven't been with a guy in so long, it feels like I've been primed for ages.

After nipping at the corner of my mouth, his heated gaze finds mine. "I can't even tell you how long I've been waiting for this—for *you*. All these weeks of just being friends with you have been both the best and most infuriating weeks of my entire existence. I didn't know what was missing from my life until you showed up. I want you so badly, I can barely think straight anymore."

Swallowing hard, I gaze up at him and weave my hands slowly through his dark hair. "I know exactly what you mean."

His lips are back on mine, but the atmosphere and this next kiss have changed with our confessions.

It's everything I know this man to be—gentle, caring, and incredibly kind-hearted, with a passion and blazing heat right underneath the surface. This moment breaks down all the walls I've built up. It strips me bare, making me feel like nothing else ever has.

Incredibly freeing.

After kissing his way down my torso, he hovers over my

breasts. I'm not sure if he's silently asking for my approval, but I push my chest toward him anyway, making it clear what I want from him.

Weeks of sexual frustration are starting to make me adventurous and more direct than I've ever been with a man.

He pulls an inch back and stares into my eyes. "Charlie, I—"

A wail rips through the room, echoing off the walls in a heartbreaking cry. I cover my eyes for a moment with my arm —trying to push away the irritation I feel about being interrupted—while Hudson lets his head fall onto my chest for a split second before getting off of me.

I immediately miss his warm body covering mine but can't hold back the small smile when he stretches out his hand to help me up.

After pulling me into him for one more soul-wrenching kiss, he takes a step back. "You go get our little monster while I start cleaning up the kitchen." He has to physically push me out of the room, slapping me on my butt at the last second.

I laugh and wiggle my finger at him. "I'll get you back for that later."

The smirk he gives me makes me sigh—because dimples. "Can't wait." To top it off, he winks at me and points toward the hallway that leads to the staircase. "Now go, before I come and get you."

If only.

We spent the rest of our day with Mira—playing with her, feeding her while having a simple dinner ourselves, and a quick bath before putting her down to sleep.

Watching Hudson read a book to Mira while she's sitting on his lap in her cute little pajamas was easily the highlight of my day. When he put her in her sleep sack and sang a song to her before handing her off to me, I was afraid my heart might just melt away at the sheer sight of it all.

When I sneak out of Mira's room and quietly close the door behind me, Hudson's waiting for me in the hallway—casually leaning against the wall like he doesn't have a care in the world.

I walk over to him, stopping when I see the big frown on his face. "Hey. Everything okay?"

After clenching his jaw a few times, he exhales loudly. "Yes. No. Gabe just called and told me he needs my help with something."

"Right now?" I put my hands on my hips and can't help but pout a little.

He nods and reaches for me, pulling me closer when I put my hand in his. We touch from head to toe, and I realize it already feels like we've been doing this forever. Whatever we have, whatever is between us, is nothing I've ever experienced before. The intensity of it is so strong it scares me a little, but I'm trying my best to tamp it down as best I can.

"I was really looking forward to our night together." His lips graze my forehead before he huffs, the frustration pouring out of every single one of his pores. "I don't even know what he wants from me, but he said it's important. I hate to ask this, but can we take a rain check?"

Even though I understand his disappointment—mine is pressing heavily onto my chest too—I'd never hold it against him when someone needs his help, especially his family. "No worries, I'm just gonna relax with a book and go to sleep early. Those seniors wore me out today."

He chuckles against my forehead before lifting my chin, so I'm forced to look at him. "I'll make it up to you. Promise."

I blink. "I know you will." Then I do something I've been wanting to do ever since I first saw him. *I* go up on my toes and kiss the hell out of *him*. It's not him initiating the kiss this time, but *me*.

And boy, does it feel good.

Hudson's hands wander down my back and have just reached my butt when I pull away for some much-needed air.

He groans. "Screw Gabe. He can figure it out by himself. I'm staying."

Swatting his chest, I laugh. "No, you won't. Go already."

After one more scorching kiss that makes sure this man will stay on my mind all night long, and quite possibly invade my dreams too, he begrudgingly turns around to walk toward the staircase.

Meanwhile, I stare at his retreating form and that fine ass of his. There's definitely nothing like it.

CHAPTER TWENTY-FIVE

THE NEXT WEEK IS MOSTLY A BLUR, HAVING QUICKLY turned into the absolute week from hell. First, Hudson is gone for most of the following day too—helping his brother with a mysterious project he apparently isn't allowed to tell me about—and then Mira and I catch the flu.

Badly.

I'm so miserable I can barely function, and I'm more grateful than ever before to have Hudson and Hannah in my life. They both help Mira and me to get through this awful misery as best as they can.

The bed dips beside me as Hudson sits on the edge, putting his hand on my forehead. "How are you feeling?"

I fight against my heavy eyes, still trying to wake up from my nap. "Finally better. Extremely happy the fever broke yesterday. It was about time for that to happen."

He nods, a small frown grazing his forehead. "I agree. I was starting to get worried about you two. Mira has been so much better today. She's been eating quite a bit, which is a relief."

That makes me smile. There's nothing worse than a sick kid, especially when you're sick yourself. At least I got lots of baby cuddles these last few days. "Thank goodness. I'm so happy to hear that."

"Tell me about it. It's funny how kids bounce back from a sickness. They can be miserable one minute, and the next one, they're jumping around again. Mira's been all smiles and babbles, playing like nothing happened."

A small chuckle manages to escape. "I've noticed that before. It's like someone turns a switch."

He grabs my hand, and I squeeze it with all my might. "Thanks so much for all the help, Hudson. I couldn't have done it without you."

"Nothing to thank me for. I hated seeing you so sick, so I'm just happy you're feeling better."

I smile at him. "Me too." One of my hands goes up to my hair, and I realize I must look worse than a scarecrow. Somehow that fact makes me laugh.

"What's so funny?"

Looking at him and his confused expression, I laugh even harder. "Are you serious? How can you even look at me with a straight face? I don't need a mirror to know how awful I must look right now." I shake my head and give him a small smile. "You're an angel for sticking around and being there for us. Seriously. You deserve a huge thank-you basket or something else crazy big."

The smile he gives me is so big and beautiful it almost blinds me. "I know exactly how you can thank me, but I need you to feel better first." He winks at me, and I almost choke on my spit.

Way to impress the crowd.

And this man.

My insides heat up at his suggestion, and I can positively say I'm on the mend. Absolutely no doubt about it.

All bodily functions are back, my libido included.

Leaning my head to the side, I look at him. "I think I just made a miraculous recovery."

He chuckles. "I was hoping you'd say something like that because I prefer sharing a bed with you a lot more than sleeping alone. So, if you're better, I want you with me again tonight."

My heartbeat quickens at the picture Hudson paints, but then reality crashes down on me. "I don't want to get you sick."

He laughs. "I think after playing nurse for the last few days, I'm a lost cause anyway. I either already have it or I lucked out this time."

"I really hope it's the latter, but just know I'd take really good care of you too if you got sick."

"I know you would." He leans in and gives my forehead a kiss, his lips lingering for a second. "Now get up and take a shower, Sleeping Beauty. I have some soup waiting for you downstairs, and Mira is gonna be up from her nap soon too. I bet she's gonna be over the moon to see you up and going again."

His scent envelops me in a blanket of comfort, the familiarity of it calming me down like nothing else. I let out a sigh when he gets up and walks to the door.

Turning around, he stretches his arms and grabs the top of the doorframe, his muscles straining and bulging like they're here to offer me a show. As if on cue, his biceps flex as he winks at me. "Holler if you need me. I'm more than happy to assist you in the shower if you need help."

Laughing at his remark feels good after being out of it for what feels like forever. "I bet you do. I think I'm good for now, but thanks for the offer." It's better to wash all this sickness off by myself.

Looking at the exposed skin on his stomach definitely doesn't make that decision easy though.

"Anytime, sweetheart, anytime." The endearment rolls off his tongue in a way that's so natural, it takes my brain a long moment to catch up. His gaze is locked with mine as he's probably trying to gauge my reaction—the one I'm still too shocked to give. "I'll see you in a minute, okay?" He gives me a small smile before he disappears.

Sweetheart.

He just called me sweetheart.

My heart can't take it.

I fall back onto my pillows, barely containing the squeal that wants to escape. But with my luck, he'd still hear me and run back to see if I'm all right. I feel too weak for that sort of embarrassment.

We take the rest of the day easy, just hanging out at home. I'm thrilled to see Hudson was right and Mira is doing a lot better. We've been cuddling a lot, both of us savoring the contact. At the end of the day, it's easy to tell the two of us feel much better, even though we're both extremely tired. I'm all for a speedy recovery, hoping to be mostly back to normal tomorrow after another good night's sleep.

"Let's get you guys upstairs and in bed before you fall asleep at the table." Hudson chuckles and starts bringing the dishes into the kitchen.

After giving Mira a quick bath, Hudson takes her into the bedroom while I clean up the bathroom. When I walk back into the bedroom a few minutes later, my heart stops at the sight in front of me. Hudson's sitting in the rocking chair with Mira snuggled against his chest, her head pressed into the crook of his neck, clearly passed out already. Hudson has his eyes closed too, his arms securely wrapped around her small body. I stand there for several minutes, watching these two important people in my life.

Committing this image to memory.

So bittersweet.

In this moment, I can't help the bursts of sadness and joy mixing in my heart—sad over what was lost while happy over what was gained.

I don't know if this will ever get less painful or easier to deal with, but I will try my best to focus on the positive since that's the only thing I can control.

Closing my eyes for a moment, I take a deep breath, trying to get my emotions back in check. When I open them again, Hudson is looking straight at me. I give him a small smile and walk over to him. As carefully as possible, I take Mira out of his arms and place her in the crib, making sure she's settled all right.

Hudson is waiting for me by the door, tucking me into his side when I reach him. "Time to get you to bed too. Go get ready. I'll be waiting for you in my room."

Heat floods me, but is quickly shut down when a big yawn takes over my body, and I nod. "Are you sure?"

"You bet. Absolutely. Now hurry." He pushes me toward my room, and we both chuckle quietly.

When I walk into his bedroom a few minutes later, he sits in the middle of the bed, slightly propped up and completely immersed in his phone. The thick carpet swallows my footsteps as I make my way over to my nightstand. *My nightstand*—is that what it is? I place my things on top of it when I notice Hudson watching me.

"Hey." He puts his phone on his nightstand before patting the spot beside him on the bed.

I barely notice though, since I'm too distracted by his chest—his very *naked* chest. The only thing he's wearing is some thin drawstring pajama pants. *Very* thin pajama pants.

I must not have been very discreet because he leans down to get into my line of sight. "Do you want me to put on a shirt? Does it bother you?"

I blink at him several times before my brain finally catches up, and then I laugh. I laugh so hard it turns into a coughing fit.

Hudson reaches around me to get my water bottle from the nightstand. "Here, have a sip."

After handing it to me, I take several gulps, trying to get the coughing under control. "Thank you."

"Of course." He gives me a moment to get my body under control. "Better now? I didn't mean for that to happen when I asked you."

Shaking my head at him, I chuckle, then set the water bottle back on the nightstand and crawl onto the bed next to him. Kneeling, I reach out and place my left hand on his warm chest, enjoying the feel of his quick heartbeat under my fingers. "*This* would never ever bother me." My fingertips start moving on their own accord. "If it was up to me, you'd never wear a shirt again, at least not when you're home."

The satisfied grin he's sporting has my heart picking up its speed, trying to catch up with my rapid breath. All it takes is one of those smiles, and I'm a total goner.

Unleash the butterflies!

He covers my hand with his, pulling my fingers up to his mouth. "I'm glad to see your spirits have returned, but it's time for you to go to sleep. I have a feeling you'll need all the strength you can get for tomorrow."

I sit back on my feet. "What's going on tomorrow? Did I miss something?"

"Nope."

"What is it then?"

"I can't tell you. It's a surprise."

A surprise? The wheels are turning in my head, trying to figure out if there have been any signs or hints about what it could be. When I come up empty, I stick my bottom lip out at him. "Hmmph."

He pushes himself up, getting right in my face. "Don't be mad at me. I know you'll like it."

"Promise?"

"Promise. Also, take your time and sleep in, okay? I'll take care of Mira, so you can get as much sleep as you need to get better." Leaning even closer, he gives the tip of my nose a featherlight kiss.

As he draws back, my first thought is that he's too good for me.

He's perfect, and I'm not sure I can keep up with him.

Then, Monica's words echo in my mind—I deserve a good guy, and I'm trying very hard to believe it.

"Thank you."

"You bet." He reaches around me and grabs the blanket, pulling it over our legs. "Now lie down, so I can properly make up for all the cuddles I've missed this week. It might just take me all night long, so we better get started."

With a sigh, I turn around and sink into his body, contentment filling me to the very brink when his arms reach around me to pull me even closer. I can't wait to feel better to make up for the lost time with him—with more than just cuddling.

CHAPTER TWENTY-SIX

WHEN I WAKE UP THE NEXT MORNING, I FEEL refreshed and energetic. Thank goodness. I stretch my limbs like a cat, excited to start the day. A big smile spreads across my face at the memories from last night and falling asleep in Hudson's arms.

I wouldn't mind doing that for the rest of my life.

"What are you smiling about?" The female voice shocks me for a moment before I recognize it.

My eyes fly open, trying to adjust to the daylight while my brain is still trying to wake up.

Am I hallucinating or is my best friend really here? In Hudson's bedroom, of all places.

"Mo? Is that you?" I prop up on my elbows and scan the room through squinted eyes.

There she is, in the flesh, sitting on the dark gray couch that's on the other side of the room, her leg propped up on the couch cushions.

"Of course, silly. Who else would it be? Last time I

checked, I haven't changed into a ghost or some other form of an apparition."

A laugh escapes my throat as I rub my eyes, willing my body to fully boot up. "What on earth are you doing here? You weren't supposed to get here for another week or so. Why didn't you tell me you were coming? I could've gotten you from the airport, I could've gotten things ready."

I sit up all the way, brushing my hand through my hair—which only ends up in me trying to untangle it because it's such a mess.

"That's how surprises work." She throws her hands up in the air. "*Surprise.*" The huge grin on her face makes my own face light up too. "Even though it looks like *you* surprised *me* instead."

"Why? What do you mean?"

"Well, I certainly didn't expect to be sent up to this bedroom instead of yours. You didn't tell me you guys were having *sleepovers.*" She wiggles her eyebrows at the last word, her grin transforming into a smirk.

Covering my face with my hands, I feel a little guilty for not having told her about me and Hudson. I didn't want to say anything yet because I'm still not sure what's actually going on either. "Yeah. About that..."

"It's okay. The last time we talked about it, you didn't want to start anything with him. At least not until some grass has grown over the whole crazy pregnancy story with his ex." She snorts loudly. "By the way, nice ass shot in the gossip magazine."

So typical. Her thoughts jump back and forth so quickly, you really have to pay attention if you want to keep up with her. Thankfully, I'm used to it, so it doesn't strike me as odd.

Monica laughs at my groan. "I'm just teasing. Relax. I was talking about the one you already told me about. There aren't any new ones—not that I know of, at least."

"Stop playing with me, I just woke up." I snatch one of the pillows from the bed and toss it her way. "Now, why are you already here, even more so, in Hudson's bedroom?"

"But that was my question to you." She points a finger at me, and I roll my eyes playfully. Her sassy expression suddenly changes, but it's hard to read her.

"What is it? Why are you looking at me like that?"

She shrugs, playing with her fingers in her lap. "I saw the note you wrote to Hannah in a pile of papers on the bar."

The note.

The one where I told Hannah that Hudson knows about my past. I needed her to not feel bad anymore for keeping it from him. It probably also inadvertently told her that we've taken things to the next level before she even saw us together the following morning.

Letting my head fall, guilt overtakes me for keeping Mo out of the loop these last few weeks. "I'm sorry I didn't tell you." I lift my head enough to look at her. "But it was time to tell him."

"It's okay. I'm glad you let him in." She nods toward the bed. "I guess it went well if you sleep in his bed."

"I wanted him to know before I could move on, I guess." My chest rises and falls on an exhale. "Mo, he was amazing. I was so scared to tell him, after everything that happened with Sebastian. I know they're completely different people but the fear of telling anyone and see them react badly hasn't gone away. Not to mention, I still get super emotional every time I tell the story. Sadly, it hasn't gotten any easier so far."

Mo gets up from her spot and hops over to the bed. On one foot.

Crap.

I'm the worst friend ever.

"Oh my gosh, I'm so sorry. Here I am, totally absorbed in my life while you're struggling to get from point A to B." Throwing the blanket back, I jump off the bed to help her.

She throws her arms around me when I reach her—something rather uncharacteristic for her. I'm usually the emotional and touchy-feely one out of the two of us, not her.

Letting go rather quickly, I help her walk back to the couch where she sits down with a huff. "It's really good to see you, C."

"Same, Mo. Always. You know I've missed you." I touch her good knee for a moment before pointing at her other leg. "You're okay now? I thought you wouldn't be here until next week."

"As good as it can be, I suppose. The plan was to fly over next week, but since I was ready to strangle my mom, I thought it might be safer for everyone to leave earlier. So, *voilà*."

Monica and her mom have always been an odd couple. They love each other dearly, but after spending a few days or weeks together, they end up at each other's throats over the smallest things. I'm actually surprised she made it this long. "I'm so sorry, even though I'm glad you're here."

For the slightest moment, I feel a hint of sadness rush through me over having to share my time with Hudson with Mo now too, especially since we just started to get closer and explore whatever it is between us.

But that's not fair to my best friend either. I'm being ridiculous.

"You're thinking about Mr. Hottie, aren't you?" She doesn't wait for an answer and just continues to talk. "I really can't blame you. We obviously both know he's beyond delicious. And oh boy, I saw him with Mira in the kitchen earlier. Holy guacamole. Now I totally get what you were telling me about those two. I really do. Everything you said about them having this crazy bond when they're together is true. He's amazing with her, and it really is quite fascinating to watch."

She sighs loudly. "He's also even better-looking in real life, you know? I don't understand how you haven't jumped his bones yet, I really don't." She studies me, her eyes going wide. "Or *have* you?"

"Not everything's about sex, Mo." I chuckle when she sticks her tongue out at me.

"I know that. But it's different when you have an exceptional piece of man standing right in front of you, even more so when he also seems like a total sweetheart. And then there's obviously the fact that you've been sleeping in his bed." She points a finger at the bed behind me, and I can't fault her logical assumption of things happening between those soft sheets.

"Oh, stop it already." Now it's my time to sigh. "But gosh, yes. He's so sweet. What am I going to do with him?"

She chuckles. "Well, you know my answer to that question. Stop worrying so much about everything. He's obviously completely crazy about you, so I'm sure you'll figure it out. Just follow your heart."

I stare at her, my mouth open.

"What?"

Shaking my head, I give her a small smile. "Nothing. That was actually quite insightful and sensitive of you. I'm impressed and a bit shocked, to be honest."

She winks at me. "I have my moments."

"Apparently, you do."

My mind is still stuck on her words, the wheels in my head spinning around and around, trying to make sense of everything.

Is Hudson really that crazy about me?

And if he is, what exactly does he want from me?

She nudges my arm to get my attention. "He genuinely seems like a good guy. Gabe said that too."

"You've already talked to Gabe about Hudson and me? When did all of that happen? You just got here." My gut clenches at the thought of them discussing us.

"When he picked me up from the airport early this morning, of course." The grin on her face looks like it's almost painful, it's that big. "And maybe we talked on the phone for the past few weeks too."

"You did *what*?" Shaking my head, I chuckle at her expression. "Ugh. On second thought, never mind. I don't want to know."

"Oh, come on. Don't be such a spoilsport. You're not the only one who can have secrets involving the Mitchell brothers."

"No, no, no." I get up and hold out my hands. "I need some coffee first before I can deal with you."

Monica laughs, knowing exactly how right I am. She's dealt with me for years, fully aware there are two sides of me.

Caffeinated Charlie, and non-caffeinated Charlie.

One of those is a lot easier to handle in the morning than the other.

She gives me a small push. "Go get your butt ready then. I'll hop back downstairs and stare at those two hunks all by myself."

I look at the crutches that lean on one side of the couch. "Are you gonna be okay getting back down by yourself? I can help you."

She waves me off. "Nope, I'm all good. Promise."

"Please call me or one of the guys if you need help, all right?" I'm still not sure how much I trust her, since Monica likes to downplay her injuries whenever possible. But short of throwing her over my shoulder, there isn't much else I can do.

"Will do. Now, let's get going. I'm ready to eat some more breakfast too. Good thing you tend to bake so much more than you need. There are always leftovers in your kitchen."

I grimace before grabbing my things from the nightstand. "If both Gabe and Hudson are down there, you better hurry up. You're actually lucky if they haven't eaten everything by now. Those two *live* for breakfast."

"They better not."

A tingle runs down my spine when Hudson waits for me at the bottom of the stairs. "There you are."

The smile on his face has my face breaking out in one too. He stares at me as if it's been days or months since he's seen me, rather than hours. The look in his eyes makes me excited and a little shy at the same time, but it's a look I'll never tire of because it's just for me.

It's *my* look.

By now, I'd also recognize his voice pretty much anywhere—it's warm and genuine, with a rasp that gives it a sexy edge—and it's actually become one of my favorite things about him that never fails to get some sort of reaction from my body.

"Sorry I took so long. I just needed a long, hot shower. I probably shouldn't have left you alone with Mo for that long."

He's standing at the foot of the staircase, gazing up at me with an adorable smile on his face. "No need to apologize, we're all good. I just wanted to make sure you're all right."

Leaning my head to the side, I study him. "You didn't run away from Mo, did you? She can be a bit overwhelming sometimes when you don't know her, but I promise she's harmless."

"What? No, I like her. She's a bit grumpy because of her leg but that's understandable. I can tell she's funny though." Coming a little closer, he lowers his voice to a whisper. "But I also quickly realized how happy I am after all that she's not staying with us. That means I don't have to share you with her, at least not all the time."

"I was just thinking about that too." I feel a little bad at my admission but also glad I'm not the only one. "I love her, and I'm thrilled she's here, but I also want to spend time with you."

Since I'm just a step above him, that puts us at almost the same height. We're close, really close, and I watch him while he studies me intently. Looking at him is one of my new favorite things to do. I mean, this man is simply gorgeous.

"How are you feeling?" His voice is low as his gaze flickers down to my mouth every few seconds.

Even though he didn't say anything inappropriate, my breathing quickens. "I'm feeling good. Very good, actually. You've done an excellent job taking care of me. Thank you."

Without consciously thinking about it, I lean in marginally, and he closes the last bit of the distance between us.

When his lips meet mine, my body relaxes instantaneously.

The kiss is light and sweet, and I want to stay like this for the whole day. What a perfect day that would be.

But reality crashes down on us pretty quickly when the noise from the kitchen filters out into the foyer.

Our lips part, and Hudson presses his forehead to mine. "You made it easy. You both did, actually. You just needed a lot of sleep and some food and liquids to get better. Mira did a lot better than I expected too. She barely woke up at night, and whenever she did, it wasn't anything that a few cuddles or a bottle couldn't make better."

Nurse Hudson. *Swoon.*

My hands stretch out, trying to find his without looking away from his face. "You are an incredible person, Hudson. Seriously. There aren't a lot of people that are as selfless and kind as you are, and I truly appreciate it." I could go on and on with my praise—he's such a polar opposite of Sebastian—but I don't want to overwhelm him.

Instead of responding, he pulls me into his chest, his lips finding mine once more. This kiss isn't anything like the one we shared before.

This kiss is deeper, more meaningful.

It makes its way straight to my heart, imprinting itself so deeply I'm not sure I can ever find anything like it again.

The need to explore that feeling further is almost too much to take.

A sudden booming of laughter breaks the connection and I sigh.

"Hudson, did you find her?" Mo's loud voice echoes through the house, making both of us groan at the same time.

I brush my hands through my still damp hair before nudging Hudson in the shoulder. "Let's go before she starts looking for us. We'll continue this later on."

"You bet we will." The promise in his voice sends another shiver down my back, and I know the anticipation will make my nerves go haywire all day long.

When we walk toward the kitchen, he brushes his hand against my lower back, reminding me he's right there with me.

CHAPTER TWENTY-SEVEN

Monica sits on the cream-colored couch in the living room with Gabe on one side and her leg propped up on the other side. Mira is on her lap, and they're looking at a book together—which basically means Mira just keeps flipping pages back and forth while Mo is trying to read the words as best as she can.

My best friend looks up when I sit down next to Hudson on the couch opposite them. Now that I'm on my second large cup of coffee, I'm a lot more relaxed and mellow.

She peeks around Mira. "Which restaurants are good around here? I'd love to take you guys out tonight."

Hudson stretches his arm behind me on the back of the couch, making me smirk into my coffee mug. "Why don't we do it here, Monica? We can easily throw you a little welcome dinner. We just get some takeout for everyone and maybe invite the rest of my family too, since they wanted to see everyone anyway. It would be easier with Mira too. That way we can put her to bed in her own room, and not worry about her getting tired when we're out and about or bringing all of her stuff with us."

He turns my way. "As long as you're okay with it, of course. Do you feel well enough to do anything tonight? If not, we can just do it another day. No big deal."

Monica's eyes are burning a hole into the side of my head, and I'm sure I'll hear about whatever is on her mind later. Right now, I can't be bothered by much though. Mira and I finally feel better, my best friend is here, and Hudson keeps sending me smiles that make my heart flutter. It's a good day. "I think that sounds like a great idea." Turning to Monica, I nod my head in her direction. "So much easier with your leg too."

She actually looks a little flustered, which doesn't happen often. "You guys shouldn't have to worry about me."

"Oh, stop it already." I'm actually getting excited. I decide to go in for the kill, singsong voice included. "I'll make you something special."

Her head snaps up, eyes wide before the big grin I was waiting for appears.

Gotcha.

"Strawberry mousse cake?" Her voice is higher than normal, and I'm surprised her tongue isn't hanging out at the sheer mention of her favorite cake.

This time, I'm unable to keep the laughter at bay. "Sure. If that's what you want."

She's already shaking her head before I finish. "No, it's too much work. I'm sure you have other stuff to do besides slaving away in the kitchen for me all day long, especially after being sick."

"Mo, I haven't been in the kitchen all week. I could totally make it."

"Of course you could, that's not the issue, but not today. Let's make that another time when it's not this crazy. How about just something simple for today?"

Leaning forward, I prop my chin up on my hand. "Oh. There's this *one* cake I've been wanting to make. It sounds fantastic and is easy to make. Might as well use the chance and try it now."

She rolls her eyes at me. "Gosh, you're evil. When have I ever been able to say no to you making anything for me?"

Hudson claps his hands together, looking satisfied. "Awesome. What do you guys feel like eating? We can order takeout, or even call a caterer and have something made for us last-minute."

Gabe shakes his head and waves Hudson off. "Don't worry, we've got that covered."

Hudson shrugs his shoulders. "It's really no biggie. It's just a phone call."

"No, thank you. I said, we've got it. You guys can figure out dessert stuff, we'll bring dinner." Gabe stands up to his full height, towering over the rest of us still sitting on the couches.

Monica looks back and forth between the brothers and their pride-pissing match before she looks at me and wiggles her eyebrows. She gives me a thumbs-up behind Mira's head and a huge grin before mouthing "Hot." At least, I *think* that's what she said.

I shake my head at her and snort. Hudson and Gabe look at me, confused—completely unaware of our wordless exchange, and maybe even their own brotherly rivalry—while Monica is trying not to laugh.

"I guess it's all settled then. Monica, let's get you and all of your stuff home." Gabe's words sound final, and Hudson rolls his eyes. "I'm sure you'd like to unpack and get situated."

"All right, grumpy." Monica gives Mira a kiss on the cheek before holding her up in the air. "Can someone take her, please?"

Standing and walking over to Mo, I snatch Mira and cuddle her as close to me as she'll let me. Hudson comes over too, playing with Mira over my shoulder. Anxiously, I watch my best friend get up from the couch, obviously struggling. I hate seeing her like this, but I know her well enough to not even try and offer my help.

Not knowing any better yet, Gabe is by her side right away, offering her a hand. It looks like he's met his match when it comes to pride because Mo dismisses him and his help immediately by waving him off.

Oh boy.

This woman can be as hardheaded and prideful as a pompous bull.

Thankfully, he lets her do her thing while staying close enough to intervene, if necessary. It'll be interesting to see how these two get along. So far, it looks like they really are two strong-willed personalities, like Hannah mentioned the other day.

Good thing they won't be living under the same roof, or I'd be worried about Gabe's sanity. I'm sure it would only be a matter of time before he kicked her out. But then, you never know. Only time will tell.

I walk Monica to the front door—taking my time so she

can keep up with her crutches—while Gabe stays back to talk to Hudson. "Are you really sure you're okay living in Gabe's guest house all by yourself, Mo? You know you don't have to pretend with me. It would be so much easier to have someone around to help. I can see you're in pain."

"I know I'm not anywhere close to normal, but I'll get there eventually. I've learned to deal with the pain. Plus, I've got some medication if it gets to be too much." She lets out a sigh and nudges my arm with her elbow. "I'm really fine, stop worrying about me."

Shaking my head, I give her a stern look. "Sorry, but that's impossible."

She rolls her eyes at me, and I have to laugh. "Gosh, you sound like my mom. Someone, please save me."

"You're such a grump when you're injured." I swat her playfully on the arm, and she smiles. "Seriously though, Mo. Promise me you'll ask for help when you need it. You can come back here, or we can find another place together."

"And take you away from your roommate? No way. He'd probably hunt me down for it."

"Mo!"

"Ugh. All right, all right. I promise." We're by the front door, and she's leaning on one crutch to swing the other one around dramatically. "Now, can I leave, please?"

I stick out my tongue at her. Monica brings that side out in me. "Of course. I'm sure your prince is ready to show you your castle."

She's trying to hide her laugh when Gabe clears his throat behind me.

He bumps my shoulder lightly and winks at me before

walking around me to open the door. "It's not a castle, but I think it's a pretty nice place."

Of course, my cheeks turn hot immediately, and I cover one of them with my hand while Mira reaches out to Monica and Gabe, trying to wiggle her way out of my arms. Monica gives us both a hug and a kiss, staying with her mouth close to my ear. "Remember what I said about Hudson earlier. He seems like a great guy. And I'm really happy to be here, Charlie. It's awesome to be close to you guys again."

For some reason, hearing her say that makes me emotional, and I nod into her neck, needing a moment to collect myself.

After giving me a second, she pulls back and grimaces. "Oh no. Prince Gabe, the waterworks show is about to start, let's leave."

Shaking my finger at her, I give her a warning. "Be nice, or I won't make you anything for tonight."

Her eyes go wide, and she gasps. "You wouldn't dare. I love you, but you know I'm no good with tears. They scare me." She shudders for a moment, making me laugh.

Gabe is looking at us like we've completely lost it. He's been acting all weird today anyway, and I wonder what's up with him.

I shoo her out the door. "Well, go ahead then. I'll see you tonight. And be nice to Gabe."

She winks at me. "Always."

Mira and I stare after them as they make their way slowly down the driveway to Gabe's car, silently hoping Gabe is as tough as he seems to be. He'll need all his strength and wits to deal with Monica.

Footsteps come up behind me, but I don't turn around,

enjoying the body heat that's radiating off Hudson when he walks right up to me. "Are you worried about her?"

I take a deep breath to calm myself and nod. Poor Hudson has dried enough of my tears this last week. "She always acts so tough and strong, but this must have hit her a lot harder than she's letting on. Not just the physical part, but also emotionally. I mean, her career has always been her dream, her life goal. Ever since we were little, she was talking about becoming a dancer. While all the other kids, me included, switched our future dream jobs on a weekly basis, Mo never did. She always just wanted to dance. And rightfully so. Watching her dance is magical. It's like nothing I've ever witnessed before."

Putting one arm around me, he pulls me into his side. Mira climbs from my arms into his, happily snuggling into his chest. "Ma-ma, ma, ma, ma." Hearing her babble her little syllables is the cutest thing. Apparently, she's already done, one of her hands in her mouth instead.

I didn't think it was possible, but these two have grown even closer over the last week—not that I should be surprised with him taking care of her so much while I was sick. "Looks like someone is ready for her nap, huh? It was an exciting morning. Monica and Gabe probably tired her out pretty good."

"No doubt." Hudson gives my forehead a soft kiss, and I lean into his body, feeling comforted by the contact. "Please don't hesitate to let me or Gabe know when you need anything for Monica. From what I've seen, she's just like Gabe, too proud and stubborn to ask herself, so that will be your job. Doctors, physical therapists, special equipment, anything. Let us know, and we'll make it happen."

I look up at him at the same moment his hand reaches out to touch my cheek. "Thank you. That means a lot to me, especially since you don't even know her."

"I don't, but I'd like to think that I know *you* pretty well by now, and she obviously means a lot to you, so that puts her on my important list too."

Blinking up at him, it takes me a moment to respond. "You're so good to me, I don't know what to say. Thank you."

He leans his head on mine. "You deserve it, and so much more. I hope you can see that one day."

A soft snore makes us both look down. We wear identical smiles when we see Mirabelle has fallen asleep in Hudson's arms.

Scratching my forehead, a bout of guilt rushes through me at seeing her this exhausted. "Poor baby. I probably should've put her down a while ago."

Hudson looks back at me. "She's okay, don't worry. Just tired from playing and getting the rest of the sickness out of her body."

This man never ceases to surprise me with his comments. "How are you so good with her?"

Shrugging, he looks down at her, his hand gently rubbing her back. "I don't know. I've always loved kids and"—the rhythmic movement of his hand stops for a moment before it continues—"I kind of read a lot about babies too last year, when I thought...you know...that I'd be starting my own family soon."

Great. Now I feel like a jerk for bringing it up. "I'm sorry, I shouldn't have asked."

"Stop apologizing, you didn't do anything wrong. It's just what it is, and it's in the past. I'm over it, really." He starts walking toward the staircase, and I fall in step beside him. "Do you want me to put her down? I mean, if you don't mind. Or you can do it. That's totally fine too, of course."

I touch his arm. "I'm good either way. You're more than welcome to, if you want. Just let me know if you need help."

He looks startled for a moment before smiling widely at me. "Sounds good. Why don't you go eat some breakfast, and then I can help you with the preparations for tonight. Look and see if you have everything, or if we need to get something from the store. And when I come back down, I'm gonna rile up my family."

An automatic protest sits on my tongue—he's been doing so much for me, for us already—but I swallow it when I see the look on his face. His eyebrows are drawn together while his lips are relaxed. I've come to read him pretty well, understanding he's silently challenging me to refuse his help again. "I'd love that, thank you."

Careful not to move Mira, he bends down and kisses me softly.

I didn't expect it—still not fully used to our open affection—but this time, I lean into him without a second of hesitation. This connection we have might feel overwhelming at times, but I can't deny how right it feels. Far too soon, he pulls back, making me miss the contact instantly.

He straightens up to his full height. "Anytime. Let me get her upstairs, and I'll be right back."

I watch him walk up the stairs with Mirabelle until he disappears around the corner, wondering if I'm being brave or stupid to allow my heart to open up like this already.

CHAPTER TWENTY-EIGHT

Hudson has been a real champ all day, helping me with my baking as well as getting everything set up for our little gathering. I love having him around, no matter what I do, even if he tries to help me with my baking and ends up making a mess. Not to mention all the stolen kisses that sweeten up my day.

It's the best.

Sadly, Hudson's parents and Hannah already had plans for tonight, but Hudson's mom left me a message saying we'll get together soon. That means it'll only be the Mitchell siblings, Monica, Mira, and me.

That might be enough anyway.

It can be a bit crazy and overwhelming at times when the whole family is together.

Monica comes into the kitchen, interrupting my thoughts. She looks at the set table and whistles. I have to say I'm a little proud of ourselves. We used the nice dinnerware, and even got some flowers and candles. "Wow, you guys.

This looks great. You're, like, the dream hosting couple already."

Rolling my eyes, I shake my head at her. "Stop it. And let's keep all the couple stuff under wraps tonight, please, okay? We haven't actually talked about any labels and all that stuff, so I don't want things to be awkward in any way. Plus, I'm still getting used to all of it and don't want to rush things either."

Studying me for a moment, she lifts one of her crutches in my direction. "You're not actually still wondering if you should give him a real chance or not, right?" She's looking at me expectantly, even though I'm sure that was a mostly rhetorical question.

I walk over to the sink to rinse off a plate, then start cleaning up the mess on the kitchen island. "Nope. I'm past that point. I have officially given up resisting him."

"Thank the unicorn."

I chuckle at my weird friend. "You and your fascination with unicorns."

She shrugs, hopping over to the plush chaise lounge Hudson brought downstairs from one of the bedrooms for her. Knowing how much time I spend in the kitchen, he wanted to make sure she's comfortable. "What? You really can't blame me. Unicorns are, like, the ultimate thing."

"Ultimate thing of what exactly, Mo?"

"*Everything*. Obviously." Her matter-of-fact tone makes us both laugh, as I watch her plop into the chaise and setting her leg up on the cushion. "Anyway, back to the matter at hand. He's going to be good for you. I'm *really* happy you're finally opening yourself up for this amazing man. Hopefully, in more than just one way." She wiggles her eyebrows, and I throw a nearby kitchen towel at her. "What? You can't tell me you haven't at least thought about it." She's holding her hands up in surrender, waiting for a response.

I don't even bother covering up my now burning cheeks, indirectly giving her the answer she wants.

She lets out a little whoop. "I knew it."

"You knew what?" Gabe's voice comes out of nowhere, making me blush even harder. I can only hope he didn't hear Monica's remark about his brother and me. That's nothing I need Gabe to think about, or worse, talk about with Hudson.

Maybe they already talk about us anyway. Yikes. *Stop it, Charlie*. Nope. Not thinking about that possibility.

"Nothing, Charming." Monica gives him a huge grin and watches his every movement as he walks over to her.

Gabe sighs in response. "Would you please stop calling me that? We talked about that earlier."

"Not a chance. I love it too much."

"What on earth is wrong with calling me Gabe? That's my name, after all."

"Nothing at all. But I think you deserve something special. And since you're my knight in shining armor, my very own Prince Charming, so to speak, it's totally appropriate."

I watch the two of them in fascination, briefly thinking this is better than TV. Gabe throws his hands up in the air and turns to face me with a pleading look.

Holding up my wet hands, I shake my head and chuckle. "Don't even look at me like that, Gabe. I can't control her any more than you can. Trust me, I've tried. She's like a wild animal, impossible to tame."

"Fantastic. You couldn't have told me that before I

invited her to stay with me. She might eat me in my sleep. Then it'll be all your fault." He points a finger at me accusingly, and I press my lips together to keep from laughing.

I've never seen Gabe this riled up over something and can't help myself but tease him a little. "I think you should be safe. She's a bit crazy, but not violent. She might nibble a little on you though, if you don't pay attention."

The kitchen towel I threw at Mo not too long ago smacks me in the face as she clears her throat. "Excuse me, you two, I'm right here. And I'm not crazy, at least not in a bad way. You're perfectly safe with me, Gabe." She gives him an innocent smile before batting her eyelashes. "Just make sure all of your doors and windows are locked at night."

He groans and turns around, but not before I can see the amused expression he's trying to hide on his face. "I'll leave you guys to it. The delivery guy should be here any minute with the food, so I'll wait in the foyer for him."

"Do you need help, Gabe?" I dry my hands off on the towel.

"Nope, thanks. I'm all good." With that, he walks out of the kitchen.

Turning back around to Monica, I start drying off the dishes. "So, how do you like the guest house? Is there anything you need?"

Her eyebrows rise in surprise. "Oh, you haven't been there yet? For some reason, I thought you'd already seen it." She gives me a big smile before continuing. "It's absolutely beautiful, Charlie. It looks like someone took the cutest little beach cottage and put it right into his backyard. He told me

260

one of his sisters decorated it for him. It's all in a nautical theme, just gorgeous."

"Oh nice. If it's anything like the rooms the girls decorated at their parents' house, I bet it's beautiful. They do have a knack for that sort of thing."

"They do." She pauses for a moment. "I just wish it was a little closer to the main house, but that's okay. I guess I need the exercise anyway, right?"

"Are you sure, Mo? You don't want to overdo it either." Naturally, I worry, planning on talking to Gabe about it later. I need him to keep an extra good eye on my best friend. The last thing we need is her getting hurt even more because she's too proud to ask for help.

Giving me an exasperated look, she pushes herself up further in the chaise. "Yes, I'm sure. Now let's stop talking about me. Tell me what cake you made."

She's looking around the kitchen with her eyes pinched into little slits, trying to see as much as she can from her position. "Where is it?"

"Such a one-track mind."

"Always. Or maybe we should call it a two-track mind? You know, food and knocking boots, of course."

My eyes widen at the unexpected comment. "What on earth is knocking boots?"

"Sex." She doesn't even blink an eye.

Shaking my head at her, I chuckle, completely used to her quirky, yet charming personality. "Wow. Your vocabulary never ceases to amaze me. Does anyone actually say that?"

"Sure. I learned that one on the road somewhere." She shrugs her shoulders as if we're discussing laundry, but I know she loves to play with me like this. She and Hudson are very alike in that aspect—they both enjoy making me all flustered.

She taps her fingers on the armrest of the chair. "Now tell me already, C. You know I hate waiting."

I stick my tongue out at her. Sometimes when we're together, it feels like we're jumping back in time, our current age completely forgotten. "I made a pink champagne cake."

"Ooh, I'm intrigued." She leans her head on the top of the chaise, giving me big googly eyes. "Please tell me more. It's incredibly sexy when you talk about your baking."

This woman.

After laughing at her comment, I walk around the corner and retrieve the cake from its hiding spot. I put it up on top of the bar, so she can see it, waving my hands around it in total presentation mode. "It's a three-layered pink champagne-infused cake, with a classic vanilla buttercream frosting. As far as decoration goes, I kept it simple and thought sugar pearls would give it a nice touch."

We're both quiet for a moment, marveling at this mouth-watering sugar concoction.

After having my fair amount of batter and frosting during prepping the cake, I know it's going to taste delicious.

Monica finds her words first. "Wow. Look at that beauty. I'm sure that would be a hit for weddings."

Nodding at her, I love that we're in tune so often. "That's exactly what I was thinking of. It's a classic with a nice twist to it, due to the color on the inside and the champagne."

Licking her lips, she keeps staring at it. "Can't wait to try it."

I'm about to snap my fingers at her when footsteps approach.

"Charlie?" Hudson enters the kitchen, and I don't have to look at Monica to know she's staring at him too.

Can I blame her? *Big, fat no.*

My first thought when my eyes land on him is *sex on a stick.*

Monica hasn't even been here for a day, and she's already rubbing off on me with her bluntness. This time, I'd have to agree with her, though.

He's freshly showered, his damp hair slicked back in a lazy way, and he smells delicious. I'm sure my mouth actually hangs open a little, but I don't care a single bit.

My best friend clears her throat while Hudson walks over to my side of the kitchen island, but my focus is completely on him.

Sorry, Mo.

"Hey, what's up?" I look at him, craning my neck back a little to see his face.

He looks at me for a long moment without saying a word, just staring into my eyes, like he doesn't have anything better to do. I smile at him in a daze, feeling—and probably looking —like a lunatic.

From the corner of my eye, I see Mo getting up, her crutches quietly squeaking on the hardwood floor. "I'll go see if Gabe needs any help."

I nod absentmindedly, not sure she even noticed.

Coming a step closer, Hudson pulls his lower lip into his mouth, making my heartbeat go crazy.

Did it suddenly get hot in here or what? I'm close to fanning myself with my shirt.

"So..." His voice is low, melodic, and soothing, making me want to close my eyes so I can focus on it better. "Grandma just told me she and Paul are going to have a night in tomorrow."

Confused by his statement, I take a moment to answer. "Oh, okay. Good for them." And I mean it. I've met Paul enough times now to know that he's a really nice guy. Both he and Hannah have been widowed for quite a while, and they seem to make each other very happy. What more could they want?

For some reason, he looks nervous, and I'm not exactly sure why. "Yeah. Anyway, she said she wouldn't mind babysitting if we wanted to do something."

Ohhhhhhh. Now we're getting somewhere, my nerves along for the ride too. "Oh."

He rubs the back of his neck before clearing his throat a couple times. "I'm not sure if this is weird, but would you like to go on a date with me tomorrow night?"

A fluttery feeling sets in my stomach as I nod, not even hesitating for a second.

That was easy.

"Yeah?"

"Yes, Hudson. I'd love to."

He beams at me, like I'm his fairy godmother and just granted him three wishes. Whatever works, I'll take it. "Awesome. Can you be ready by six?"

We grin at each other while my heart speeds up wildly at the thought of having a date with him in a day. "Absolutely."

The doorbell rings in the background and someone's arguing, but I just can't seem to care at the moment. All I want to do is stare at this man in front of me some more.

"Perfect." His voice is low and raspy, making the hair on my body stand up in anticipation.

He lifts his hands to caress both of my cheeks softly before bending down to give me a tender kiss. My lips tingle with a longing for more, but I know this is neither the right time nor place for it.

Sighing heavily when the contact breaks a moment later, I'm also relieved because two seconds later, Monica and Gabe walk into the kitchen.

"I can't wait for tomorrow." He says it low enough so only I can hear it.

Me neither, Hudson. Me neither.

CHAPTER TWENTY-NINE

Almost two hours later, we all sit at the big table that's filled with leftovers of the most delicious Italian food I've ever had.

"You seriously are the cutest thing ever." Monica coos at Mirabelle, who's happily sitting on her lap. "And I think you totally know it too. Good for you, girl. Own it."

The two of them have been glued to the hip whenever Mo is around, but I'm not surprised—Mo is definitely the funny aunt type.

Needless to say, my little girl is eating up the attention everyone's been giving her. She's soaking it up, trying to play with everything and everyone she can possibly get her fingers on—preferably Mo's strawberry blonde hair or Gabe's fun shirt sleeve.

She's alternatively playing with both while they sneak little looks at each other. After Gabe's grumpy mood earlier, I was actually surprised he willingly sat down next to her. Having Mirabelle around seems to have softened him some, bringing him back to what I've come to consider his normal self.

Hudson and Gabe's sister, Dahlia, is sitting across from them, her long, blonde-dyed hair all waves and braids. She'd be the perfect model for a hippie photo shoot. Absolutely stunning.

Pulling apart a piece of baguette in her hands, she looks up at Monica. "Gabe said you broke your thigh bone during a car accident? I hope it's not half as bad as it sounds. What did the doctors say about your recovery? Did they tell you how long it will take to heal?"

The table is still filled with dirty dishes, but everyone seems to be engaged in conversations, not wanting to deal with the aftermath of this big meal yet. It's been such a fun time that neither Hudson nor I have wanted to get up to clean the mess either. Thankfully, no one seems to mind.

Monica sighs, absentmindedly playing with the palm tree-looking ponytail on top of Mirabelle's head. "They said on average it takes about three to six months to heal, sometimes longer. The fact that my bones were broken in several places makes it a lot harder to predict. Time will tell, or so I've been told, at least. The hardest part will probably be staying off my leg for a while, it's already driving me absolutely crazy. And of course, it all depends on how diligently I'll follow my physical therapist's orders. I'm going to meet up with mine tomorrow. He came with stellar recommendations, so hopefully he's as good as everyone says he is."

"What's his name?" Dahlia's twin, Rose, leans forward now too—her dark hair such a stark contrast to her sister's—

stopping the round of peek-a-boo she was playing with Mirabelle.

"Alex Brown."

Rose leans back in her chair, chuckling in amusement. Dahlia joins in, making them look more similar than I've ever seen before.

Rose is the first to speak again. "Well, if anyone should be able to fix you, it's him. Plus, he's one of the most gorgeous men I've ever seen in my life. And you have a legitimate reason to stare at him for copious amounts of time now. For that alone, it'll all be worth it."

Gabe groans from the other side of Monica.

Dahlia points at Gabe. "You used to be best friends with him, right up until college. I don't think you've ever told us what happened."

"And there's a reason for it, so drop it." Gabe's reply is sharp, the annoyance clear in his voice. It reminds me of his earlier behavior, and I wonder if Monica brought up her physical therapist before with him, unknowingly hitting a nerve. Apparently, he's had enough of it because he gets up from his chair, silently picking up dirty dishes to carry over to the kitchen.

The twins share a look, probably having heard that answer before. Monica looks after him, a deep frown etched on her forehead.

Rose waves him off, leaning toward Monica again as if she's getting ready for round two of her interrogation. "Just ignore him. He always gets grumpy when someone brings up Al—"

"Dahlia, how's your little project going?" Hudson interrupts, and I wonder if he's trying to change the subject.

The smile that breaks across Dahlia's face reminds me of Hudson when he talks about his music. It's mesmerizing. "It's going really great."

He turns to me. "Dahlia opened up Brooksville Academy of Arts last year, and from what I've heard, it's becoming quite popular."

She nods in response. "It's certainly keeping me busy, I can tell you that much. It's exciting though, I love it. So far, I've been mainly focusing on kids. The classes are so much messier, but also so much more fun. It's a nice reminder of why I love art so much. Seeing the excitement on those little faces is pretty much the best thing ever." Her eyes sparkle, and I'm sure her beaming smile could light up a small planet. I always think it's special to see someone be so passionate about something they love.

Who knows? Maybe that's exactly the way I look when I talk about my bakery.

Her hands fly through the air as she continues, moving as fast as the words come out of her mouth. "There are so many things I'd like to do. I want to get a bigger building and expand the courses I'm offering. Maybe we can even get some other creative areas incorporated too. There have been lots of studies that show that art, and other creative outlets, can help children that struggle in school, or even help with battling health issues. I'd like to work with schools and support them however possible. And I've also been thinking about a summer camp." She takes a deep breath, chuckling nervously. "Sorry, I've been having lots of ideas, but it's still in the beginning stages. It's very exhilarating."

I'm in awe, pure awe.

What she's trying to do with her academy sounds

inspiring, even more so when children are the main focus and how to help them.

When I look at Hudson, he's still staring at his sister.

He seems a bit shocked by her little speech. "Wow, I don't know what to say. I'm thrilled for you and your plans, and that it's all going so well. I had no idea you were this serious about it. It's great, Dahlia. *Really* great. I hope you're proud of yourself."

"Thank you." She looks down at her hands for a moment before gazing back up at him.

Hudson leans closer to her across the table. "Please let me know if you need any help with anything, okay? Anything."

She shakes her head before he can say more. "No, no. You have enough on your plate already. Plus, aren't you going to leave again soon? Usually, you only stay for a short while before you head back out again."

A sudden commotion takes place under the table, followed by an outcry of pain from Dahlia and a silent staring contest between the twins.

"Excuse me." Dahlia stands up, after mumbling a lame apology, and joins Gabe in the kitchen.

It looks like she's limping a little.

Limping?

What on earth?

Wait. Did Rose just *kick* her, because of what she said about Hudson leaving again soon?

For some reason, I didn't even think about that statement. I mean, in the end, isn't that exactly what Hudson told me when we first met? That he's home for a break from his music and to write before going back on the road?

That definitely didn't sound like an extended trip.

As if he knows he's on my mind, Hudson's hand squeezes my thigh gently under the table before he entangles our fingers. "You okay?"

I nod because I'm not sure what to say to him right now. Obviously, it's not my place to tell him to stay, not that I could ever ask that of him anyway. He's got a big career and being on the road is a huge part of it.

No news there, regardless of how much I dislike the thought of it.

Instead, I try and focus on the wonderful company tonight. Spending time with this awesome family and getting to know them better has been great. No matter what happens with Hudson when he leaves town again at some point, I will still stay in Brooksville. Having a few friends will be good, and necessary.

This situation makes it blatantly clear, though, that Hudson and I have to talk about us, what we are, and where we're going. For now, I try and focus on the positive, like this wonderful evening and our date tomorrow.

Three long hours later, I finally close the front door behind the last person leaving. "Gosh, they can be exhausting."

Hudson chuckles next to me, silently agreeing with me. He takes my hand and turns me around. "Come on, you party animal, time for bed."

I stifle a yawn and nod. It's late, and sleeping does sound good, especially when it's in his really big and extremely comfortable bed. Even more so when he's in there with me.

Without any protest, I let out a long sigh and follow him up the stairs.

"Charlie?"

"Huh?" Apparently, I spaced out for a second.

Hudson chuckles. "Are you gonna get ready in your room? You know, it might be easiest to just get some of your stuff and put it in my bathroom and bedroom. I mean, just, if you want, of course."

It's a simple statement, but it has so much meaning behind it. At least, that's what it sounds like to me, and as weird as it sounds, it's something I've never been asked before. Even though Sebastian and I spent some nights together, we never intentionally left any personal belongings at the other person's place. It never even occurred to me, if I'm being honest. I was a good little visitor, taking everything back home with me when I left. Oddly enough, it felt right. That should have been a sign right there.

Realizing Hudson is still waiting for an answer, I nod. I feel like throwing my arms around him and thanking him for being this awesome person. He makes all this intimacy stuff so easy, something I never knew could be like that. "I was gonna jump in the shower quick, wash all this food smell off me."

"How about a bath?" The words shoot out of his mouth, as if he's been waiting to say them for hours. "You deserve some nice relaxation time after this week. I can run it for you in my bathroom. I mean, my bathtub is a lot bigger."

Interestingly enough, I feel a little disappointed at his lack of flirtation right now, which can only mean he's actually planning on letting me have the bath by myself.

Something in me clicks in that moment, bringing out a

hidden part of me, and I open myself up to a need I've never felt before.

Seduction.

Taking a step forward, I lean into his body, both of my hands firmly pressed against his chest. I look up at him from under my eyelashes, hoping I'm not making a total fool out of myself. I'm not sure I'd recover from that. "A bath sounds perfect, but only if you join me."

His eyes go wide for a moment before he wraps his arms around my waist. "That's not what I meant, but I'd be a fool to refuse."

"Well, then you better not be one."

"Oh, Charlie. What am I gonna do with you?" He's close enough for me to feel his warm breath on my face.

"So many possibilities." I grin and go up on my toes, closing the last bit of space between us to seal his lips with mine. "Give me one minute. I'll be right back."

After getting everything I need from my room, and checking on Mirabelle one more time, who passed out hours ago, I make my way back to Hudson's room, my nerves on full alert.

When I walk into his bathroom, there's a sea of bubbles rising in the bathtub. Hudson stands in front of the bathtub with his back to me. I put my things on the large counter and quietly walk over to him. Circling my arms around his middle, I rest my head between his shoulder blades, taking in a deep breath. I love his scent, it's familiar and soothing, the sound of the running water an added balm for my soul.

He turns around in my arms to face me, and after a long moment of staring into my eyes, he cups my face with his hands, pulling me in for a kiss. His lips are soft, his tongue unhurried as it delves into my mouth. Since I can't ignore the tense back muscles under my hands, I'm convinced he's taking things slowly for my benefit. I can't find it in me to complain, though, because this is perfect. This is exactly what I needed, and I'm sure Hudson knows that.

My hands drift under his shirt before tugging it up at the edges. Hudson gets the memo and lifts his arms for me to pull off his shirt, revealing his beautiful chest in the process. My hands have a mind of their own, exploring his naked skin—dips and curves of his muscles included—with a tenacity I don't usually have.

I'm slowly starting to realize Hudson brings that out in me. He's already been such a big influence in so many aspects of my life. It's almost like he has a direct connection to my inner self, sometimes knowing what I need before I even know it myself.

After stripping off his jeans, leaving him in only his tight black boxer briefs that do nothing to hide his erection, he kisses me again until we're both breathless. "Your turn."

Lifting my arms over my head, I let him pull up the dress I'm wearing, my eyes never leaving his as he takes in every new inch of skin he's revealing. The awe and pure lust in his gaze is a turn-on I've never experienced before, making me tingle in places I haven't felt anything in a very long time.

"Oh shit." Hudson drops my dress and jumps away from me, leaping to the bathtub to turn off the faucet. "That was a close one."

I have to laugh at the fact that we almost let the bathtub water overflow, and therefore flood the bathroom. Just shows how distracted we were.

"We should probably get in there before it gets cold."

I gulp, nerves making my stomach clench, and I think Hudson is able to see it as clear as day.

"You're sure you're good with this? It's okay if you've changed your mind." He comes back over to me and takes my hands in his.

"No!" I almost yell at him and decide that honesty is the best policy, as usual. "I'm just a little nervous, I guess. I haven't been with anyone since, you know, last year, and even then, it never felt like this before. Everything is just so intense with you."

"I know exactly what you mean." He reaches up to brush my hair back, giving me a soft kiss. "I actually just remembered something. Why don't you get in the tub already? I'll be right back, okay?"

Nodding at him, I don't even care if he's telling the truth right now or not. The fact that this man cares enough to *want* to ease my nerves is something I don't take lightly. There are a whole bunch of people out there that wouldn't have cared one bit about my discomfort or would have been pushy, or maybe even annoyed instead. Even though we all want the same thing, it's the way we treat others to get to that goal that matters. Sadly, a lot of people have no clue what that actually means.

Thankfully for me, Hudson is an expert in not only reading me, but in being a decent human being in general.

Once he's gone, I discard my underwear and bra, slipping into the hot bathwater with a sigh. The bubbles cover me immediately, enveloping my body like a silky cloud, while the delicious smells of lavender and vanilla surround me, relaxing me instantly.

A moment later, Hudson comes back, two glasses and the

bottle of champagne I know was in the fridge in his hands. "I remembered you liked this one, so I thought you might want a glass?"

"I'd love one, thanks."

Hudson pops the cork and pours us both a glass before giving one to me.

"Thank you." I take a deep breath as he stands right next to the bathtub, silently swallowing my nerves. I move forward in the bathtub to make room behind me. "Come on in already, the water is perfect."

Rather than looking at him, I focus on the glass in my hand, watching the little bubbles in the liquid sparkle. He climbs in behind me, the water sloshing all around me from the movement. After settling in, his long legs on either side of me, he places a kiss on one of my shoulders, and I lean into the caress without a second thought.

His touch makes me feel *everything*—especially the overwhelming sensation of losing control that I always feared but secretly missed regardless. It's filled with passion, emotions, so much affection, and earth-shattering lust that I'm not sure I know what to do with it.

"Come here." Hudson takes my glass and puts both on the large windowsill next to us before wrapping his hands around my waist to pull me back against him.

Nothing between us.

Skin to skin.

Unable to cover the gasp of surprise that escapes my mouth, I lean back, my head resting on his shoulder, while I try to commit every sensation to memory.

The mixture of the hot water lapping around, his warm body behind and around me, and his warm hands now on me too—not to forget his erection that's pressed against my butt. It feels so good I want to stay here forever.

My body is on high-alert, so sensitive to everything going on that I involuntarily jerk when Hudson's hands begin to move on my stomach.

After giving my midsection some attention, they move further up, and the anticipation of him touching me intimately almost makes me jump out of my skin. When he finally reaches my breasts and cups them, I'm pretty sure I'm ready to see stars.

Hudson groans behind me as he gently pinches my nipples, rolling and rubbing them to his heart's content, while I start to get more and more restless. He chuckles behind me and leans forward, removing a hand from my breast and guiding my face toward his.

"You feel so good." He stares into my eyes, his other hand still firmly on my breast, squeezing it when he gives me a kiss so passionately, I forget where left and right is. His erection throbs behind me when his hand leaves my face to move down my body.

This time, he doesn't stop at my breast or belly. Instead, he moves beyond it to where I need him the most right now.

"Hudson." His name falls from my lips right before his fingers touch my bundle of nerves, eliciting a loud moan from my throat. For a split second, I'm not sure if I should be embarrassed about it, but then I push the self-doubt away. It's been so long since I've felt anything remotely like this—if ever, really—that I can't bring myself to feel any kind of shame.

He rubs me halfway into oblivion, knowing exactly what I need before he plunges deep inside me with his fingers. He fills me, over and over again, while still taking care of my now almost quivering nub. "I love how responsive you are."

The combination of hearing his sexy voice and the never-ending stimulation sends me flying over the edge so hard, I'm not sure I'd stay upright if it wasn't for his secure grip on me.

After gently bringing me down from my orgasm, he kisses me with a fierceness that makes it hard for me to tell if the tingles in my lower body are after-tremors or new ones.

He nibbles on my lower lip, and I close my eyes at the feeling of it. "You're so incredibly sexy. I can't wait to do that all over again."

Somehow that makes me chuckle, since the pleasure was very obviously—and loudly—all mine. "Me too."

I turn around in his arms, shaky legs and all, and look into his eyes.

I can't wait for more with him, fully intending on returning the favor tonight.

CHAPTER THIRTY

"Where are we going, Hudson?" I can't decide where to look, switching back and forth between the beautiful greenery we're passing and Hudson's handsome profile.

He chuckles in response. "You already know I won't tell you, so stop asking me."

We've been in the car for maybe half an hour, but it feels like forever. After this last week and everything that's happened between us—especially last night in the bathtub—I shouldn't feel so on edge, but my nerves are shot, and my anticipation is through the roof.

Hudson grabs my hand across the middle console and squeezes it. "I can tell you, if you really want to know."

Now I feel bad.

I'm sure he can see the slight panic on my face from a mile away, even though I realize I don't really have a reason for it. "I'm good, sorry. Just a bit nervous, I guess."

"If it makes you feel any better, so am I." He pulls my hand up to his face and gives it a gentle kiss.

Just like that, everything in my world is right again. The nerves aren't fully gone, but his admission puts everything back in perspective.

This beautiful person wants to spend time with me and surprise me with our date.

Time to relax.

I take a deep breath and tighten the grip on our hands. The smile that crosses his face makes my heartbeat speed up, and I have to grin too.

Putting on the signal, he turns left and heads up a little mountain. "We're almost there, I promise."

Trying not to stare at him nonstop like a stalker, I nod and turn to look out the window again. We left the city—or rather, town—a little while ago, and all that's left is the gorgeous landscape. The car turns onto a dirt trail, slowing down to accommodate the road condition while also allowing me to really take in the beauty that's all around us.

I haven't been out of Brooksville since we moved here, so I'm equally excited and mesmerized by everything I see.

The car comes to a stop. "We're here."

As promised, Hudson stops the car a few feet later, and I gasp at the sight in front of us. Nestled in between the magnificent trees and flowers is a little cabin. It looks straight out of a fairy tale. We both get out of the car, and Hudson walks around it to stand next to me as I take in the surroundings some more.

The area around the little brown wooden house seems well taken care of. A big blanket is spread out on the front lawn, with beautiful flowers surrounding it. The sight of it makes me a little emotional. It might not seem a lot to some, but no one has ever done anything like this for me.

Turning to Hudson with a timid smile, I feel a little overwhelmed by all the attention, and I can't deny it's doing funny things to my heart and stomach.

"Is that where you went this morning?" I shake my head at him. "You really didn't have to do so much."

"I wanted to do something special for you." He studies me for a moment. "Does that mean you like it?" His voice sounds a little rough, making me wonder if there's uncertainty behind it, which would be crazy.

"Are you kidding me? I love it. Thank you." I close the distance between us, and his eyes widen in amusement and anticipation.

Our bodies touch, little bursts of energy tingling everywhere. My hand lifts on its own accord, drawn to the stubble on his strong jaw. I slowly move my fingers over it and make my way around to his neck. His hair is long enough for me to bury my hands in. I tug on it, and thankfully, he understands my signal and bends down just as I go up on my toes. We meet in the middle for a kiss that quickly turns into more.

"Charlie." Hudson sighs his approval against my lips.

Both of my hands are at his neck, trying to pull him even closer to me while his hands move around my waist, pressing into my lower back. The little flickers inside my veins have turned into gigantic sparks, urging me on even more.

This man is his own kind of addiction I can never get enough of.

He seems to feel the same way as our kiss turns more frantic by the second.

I've never been much of an initiator, but Hudson makes me want to climb on top of him right now—no matter if we end up on the ground, the car, or whatever other surface we can find within a two-foot radius.

"Wait." He pulls back, both of us breathing hard.

It takes me a good minute before I can think straight again, let alone get a word out. "I'm sorry, I didn't mean to jump you like this." I cover my face with my hands before peeking through my fingers at his smirking face.

Prying my hands from my face, he shakes his head. "Did I give you the impression I minded it in any way? You can attack me like that whenever you want, day or night." The wink he gives me nearly does me in.

"Not really first date material though, huh?"

"I don't think anything between us has been going according to any sort of normal timeline anyway, so I think we're safe to do whatever we want, whenever we want it."

Well, isn't that a nice way to look at it? Even though, he's right. We have been doing things completely out of order, which makes me chuckle.

Since it feels good to have that off my chest, I instantly relax. "I guess you're right. No normal rules for us then?"

"Nope." He gives me another kiss but doesn't linger this time. Instead, he pulls on my hand and walks to the trunk. "Now, let me show you around and feed you before I change my mind and eat you up instead."

"Some people do prefer to have dessert *before* their main meal."

He stops and spins around, and it's hard to tell who's more shocked right now—him or me.

My eyes are wide as saucers as I clamp my free hand over my mouth, slowly shaking my head. "She does that to me. I swear, this is all her fault." The words come out muffled through my fingers.

Hudson throws his head back and laughs. "I'm guessing we're talking about Monica?" He taps the tip of my nose with his index finger before leaning close to my ear. "I wouldn't consider that a bad influence, though. Actually, I really like it —even more so, since it makes you blush."

With that, he trails little kisses along my jaw before claiming my mouth once more. At this pace, we'll never even make it close to the little cottage. When we come up for air, I can see the strain it takes him to stay away from me this time.

Closing his eyes for a moment, I listen to his breathing as he tries to calm down. "Phew, this is a lot harder than I thought it would be."

"I'll behave now. No more distractions from me."

He shakes his head, like I have no idea what I'm talking about. To be honest, I'm not sure how much I comprehend right now. I feel like I'm walking through some sort of haze, my main focus being Hudson and those delicious lips of his. Nothing else registers, not even a bit.

I quietly chuckle to myself, realizing this is probably the first time I truly understand what Monica's one-track mind is all about. No wonder she talks about this stuff constantly. It already feels utterly addicting.

My thoughts jump to my past for a moment, wondering what all of this says about my previous experiences with guys, because *nothing* was ever close to being this exciting or worthwhile before.

Nothing.

Not a single encounter.

Hudson squeezes my hand before letting go. Opening the

trunk of his big SUV, I'm surprised to see it's filled as far as the eye can see.

What on earth does this man plan on doing out here with me?

The sight makes me chuckle. "How long were you planning on staying here? A month?"

One side of his mouth quirks up, making his dimple pop out. "I just wanted to be prepared, that's all. Plus, I want to spoil you, and also make sure you won't get bored, so I brought lots of entertainment."

Grasping his arm, I turn him around. "I really hope you don't mean that. I can't even tell you how much I've been looking forward to spending some time with you alone. No baby monitor or people that can come home and interrupt us. Just you and me. That's all I need and want right now. There will absolutely not be any need for other forms of entertainment. Believe me."

The smile he gives me in response is one of the most genuine smiles I've ever seen on his face. It reaches his eyes in a way that makes the butterflies in my stomach go completely crazy. "Oh, Charlie. What am I gonna do with you?"

I shrug my shoulders and smirk at him. "How about you kiss me again?"

"I think that can be arranged." The heat in his eyes has grown even more since our last lip action, and I feel the reciprocal buzz in my veins from it. My whole body is humming in anticipation, wanting more and more of this intoxicating feeling whenever he touches me.

After a few minutes in paradise, he pulls back. "Okay. I keep saying it, but let's stop right there. I want to do this the right way, and you deserve to be spoiled first."

Obviously, this means a lot to him, so I try to be good, holding out my hands in front of me. "Let me carry something."

After giving me a few bags, he grabs the remaining basket and his guitar case, and shuts the trunk.

We walk over to the cabin in silence. As much as I want to jump his bones right now, I'm also curious about this beautiful place he picked, and what he has planned.

Hudson pulls the keys out of his jeans pocket and unlocks the door, pushing it wide open. It creaks a little, which only adds to the charm of this place. Letting me step in first, I can feel his eyes on me as I look around.

It's nothing fancy or big, but it's warm and cozy. There's a small sitting area in front of a fireplace, a tiny kitchenette in the right corner, and it appears a big bed is just on the left side that is mostly hidden from sight. I take a few steps further into the room to get a better look, definitely drawn to it. The big four-poster bed looms around the corner and looks just as inviting as Hudson's bed back at the house.

You're in trouble, Charlie. So much trouble.

"Do you like it?" His voice comes from right behind me, causing a shiver to run down my spine.

I turn around and beam at him. "I love it. It's beautiful. Is it yours?"

He nods. "Grandma and Grandpa had one just like this when I was younger. It was very old though, and Grandma sold it after Grandpa died. But I always loved their cabin, so I knew I wanted to have one eventually too. It's been a nice place to escape to, when I'm in need of some real quiet time."

Somehow, that makes this place even more special. "Thanks for sharing it with me."

"Of course." He gives me a smile before nodding over to the kitchenette. "Let's go put the stuff away we don't need right now. And then we can go outside and eat if you want? The sun should start setting in a little bit."

His words make me feel all warm and fuzzy. "I'd love to."

"Let's do it then."

After putting a few things in the fridge and cabinets, Hudson pulls me back outside toward the blanket, carrying the basket and guitar case.

Is he actually going to play for me?

CHAPTER THIRTY-ONE

It's official. Sitting between Hudson's legs is my new favorite place to be. We just had the most delicious picnic while watching one of the most magnificent sunsets I've ever seen.

Perfect doesn't even begin to cover tonight.

To make things even better, he's now sitting behind me on the blanket, his arms tightly wound around both me and his guitar—which is safely propped up on my lap.

"Are you ready?" Hudson's mouth is right next to my ear, his breath making me shiver.

Am I ready?

Absolutely. It feels like I've been waiting for this for a long time.

I nod, excited about what's to come.

When he starts strumming the guitar, I have to laugh at the sensation. The vibrations of the tones are everywhere in my body, and it's an incredible sensation.

He chuckles, making us both shake even more. "Hold

still, silly." His hand stops strumming as he presses his lips to my neck. "I'm not sure this is going to work."

"No way. I'll hold still now, I promise." Pretending to be a statue, I sit completely still, not moving an inch.

His fingers start moving again, his left hand finding the chords while his right hand strums continuously. I close my eyes in contentment and lean my head back on his shoulder.

We sit like this for a while, and I'm certain I could listen to him play for the next few years.

Who am I kidding?

More like the rest of my life because this man is incredibly talented. He's currently playing the most beautiful melody I've ever heard, evoking all sorts of feelings in me. It's the same song he was humming to me when I told him about my past.

Thinking of that night still makes me feel a bit raw, but this song makes it all better. It's like my own personal connection with Hudson and the most beautiful thing that's come out of dealing with my past yet.

The song has me completely enthralled, playing at my heartstrings in the most marvelous way.

"This is your song, you know?" Hudson stops for a moment. "I'm still working on the lyrics, but I like to play it often because it makes me think about you."

I arch to the side to look at him.

"And just for the record, I like thinking about you—not that I have much of a choice anymore these days, since you've pretty much taken over my mind."

I think my insides just melted a little. I love how blunt Hudson is. It always seems like he says exactly what's on his mind. Usually, his thoughts mirror mine, but I'm too chicken to tell him that.

After placing his guitar next to us on the blanket, he bends down to give my nose a kiss before going straight for my lips. It's a quick one but one I enjoy nonetheless.

Hovering over me, he gently brushes the hair out of my face. "Are you ready to go inside? It's starting to cool down, now that the sun is almost gone, and I don't want you to get cold."

I was so distracted by him, I didn't even notice the temperatures dropping. "If you want to, sure. I'm okay either way."

"We can turn on the fireplace inside and make out on the rug in front of it." He wiggles his eyebrows at me, making me laugh.

I slap his arm gently, still chuckling. "What are you? Sixteen?"

"With you, it seems like it. I just want to eat you up all day, every day." He slowly comes closer again, and I expect him to give me another kiss. Instead, he goes for my throat, gently nibbling his way from my ear down to my collarbone.

That touch elicits a string of feelings in my body that make it hard to know what's going on anymore. "Your idea sounds better and better by the second."

He finds a soft spot on my neck, sucking on it until I gasp, ready to melt into a puddle right this second. "That's what I thought." After staring at me for a moment, he swipes his thumb over my cheek. "Have I told you already how much I like having you here with me? Because I like it *a lot*."

Letting my head fall back into the curve of his shoulder, I nestle into his neck as much as possible. The mixture of his signature scent mixed with the forest smells from around us is like my very own aphrodisiac. "I do too. I enjoy every minute with you."

"Let's go inside then and see if we can make it even better." After standing, he holds out his hand to help me up.

The butterflies in my stomach are happily throwing a big celebration party, not helping my nerves one bit.

After getting everything back into the cabin, Hudson goes straight for the fireplace, turning it on with practiced ease. My body has finally gotten the memo about the lower temperatures, so I'm looking forward to the warmth the fire will provide.

"Are you all right?" He walks over to me and pulls me into an embrace.

I guess I zoned out for a moment while I watched him.

Smiling up at him, I snuggle further into his body. "Absolutely."

"Good." He looks at me so intensely I wonder if he's trying to read my mind. "What do you feel like doing? Do you want to sit down on the couch and talk? We could have some more wine too, if you want to."

"That sounds lovely."

He starts walking away but pauses after a few steps, turning back to look at me for a moment before he focuses on his feet. He's biting his lower lip in a way I've never really seen him do before. Is he nervous about something? Or guilty?

After clearing his throat several times, he looks back up at me, his eyes going back and forth between mine.

A ball of anxiety tightens in my belly, and I'm starting to feel nervous for a whole different reason. "What is it?"

"Well, I kind of did something, and thinking about it now, makes me a little unsure if I might have overstepped my boundaries and ruined our night. Which would be the last thing I'd want."

That doesn't sound good at all. "Just spit it out." There's an edge to my voice, and I'm not sure if it's anger or slight hysteria. My emotions are so all over the place it's hard to control them right now.

He shoves his right hand roughly through his hair. "I might've been a little presumptuous—or maybe I should say, hopeful—and asked Grandma if she'd be good to stay by herself with Mira until tomorrow." There's the slightest bit of color showing on his cheeks, making him look like the most innocent person in the world.

After giving my body a minute to relax again, trying to keep my heart from tripping all over itself while also calming down my breathing, I go over to him and grasp his face with both hands, staring intently into his beautiful eyes. "You just gave me a mini heart attack. Next time, just tell me, okay?" I let out another big breath after he nods. "I'd love to stay the night with you, even though I'm slightly mortified about what Hannah must be thinking."

He only shrugs his shoulders. "It's my grandma we're talking about here. She'd probably be the first one suggesting and advocating it anyway."

Well, he's got me there. "You're right. Oh gosh. I just love her. She really is the best."

"Yup. Grandma has some weird tendencies sometimes, but she's awesome. I wouldn't change her for the world."

"Can't blame you."

We fall silent again until Hudson takes my hands in his.

"You're really good with staying overnight? We really don't have to. It's more than okay if you'd rather head back home tonight."

I nod without having to think about it again. "Yes."

His smile is addictive, making my own butterflies appear immediately. Anticipation of what's to come ripples through my whole body, increasing my inner temperature by several degrees—or at least that's what it feels like.

"Awesome. Do you want me to call Grandma, or do you want to?"

I cringe before I laugh. "Oh no, that's all on you. This is too embarrassing to talk about with her."

He chuckles and takes his phone out of his pocket. "All right, I'll do it then."

Putting my hand on his arm, I swallow past a small lump in my throat. "Would you do me a favor though, and ask her if Mira's okay, please? Maybe she can send some pictures? Or a video? And tell her to call if she needs anything. She knows where all of Mira's things are, but if she can't find something in her room, it's probably in mine. Also—"

His hand goes under my chin to tilt it back far enough for me to look up at him. "Hey! Take a deep breath, okay? Mira is going to be fine. And I know Grandma would call the second she needs us." He frowns down at me before shaking his head. "Let's just forget about it and go home. I don't want to stress you out. It's not worth it."

"No!" I half yell at him, my emotions a mess. "Just give me a moment, so I can get used to this idea. This will be my first night away from Mira, and it's a strange feeling to know I won't be there when she wakes up."

I take a deep breath because I truly want this, all of it. I want to relax and enjoy this extraordinary night with Hudson. There really is no one better than Hannah to trust with Mirabelle, and we have our phones on in case we're needed.

I make a shooing motion with my hand before I point down to where he's still clutching the phone. "Go call her, I'll be fine. I'm gonna go over to the couch and sit down."

"You're absolutely sure?"

"Yes." I nod for emphasis before starting to walk backward, making a calling motion with my hand by my ear.

He still doesn't look fully convinced but nods, pressing around on the screen of his phone.

I walk over to the couch while he puts the phone up to his ear and grabs our bags from where we left them to set them on the kitchenette.

The coffee table in front of me distracts me, and I bend down to look at the few random magazines and something that looks like a photo album. Curiosity wins and I grab it, opening it on my lap.

What I find inside warms my heart—family pictures, lots and lots of them.

There are camping trips, treehouse adventures, all sorts of sports activities, and some fun candid pictures. All four siblings with their parents, looking like they're having the time of their lives. A few pages in, one picture in particular catches my eye, and I have to laugh. It's Hudson in just a pair of underwear with a cape around his neck and a guitar swung around his bare shoulder. He's smiling at the camera, proudly showing off a missing front tooth.

"Ahh. You found *that* picture, huh?" He sits down next to me, handing me a glass of wine. "Here."

"Thank you."

"You're very welcome."

After taking a sip, I put the glass on the table. "Everything okay back at the house?"

Chuckling, he puts his glass next to mine before pulling his phone out of his back pocket. "Oh yeah. Grandma said they're having a blast. Mira just took a bath, and she's getting her ready for bed now."

He turns the phone my way to show me a picture of Mira wrapped up in a towel like a cocoon.

"Aww. So cute."

"Grandma thought you'd like that, and she said to tell you to have fun."

"Oh gosh. I'm not sure I can ever look her in the eye again."

Hudson pats my leg and chuckles. "You'll be fine."

"Hopefully." Looking down, I catch sight of the cute picture of Hudson again. I point to it. "I hope it was okay to look at this."

"Of course. There are some great pictures in there."

I tap on the one I was looking at. "This one is my absolute favorite so far."

"I can see why." He chuckles, leaning closer to get a better look. "Very sexy."

"You were adorable." I study him, excited to learn more about him. "Was that your first guitar?"

He stretches his arm over the back of the couch and starts playing with a strand of my hair. "Yeah. Grandpa gave it to me."

"Seems like it was meant to be."

"Yeah?"

I nod, not a doubt in my mind. "Have you already figured things out about your future, and what you want to do? We haven't talked about it in a while but at dinner yesterday... I don't know. I guess the conversation about you leaving soon got me thinking. Will you get back together with your band?"

He groans in frustration, and I'm afraid I ruined the mood.

I hold up my hands. "I'm sorry, forget I said anything. I shouldn't have brought it up."

His hand brushes over my hair, the motion incredibly soothing—just like his voice. "No, you didn't do anything wrong. I just have a lot of people breathing down my neck about it right now, so it's a touchy subject for me. I'm seeing the boys in a couple weeks, so we'll talk about it then. I know what I want, but I'm not sure yet if I can get it."

"Okay."

"Speaking of seeing them, I've been wanting to ask you something." His fingers interlace with mine, his thumb tracing imaginary patterns on my skin.

Pulling my gaze away from our hands, I look back up at him. "What is it?"

"One of the guys from the band, Elijah, is getting married soon, and I was wondering if you'd like to come with me? The wedding is in Los Angeles, and we can take Mira with us."

I blink before blinking some more. "You want me to come with you to your friend's wedding?"

"Yeah." The simple word comes out of his mouth so matter-of-factly as if it's the most normal thing to ask.

Heck, maybe it is.

My mind is going into overdrive, trying to work through

the situation. This probably means it'll be a bigger wedding, or at least other celebrities will be there, which will also mean paparazzi.

Hudson and I will be there together. Like, together *together*.

In *public*. For *everyone* to see.

Am I ready for that?

It's the exact thing I've been shying away from—the whole public side of being with Hudson. Besides that one incident, it's been pretty simple to live with him in Brooksville. But once the cat's out of the sack—and the pictures out in the world—I'm not sure if, or how, things will change.

Back then, I was incredibly attracted to Hudson, but we weren't that close yet. It was easier not wanting to risk my private life for someone I didn't know very well.

But things are different now.

So different.

We've grown incredibly close, talking all day long about everything and anything. He's become my person in life—the person I told about my past, and who I trust. What started out as lust between us quickly morphed into something more, especially with how much time we spend together on a daily basis.

It's been impossible *not* to form a bond.

If I really want to see where things go between us, I have to push these worries and fears aside and take that leap into his world. Since it's a part of him, it's either all of it or nothing at all.

And the thought of not having him, of not being with him, hurts too much.

I'm glad he gave me a moment to ponder over it, already knowing I can slip into my own mind sometimes. "I'd love to come with you."

"Perfect." He looks satisfied and happy, which makes me happy too.

What makes this moment even better is our next kiss.

It's filled with emotions, with promises, pulling me immediately under his spell, my whole focus shifting in an instant.

When we part, I do something that is very atypical for me yet feels entirely right—I get up from the couch and walk over to the fireplace with slow, deliberate footsteps.

I find his eyes on me, as I expected them to be, when I turn back around to look at him. Slowly unbuttoning my cardigan, I keep my gaze on his as I undo button for button.

"What are you doing?" Hudson's voice sounds hoarse, like he's having a hard time getting the words out.

With my cardigan now completely undone, I start sliding it down my shoulders, almost painfully slow. "I believe you promised me a make-out session in front of the fireplace, didn't you?"

Like he has no time to waste, he jumps up from the couch and walks over to me, a predatory gleam in his eyes.

At that moment, I'm absolutely convinced this is going to be one of the best nights of my life, and nothing can ever take that away from me.

CHAPTER THIRTY-TWO

When I drop my cardigan to the floor, Hudson's eyes stay glued to my chest and the tight tank top I'm wearing. After an audible gulp, his gaze moves up to my face, his eyes blazing with unfiltered lust.

My chest is rising and falling rapidly when he steps closer. To my utter dismay, he stops a foot away when all I want are his hands on me.

He exhales loudly. "Dang, Charlie. You're driving me absolutely insane."

A big smile spreads across my face, and I can't help but grab a handful of his T-shirt to pull him closer. "I'm glad because you're doing the same to me." My lips feel suddenly dry, and I wet them with my tongue, my focus shifting down to his mouth.

The last bit of his self-control snaps as his hands find their way into my hair, his body pushing against me.

His body. I don't think I can ever get enough of it.

I feel him everywhere as we touch from our toes all the way up to our noses. His lips are devouring mine, his tongue so skilled, I'm afraid I'll start swaying soon. I'm mesmerized, absolutely enthralled. My skin is tingling everywhere, almost like I just received a shock that's still buzzing through my system.

His lips are relentless, sucking on mine in a way that is so sexy, I want to push him to the floor right this second to have my way with him.

On second thought, he might not even mind.

Our breaths are erratic when we both gasp for air a moment later.

His hand rubs up and over my shoulder before going down my back and to my butt. He squeezes it hard, pulling me into his pelvis.

Oh. My. Goodness.

A sudden panic rushes over me that I won't be good enough for him. It's been a while since I've had sex, and even then, I never did anything adventurous either.

What if I suck at this? And I don't mean that literally.

As if he knows exactly how close I am to freaking out, he moves his hands back up to my face, kissing me with a tenderness that makes my heart sigh in pure happiness. When he pulls back, he rests his forehead against mine, his hands still cradling my face. "I hope you know I'd never push you. All you have to do is tell me what you want, and I'll enjoy every second of whatever you're willing to give."

It's undeniable this man has a direct connection to my heart, his words sinking in so deeply, I'm starting to believe they'll forever be imprinted there. "I want you. All of you. Every last bit."

His chuckle makes me grin, and I love that things with him are so easy. He's direct, and has been nothing but honest and genuine so far. No games, no lies. Just him being him.

"I'm glad to hear that because I'm dying to finally have all of you too." Rubbing his nose up and down mine, he leans in for a deep kiss.

My hands have a mind of their own, running back through his hair and tugging him so close to me I've lost track of where I end and he starts.

I'm starting to get impatient and somehow manage to pull my top over my head without stopping the kiss for more than three seconds.

But it's still not enough.

I need more, so much more.

Tugging on the hem of his shirt, I try and pull it up as far as I can without breaking our contact. He chuckles against my lips, clearly amused by my frenzied movements and my obvious desperation.

Once his shirt is off, I take a moment and marvel at the sight. No matter how often I see his naked skin, I still enjoy the view as much as I did the first time. I reach out, my fingers raking up and down his chest and stomach before I dig them into his skin, tantalizingly slow.

His hands are by his sides, twitching slightly in response, and I wonder if he's itching to touch me too.

My black lace bra suddenly feels too tight under his gaze, and my breasts ache for him, heaving up and down with my already quickened breath.

"You're so beautiful." His hands finally move up my arms and down the sides of my body, and I sigh in relief.

Shivering under his touch, I watch as his fingers slowly make their way up my stomach before they pause just under my bra. He traces the outline underneath my breasts, and my breath hitches in anticipation.

"Hudson, please." The whimper comes out of my mouth with such desperation, I'm surprised I haven't spontaneously combusted yet.

Looking into my eyes, I wonder if he sees the same fiery blaze in mine that I see in his. "Please what, Charlie?"

"Touch me. I... I need you to touch me."

If he's surprised about my directness, that makes two of us, but I'm so lost in this tension between us, I'm not above begging anymore.

Thankfully, he's only too happy to oblige, moving his hands up to cup my breasts through the bra. My eyes close on their own accord at the exquisite sensation that only intensifies as he brushes his thumbs over my taut nipples.

My head rolls around on my shoulders, and a tiny moan escapes my lips. "I need more."

I want to protest when his hands leave my chest, but thankfully, he only moves them to my back, releasing the clasp of my bra.

The sudden rush of air makes my nipples pucker up even more when my bra falls to the floor.

Hudson pulls me close, and I revel in the feel of my naked breasts pressed against his naked chest. It's impeccable but still not enough. Not even close.

Our mouths find each other and just like that, we're lost again. Soon, our hands join the craziness, moving around our bodies almost carelessly, like we can't touch enough skin fast enough.

A big breath of air escapes him when he slowly pulls back from me, trailing kisses down my neck, to my collarbone, and *finally* making it to my heavy breasts. He nibbles on my skin until he finds his way to my nipple—sucking and biting before soothing it with his tongue.

My back arches of its own volition, pressing my chest into him because it's never enough.

Never. Enough.

The feeling is so strong my knees wobble, and a string of words comes out of my mouth, even though I have no idea what I'm actually saying.

When I can't take it any longer, I reach for his jeans, fumbling around for the button.

He snatches my hands and pulls them away from his pants. "Should we go over to the bed?"

Looking up at him, it takes me a moment to snap out of the haze I'm in and for his words to sink in. I pout for a moment before shaking my head. "No. Let's just stay right here. The rug looks perfectly fine to me."

Wiggling his eyebrows, he smirks at me. "You're turning into a little sex kitten. I like it."

Pulling my lower lip into my mouth, I still feel little bouts of uncertainty course through me, but I try to ignore them as much as possible.

Instead, I try to focus on everything that's going on between us, like the rest of our clothes. There's way too many of them.

I point at his jeans. "Time to get rid of these."

"Not sure that's such a good idea right now." He chuckles and pulls my hand up to his mouth. "I wasn't kidding earlier. I do feel like a teenager when I'm around you, and I really don't want to end the party too early."

My eyes go wide for a moment before the ever-telling heat rushes into my cheeks.

"But"—the smirk he gives me is so naughty my whole body almost vibrates in anticipation—"I can help you with *your* pants."

I gulp. "Okay." That's all I manage to say, and it's all the invitation Hudson needs.

His hands are frantic, pulling at the top of my black pants. He releases a groan of appreciation when he finally manages to slide them down my legs.

Stepping out of them, I almost lose my balance when he unexpectedly starts kissing his way up my legs—not stopping until he makes it to my black lace panties.

After a kiss through the soft material, he stands back up, his lips on mine in a nanosecond. His mouth ravishes mine, swallowing a loud moan when he starts rubbing my most sensitive parts through my underwear with his fingers.

My body has a sudden mind of its own, rhythmically moving against his hand, fixated on pushing this ecstasy that has taken every inch of me to a whole new level.

When he pulls the small piece of material to the side and comes in contact with my bare skin, I have to hold on to him for dear life. The groan that escapes his lips is so sexy I'm not sure how much longer I can take it. His attention is back on my sensitive nub before he seems to get impatient, inserting a finger inside of me.

"Yes! Just like that." My voice sounds as impatient as I feel, my movements getting more desperate by the second, racing this electric current that's getting stronger and stronger the more time passes.

His free hand moves up to my breast, squeezing it while

his fingers keep exploring and working me so expertly, I want to cry out.

The pressure is getting intense until I can't take it any longer. "Oh gosh, I'm going to—"

My insides tighten around his fingers before I even have a chance to finish the sentence, not that he would have missed my moans anyway.

When I open my eyes again, I'm not sure what to expect. Having him touch me like this is still new, making me feel extremely exposed, not only to his touch but also to his reaction.

All is well in my world—pretty much perfect right this second—when I see the big, satisfied grin on his face. The look he gives me is so intense a renewed excitement starts to tingle in my lower belly.

"I want to make you feel good too." The words are barely loud enough for Hudson to hear.

"Later, sweetheart. Right now, I just want to be inside of you."

He doesn't give me time to react to his statement before he pulls down his pants, boxer briefs included. Even though we took a bath together last night, he was quick to wrap a towel around his hips when we were done. To my utter dismay, he tucked me into bed right after, telling me I needed all the sleep I could get.

Now I understand why, as I openly stare at his lower body.

To say I'm impressed doesn't even cover it.

"Do you like what you see?" His confidence apparently knows no boundaries as he takes himself in his hand, stroking once, twice.

304

Instead of blushing a profuse shade of red, I laugh. He keeps surprising me in the most entertaining way, and I love it. "Of course I do, silly. How can I not like it?"

Spurred on by his grin—complete with dimples—I push down my own underwear and let it drop to the ground. Taking a step toward him, I put my hands on his chest. "And just so we're clear, I want all of you."

"Yeah?"

I put a finger on his lips, and he slips his tongue out to lick it.

Gasping at the unexpected contact, I tell him the truth. "I've never been so sure about anything in my life."

"Thank goodness." His lips are back on mine while he lowers both of us slowly to the rug. "One second." He gets up quickly to snatch some pillows from the couch and protection from his pants.

After getting my fill of watching his glorious butt move around the room, he places the pillows under my head and back. Then he lies down next to me, exploring my whole body some more with his hands and his mouth until I'm ready to explode from all the tension.

"Now, Hudson, I can't wait for another second."

My raspy voice probably screams of desperation, but I couldn't care less.

After rolling on the condom, he settles himself between my spread legs, his gaze solely focused on mine.

He eases himself slowly inside me, and we both moan and groan simultaneously. Without even thinking about what I'm doing, I wrap my legs around his back, urging him on with my movements. Before I know it, we've settled into a rapid pace, neither of us having any patience left to draw this out even a moment longer.

My next orgasm is right around the corner, the buzzing already so strong I'm almost afraid to go over the edge.

"Come for me, sweetheart." His hand moves between us, rubbing me until I'm a goner.

I explode around him, pushing him right over the edge with me as I experience the most intense orgasm of my life.

Without warning, Hudson collapses on top of me while we try to get our frenzied breathing under control.

As he nestles into my neck, his low voice tickles my sensitive skin. "I'll get right off you. I just need a minute."

Laughing, I squeeze his butt lazily. "Don't you dare. I like having you here."

He turns his face my way, our gazes locking. "What am I supposed to do with you?"

"I have an idea or two. Maybe more."

"I bet you do." He brushes a strand of hair out of my face and places a kiss on my nose. "And trust me, I want to hear about every single one of them."

We stay there for another few minutes, waiting for our hearts to slow down before starting all over again.

I don't think the high from all of this will wear off anytime soon, but I'm more than okay with that.

CHAPTER THIRTY-THREE

"Gosh, I could just eat you up. Look at you and those cheeks of yours. Charlie, have you seen her cheeks?" Hudson is sitting on a stool in the bakery, Mirabelle perched on the big working table in front of him. He has his arms around her like a cage, making sure she's safe while they're playing together.

Since the bakery opening is getting closer, the three of us spend as much time together here as possible, even though I have to be honest and admit that my mind hasn't been as much on the bakery lately as it used to be. What was once my sole focus—besides Mira, of course—has quickly given way to Hudson, and the rest of his family too.

I'm still extremely excited about the opening, but now I know it won't be responsible for most of my happiness. Others things—or rather, people—have snuck into my life, mixing up my priority list a little. I quickly realized there's nothing wrong with that, though. Now I'll be able to enjoy both my business and everyone that has come to mean so much to me in my life.

Hudson's looking at me expectantly, and I have to chuckle. "Mmm, let me think. I might have noticed those cute cheeks a time or two, silly."

"Listen to your mama, Mira. She's being all sassy since we've, you know, done some grown-up stuff." He wiggles his eyebrows at me, and I gasp.

If it wasn't for Mira being right in front of him, I'd have thrown something at him.

"Would you stop it already?" I giggle and walk over to him, squeezing his arm, though I'm not sure if that's supposed to be punishment for him or enjoyment for me. I know I'd be mighty fine feeling his muscles all day long. "You can't keep making those remarks all the time."

He looks at me like I just told him I lost his favorite toy. "What? Why not? I want everyone to know you're mine."

I give him a look I hope conveys all the happy feelings that are coursing through me whenever he's around, or when I think of him. "Maybe try a more subtle way? Not everyone needs to know what we do behind closed doors, you know?"

"Or against a tree."

This time, I almost choke on my own spit. "I can't believe you, you're incorrigible." I grip his arm with some more force now, but am unable to hold back a chuckle.

He's laughing loudly, clearly enjoying this little game of his. "You know I'm just kidding. I'll keep the details to myself, don't you worry. I'm way too selfish to share you with anyone, in any way. Although, I do hope I can tell the whole world about how awesome you are at some point—how awesome you *both* are."

I lean back against the table next to Mirabelle. "You really want to do that? That's kind of a big deal."

Apparently, Mirabelle likes having us both so close. She's giggling and swinging her little toys around, hitting Hudson with them more often than not. As always, he's a good sport about it.

Lucky us.

Hoisting her up on his arm, he stands up to get closer to me. "You bet I do. I'll zip it for the public, for now, but in no way will I back away from you in our normal life, now that I finally got you. I want to be with you whenever I can and not worry about the media possibly seeing us. Can you handle that?"

Taking a deep breath, I nod. It's not like I haven't thought about this exact thing before. I know who he is, and I'm aware it's all a big part of his life. I'd never have started anything with him without making a conscious decision about his mostly very public life. I've realized I don't have to love it, only accept it for what it is and be okay with that.

Nestling into his other side opposite Mirabelle, I look up at him. "That's only fair, I suppose. It's not like I can keep my hands off of you anyway." I stick out my tongue at him, and he winks at me in return.

I like our exchanges. They bring me so much joy, I want to pinch myself sometimes.

This lightheartedness was exactly what was missing in my life.

"That's what I like to hear, sweetheart."

Hearing Hudson call me sweetheart still makes my heart go into overdrive every single time.

He bends down to give me a soft kiss when Mirabelle starts banging her toys on both our heads.

"Little stinker, you." Hudson takes his hand from around

me and starts tickling her, making my heart explode at the sight of them.

"Aww, Charming. Look at them! All unicorns and rainbows here." Monica's distinct voice sounds behind us, and I turn around to wave at her and Gabe.

"Hey, guys. What are you doing here?"

Gabe points at his brother. "Didn't Hudson tell you he requested a man talk with me?" He chuckles when Hudson shakes his head. "Plus, I could use a much-needed break from this one here." He nods toward Monica, who blows him a kiss.

Those guys have the funniest dynamic I've ever seen between two people. I have absolutely no idea what's going on there, but they sure are entertaining.

She pokes him in the chest. "Be nice or I won't make you dinner tonight."

"All right, all right. I promise I'll behave now." He holds up both of his hands in defense, and I understand why.

Where I'm good at baking, Monica's good at cooking, even though she barely does it with all the traveling and mostly living in hotels.

Hudson ignores them and moves in front of me, blocking me from view. "Is it okay if we take Mira for a walk? I thought she'd like that."

"Of course, she's gonna love it." I give him a big smile, feeling all warm and fuzzy about the way he takes such good care of my baby girl. I never knew how incredibly sexy that could be, and I plan on showing him later on exactly how much of a turn-on it is.

I lean in to give Mira a kiss and some snuggles, chuckling when she already starts waving bye-bye.

"We'll see you in a bit, sweetheart." Hudson bends down to kiss my cheek before walking over to the back door to put Mirabelle in her stroller.

Monica hops over to stand beside me as we watch Hudson pack up some of Mira's things while Gabe entertains her.

What a sight.

I nudge Monica with my elbow just as both men look up. When they see us watching, they smile, satisfied with themselves.

Such guys.

They leave a minute later, looking as adorable as they possibly could.

Not a second after the door closes behind them, Monica turns around to face me, an eager expression on her face. "So, spill the beans, *sweetheart*."

"You heard that, huh?" Before going back to my workstation, I pull over the big recliner Hudson brought from the house for Monica.

"Of course I heard that, silly." She sits down in the chair, letting out a big huff. "Thanks."

"Welcome." I look at her, trying to get a good read on her. "How are you feeling?"

She doesn't like talking about herself a lot, but I don't need her to tell me how crappy she's sleeping to know it's true. The dark circles under her eyes say it all.

Shrugging her shoulders, she gets comfortable in the chair. "I'm okay. I'll get through it, and that's all that matters. Now stop distracting me, and clue me in."

She studies me like a hawk, trying to find a hint of an answer on my face. "You totally screwed the rockstar, didn't you?" Her eyes go wide. "Oh my freaking gosh, I can't believe it. You really did."

I chuckle at her expression, unable to deny that I'm torn. On one side, I want to tell her everything, but on the other, I want to keep it all to myself. Using a middle ground might seem like the way to go. "No, I didn't *screw* him, Mo."

Her excited expression falls at once, and I have a hard time trying not to laugh. Goodness, I actually feel a little bad for her right now.

Taking pity on her, I train my eyes on her face. "But I might have had sex with him."

Her head falls back on the chair, and she laughs, hitting the armrest hard with her fist. "I knew it." She points her finger at me, wiggling it around. "Tell me everything, no matter how small a detail it is."

Shaking my head at her, I finally chuckle. She knows I'm so not a kiss-and-tell person, not even with her.

She sticks her tongue out at me. "Ugh, you're so lame. You know I haven't gotten any action in forever, and there's no end to that drought in the near future either. Come on, help a friend out here. I have to vicariously live through you now."

"Always so dramatic."

She shrugs her shoulders, and I know she doesn't mind comments like that, since she knows I'm right. "Was it good, at least?"

I sigh, finishing up the dough I started before placing it in a bread form. "Very."

"Everything you thought it would be?"

That's an easy nod from me. "Pretty much, and then some."

"And you want lots more of it?"

"Mmm yes, please." I have to laugh at her continuous inquisition.

She smirks at me, satisfaction evident on her face. "I thought so. Good for you. About time you got a good guy."

"Thanks, Mo." I stop laughing and smile at her.

This woman might be a dramatic goofball at times, but there's a reason she's my friend. She's loyal and incredibly supportive, always looking out for me and wanting my best.

"I'm serious. You deserve this more than anyone I know. You've had a crapload of stuff to go through in your life. Now it's finally time to be happy with your adorable baby and a good guy by your side." She sighs, something I don't see her do very often. "And he's obviously got it bad for you. Plus, he adores Mira, so he gets my approval."

I snort, but on the inside, I try to keep my emotions in check after everything she just said. "Thank goodness."

"Don't get all cheeky with me, I'm serious."

"I know, I know. We just haven't really talked about us yet." I know we have to do this at some point soon. I need to know exactly where we're standing, but just thinking about having *the talk* with Hudson gives me an anxiety attack. Even though he did mention wanting to tell everyone about us and not wanting to share me either.

"Everyone who's been around you two knows you guys are meant for each other. Just bring it up next time." She says it so nonchalantly, I have to laugh. Monica would do something like that, just *bring it up* in the middle of a normal conversation.

I'd probably pee my pants.

Her comment makes me pause for a moment, though,

wondering if she's actually right about Hudson. I mean, I'd like to think so, but I also just had lots of sex with the man, so I'm not sure if my observation skills are very spot-on when it comes to him.

"Please, just remember I look awful in pink." Her eyes are wide, and she shivers slightly, as if she's trying to shake off a bad memory.

I laugh at her remark and her expression, but I'm also a bit confused. "I will never forget that, trust me. That bubblegum party was cute, though. Your mom meant well. Why are we talking about this?"

Tilting her head to the side, she gives me a pointed look. "For my bridesmaid dress, of course. Come on, C. Keep up."

"You're unbelievable. We're not talking about my wedding. There is no wedding to talk about."

"Maybe not right now, but definitely in the future."

"You're crazy." I take a new ball of dough out of a container, and knead it over and over, trying hard to ignore her. As usual, she won't have it, calling my name until I finally look back up at her. "All right. What do you want, Mo?"

"In the end, it's all really easy, you know." She pauses for a moment before continuing. "It all comes down to one thing."

Another dramatic pause where she stares me down.

"Are you in love with Hudson or not?"

Her question hits me right in the chest, and I stop breathing for a moment. Fleeting thoughts of affection, or having a crush on him, have floated around in my mind for a while now. But until this moment, I haven't really thought about the big "L" word, and I'm not sure I'm ready for it yet either.

CHAPTER THIRTY-FOUR

My conversation with Monica from the other day has been pretty much replaying nonstop in my mind, making me unable to think about much else. It's gotten to the point where I listen to Hudson sleep next to me while I lie awake for hours at night, my brain going in circles over and over again. I'm exhausted, to say the least, and I know I need to do something about it.

Hannah sits down next to me on the couch, her presence pulling me back to reality. After taking a sip of her drink, she smiles at me. "Penny for your thoughts?"

I close the laptop perched on my legs with a loud *thud*—it's not like I was getting anything done anyway. After putting Mirabelle to bed a little while ago, I tried to get some work done, but I should have known better. I'm a lost cause right now.

Looking over at Hannah, I'm not sure how much to disclose to her. She *is* Hudson's grandma, after all. Surely, she'd take sides, wouldn't she? "I don't know. Just a lot of stuff going on, I guess."

Hannah has quickly become one of my favorite people in life. She's been nothing but wonderful to me and Mira, and has also been one of my biggest supporters from the very beginning. I know, for a fact, I wouldn't be so close to fulfilling my dream of opening my own bakery if it wasn't for her, nor would I be emotionally in the place I am right now without her guidance over the last year.

I can't exactly go and tell her I'm trying to figure out my feelings for her grandson, now can I? The last thing I want to do is cause any tension between us—I don't think I could take that.

She only nods, ever the calm person. "Is there anything I can do to help?"

I shake my head. "You're already doing so much. I couldn't have handled everything without all of your help in the bakery and with Mira. You've truly been a lifesaver, in more than one way."

"Oh, stop it already, it's nothing. I love you guys, you're family. Of course I'll help you whatever way I can. There's nothing special about that."

"It's very special to me. Trust me, I'll be forever grateful for everything you've done for us. I wouldn't be *here* if it wasn't for you." I give her a big smile, really wanting to convey that I mean it.

"You're very welcome, dear. I know you're stressed about the bakery opening coming up, but it's going to be great. You've worked hard for this and almost everything is ready. All you need to do now is show up, and bake some delicious things for everyone. Easy peasy for you." She pauses for a moment and studies me. "That's not all that's going on though, is it?"

Putting my laptop on the coffee table in front of us, I grab my wine glass instead. "Not exactly." I sink back into the soft couch cushions and let out a loud sigh.

"That bad, huh?" Hannah chuckles softly.

I shrug my shoulders several times. "Maybe. Yes. Probably not. I don't know." That sentence is the perfect depiction of how crazy my thoughts are right now.

They're all over the dang place.

She has that knowing look in her eyes, that's somehow intimidating and reassuring, all at the same time. "This is about my lovely grandson, isn't it?"

Somehow, I'm still surprised by her uncanny ability to know what's going on, even though I really should be used to it by now. "Yeah."

"And since you two have been inseparable, I'm guessing your problem is a matter of the heart?"

This woman.

My eyes go wide as I stare at her. Either she can read my mind, or she has some other supernatural power.

She laughs at my expression. "As much as I like to pretend otherwise, I've been around for a while now, sweet Charlie. I've experienced a lot and have seen even more. And knowing your history, I was actually just waiting for you to come to this point."

Closing my eyes for a moment, I'm willing the emotions away that are trying to bubble to the surface. "I'm not sure what I want. I don't know what the right thing to do is."

She pats my arm gently. "You know, doing the right thing when it comes to love is tricky because it's not the same for everyone. What's good for one person isn't necessarily good for the next. What's going too fast for some people might be taking too long for others. Love has its own, very non-conforming way for all of us—it's unique, just like every human is."

Taking a moment to process all that info, I study her curiously. "You really think so?"

She laughs loudly. "Oh, you bet. Back when I saw my old Frank for the first time, I knew right then and there that he was it for me. I was sure there would never be a man in my life that I'd love as much as I loved him, and I was right. I loved him with all my heart until his very last day. Things now with Paul are completely different. We've been friends for years, but sparks didn't start flying until last year—it came somewhat out of the blue. For me, at least. And I know I can't compare these two people and relationships in any way, but I do know they're both wonderful."

"That makes sense, I guess." As embarrassing as it is—and I wouldn't admit it out loud either—I've gotten most of my love information and advice from books and other media forms. No one in my family has ever been very successful when it comes to love and relationships. Mo has been my only close friend growing up—and her main love has always been dancing.

"Love is a gift we should enjoy as much as we possibly can when we're given it. Take it as it is—one of the best and most beautiful things that can ever happen to you if you find the right person." She can probably hear my wheels spinning, because she gives me a moment.

I trust Hannah and her advice in a way I don't trust anything else, so I'm trying to make a real effort and take her words to heart.

"There are a few things you should ask yourself, Charlie.

Do you want to fall asleep and wake up next to that one person for the rest of your life? Do they make you happy? I mean, *really* happy and also a better person? Do they treat you well? Are they the first person you want to tell about your good day or when something exciting happens? And are they the first person you want a hug from after a bad day? All very simple questions, but the answers are not only crucial, they also make all the difference."

She looks at me as if I should know all of the answers right now. Is that the problem and what I'm so hung up on, or do I already know all the answers?

"Hey." Hannah nudges my shoulder. "I know this is freaking you out. You're still so young, and you've already gone through so much in your life. I get it. I'd be scared too. But that's exactly the reason you have to look for these answers and follow your heart. Because if you never do anything you're scared of, you'll never truly live either. And you, my friend, deserve to live life to the fullest. More than anyone else I know."

Her words hit me so deeply, bringing back all the pain and hurt from growing up in a messed-up family, to losing the only family I had left and unexpectedly becoming a mother in the same moment, just to be left by my fiancé the day after.

All of that has made me more wary of life than anything else ever has. The question now is, will I let the fact that things can end badly at any moment rule my fears or my desire to live life to the fullest?

Turning to Hannah, I let out a big breath, trying to calm myself down enough so the overwhelming emotions won't turn into tears. "Thank you. Seems like I have a lot to think about."

She nods, giving me her signature grandmotherly smile that's both reassuring and calming. Before she can say anything else, Hudson's voice comes from behind us.

"Ah, there are my two favorite girls." He walks around the couch to stand in front of us. "Well, there's one more, but she's sleeping right now, so I guess that leaves you two."

"You charmer, you." Hannah looks amused, wiggling her finger at her grandson.

Hudson bends down between us on the couch to kiss our cheeks. "It's true, Grandma. I swear." He winks at me. "I'm gonna get something to drink. Do you guys want anything?"

I shake my head while Hannah pushes herself off the couch. "I'm good, honey, but thank you. It's late, so I'm going to leave you kids to it and try to get some sleep. It's been a busy week."

"Goodnight, Grandma." He kisses her cheek one more time before wandering into the kitchen, leaving me and Hannah alone again.

She lowers her voice so only I can hear her. "I'm here for you, no matter what, even if you just want to talk some more. Believe in yourself, because I think you know exactly what you want, sweetie. Don't be afraid to get it and hold onto it tightly." She walks around the couch and squeezes my shoulder once more when she passes me. "I'll see you tomorrow. Have a good night."

"You too, Hannah. And thank you, again."

"Always." She waves me off, slowly walking out of the room.

Hudson strolls back over after a moment, a bottle of beer and a bowl of grapes in his hands. "Everything okay? Grandma had her lecturing look on her face."

Choking on the sip of wine I just took, I put the glass back down on the table so I don't spill anything.

Not even waiting a beat, he sets down his bottle and bowl and puts his arm around me, gently rubbing my back until my coughs finally subside.

As if it's second nature, I lean into his touch, immediately feeling comforted by his presence.

His phone vibrates in his pocket, and he lets out a big sigh. "Let me turn that off quickly."

"Maybe it's important." I try and move out of his embrace but he holds onto me.

"I'm pretty sure it's my manager, again. He's been driving me crazy these past few days. He calls me all the time. Apparently, he thinks my time's up and I need to make a decision. Even though he knows we'll tell him as a group next week, after we see each other at the wedding."

"I'm sorry. Hopefully he can understand." I give his arm a squeeze. "Are you excited to see everyone again?"

He shrugs his shoulders, as he starts playing with my fingers. "Yes and no. I do miss my bandmates and playing with them, but I don't miss all the stress surrounding it. Plus, I've been really enjoying being here too—with you." With a sparkle in his eyes, he leans down to kiss me.

His lips are very loving, soft and sweet against mine, and my heart responds immediately. My heartbeat increases, and it distracts me so much that it pulls me out of the moment, my thoughts going back to my conversations with Monica and Hannah.

"Everything okay?" His eyebrows furrow as he looks at me with concerned eyes.

"Hudson, we need...I think we need to talk."

He nods. "Good. Because I wanted to talk to you too."

CHAPTER THIRTY-FIVE

WHY ON EARTH DID I AGREE TO HAVE OUR TALK IN THE bedroom? I've clearly lost my mind because that just screams *bad idea* from miles away. Looking everywhere in the spacious bedroom except at Hudson, I continuously wipe my hands on my pants. My stomach is tied up in knots, cramping, and making me feel nauseous.

Please, don't let me get sick. That's definitely the absolute last thing I need right now.

Hudson pats the spot next to him on the couch. "Come over here and sit down with me, please. You're starting to make me all nervous."

After taking a deep breath, I walk over to him, my thoughts still going in one big dizzying loop.

Do I really want to have this talk with him? Maybe we can just keep going like we have been. It seems to have worked pretty well so far.

And what on earth does *he* want to talk to me about?

Maybe he wants to end things, while I'm contemplating taking the next step.

"Charlie." Hudson's voice is low, and I realize I stopped walking toward him. Instead, I've been pacing back and forth in the middle of the room, probably making him think I've really lost my marbles.

Getting up from the couch, he walks over to me, his steps slow and cautious. The look on his face reminds me of a person approaching a scared or injured animal, something that looks ready to run at any moment.

Well, that *does* sound kind of appropriate, I suppose.

"What has you so upset?" He's a few feet away from me, apparently planning on giving me some space, and eyeing me warily while scratching his chin. "Did something happen? Are you not feeling well?"

Closing my eyes for a moment, I take a deep breath. Right then and there, I decide to do something that is completely out of character for me, but it just feels right. I might possibly regret it in about two seconds, but I'm not going to beat around the bush.

Full-on honesty, no holding back.

"Mo asked me if I'm in love with you."

Well, how's that for directness?

A quiet "Oh" is all I hear from him before there's only silence again—just absolute, soul-piercing, heart-wrenching silence.

In fact, it's so quiet, I'm sure I could hear a feather fall to the ground. I look down at the floor, absentmindedly tracing an imaginary pattern on the rug with my foot. I can't look at him, my brain contemplating if it might be best to just leave and sleep in my room for the night.

My breath hitches when his feet appear in my line of vision, stopping right in front of my own—toes to toes.

His fingers move under my chin, gently pushing it up until my eyes meet his beautiful brown ones. "Hey." He brushes a few strands of hair out of my face and gently caresses my cheek. "Why does that have you so tied up in knots?"

Grabbing my hand, he leads me over to the couch, not leaving any room between us when we sit down. "Please look at me." His voice is soft yet commanding, making me peer up at him. "I think you know by now that I'm pretty straightforward and honest, right? I just don't see the point in holding back."

I nod because he's right, that's all he's ever been since we met.

He runs his hand through his hair before looking at the ceiling for a moment, blowing out a big breath. "Man, this is harder than I thought it was going to be."

Well, *that's* certainly not helping with my nerves.

He's totally going to say this was fun, but he's not looking for anything more, isn't he? I should have walked away earlier when I still had the chance.

"I'm falling in love with you, Charlie."

Wait. *What?*

My lips are moving but no sound is coming out.

All the while, Hudson is staring at me, probably waiting for a reply, or at least some sort of reaction.

"You what?" My voice doesn't sound like my own. It's several octaves higher, and my throat feels like it hasn't felt any liquid in ages.

Taking my hands in his, he gives me one of his breathtaking smiles I can't ever get enough of. "I've been falling for you for quite a while now. It's been getting more and more intense every day, and I just need you to know. You deserve to know how I feel about you."

The butterflies in my belly act like they're on steroids. I'm about to smile back at him, when I see a sudden dull in his gaze—right before his smile drops a little too.

"Why do I feel like there's a but coming?" My insides start cramping up, not wanting to hear anything negative after the beautiful words he just said. My stomach is churning, making me wonder if I could actually make it to the bathroom in time if I had to.

Clearing his throat, his eyes fixate on mine. "You've been on my mind from the very first moment I laid eyes on you—and not just because of the whole music thing. You're different than any woman I've ever met, and once I got to know you better, I was completely under your spell. And you didn't even notice it nor did you seem to care much about it either. Being with you has been incredibly refreshing, and I can't even begin to tell you how much I enjoy every single minute we spend together." The look in his eyes is warm and soft, but my body doesn't want to relax yet.

I'm still unsure if his admission makes the situation better or worse right now, knowing there's still something bad coming—at least that's what it seems like.

There's a sudden sparkle in his eyes that wasn't there before. "And then there's Mira, making this whole relationship with you and what we have even more special."

I'm starting to lose the battle with my emotions, his words hitting me straight in the heart. I can't take it any longer, my throat starting to clog up, my voice already sounding scratchy. "Hudson, please. Just tell me what's going on."

He clears his throat again. "You guys mean so much to

me, which is why I don't want to hurt you, especially after knowing what you've already had to go through before."

Tears form in the corners of my eyes, and I try my hardest to hold them back. I'm still utterly confused, and my patience is starting to dwindle too—the tension and anxiety in my body is threatening to take over. "Say it already. I need to know."

Shaking his head, he scratches the back of his neck. "I'm not doing a good job right now, am I? I've actually been wanting to talk to you about all of this for a while, but I didn't want to scare you off. And now I'm making a complete mess of things."

I can't help but exhale the breath of frustration that's been lodged in my throat.

Dropping my hands unexpectedly, he gets up and starts pacing in front of me. "Crap, I'm really bad at this. All right. Let me start over again." He stops and goes down on his knees in front of me. "Charlie, I'm utterly in love with you, and I want nothing more than to be with you and Mira, for us to be a family. The time with you two has been some of the best of my life, and I can't remember the last time I was this content and just...happy. But, I don't know what my future holds right now, and I'm not sure you want to deal with my crazy life, not knowing what's going to happen with my career either."

"What on earth are you talking about?"

"I want to give you everything you deserve. A partner by your side to help you fulfill your dreams, and someone who can help raise Mira. You should wake up next to someone every morning and go to sleep next to that same person every night, not spend endless nights alone in bed. I don't want you to go through that. I can't do that to you. You deserve more than that."

With that confession, I lose my emotional battle. A few tears flow down my cheeks as I try to keep my sniffles at a minimum.

"No, no. Please don't cry, sweetheart." He captures my face in his hands, wiping away my tears with his thumbs. "That's the last thing I wanted."

Once I think I can manage to speak again, I hardly recognize my voice, the words barely making it past the big lump in my throat. "Does it not matter at all what *I* want?"

Pausing mid-wipe, he looks at me with his brows furrowed. "Of course it does. You're what matters the most. I know we haven't known each other for very long, and you might think I'm crazy, but you're *it* for me. I don't think I can ever find what I have with you with anyone else. We've been spending almost every free minute together from the moment we met, and I've never formed a bond like this with another person. What I want more than anything else though, is to see you happy because that's what you deserve."

My hands are shaking, and I press my lips together so hard to keep them from trembling they must be as white as a sheet. Closing my eyes, I try and get a grip on my emotions. "*You* are what's best for me, Hudson. *You.*"

He starts blinking feverishly. "You want me, all of my crazy life included? Even if I can't be with you all the time?"

"Are you kidding me? Of course. This is your career, your dream. It's all a part of *you*, and I know we're going to figure it all out—together. Of course I won't like being away from you, but it's better than the alternative. Every day with you is so much better than any day spent alone or with someone else."

This is it.

Taking a deep breath, I try to listen to my inner voice that keeps telling me I can say the next few words. "Because I'm utterly and totally in love with you too."

Without a word, Hudson lunges for me and scoops me up, carrying me over to the bed. Ever so gently, he lays me down and stares at me like he can't believe I'm really there. "This is the best thing anyone has ever said to me."

He lowers himself on top of me until his head is against my chest. He stays there for a few moments, listening to my erratic heartbeat, this special moment forever imprinted in my memory.

Wiggling my hands out from between our bodies, I brush over his face and hair until he crawls further up. His eyes are full of emotions and close briefly as I trace over his eyebrows, down his nose, and finally across his lips. They are soft and automatically open as I touch them with my fingers. It's not a big movement, but it has my heartbeat accelerating like crazy.

When his eyes open lazily, he studies me in this quiet and serene moment. "I can't tell you how incredibly happy you make me."

I smile at him—a big, wide, beaming smile—hoping it silently tells him all the crazy feelings my heart is trying to express. "I think I have a pretty good idea because you make me just as happy."

Brushing his nose against mine, he whispers his first, "I love you," before capturing my lips in a deep kiss, showing me for the rest of the evening just how much I mean to him.

CHAPTER THIRTY-SIX

"You're so incredibly beautiful." Hudson's raspy voice tickles my neck from behind as I stretch like a cat.

Opening my eyes slowly—a huge grin on my face—I look back to see him propped up on one side, giving me the absolute best smile I could ever ask for. Waking up next to this gorgeous man never gets old, bringing a flurry of emotions with it every single morning. The last few days since our "love talk," as I like to call it, have been absolutely blissful—perfect, really.

I can't remember ever feeling this happy before.

"Good morning." I blink at him, my eyes still needing a moment to fully wake up. My body is quite the opposite, already tingling in all the right places as his hands start wandering down my body and under the blankets. Shaking my head, I chuckle. "You're insatiable."

"When it comes to you, absolutely. There's nothing better than having you under me, on top of me, or any other way I can have you—morning, noon, and night." He winks at me, probably feeling really smug.

Can't argue with that, though.

Being with Hudson feels like nothing I've ever felt. I'm close to the point of admitting I didn't even know what it meant to be intimate with someone before him—but it's silly and a little embarrassing to say that out loud, so I keep that little realization to myself. He's made such a big impression on me and my life—allowing me to enjoy the simplest things, just because everything is so much more fun with him by my side.

Raising my eyebrows at him, I start to push myself up on all fours and slowly crawl over until I'm hovering above him. "Oh yeah, is that so?"

That's another thing that has changed dramatically. I've started to be more confident and take things more into my own hands, so to speak. He spurs me on even more with the way he looks at me, especially when he does that little growl, right before he can't take it anymore and pulls me close to him.

Having his eyes darken with lust—just like right now—is a confidence booster like nothing else. I throw my leg over him, straddling him lazily while his hands roam up my legs and stop at my butt.

A moment later, he pulls me down onto him, groaning into my neck. "You're so damn sexy, you're driving me absolutely insane."

I lean in for a kiss, and our lips starting to move together in perfect sync when Mirabelle's babbling comes across the monitor. I close my eyes, as both Hudson and I groan in frustration.

He kisses me one more time before rolling us over so he's above me. "I love that girl, but sometimes her timing sucks.

Good thing I got my fair share of you last night, or I'd be really bummed right now." Looking at the baby monitor, he reaches past me to the nightstand to turn it off. "Why don't you go and get ready while I grab Miss Mira and make us something to eat?"

"Would you really?" I give him a big smile, feeling like I could explode with happiness. "You're the best, thank you."

"It's nothing. Let's get ready, and then we can have a relaxed breakfast together."

I nod. "Sounds great."

"See you in a few." One more kiss and he hops off the bed, my eyes following his every move as he leisurely walks over to the door in just his shorts. Before he slips out, he turns around one more time. "Hurry up, sweetheart, there's something I wanted to show you."

Begrudgingly, I get up a moment later, walking over to the en suite bathroom we've been sharing. It's a huge bathroom, almost as big as my tiny—and ridiculously expensive—apartment in New York used to be. It's easily big enough for both of us and then some, and I smile as I make my way over to the tiled walk-in shower to turn on the water.

When the temperature is good, I take off my pajamas and step under the warm water sprays. Several showerheads surround me, making this feel more like a spa experience than just a normal shower. My thoughts go to Hudson almost automatically, since he's quickly become one of my favorite things to think about—no matter if he's around or not. I'm still trying to wrap my head around how things have changed between us.

My mind can't help itself, jumping back to Sebastian and how different things were with him. I don't think I've ever realized how much was truly missing in our relationship until I met Hudson. It's so easy to dismiss relationships in general —especially after practically seeing every single one of my family members ever had fall apart—but now, I finally see things in a different light.

Now, I know all it takes is finding the right person.

A person that makes you—the real you, not someone you pretend to be—smile and happy at heart, even on bad days.

This euphoric feeling of being in love with someone that's right for you feels like magic. It's cloaking me in some sort of bewitched haze that makes me smile like a moron almost nonstop.

It also feels like my heart might explode at any moment, and I welcome both sensations with open arms.

Once I'm dressed, I go downstairs, coming up short when I enter the kitchen and see that Hudson and Mirabelle have a little party going on. Hudson is singing along to the music while Mirabelle is hopping in her little bouncer—in sync with the music, giggling almost uncontrollably every time Hudson leans down to directly sing to her.

My hand immediately goes to my chest because talk about the cutest sight ever.

Leaning against the doorframe, I enjoy the show as long as possible before they see me.

Boy, I've got it bad.

Oh yes, I do. And there's nothing wrong with that at all. Right?

The song ends, and when Hudson turns around to continue whatever he started making on the kitchen counter, he looks up at me. He smirks, knowing full well I was enjoying their little performance.

Show-off.

Mirabelle finally spots me too, shrieking and throwing her hands up in the air. She jumps as fast as she can, making the toys on the bouncer rattle and shake.

I walk over to her, crouching down on the floor to be on the same level. "Hi, cutie pie, did you have a good night?" I lean in to shower her with kisses until her little giggles are all I hear. We give each other the same happy smiles before I grab her under her arms to lift her out of the seat.

Walking to Hudson with Mira on one hip, I bump his with my other. "Hey, rockstar, nice performance you did there."

He chuckles, stirring some eggs in one pan before flipping a pancake in another. "Don't even try to pretend you didn't like it."

I shake my head and snort, snatching a piece of banana from the cutting board and sharing with Mira. "Never. It was awe-inspiring."

He leans over to give me a soft kiss on my lips before kissing Mira on the cheek too. "Good, good. That's what I like to hear, pleasing the crowds." He nods to all the food everywhere. "Breakfast will be done in a minute. Why don't you put Mira in her chair? I'll bring everything over."

I nod, leaning my head on his shoulder. "Thank you."

"Welcome, sweetheart." He gives my forehead a kiss before I move away. "Anything for you."

The butterflies and hummingbirds in my belly feel like they might break out at any moment, they're fluttering that hard.

Mira and I walk over to the table—the one that's already set, thanks to Mr. Rockstar. I put her in her chair, tie her bib, and click the tray in place. After putting a few pieces of cereal on her tray, I walk back over to the kitchen.

"I said I was gonna bring it." Hudson shakes his head before handing me a plate with toast and a bowl full of scrambled eggs, while he snatches up the plate of pancakes and a bowl of fresh fruit.

"I know, but I want to help." Everything smells delicious, and I inhale deeply. "It looks yummy. You didn't have to make all of this."

He blinks at me. "I know, but I wanted to. Now, let's go and sit down before it gets cold. I'll feed Mira."

Bossy rockstar. "Okay."

I sit down in my chair and watch Hudson as he heads back into the kitchen to get Mirabelle's bowl. Once he's seated, he starts feeding Mira her oatmeal while eating his own food at the same time.

Stopping mid-bite, he looks over at me. "What's wrong? You haven't touched your food yet."

"Oh," is all that comes out of my mouth before I shake myself out of my trance. "Sorry, I was just lost in thought. I guess I'm still amazed that you take such good care of not only me, but Mira especially."

He puts his fork down. "Does that bother you? Am I taking over too much? I never meant to push you out of the way."

"What? No, no. That's not at all what I meant." But what exactly am I going to tell him? That I'm still afraid this is all just a dream I'll wake up from at some point because let's be real, Hudson seems like the perfect guy. I don't think I'm not worthy of a great guy, but I also know—sadly, firsthand—that not every guy wants a woman who comes with a baby in tow. It's a lot to take on. "You're amazing, that's all. I just have those moments when it hits me, and I'm not always sure what I did to deserve you."

Self-doubt is a total bitch, creeping in at the worst and utterly unwanted times, and I hate her from the bottom of my heart. Sometimes I wish I could just turn off my brain to escape those thoughts, for a little while, at least, but I think we all just do our best to move on from them.

"I keep asking myself the same thing." His voice is soft and gentle, as he cocks his head to the side and reaches out to touch my hand. "Without a doubt, you two are the very best things that have ever happened to me, and I don't want you to ever doubt that for even a moment, all right?"

I nod, my emotions clogging up my throat too much to speak.

After squeezing my hand, he gives me a small smile. "Now, let's eat up, there's something I want to show you."

I totally forgot about that, and give him a small smile. "Okay."

***

Once we're done with breakfast and everything is cleaned up, Hudson leads us upstairs to one of the spare bedrooms. I've never been in here, except that one time when Hannah put a few of our things in here we didn't need.

When Hudson opens the door for us and walks in, I'm confused at what I'm seeing. Half the open space is covered in all sorts of baby things. Lots and lots of boxes and unpacked items.

I close the door after us so Mira can't get out before walking over to him. "What is all of this?"

"Well"—he scratches the back of his neck and grimaces when he looks at me—"I came in here this morning to get our suitcases for the wedding next week, and stumbled across a few boxes in the back of the closet that I'd totally forgotten about."

Clearing his throat, he opens his arms toward the big pile in front of us. "This is the result of me going overboard when I thought I was going to be a dad soon last year. Obviously, I can easily see now that I went a little crazy. I put all of the stuff in the corner of the closet after Addy and I broke up and just tried to forget about it."

"Oh." I'm not sure what else to say. Seeing this huge heap in front of us makes my heart hurt once more for Hudson. That stupid excuse of a woman. I'll never understand how she could do that to him, especially since she knew how much he wanted to be a father.

I stay quiet, but take his hand in mine to let him know I'm right here for him.

"Maybe I should've returned things last year, or donated them, but I guess I wasn't ready to let go of it yet." He turns around to face me while Mira is inspecting everything at our feet. His eyes are full of emotions when he looks at me. "If it's okay with you, though, I'd like to give a few things to Mira. There are a lot of items for little babies, but some are for toddlers and little kids too. I can put the baby stuff away again, but thought I could give some of it to Dahlia for her art classes. I'm sure the little kiddos would be thrilled to have something to play with while they wait for their classes to start."

"I bet they'd love that." Seeing him like this is doing something to my heart, something permanent no one can ever undo or change. Looking down at Mira, I smile. "And I bet she'll be happy about a few new toys too."

"Perfect."

He's letting go of his own troubled past that hurt him so much because he wants to make all these other kids, and my little girl, happy instead. And who am I kidding, Hudson and Mira have each other so tightly wrapped around their fingers that she's well on her way—if not already there—of becoming *his* little girl too.

I'm in so deeply, I'm not sure there's ever going to be a way out for me again—not that I'd want that.

CHAPTER THIRTY-SEVEN

Knowing about Hudson being famous is one thing, but actually experiencing it firsthand, is totally different. Not only did his fame hit me in the face like a bat out of hell, but also his wealth, and I'm not sure I can ever get used to either.

I definitely know I wasn't prepared for what was waiting for me on our trip to Los Angeles for the wedding—not one bit.

Hudson had to all but drag me onto the airplane when I noticed it was a private jet. I stood there, frozen, not knowing where to look first. He quickly told me it wasn't his, just a loan from a friend—as if that would make it all better.

Okay, maybe it did make a teeny bit of a difference.

Once we landed in L.A., we were joined by two huge bodyguards—Tommy and Mason—who didn't leave our sides as we made our way to the super popular hotel. They both tried their best to keep us as guarded from the paparazzi as possible, who seemed to be expecting us at the back entrance of the hotel when we arrived.

When we finally make it to our hotel room, I feel like I've been taken through the wringer.

After putting away our most important things, I plop down on the huge bed with Mira, looking around the ginormous suite we're staying in, and let out the biggest sigh ever. "What a trip."

Hudson is quiet, studying me like he's been doing ever since we left the house. I'm not sure if he thought I wouldn't notice his eyes on me, but I feel them constantly.

He walks over and sits down on the edge of the bed, making sure Mira won't fall off. "You're okay? Getting into the hotel was a bit more intense than I thought it would be. They told us there wouldn't be any photographers at the back."

Mira hoists herself up on my belly, moving her little hips and dancing to some sort of rhythm only she can hear.

"Hi, sweetie." I brush back the hair that keeps falling into her face before I try to secure the little hair tie at the top of her head again.

Hannah offered to babysit Mira so we could go to L.A. by ourselves, but Hudson all but insisted we bring her, which made me happy. I don't think it would've sat well with me to just leave her back home like that. I already feel guilty enough for spending so much time away from her, with all the bakery stuff going on.

Except, I've been neglecting that too, since things got more serious between Hudson and me. Thankfully, I wasn't in an extreme rush with the bakery anyway, so I just pushed the opening back a little. Now it's only a week away, right after Mira's first birthday. I thought it would be fun.

"Do you already regret coming here?" Hudson's voice

pulls me out of my thoughts, and I look up at his face. If he frowns any more, those lines will be etched in his skin forever.

Snatching Mira, I snuggle her to my chest and look over her shoulder at Hudson. "Stop worrying so much. I thought that was my job."

He exhales in a half-huff, half-chuckle, and I realize he already seems to be in a funk about it.

Is that why he's been watching me so intently this whole trip? To gauge my reaction?

Is he expecting me to freak out?

Reaching out, I snatch his hand from his bouncing leg and intertwine it with mine. "We're here, and we're gonna have fun watching your friend tie the knot, all right?"

One corner of his mouth pulls up before it morphs into a small smile. "Yeah. I think I've been gone for too long already from all of this, so it's stressing me out more than usual. I can't handle the thought of one of those paparazzi douchebags looking at you the wrong way, or making a rude remark."

"Hey. I'm a big girl, and I can take care of myself."

"I know." His fingers play with mine as he avoids my gaze. "I still don't like it."

"Hudson."

His gaze snaps up to mine, and the vulnerability is clear as day.

I pull my hand from his and brush it over his cheek. "I'm here because of you. *You're* what's important in this whole scenario, not any of the other stuff. But I'll get used to that too."

Mira chooses that moment to lean her head back and

yawn. Poor thing hasn't slept since we left the house this morning.

Hudson kisses Mira's forehead before getting off the bed. "Why don't you put her down, and I'll jump into the shower quickly."

I nod. "Sounds good." I get up but pause before going into Mira's adjacent room. "Okay, remind me again. The rehearsal dinner is at five tonight, and the wedding starts at eleven tomorrow?"

"Yup."

"Is that normal to have a wedding that early? I've never been to one before."

He drops the hem of his T-shirt he'd just started to lift.

Dang it. Bad timing.

It never gets old to see him without clothes.

Hudson walks over to me, tilting his head to the side. "You've never been to a wedding before? Really?"

Shaking my head, I shrug my shoulders, making Mira move around in the process. "Nope. Never known anyone pregnant either—in case you were wondering."

Closing his eyes for a moment, he smirks at me. "Smartass. I guess I've just never thought about the possibility that not everyone's going to these things."

He's close enough that Mira can smack him in the face before she does the same to me. Hudson snatches her little hand and showers it with kisses. "Someone's getting grumpy, better get her to bed fast." After another kiss for Mira on the cheek, he leans in to give me a quick peck too—but not before Mira smacks him over the head one more time. "Save me from this wild baby. I'll see you in a minute."

This time, I don't interrupt him as he pulls up his shirt,

tossing it on the bed on his way to the bathroom. Mira's whimper makes me sigh, my focus snapping back to her as we make our way into her temporary room.

She passes out the second her head hits the mattress, and with the baby monitor in hand, I rush back into our room, making a straight beeline for the bathroom. Thankfully, Hudson's been taking his time. After I manage to strip off my clothes in record time, I step into the shower behind him.

He sighs loudly when I slip my hands around his middle, kissing and nipping at his back until he turns around. His hands cup my cheeks as he pulls me into him, his hardness pushing into my belly. With his hands, mouth, and tongue everywhere, I'm hot and ready in no time at all, feeling like I might combust at any moment. Hudson seems to feel the same when he whispers, "I need you," in my ear.

A minute later, I'm hoisted up against the shower wall, listening to Hudson's guttural grunts as he pushes himself into me, over and over. Thank goodness we had the whole birth control talk last week. I've quickly realized having sex without a barrier between us brings the experience to a whole new level. It still surprises me every single time how good it feels.

Hours later, I'm holding my belly, unable to remember the last time I laughed this much. The rehearsal dinner has been a ton of fun, way more than I expected. Most people have already left, leaving only us and Hudson's band members, plus their significant others.

Hudson just told everyone how we met, even though I'm

still not sure why. Not only did I attack him, but I also didn't recognize him. You'd think that's something he wouldn't want to tell his friends, but here he is, with the biggest smile on his face while everyone around the table howls with laughter.

Jodie—the bride-to-be—clasps my arm while wiping tears away. "This has got to be the cutest and funniest way anyone has ever met." The others around the table calm down and start talking about something else while Jodie continues her conversation with me, her voice hushed. "I hope you don't mind me saying this, but I'm so happy Hudson's found you— both of you." She looks at Mira, who's happily bouncing on one of my legs. "I've never seen him this happy, and even though the guys try to be all tough and manly, I know they're thrilled for him too."

"Thank you." I give her a smile that I hope shows my gratitude. I've tried really hard to hide it from Hudson, but my nerves were pretty shot at having to face the very people he usually spends most of his time with.

Worrying about fitting in, and people liking and accepting you never seems to get easier, no matter how old you get. Sometimes, it even seems to get worse.

She squeezes my arm again before letting go. "You guys make a great couple, and I'm so glad I finally got to meet you." Her mouth stays open like she wants to say more, but she's interrupted by a loud noise.

My eyes go wide, and my head automatically snaps over to look at Hudson.

A silent moment passes between us, where I'm still trying to figure out if I should be mortified or laugh about what's happening.

Hudson's lips are pressed together, the corners of his mouth twitching. "Was that what I think it was?"

We both look at Mira and her tomato-red face as she's grunting, clearly preoccupied.

Hudson claps his hands together before pushing his chair back. "Well, guys. This was fun, but it looks like we just got our cue to leave."

Just then, Mira lets out another groan, and it feels like her little bum is vibrating on my leg.

Poor baby. Pooping when you're sitting on something just seems to be the most uncomfortable thing ever, yet it's her favorite position to do it in.

Everyone around the table laughs as they catch on to what's going on, and we quickly say our goodnights. We make our way out of there and back up to our room as fast as we can before we start stinking up the whole place.

CHAPTER THIRTY-EIGHT

"Are you sure you're okay?" Hudson rubs my back for what must be the three hundredth time today.

Nodding through my sniffles, I see him biting his cheek and have to chuckle. "Stop it."

"What?" He's laughing now, holding out his hands in surrender. "I didn't say anything."

"You didn't have to." I wipe at my eyes, crossing my fingers I don't look like a raccoon, or worse. "Plus, it's not really my fault, you know?"

He shakes his head, trying to keep a straight face. "Of course not."

Gosh, he's so freaking cute, I could kiss his face all day long. I would, if it wasn't for a baby in my arms, and the fact we're currently standing in the hotel lobby. I needed a moment to collect myself after witnessing the most beautiful wedding I've ever seen before we head to the wedding reception. "It was so much better than it is in books or movies. I mean, gosh, did you see them?"

Hudson wraps his arm around me and gives my forehead

a kiss, quietly grinning against my skin. "I did see them. It was a great wedding."

I sigh loudly, leaning into his body, and let the familiar scent and warmth comfort me. "So beautiful. Makes me wanna go to a wedding every day."

He laughs into my hair, and I get it. Most men are probably not as much into weddings as women. For a lot of women, it seems to almost be a part of the female DNA; a built-in wedding strand, so to speak. But I'm okay with that—more than okay, actually. Witnessing Elijah and Jodie exchange their wedding vows and seeing their love for each other was one of the most extraordinary things I've ever seen. It was almost like another person in the room, it was that visible.

A wedding spirit.

I think it got to me.

Hudson squeezes my shoulder before letting go, taking Mira out of my arms. She's been trying to crawl to him for the last minute or two, impatient as ever. Hudson tickles her before looking back at me. "Do you think Mira is going to be okay for a while longer, or should she have a nap first and then we go to the reception afterward?"

"We should be good. It was really perfect timing this morning, with the wedding starting shortly after she woke up from her morning nap. And it didn't take too long either, so she should still have some time in her before she needs to go back down."

"Sounds good. Let's go get something to eat then." Hudson grabs my hand and pulls me in the direction of the ballroom, where the reception is being held.

"Charlotte?"

My feet stop, and I'm suddenly unable to breathe. My eyes grow so wide, they start burning, while my stomach rolls in a way that makes me look around in alarm, not sure I'll be able to keep my breakfast down.

My hand goes limp, slipping out of Hudson's, and my eyes close briefly. I force myself to focus on breathing in and out before my body fails me. The panic that has taken over is a living thing, trying to crush me from all possible sides, and I feel extra weak, afraid my heart won't ever recover from this shock.

"Charlotte." This time, the voice is louder, closer, and I cringe.

When I open my eyes, Hudson is right in front of me, a worried expression on his face that makes me swallow loudly. I whisper, "This can't be happening," under my breath before turning around, facing the inevitable.

And there he is.

Sebastian—in the flesh.

My stomach churns again as I try my best to keep the threatening nausea at bay. His blond hair is slicked back, and he's wearing a gray designer suit—his favorite piece of clothing. He's still handsome, but it's suddenly blatantly clear I have no idea what I ever saw in him. There's no warmth in his eyes, just cold disapproval. The hard lines on his face dominate everything else, intent on overpowering any softness that could possibly be there.

Hudson is tense behind me, and I'm worried he's going to push me aside at any moment.

I can't let that happen.

We both know exactly how that would end, and it would be a terrible headline for Hudson. I blindly reach for his arm behind me, and instinctively, I also move a little to the right to stand in front of Mira as much as possible.

Giving myself the fastest inner pep talk ever, I tell myself to be strong.

There's *no* reason to be intimidated by him.

I'm *not* the same person he left last year.

Staring him straight in the eye, I lift my chin slightly. "What are you doing here, Sebastian?" I'm thrilled my voice is strong and steady, nothing like the turmoil that's going on inside of me.

Hudson's arm started shaking the second Sebastian's name left my lips, and I tighten my hold on him reflexively. Never have I ever been so grateful before for him holding Mirabelle. I'm pretty certain she's the only reason he hasn't jumped my ex-fiancé yet.

"I'm attending a conference in town." He studies me from top to bottom before his gaze flickers to my hand on Hudson's arm and over to Mira—who, of course, keeps leaning around me to see what's going on. His chin nods toward my baby girl, and my teeth clench in response. "Is that—?"

"None of your business." My voice comes out in a low bark, my temper slowly rising as all of those old emotions come back, one by one. I didn't realize there was still so much anger left over what happened, but then, I've never been able to get full closure either.

He doesn't flinch, like other people would. Instead, he cocks his head to the side and studies me like I'm some science experiment he can't figure out. "You've changed since I last saw you. Must be this whole new life you're living now." His voice does this deadpan thing again before his gaze flickers over to Hudson for a second, and I want to knee him in the balls—so badly.

Ultimately, this is one of the reasons why he's such a good lawyer. It's just too bad he can't turn that persona off when he's not in court, or I guess that's just who he is at the end of the day.

Even after all the years I spent with him, I'm still not completely sure.

Still hyperaware of where we are, I keep my voice low. "All I want is to live a *normal* life, you know that. And of course I've changed—I had to, after you left me alone with a baby. Not only did I become a mom overnight, but a single mom on top of that."

It takes him a moment to digest my accusation. His voice is still the same, completely level and in control. "I wasn't ready to be a father, especially not like that. Not with a baby that wasn't mine."

Laughing without a trace of humor in my voice, I want to shake this man to see if there's any humanity in him at all. "And you think I was ready? Do you think I wanted my sister and grandma to die—the only family I had left—so I could be thrown into motherhood in the same breath? Do you know how hard it was for me to grieve the loss while simultaneously trying to be strong and happy for my little girl? It's a miracle she survived that accident in the first place. She should be the last person to ever be punished for what happened."

"She's not *yours*." His words are so matter-of-fact, it takes me a moment before they sink in.

Hudson growls and curses under his breath behind me, and I know he's absolutely ready to take over.

If it wasn't for the place we're in, and him holding Mira, there would be blood. I have no doubt about that.

I hold back the angry tears that threaten to run down my face, and point at the excuse of a man in front of me, my hand shaking. "Fuck you, Sebastian. Fuck you. How dare you say something like that. Of course she's mine, through and through. She's been a real blessing for me, teaching me more about life and myself than anything else ever has. She's played a big part in me becoming who I am today, and I couldn't be more proud of her, or myself. Mira deserves the best life and people that give her all the love she deserves. She's already a million times more humane than you'll ever be."

The tension in the room is so thick, I see people stopping around us to watch.

I glare at my once almost-husband, the man I so foolishly believed I loved at one point. I secretly challenge him to try and counter my words, just so I can prove him wrong. All this time, I thought he still had some invisible hold over me, that he broke something inside of me that couldn't be fixed.

But this moment changes *everything*.

There is nothing left between us, absolutely *nothing*, and it's freeing to finally realize that.

When he opens his mouth to speak again, I shake my head. "No, we're done. There is nothing else I want to say to you, and judging by the few things that have come out of your mouth the last few minutes, I can tell you, *with absolute certainty*, there's nothing I want to hear from you either." I don't care if my behavior is rude, or if he thinks I'm insulting. All I know is that I want to get away from this man. "Goodbye, Sebastian."

Not waiting for a reply, I turn around and pull Hudson and Mira with me—which isn't easy at all. Pulling on Hudson feels like I'm tugging on dead weight, and one look at him explains why. He's still turned into Sebastian's direction, quite obviously not as ready to leave this situation as I am.

He's like a bull, ready to charge, willing to go into battle. His jaw is clenched, nostrils flaring, and his eyes are pressed into tight slits. "I want to hurt him so badly, I can't even think straight."

I stop walking, so I can push him over into a corner instead. Turning his chin, I silently beg him to look at me. "Hudson, listen to me. He's not worth it, not one tiny bit. All I want is to forget about this man, to completely wipe him from my memory. Because we—you, me, and Mira—are what's important. I don't want him to taint our life in any way."

Leaning in until our foreheads touch, we both exhale a big breath. Mira leans in too, but a little harsher than necessary so she ends up banging her little head on ours.

This moment is so surreal, I have to chuckle. It helps like nothing else to bring me back down from my rage-infused high because this is exactly what I just said to Hudson.

We are what's most important.

Us three.

I kiss Mira first and then Hudson before grabbing his hand to hold on as tightly as possible. "Let's go. I need a huge piece of cake and a drink."

CHAPTER THIRTY-NINE

WE MANAGE TO ENJOY THE RECEPTION AS BEST AS WE can despite still being a little shaken up for the rest of the day. When it's evident that Mira needs to go to sleep, we say our goodbyes and head up to our suite.

Hudson gets out of the elevator first, and I almost run into him when he abruptly stops.

"Oops. Sorry." I peek around him just as one of his bodyguards walks toward us, a grim expression on his face.

"Sorry, boss. We were hoping to get this taken care of before you came back up."

"What's going on, Tommy?" Hudson's voice is low, and there's an edge to it I can easily detect now.

The massive man looks back and forth between Hudson and me before bending down a little. "We had a little incident with a fan."

Hudson's head snaps up, and Tommy flinches, leaning back a few inches. "What happened?"

The big mountain of a man rubs his neck, his voice deep. "One of the hotel staff caught a chick trying to break into your suite. Police were called and everything's been taken care of."

As if on cue, two officers walk toward us with a woman between them in handcuffs, followed by a hotel worker and the other bodyguard. I instinctively try and hide a little behind Hudson when they pass, but not before catching the woman's eyes. They are so full of hatred, I shudder involuntarily.

They all enter the elevator, but the woman's eyes stay trained on me. Her lips curl into a snarl as she tries to get away from the officers. "You're never gonna make him happy, bitch. He's mine."

One of the policemen says something to her in a harsh tone, and then the elevator doors close.

I'm so shocked, I stare at the closed elevator doors for what feels like hours while Tommy and Hudson talk in hushed voices.

Hudson's hand comes around my waist as he gently guides me down the hallway to our suite. The other bodyguard, Mason, stands outside the door again, and nods at us when we get there.

Once we're inside, Hudson comes to stand in front of me. "Are you all right?"

I blink at him. "That was a bit freaky, but yeah, I think so."

He nods, his face an unreadable mask. "I need to go and take care of a few things with the police. Tommy will come with me, but Mason will stay in front of the door. Are you going to be all right by yourself? I'll be back as soon as I can."

"Okay."

After a quick kiss on the forehead for me and one for

Mira—who fell asleep at some point during this crazy trip to our room—Hudson is out the door, leaving me with a weird feeling in my belly.

Thankfully, Mira is conked out so hard, she doesn't even wake up when I put her in her PJ's and sleep sack before laying her down in the crib. With the baby monitor in tow, I take a long, hot shower, trying to relax as much as I can before climbing into the big bed by myself to read until Hudson gets back.

I must have fallen asleep at some point because the next thing I know, I'm waking up the next morning. The shower is on in the bathroom, and my foggy brain is trying to deal with the emotions that are coming back from last night's events, plus the confusion about Hudson not waking me up when he got back.

At least I think he got back to sleep here.

Trying to shake off the uneasiness, I grab my things from the suitcase—after making sure Mira's still asleep—and make my way to the bathroom just as Hudson opens it from the other side.

He looks tired, utterly exhausted to the ninth. "Hey."

Something about him is off.

He looks reserved and withdrawn.

"Hey. You okay?"

All I get is a curt nod. "Yeah. Just didn't sleep well." We stare at each other for a moment before he takes a step around me. "Are you okay to leave in a couple hours?"

My stomach churns at his odd behavior. The loss of

affection is so distinct, I suddenly feel slightly nauseous. "Sure. Just let me get ready quickly, and by the time I'm done, I'm sure Mira's going to be awake too."

"Okay." He pulls his phone out of his pocket and walks toward the couch. "I'll get us a car and let the flight crew know we'll be ready to leave soon."

After watching his retreating back for a few moments, I slip into the bathroom and close the door behind me—my eyes burning hot with unshed tears, and my chest feeling heavy and tight.

The next few hours are a total blur as I try my hardest to stay as present as I can be, for Mira's benefit. Even though Hudson sits next to me in the car to the airport and the entire plane ride, he isn't *really* there.

We're back at the house before I know it, and I try to keep it together as I unpack our suitcase while keeping Mira entertained too. Thankfully, she's happy as a clam playing in the suitcase for now, as I put everything away.

"There are my girls." Hannah's voice makes me both happy and sad—happy because not seeing her for the whole weekend felt like forever and sad because it's not Hudson.

I guess I was really hoping he'd come around and tell me what on earth is going on with him.

Hannah comes over to where I sit on the floor next to the suitcase and crouches down too. "Did you guys have fun? I just talked to Hudson in his studio for a moment, but he wasn't very talkative."

"The wedding was absolutely beautiful." There, that's

the truth. For some reason, I just can't bring myself to tell her about the other things that happened, even though I'm sure she knows something is up. The fake smile on my face probably wouldn't fool anyone.

Mira is climbing out of the suitcase, squealing as she makes her way over to Hannah. The two reunite like they haven't seen each other in years, and it's adorable to watch.

Hannah really has become not only a stand-in grandmother but also a stand-in great-grandmother—the very best at both.

Pulling Mira into her arms, she looks over at me. "Want me to take her for a walk, or does she need to go down soon?"

Checking the time on my phone, I shake my head. "She slept on the plane, so she still has a few more hours. I'm sure she'd love to get out for a bit."

"Perfect." She gets up with Mira and waves at me. "Say, 'Bye-bye, Mommy, we'll see you in a little bit.'" Mira swings her little hand around like it's made of gummy and gives me a big, toothy grin with drool running down her chin.

Smiling at the sight, I wave back. "Bye, girls. Have fun."

Before they leave the room, Hannah turns one more time. "Did I mention Hudson is in his studio?" She gives me one more pointed look, and then they're gone around the corner.

Hannah, subtle as always.

My shoulders sag, and I let out a loud sigh.

Looks like I have a rockstar to find.

When I make it down to the studio, though, it's empty. Disappointment courses through me, but I try to not let it get to me too much. I'm already anxious and exhausted enough from the last twenty-four hours.

There's nothing wrong. Everything's going to be okay.

I repeat the words over and over in my head as I walk across the room to sit down on one of the black leather couches. A piece of paper falls to the floor, and I pick it up absentmindedly. I'm about to set it back down on the cushion next to me when my eyes land on the two words at the top of the page.

Charlie's Song.

My hand flies to my mouth as I debate for less than two seconds if I should read it or not, because who am I kidding? There's no way I can put down a piece of paper with my name on it without taking a peek.

Especially after everything that's happened.

After taking a deep breath, I start all the way at the top, my eyes going over my name again.

Charlie's Song

Life hasn't been the same since I met you
Because you are my heart, my reason for smiling
I won't live without you, don't want to, just can't do
You own me—my love, my soul, my everything

My new goal in life is putting that sparkle in your eyes
Because seeing you sad causes me pain I've never known
before
I would do anything to protect you from any lies
Just give me a chance and I'll prove it to you

Having you in my life has changed me in such a short while
Your touch, your love, you make my heart smile

JASMIN MILLER

I feel like I'm nothing without you
Just like a broken shell—I hope you need me too

Loving you has become my drug, my new favorite thing
All I want is to have you by my side
To feel you, to breathe you in
Sweetheart, please stay with me before I fall apart inside

A fat teardrop falls onto the paper, missing some of the words by mere millimeters. Using the corner of my sleeve, I wipe away the tears and sniffle some more.

The combination of the raw pain and love in those lines claws at my chest, and a lone sob breaks through before a pair of strong arms surrounds me like a cage, pulling me into the warm and safe embrace I've come to love so much.

"I'm so sorry, please don't cry." Hudson's words are a quiet whisper in my hair, and for the first time in a while, I let my emotions get the better of me until I'm all cried out.

The tears are for so many things—happy tears for the love I feel for Hudson while I'm also beyond terrified to lose him, happy tears for Mira's birthday coming up and the sheer miracle of her being alive while still mourning the family I lost, and frustrated tears for myself and all the mistakes I made in the past but trying to forgive myself for.

"Shh." Hudson rubs my back in rhythmic circles. "I'm so sorry I was such an ass. Everything happening the last twenty-four hours threw me in a bout of self-doubt, and I was so scared of losing you that I just shut down. I shouldn't have done that, I should've talked to you instead."

His admission snaps me out of my moment, and after wiping my eyes—and my nose too, with a very unladylike

360

swipe—I look up at him through wet eyelashes. "What are you talking about?" My voice sounds strange when I push the words out.

"You told Sebastian yesterday that you just wanted a normal life. I thought you might change your mind after all, that being with me is just too much for you to handle. The whole weekend was already a lot to take in, and then that crazy fan showed up on top of it. It couldn't have been more opposite of a normal life. I'm so sorry I can't offer you the life you want."

Another single tear rolls down my cheek, but this one is for Hudson and his beautiful soul. "You are everything I want and need. You are my normal, and don't think for even a minute that you can get rid of me that easily. Just like you told me a few weeks ago that I'm it for you, *you* are *it* for me too. There won't ever be anyone I'll love as much as I love you. No one will ever fill that spot in my heart and soul the way you do."

His eyes are shiny under the studio lights as he crushes me to him. "I love you so damn much, and I'll try my best to give you everything you need."

"You already do."

We hold each other for a long time, my heart so full I'm afraid it might burst at any moment.

CHAPTER FORTY

Letting out a big huff, I plop down on one of the bakery stools and can't help but laugh at myself. "I have to get used to working this much again. It's barely past noon, and I'm exhausted."

It's only been a few days since we got back from Los Angeles, and everyone's been working their butts off to get ready for the bakery opening tomorrow.

"You're doing just fine." Max—the only baker I've hired so far—is on the opposite side of the kitchen work table. He's proven to be worth every single penny I pay him since he has yet to make something that doesn't taste like pure magic. He's, without a doubt, a genius in the kitchen, at least when it comes to baking, and I'm thrilled to have him on my team.

"I'm your boss, you have to say that," I tease, and get a chuckle from him in return.

"Come on." He adds another baking sheet to the already half-filled pan rack before looking at me. "If we hurry up, we can get things done early. We have to be here in the middle of the night again, after all."

I push myself off the chair, raising my messy hands in the air. "I know, I know. Hopefully, I can hire someone else soon too, if the bakery does well. That way, we'd have one more person to share the early morning shift with."

"That would be nice but no worries. I really don't mind the mornings. I actually like to be out and about when everyone else is still sleeping. It's quiet and rather peaceful."

My mind mulls over that for a moment, and I have to agree with him. "That's true. Alrighty, let's finish this up."

We bake in pleasant silence, both of us in our element, with the local radio station quietly playing in the background. We work great as a team without being in each other's way, both of us knowing exactly what we're doing.

"Look, birthday girl." Hudson's voice sounds behind me, and I turn around with a grin on my face. "There's your beautiful mama."

The sight in front of me does funny things to my stomach while my heart is trying to speed away. Hudson looks beyond sexy in his simple dark jeans and a light gray T-shirt, his dark hair hidden under a black hat. It's a sight to behold, and I'll never, ever tire of seeing it. But what makes him look the absolute best is my little cutie pie strapped to his chest in a baby carrier. Mira is all flailing arms and legs when I walk over to them for snuggles and kisses.

"Ma-ma, ma-ma." Mira's smile is so wide, there's nothing left of her eyes but little slits.

Hearing her say those two little syllables still brings tears to my eyes. It's a feeling I can't fully describe. All I know is that it does something incredible to my heart, and that feeling will never get old, no matter how often she says it.

I take a deep breath, wiping my hands off on my apron. "What are you guys doing here?"

"We thought Grandma could use a break, so we went for a walk." He looks around the kitchen and waves at Max. "We were also hoping we'd be lucky enough to steal you away, so we can take you home with us early before everyone gets there for Mira's birthday party."

We've organized a little birthday party for Mira, and I can't wait to give her the little cake I made for her. Even though I did cut back on the sugar, making something healthier for her. The last thing this energetic girl needs is lots of extra sugar.

I start to shake my head, but Max speaks up before I can get a word out. "You should go, Charlie. I can easily finish by myself. We're almost done anyway."

I turn around to look at him. "Are you sure?"

"Absolutely, *boss*." He winks at me, and Hudson chuckles next to me.

"Looks like you're outnumbered, sweetheart."

"All right, all right." I look around my workstation before I smile up at Hudson. "I only need to finish up what I started, get things cleaned up, and talk to Claire up front, to make sure she's all set for tomorrow."

"No problem." He thinks for a moment. "How about Miss Mira and I go over to the new place that just opened to see what they have to offer?"

"The waffle place?"

Hudson nods eagerly, his eyes wide in excitement. "I've heard good things about them."

"Sounds good to me. Go satisfy your sweet tooth."

"You know it. We'll be back soon." He bends down for a quick kiss, and then they're out the door again.

Clapping my hands together, I get back to work. "Okay, let's get this show on the road."

Before I know it, Hudson and Mira walk back in the door, just as I'm taking off my apron. Hudson has a huge grin on his face as he holds up a big paper bag.

"What did you get?" The delicious smell coming from the bag is enough to have me curious.

"Lots of good stuff. I really wanted to try their waffles and ice cream, but with this early summer heat, it probably wouldn't have survived the journey. Instead, I got us waffles with whipped cream and berries." He places the bag on the counter and sorts the items inside.

Mira is trying hard to grab the bag, but Hudson keeps it just out of her reach. She's starting to get frustrated, which means we have to hurry up before she has a meltdown.

He's pulling out all sorts of containers, and my stomach growls at that moment, as if it just realized I've barely eaten today. "Yum."

Hudson's waving at me. "Well, go get your stuff so we can go home quickly. I need to tell you how the conference call went."

Of course. That right there is the problem with being hungry; everything else just slips my mind sometimes. I definitely want to know about the call he had with his bandmates and management team about the band's future. We've been waiting for this for a long time.

I hold up my finger. "Give me two seconds."

He chuckles as I rush around like a crazy person, grabbing my purse and cardigan from my office. In the meantime, he takes two little packages from the bag and brings them to Max and Claire.

How sweet.

Catching me staring at him, he smiles at me and holds out his hand. "Ready?"

"Yup." I beam at him and run over to his side before turning around to wave goodbye to Max and Claire. "See you in the morning, guys. Thanks again for everything."

Hudson dropped me off this morning, knowing I wanted to walk back home from the bakery. It's too nice outside to sit in a hot car if I don't have to.

The three of us walk down the back alley, hand in hand.

"So?" I turn to Hudson, clearly impatient.

"Do you think you can make it until we're home?"

"If I have to." I can't hold back a sigh and he chuckles.

Thankfully, it's only a fifteen-minute walk.

After putting Mira down for a nap, I join Hudson in the kitchen. Playing with Hannah half of the day before taking that walk with Hudson clearly tired her out.

The thought of her strapped to Hudson's chest makes me smile all over again. I'll have to take a picture at some point. That cute sight is definitely something I never want to forget.

"Are you thinking about me?" Hudson pushes off the counter he was leaning on and walks over to me, his stride casual and relaxed.

"What?" I laugh in reply. "Why would you think that?"

He's in front of me now and grabs me by the belt loops of

my jeans to pull me closer. "Because you had this dreamy look in your eyes and a big smile on your face."

Raising my eyebrows at him, I can't hold back a smirk. "So, it has to be about you then?"

"I sure hope so."

I chuckle at his smugness, secretly enjoying this little banter between us. Then I throw my hands up in the air. "Fine. It was about you. Happy now?" I stick my tongue out at him.

"Very." He bends down to give me a long, thorough kiss, and I melt into him immediately.

I'm close to tugging off our clothes right here when thoughts of his phone call cross my mind again. "You. Phone call. Talk." That's all my brain can produce right now, still fuzzy from his kiss. I pull back and shake my head. "Never mind, I think it's better to wait a minute, so I can clear my head first."

He chuckles, looking as self-assured as always.

I slap his arm lightly. "Oh, stop it already. You're driving me crazy."

His warm breath tickles my ear when he comes closer. "Trust me, sweetheart, I'm planning on driving you completely crazy tonight, over and over again." He nibbles gently on the shell of my ear, making his way down my throat until I gasp out loud. "But let's talk first."

Closing my eyes for a minute, I let all the sensations run through my body. Once I'm confident enough I've got it all under control—mostly, at least—I open them back up and stare at him. "You're such a tease, you big meanie."

I grab some cups from the cabinet and juice from the refrigerator, then walk toward the patio door, purposefully swinging my hips a little more than usual. "Are you coming?" I turn around and wink at him over my shoulder, almost unable to hold back my laughter.

"You little minx, you." He runs after me, reaching me in no time.

I squeal when he picks me up and carries me outside while I snuggle as close to his chest as the cups and bottle allow. "Mmm. I could get used to this."

"You better." He puts me down in front of the outdoor couch and gives me another long and passionate kiss that leaves me longing for more.

When I sit down, I purposefully scoot to the other side of the couch, holding my hands up in front of me. "I'll stay right here until we're done talking."

Hudson chuckles, his eyes bright, both of his dimples popping out. "I promise I'll behave now."

"I believe it when I see it." Shaking my head at him, I grin. "Now spill the beans. We don't have long before people start arriving."

"You're right, sorry." Leaning forward with his elbows onto his knees, he focuses on me. "You remember I'm due for another album, right?"

I nod, remembering one of our conversations about his music. "Which is why you were so freaked out about not being able to write."

He flinches at my words but nods. "Exactly. The good thing is, they loved the new music I wrote. More than loved it, actually. They said it was some of the best music I've ever written." He stretches forward to tap my nose with his finger. "All thanks to you, of course."

I shake my head at him, knowing full well I didn't

actually do anything. "I'm so glad they liked it. Why do I hear a but coming, though?"

Hudson lets out a big breath. "Because they wouldn't let me out of touring for that next album."

I swallow loudly, knowing what that means—a lot of time away from Hudson, for at least the next year. "But we were able to meet somewhere in the middle. I'll only tour in a few major cities and won't be away for long at a time. And maybe you could even come with me for a few gigs, if you want to."

"Wow. It's not perfect, but it doesn't sound too bad either." My heart feels like it weighs ten pounds less. "I'm so happy."

He gives me a big smile. "Me too, believe me. They were actually a lot more lenient and welcoming to my ideas than I thought they would be. I made it clear this would be the last tour I'd be doing for them, but that I'd still love to record for them in the future if they were interested, and they agreed."

"For real?" is the only thing that comes out of my mouth.

"Yup."

There's a lot of stuff I still have no clue about in the music world—especially the business side of things—but I know we were really lucky with this outcome.

He pours us both some juice and takes a sip. "I told them I'll be busy with my new project, and they know how excited and passionate I am about it. Surprisingly, they were very accepting of that too. I think they were afraid to lose all the money versus just some of it. But in the end, it works for me. So, I'm all for it."

Now it's me closing the distance between us, putting my arms around his neck to give him a big hug. "That all sounds great. I'm thrilled for you, for me, for all of us."

"Thank you, sweetheart, me too."

I pull back, studying his face. "But wait, what new project were you talking about? Have you been keeping secrets from me?"

"Maybe a little, sorry." He beams at me, a slight blush on his cheeks, but it's obvious he's very excited about whatever it is. "I've actually been thinking about it for a while, but I wanted to be sure first that I could work things out with my management team. I didn't want to disappoint anyone, in case they made things hard for me."

"Well. What is it?" My thoughts are so all over the place I'm drawing a blank.

"I want to work with Dahlia at the Arts Center. Remember when she was talking about wanting to expand and integrate some other areas too?" He pauses to point a finger at himself. "Well, I'd love to handle the music part. I think it would be so awesome to work with the kids and to help out wherever I can."

My heart squeezes, and I lean in again to kiss him. "That sounds wonderful, and you'll do so great. And the kids! They are going to be over the moon to learn from you."

He shrugs. "I hope so. Dahlia doesn't know yet, so I hope she'll be happy too."

I stare at him in bewilderment. "Are you kidding me? She'll be out of her mind happy. Not just to have you working at the academy, but also because you'll be around so much more. Your whole family is going to be ecstatic."

"Are you okay if I tell everyone tonight when they're here anyway? I don't want to take away from Mira's birthday."

Always so thoughtful. "Of course, silly. That sounds perfect."

"And I was hoping that we can tell them about us too?" He leans back, pulling a little box out of his pants.

His hands shake a little as he gives me the box.

"Hudson?" My hands tremble too, and I think I'm starting to sweat.

Putting his hand on the box, he keeps me from opening it. "It's not what you might think it is. Not because I don't want to, but because I don't want to overwhelm you and go too fast. Regardless though, don't doubt for even a second that you'll get *that* box too, at some point. But this"—he taps on the box in my hand—"is my way of telling you that I want you. Just in case there was any doubt left in your mind."

I slowly open the lid, not wanting to wait for another moment. I stare at the silver key that's nestled in the middle of the box.

"I know you already have one, but I wanted you to have your very own, not just a spare. Because without you guys, this place is just a house. It's you two that make it a home, my favorite place I can't wait to get back to whenever I'm out. I want you with me, day and night, for good. Both of you. Always."

"You want us to stay with you? For real?" My brain is fuzzy again. Conversations with Hannah float around my mind, and her telling me she's moving back into her place soon. Now that I think about it, she'd never mentioned us.

"Heck yes. I couldn't think of anyone better to share this place with than you two. Just imagining the house all empty and quiet without you is more than depressing and just impossible to accept. We can get Mira's room all made up just for her, and you can get whatever you need for the kitchen. Anything. It's yours."

Taking the key out of the box, I hold it up, noticing several key tags on the key ring. My eyes become teary as I inspect them closer, and the laughter bubbles out of me when I read *I love Hudson* and *Hudson and Charlie forever*. But my favorite might be *Hudson, Charlie, and Mira* with a big heart around it.

My head is moving up and down—I think. Everything is a bit fuzzy and surreal right now.

Cupping both of my cheeks with his hands, he holds my head steady. "Is that a yes, sweetheart?"

I laugh and nod as much as I can. "Absolutely. Yes, yes, yes. I feel the same way about you and our life. I tried not to think about moving out because every time I did, I just wanted to cry. I can't imagine living without you anymore either, and I know Mira feels the same. She adores you so much."

"Good, because I feel the same about her." Our gazes lock, and I can see my future play out in Hudson's eyes— offering me everything I could ever ask for and then some. "I love you, sweetheart."

A very happy future indeed.

"I love you, Hudson. Forever."

"Forever."

EPILOGUE
ONE YEAR AND ONE DAY LATER

"HAPPY ANNIVERSARY, SWEETHEART." HUDSON'S ARMS wind around my waist from behind, still making my heart speed up, just like day one. "I'm so proud of you." He nudges my throat with his nose, sending a little shiver up my spine.

I turn around in his arms to face him, catching our reflection in the bathroom mirror. "I haven't really done much. The bakery has only been doing so well because these awesome people come in to buy our food every day. It's all because of them."

Leaning down, he kisses first one cheek, then the other, before moving to my lips. I feel like I might melt into a puddle if he keeps doing that. "Yes, but someone needs to make all those delicious goodies for those awesome people to buy."

I chuckle at his insistence. "Okay, I'll take it. Thank you. I can't believe it's already been a year since I opened."

Gazing up into his eyes, I want to get lost in them like I do pretty much every time. Opening a bakery has always been a dream of mine, and it was fantastic when it finally happened. I'm definitely excited about the first anniversary and about celebrating it, but right now, I'd rather spend some more time with Hudson. Especially since he just got home from the last concert of his tour yesterday—just in time for Mira's birthday. I'm not sure who was happier to see him.

Sounds like that deserves a celebration too.

Pouting, I lean into him. "Do we have to go? Can't we just stay home for a bit longer?"

He smiles at me, his eyes sparkling mischievously. "Well, we could, but just think about all those poor people that woke up today wanting to eat some of your delicious cake or pastries."

"All right, all right." I mindlessly brush my hands across his chest while still gazing up at him. "I'm so happy you're back for good now."

He lets out a big breath, staring at the white ceiling. "Tell me about it. I was seriously counting down the hours. I'm not sure if I was happier when we were done, or the rest of the tour team. Apparently, I've been getting on everyone's nerves a bit."

That makes me chuckle, especially since I've come to know all of the bandmates and most of the tour crew pretty well over the last year, joining Hudson for his concerts whenever it was possible. "I can just imagine you guys. Even though we all know they missed their other halves just as much as you did."

He puffs out his chest, looking pretty proud of himself. "You're absolutely right. At least I'm not ashamed of admitting I've missed you guys the most."

"I can certainly live with that. We missed you too. A lot." A snicker rumbles through my body. "Particularly Mira. I can't even tell you how many times I've heard 'Daddy' here, 'Daddy' there, especially since she started talking so much more over the last few months."

"Good. I can't wait to spend more time with her. Maybe she can come up to the academy with me sometime next week? I already have a few music sessions planned."

I nod enthusiastically. "She'd absolutely love it, no doubt about it."

"Perfect. Now let's go." He pulls me out of the bathroom, through our bedroom, and down the stairs.

"What is going on with you this morning?" I laugh at his unusual behavior, trying to keep up with his rushed steps. "Usually you'd be the first one to say 'screw everyone,' and have me pressed up against a wall."

"Later, sweetheart." He squeezes my hand and turns around to grin at me. "It's a big day, so I'm excited."

I sigh loudly, knowing exactly how right he is.

Today *is* a big day.

"Hudson, stop for a second. There's something I need to—"

My words trail off as we walk into the kitchen, and I stop at the sight in front of me.

The whole room is filled with flowers. Tulips, to be exact. My favorites. They're everywhere—on the kitchen bar, the big island, the countertops, the bar stools. Wherever the eye can see, there are tulips in all possible colors.

It's nothing like I've ever seen. So beautiful.

"Wow, I..." That's pretty much all I can think of saying.

"Shh." Hudson chuckles as he holds my hands, exhaling loudly as he slowly goes down on one knee. "My turn first."

Despite the situation, we both have to laugh, and I'm already loving this moment more than I ever thought I could.

Even though I can't believe *this moment* is really happening.

"Charlie, right here in this kitchen is where we first met and where our journey began. You had me mesmerized from the first second, even when I only caught a glance of you before you threw a ball of dough in my face. You're beautifully different and everything I could've ever dreamed of finding in a partner. You've brought me so much joy by not only being the wonderful person you are, but also by enriching my life even more with our beautiful girl." He pauses to take a deep breath and reaches into his pocket.

Even though I know what's coming, my breath still hitches in my throat, my hands shaking like trees in the wind. A sigh escapes my mouth when his hand appears in front of me, but this time, he's holding a beautiful ring between his fingers.

"Sweetheart, there's never going to be anyone more perfect for me than you, and I can't imagine the rest of my life with anyone but you and Mira. Would you do me the honor of becoming my wife and letting me officially be Mira's father?"

Tears run down my cheeks as I look at this beautiful man in front of me. Seeing him down on one knee brings out emotions I didn't know existed—they're so overwhelming that my knees start shaking too. I was certain I'd cry today, I just didn't know it was going to be this early on or for this reason.

He's still looking up at me expectantly, making me realize I haven't given him an answer yet.

"Yes, yes, yes. Absolutely yes."

Before he can get back up on his feet, I throw myself into his arms, making both of us topple over onto the floor. "Of course I'll marry you."

He laughs and pulls my face to his, showering me with impatient kisses.

After a few minutes, he pushes me back gently so we're both seated on the floor.

He gently lifts up my hand. "May I?"

I nod eagerly, spreading out my fingers in anticipation. Once the ring is on my finger, I pull it close to my face to get a better look at it. It's different than anything I've ever seen, but somehow it looks familiar too. I don't know much about jewelry, but it looks like it's vintage with a modern look to it.

It's absolutely breathtaking.

"Do you like it?" Hudson's voice is filled with uncertainty. "We can get you something else if you want. No worries at all. I know it's nothing big and fancy, but I thought it would—"

"Shh." This time, I interrupt him. "Thank you so much, it's absolutely perfect. I can't imagine anything more beautiful, so give me a moment to fully take it in."

"I'm glad you like it. It's a very unique piece, just like you." His next words come out in a soft whisper. "It's your grandma's ring. Well, at least part of it. My grandma found it in her belongings and thought you might like it. The band was pretty demolished, so we had that exchanged for something more modern. But the stone was still in great condition, so we used that in combination with the new band."

"Oh, Hudson." I throw myself at him again, burrowing my face into his shoulder. My sobs are quiet but heartbreaking. I will never be able to tell him how much this gesture means to me. This will be one of my most treasured possessions, I'm absolutely sure of it. "Thank you so much."

"Anything for you. I'm just happy you like it and that you said yes." He gives me a big smile, gently wiping my tears away with his thumbs. "What an awesome day."

Giving him a small smile, I reach into the back pocket of my jeans to hand him the small package I put there earlier. "Maybe we can make it even better?"

"What?" The smile falls from his face as he stares at the small rectangular box in my hands, looking at it like it might bite him at any moment.

I push it toward him, nudging his hand with it. "Here, I've got something for you too. Open it."

"Are you sure?" His eyes are as wide as saucers, and I have absolutely no idea what's going on in his mind right now.

"Yes, of course I'm sure." I pull it back an inch toward me, the shape poking my belly. "Or do you want me to open it?"

He shakes his head, almost grabbing the package out of my hands with a newfound eagerness. "No, no. I'll do it."

Getting to work immediately, small pieces of paper fly in all directions, making me chuckle.

And then Hudson stares at the contents in his hands for a long time. "Is this for real?"

I nod, unable to hold back the gigantic grin on my face.

"We're really going to have a baby?" He holds up the pregnancy test I wrapped for him, his voice completely in awe.

"Sure looks like it." I can't help myself and squeal a little.

This time, I'm the one being tackled to the floor. Hudson

hovers over me, carefully holding my face in his hands. His eyes are watery, gazing into mine with so much affection that mine automatically start tearing up again too.

He bends down to smother my face with kisses before settling on my lips for good. "I can't believe we're going to have a baby. Mira is going to be the best big sister ever." He keeps shaking his head. "A baby. I can't wait."

A second later, he's up on his feet, holding out his hand to me. "Come on, let's go. Everyone's waiting at the bakery to celebrate with us. Boy, they don't even know half of it. They are going to flip." He chuckles softly to himself before pulling me closer. "I love you so much."

Snuggling into him as close as I can get, I let out a deep, relaxed breath before kissing him deeply. "I love you."

When we pull apart and I look up at his face, I'm pretty sure his smile could light up an entire continent, and I can't get enough of it.

Lifting me up, he spins me around in a bed of tulips. "Best day ever."

I laugh because I couldn't agree more. "Definitely best day ever."

AUTHOR NOTE

Thank you so much for reading my words!

If you enjoyed *Baking With A Rockstar*, it would mean the world to me if you could leave a review. Word of mouth and reviews go a long way, and I'd appreciate it so much.

For more books and bonus scenes, please visit my website www.jasminmiller.com

ACKNOWLEDGMENTS

This novel. Hudson and Charlie. Mira and the rest of the Mitchell family. None of them might have ever seen the light of day if it wasn't for a bunch of people in my life.

So...let's buckle up and throw around some well-deserved lovin'.

To my husband — You're my biggest supporter, no matter if you listen to my rambling, help with my plotting, comfort me when I'm exhausted or want to throw my laptop at the wall (while easing my frustration with ten pounds of chocolate). You're there for me. Always. You're my cheerleader (without the pom-poms and cheers), and I'm incredibly grateful for you. You encourage me to go after my dreams, knowing exactly how much I need that extra push sometimes. Thank you for knowing exactly what I need, and for being selfless enough to let me do my thing. You (and our monsters) own my heart. Forever.

To Suze — Where am I even going to start with you and this story? Thank you for loving Hudson and Charlie as much as I do, and sometimes maybe even a little more. Your constant support and encouragement push me even when I don't want to do another thing. You're an amazing friend and CP, and I'm beyond grateful that life has thrown us together.

To my betas Melissa, Kristen, Stephie (plus two anonymous ones) — Thank you guys so much for not holding back and for taking the time to improve my story. It wouldn't be the same without you, and I appreciate your feedback to no end.

To Jenn Wood — I love how your words flow so effortlessly with mine. Thank you for taking this story to the next level and beyond and for helping me fall in love with it again.

To Judy Zweifel — You keep impressing me with your excellent proofreading skills, and I'll be forever grateful you caught all the things you did. I'm sure you saved me from a meltdown or two. Thank you!

To my family and my lovely friends Kaylyn, Brooke, Chelli, Kirby, Lia, Becca, Holly, and Lorraine — You guys have been by my side for most of this journey, and I can't ever thank you enough for all the love and support over the years. Your encouragement has helped me more times than I can count.

To my Awesome Peeps, my fantastic reader group — Having you guys by my side has made this adventure all the better. Your love and support mean more than I can ever put into words.

And last but certainly not least.

To my readers — You guys are the reason I do what I do. Knowing you are out there reading my stories keeps me going, and I can't ever thank you enough. You warm my heart.

ABOUT THE AUTHOR

Jasmin Miller is a professional lover of books and cake (preferably together) as well as a fangirl extraordinaire. She loves to read and write about anything romantic and never misses a chance to swoon over characters. Originally from Germany, she now lives in the western US with her husband and three little humans that keep her busy day and night.

If you liked *Baking With A Rockstar* and would like to know more about her and her books, please sign up for her newsletter on her website. She'd love to connect with you.

www.jasminmiller.com
jasminmillerbooks@gmail.com
Facebook.com/jasminmillerwrites
Instagram.com/jasminmiller
Twitter.com/JasminMiller_
Facebook.com/groups/jasminmillerpeeps

Made in the USA
Coppell, TX
02 July 2022

79514689R00229